A RUINED WORLD

ALSO BY STUART THAMAN

The Goblin Wars Series
The Minotaur King
Siege of Talonrend
Death of a King
Rebirth of a God

The Umbral Blade Series
Shadowlith
Mournstead
Umbral Blade Collector's Edition

Killstreak Series
Respawn
Heavy Armor
Kingsgate

Forsaken Talents Series
A Dark Path
A Black Soul
A Ruined World
A Buried God

Realm Online Series
Oathbreaker
Citadel Deathgaze

Chronicles of Estria
Blood and Ash

Short Story Collections

Dragonband Tales Volume 2: The Hunters and the Hunted

Unsheathed

Against All Odds

Blades & Bullets

With Sena Andeo

Steamship Brass Anchor

A Ruined World(Forsaken Talents Book 3)
Copyright © 2019 Stuart Thaman
Nef House Publishing
www.stuartthamanbooks.com

All rights reserved. No part of this publication may be sold, transmitted, reproduced, or stored in a retrieval system without the prior written consent of the publisher, except in the case of brief quotations embodied in critical articles and reviews.

This is a work of fiction. Names, characters, places, brands, and incidents are products of the author's imagination or are used fictitiously. Any resemblance to actual events, locales, organizations, or persons, living or dead, is entirely coincidental.

ISBN: 978-1-965393-12-3

Cover by J Caleb Clark (www.jcalebdesign.com)
Interior layout by Bodie D Dykstra (www.bdbookdesign.com)

A RUINED WORLD

FORSAKEN TALENTS

GRIMDARK LITRPG

STUART THAMAN

FOREWORD

This is Stuart Thaman. Welcome back to Forsaken Talents. First and foremost, please accept my apologies for the years that have elapsed since *A Black Soul* was released in 2019. A lot of things have happened in the interim, some good and some bad, and this series got away from me. Then, around 2023 when I sat down to finally write *A Ruined World*, I realized my entire note document was simply gone. Recreating that document was a necessary task to completing the novel, and the daunting nature of it all made me hesitate. But here it is. *A Buried God* is in the works. Right now, I anticipate the fourth installment to be the last.

Anyway, if you're wondering what happened in book two, you probably aren't alone. Ben sacked Echelon, but the old resurrection orbs of Wonder have been reactivated by the developers. Vic has been captured, Hel has been transformed by Lady Kalma, and Ben's closest allies are players he can barely trust. Though Ben's mind slips more and more every day, his goal is clear: humanity is a disease, and the only cure is extinction.

Welcome back to Forsaken Talents. I genuinely hope you have as much fun reading *A Black Soul* as I had writing it.

As always, this one goes out to everyone who has left a review. Thank you!

Bright were the castle buildings, many the bathing-halls,
high the abundance of gables, great the noise of the multitude,
many a meadhall full of festivity,
until Fate the mighty changed that.
Far and wide the slain perished, days of pestilence came,
death took all the brave men away;
their places of war became deserted places,
the city decayed.

- Excerpt from the "The Ruin of the Empire" contained within the Exeter Book, 10th century A.D.

CHAPTER 1

So much work to do. So much to accomplish. So much . . . to conquer.

Vic barely registered as a flicker in my transformed mind. I had changed so much that I barely recognized my own consciousness. Some of that was for the better, I knew. Some . . . for the worse. I'd set my thoughts to more profound ventures than simple revenge. Lady Kalma had given me visions of the world to come—of death and destruction on a scale that no mortal was truly capable of comprehending—and those visions now drove my footsteps and guided my squid-like arms. But still, Vic would die. I would give him the glorious gift of true death just the same. And the sand in his small hourglass had already run dangerously low.

I stood amidst a legion of my undead minions. We were several miles outside Echelon, on the other side of the city from my necropolis, and things were steadily going according to plan. According to Lady Kalma's plan.

I knew the last remnants of survivors would either flee or try to mount a resistance—what other option was before them? Most of them fled Echelon's walls before we arrived, and they were of no concern to me now. For the moment, my focus was honed on Elyk. The crazed murderer wore my armor and wielded Infernum, the most powerful relic I had ever seen. He was a whirlwind of fire, steel, and death, slowly creeping toward the outer limits of my vision. The battle had only barely begun, and already the field of corpses left in Elyk's wake was wide and deep. The man was unstoppable, an inexorable plague of violence that no blade or arrow could hope to slow. And every kill only fueled his strength, leveling his physical stat and giving him a handful of new abilities after every single battle.

I watched the harvester with a smile of admiration like a father pleased with the performance of his beloved son. And I was. Everything Elyk had become was because of me. Not only did I give him an incredible set of equipment—I had given him a home and a life. If I hadn't taken him under my dark wings, he would be either dead already or fleeing Echelon right now with the rest of the refugees, never learning his true potential. And what was a man without potential? Without success? *Nothing*. A husk of life not fit to draw breath. No better than the hundreds of corpses littering the ground, each one a universe of possibilities cut short. But they would respawn. Like wheat in a field, they would be reborn only to be hewn again, either by my own hand or Elyk's wicked blade.

My mind turned next to Helvegen.

I missed her, or at least some part of me did.

I . . . I didn't love her. No, I did not believe what we had was ever love. Perhaps we had approximated the notion of love, but we never attained it. Now we had something else. A rivalry? Perhaps. I wasn't sure, and I hadn't thought to ask as her blood dripped from my tentacle arm to the floor next to my bed. No matter what, the two of us were connected. We shared a bond of closeness and animosity that could not be denied.

And she was here. I felt it in my bones. I *knew* beyond a doubt that she was here.

"Elyk is about to break through," Xia said quietly, interrupting my silent thoughts for the first time in some hours.

I nodded. "Almost to the core," I replied. More than Helvegen, I felt the core's presence. It called to me, beckoning with a sick mockery of life and death. The regeneration core was unnatural, unholy. It defied man's true purpose. It was an abomination, and it churned my stomach to be so near to it.

Luckily, I was fit for the task of bringing it down.

The harvester, leading over a hundred verdantly augmented undead, pushed toward the resurrection beacon outside Echelon. It controlled the souls of all those who died on the entire continent, bringing them back in fresh bodies and seeing them go on their way. The whole concept was disgusting—an afront to Lady Kalma and her sisters of death.

I hadn't given the defenders much time to prepare before marching my soulless army to their doorstep. We'd moved in less than a day, but still they were at least partially entrenched. In the end, the defenders of Echelon, their barricades and bulwarks, would all be inconsequential. Echelon was the easy city to conquer. My citadel was right next door, and we gave them little time to prepare. But the other cities . . . they would be difficult to capture. They would have time, and they would know exactly what was coming.

Just then Elyk broke through the line of defenders, and what had begun as a pitched battle with clearly drawn lines devolved into a chaotic rout. Those brave souls defending the beacon knew their time was up. My zombies flooded through their ranks, and within moments I could no longer tell where my troops ended and the defenders began.

"We need to move closer," I told my lieutenants. "I want a better view."

My cadre of elite players and NPCs began the slow march toward the front lines. I didn't want to enter the fray myself, but I needed to see what the resurrection hub looked like. I needed to know its appearance exactly—and know what kind of area or building it was kept in—so I could easily find all the others spread throughout Wonder.

We neared the cacophony of the front lines, stepping over ruined bodies and shattered undead, and something struck me as impossible.

Somehow, my soldiers were losing.

In a matter of moments, the tide had turned. They had broken through the defenders' lines, but they weren't gaining any more ground. In fact, they were rapidly giving it up. I stood maybe thirty or forty paces from the action, and I struggled to find Elyk among the chaos. He was badly wounded—it looked like a spear was lodged in his shoulder through his breastplate. His helmet was missing as well.

"Sir . . . what do we do?" Xia asked. She sounded scared. And the warlock *never* sounded scared.

I had to think for a moment. If I called for a retreat, we could regroup, reassess the defenders, and then make a new assault with better planning and more information. But that would give my enemies just as much time to do the same, and if our surprise attack failed now then so would a planned attack later. The moment was all or nothing.

"Tell the zombies to pull back. Bring Elyk here as well. We'll retreat, but only for a moment. Then I'll lead the charge," I commanded.

Xia obeyed my orders at once. She called the zombies, bringing back what few of them were left intact, and soon enough I saw Elyk staggering toward me. The harvester was bloody and haggard, using Infernum as a cane to support his body weight.

As soon as he was close enough to be heard, he started yelling at me. "What the hell are you doing?"

I was instantly taken aback. The man looked like he was on the verge of death, and he questioned my order for retreat? "We're losing too many!" I yelled. The answer was obvious. How could he not see it? "We have to regroup. We'll make another push!"

Elyk shook his head. "We almost have them! Send the zombies back in! You're letting them escape and respawn!"

I shook my head. Something didn't make sense.

Elyk took another few steps closer to me, and his appearance instantly changed. He stood upright, his helmet returned to his head, and he now held Infernum in a steady grip. And he wasn't impaled by a spear. He was fine. More than fine. Covered in gore, yes, but none of it was his.

"What the hell?" I struggled to wrap my mind around what was happening.

Elyk continued to berate me. "Send them back! Every second of delay is going to cost us more undead. They're respawning back there, and most of them are fleeing now. We won't be able to catch them all."

He was right. "Back through the lines!" I yelled as loudly as I could. "Kill them all!"

"What's happening?" Xia asked at my side. She had readied a ball of magic between her hands, but she let it dissipate as our zombies turned back toward the breach in the bulwarks.

Elyk readjusted his grip on Infernum's hilt and charged. When he cleared the first two destroyed barricades, his appearance instantly reverted back to what I had seen before. He was battered and bloodied, barely clinging to life. I charged along behind him. When I was close to him once more—shoving zombies aside to make my way through the rotten, disgusting swarm—I could see him as he truly was.

Finally, it dawned on me.

Just as I had felt before, Helvegen was somewhere on the other side. The painter was using her immense skill to change what I saw. For the first time, *I* was the target of her powerful magic.

"Fuck. That's not good," I said to no one in particular.

"What is it, master?" Xia asked.

"Hel is painting the battlefield. She's making it look like we're losing. But we aren't. We're fucking slaughtering them all!"

I caught sight of a defender struggling to breathe through a broken jaw. He leaked blood from a dozen or more gashes and gouges, but he was still alive. I went to him, towering above him on the ground, and wrapped my tentacles around his bloody neck. I hoisted him up to eye level so I could capture his entire attention.

"Where is Helvegen? Tell me where she is, and I'll let you live," I said evenly.

The man only looked terrified. His mouth moved slowly, though no words came out. He was too wounded and shell-shocked to be of any use.

I crushed his esophagus in my hand and tossed him over the earthworks toward the rest of my army. After the battle, he would be converted into another mindless undead to swell my ranks.

I needed to find someone with a little more life left in their bones. Elyk was deep in the thick of the battle ahead of me, cleaving left and right with impunity. Half of his strikes were so powerful they blasted apart two or three combatants in a single stroke. And he wasn't always hitting our enemies. Zombies who got too close were torn to ribbons just the same as the defenders. So be it.

We reached the end of the hastily built bulwarks, and what resistance we had faced trickled down to nearly nothing. Everyone still alive was running. At the end of the barricades and earthworks stood a stone and mortar building about two stories tall. It had no door, but rather each of the four walls were completely open between marble pillars supporting the roof. In the center, a red orb slowly oscillated about four or five feet above the ground. It dripped a pinkish liquid that looked like watered down blood or thin paint, and the liquid disappeared between cracks in the stone floor.

Before, dying had meant respawning at home. I would wake up in my bed or near it, usually with a headache and a growling stomach. Now, I watched in awe as the orb flashed and produced a living being: a young woman who took off at a sprint the moment her feet hit solid ground. Three more quickly materialized behind her and ran the same direction.

Then the orb's magic died down, and the last defender expired and respawned.

My zombies spread out around the stone pergola in a defensive formation, Elyk standing next to the orb with a sheen of blood reflecting from his armor.

"We have it," the harvester said.

I watched the rotating orb with fascination. It shimmered and shined, dancing in the strong light of the day.

"How do we destroy it?" Xia asked.

"One good hit should do it," Elyk responded. He readied Infernum above his head like a lumberjack about to split a piece of wood. I had no doubt the legendary sword could rend the orb in half, but another plan formed in my head.

A buzzing sound rang out from the orb, short and punctuated, and I held up a hand to stop Elyk's movement. Everyone waited in a silence. A few seconds later, a shimmer obscured a man-sized patch of air right next to the orb. Then the man himself appeared. He was tall, perhaps in his late twenties, and the name floating above his head was George.

Something about witnessing several resurrections within the game gave me pause. In a way, it was beautiful. But at the same time, I hated everything it meant and everything it could do. Resurrection was *not* the will of Lady Kalma. It was not meant to be.

George blinked and held a hand to his eyes against the light. He was only level eleven. His class showed him as a crossbowman, but based on his clothing I guessed his stats and abilities were designed more for economics or crafting than combat. The man didn't speak. He only stood with his hand to the sun and watched, his entire body trembling with fear.

Another vibration jolted out of the orb. Seconds later, the man I had killed and thrown beyond the bulwarks reconstituted in front of my eyes.

I looked to a handful of the nearest zombies. "Push the orb," I commanded them.

They obeyed my order at once, lining up shoulder to should and reaching their foul hands to the orb. They touched it, then began to push, and the orb moved, though not much.

"More," I said, pointing to another pair of zombies that looked a bit stronger than the first set. Thick vines wrapped around their arms and legs, and they hadn't been nearly as damaged during the battle as some of the others. They joined the first four, and the six of them pushed the orb with all their strength.

Finally, the orb snapped out of place. It jolted to the side like someone had cut a taught string delicately balancing it in place. At once, the color of the orb faded to dull gray, and it lost all its luster and shine. Though it still hovered above the ground, it looked like a plain ball of metal or maybe painted wood. Everything that had made the orb so captivating was gone.

George shifted nervously from one foot to the other.

The other man, his name printed in an alphabet I couldn't recognize or pronounce, looked like he was about to bolt. His eyes were glued to the space between a pair of zombies, and he had all his weight on the balls of his feet. He was so close to running that he was nearly falling over. Honestly, he looked ridiculous. Escape was impossible.

"We need to perform a test," I said to the nervous man. "You understand, right?"

I rammed my pointed tentacles through his chest before he could respond. He gagged, sputtering blood and truncated gasps of air from his ruptured lungs. I spread my fingers inside his chest, and he stopped squirming. George looked like he was going to piss himself. I shook the corpse from my arm and waited.

"Well?" Elyk said after a moment.

The orb was silent.

"I think we got it," I answered. I turned to the zombie moving crew and commanded them to push the orb all the way back to Undercroft Citadel. At once, they began maneuvering the object back through the bulwarks toward the breach and out of sight.

That left only George. He still hadn't said a word.

I fixed the man with my eyes. "Well? What's it going to be?" I asked. Truth be told, he probably wasn't useful enough to bother saving. He would serve my cause better as a mindless slave, someone I would never have to worry about again.

George took a moment to gather his wits. "I'm . . . I'm George," he said quietly.

"I know that much," I said with a laugh. "But what's going to happen to you, George? Are you useful to me, George? Are you going to beg for your life and come back to my citadel to serve me? Or am I going to kill you here, George, and then drag your corpse back to my necromancer to serve me that way?"

George nodded, though I wasn't exactly sure why. "I'll go with you, I suppose."

"But what makes you useful? Why do I need to save your life?" I demanded.

He thought for a moment. "I'm not very strong. I can make crossbows, but I'm not a great fighter."

"Well, George, at least you're honest. Anything else?"

"Back . . . back home I was a professor. I never played the game much. Always working."

He was becoming less and less useful every time he spoke. Unless he taught courses in bomb making or military strategy, I was going to kill him. "What did you teach, George?"

Finally, he managed to look me in the eye. "Classical philosophy. Mostly to freshman and sophomores. I only got my doctorate two years ago."

"Like . . . Plato and shit?" I never cared much for ancient books and their confusing prose. In the game, I cared for it even less.

George looked back to his feet. "Not Plato," he said meekly. "Xenophon and Diogenes. And some Eastern writers, but not many."

"Fucking useless," I muttered. I made my arms into something of a sledgehammer and swung hard for the man's chest. His bones caved inward beneath the strength of my limbs, and he collapsed to the ground with his back against one of the four stone pillars supporting the roof of the pergola. I stepped in front of him and slammed his chest again. Crushed between my combined fists and the stone pillar, he died without a sound. I waited again for the telltale humming and vibrating of the resurrection module, but none came.

Perhaps saving the man and forcing him to build crossbows would have been the smarter decision, but I didn't care. Testing the orb a second time was just as valuable. And plucking hapless soldiers from death wasn't on my to-do list.

Gazing around the silent pergola, it dawned on me: we won. True death was back, at least in part of Wonder. *That* was what mattered most.

"Alright, back to Undercroft. Everyone will be fleeing to the other cities and their resurrection hubs. I highly doubt we'll see anyone else trying to resist on the entire continent." I looked to Elyk, his smile as broad as my own. "We have a lot of work to do."

CHAPTER 2

Undercroft Citadel was truly a sight to behold. I thought back to the simple trappings of Whitechapel, the village where it all began, and smiled. Even the dark citadel I lorded over only a few weeks ago paled in comparison. What we had now was a proper city. Streets laid out in an organized grid, plenty of housing, workshops for virtually anything, and towering walls of stone, iron, and bleached bone. Much to my delight, the orc encampments were still outside the primary defenses, so the risk of accidental cannibalism was at least minimized. I watched from my high vantage point as a pair of mindless undead worked the minecart door. The cart, heavily laden with raw ore, rumbled down the tracks where it entered Geirr's workshop.

Next to the forge was a large, terraced farm, though at least half the crops were unnatural. Kinglsey was nearby, prodding the soil with a battered old shovel that someone must have brought back from Echelon or Riverside. Several streets in the opposite direction was an archery range complete with a wooden viewing pavilion. It reminded me of something we could use for a tournament, though how much fun it would be with undead competitors was an issue for another time.

The ossuary, perhaps the most impressive section of Undercroft Citadel, now emanated dark energy. Despite no overhanging ledges or awnings, deep shadows jutted forth from the doors and completely obscured the intricate carvings on their faces. Investigating the ossuary would be high on my priority list, though not the first thing I needed to do.

Since becoming Bentalÿk, I hadn't had an opportunity to review my stats, make talent selections, or take care of all the other housekeeping functions that were so vital. Basking in the warm morning light, I took a seat on the marble stairs, leaned back, and pulled up my stats.

Bentalÿk, Level 20 Blight of Deep Waters, Defender of the Necropolis, Host of Blasphemies, Scourge of Echelon

Physical: 38

Cunning: 40

Influence: 37

Renown: 58

Investigation: 9

Trade: 10

Craftsmanship: 10

Fortune: 14

Infamy: 684

Status: unstable, feared, hated and feared by Echelon, hated by Imps (wild beasts), blessed by Lady Kalma, active bounty (global)

Holdings: Undercroft Citadel (Raid), Tendershoot Mine

Allegiance: Lady Kalma, the Stench of Corpses

I had gained two levels since activating *Host of Blasphemies* thanks to the points in cunning that had apparently come with the talent. Level twenty meant I was becoming significantly formidable in my own right. Even without Infernum and the legendary armor Elyk now wore, even without an army of the undead to command, I would be hard to kill.

Somewhere around level sixteen or so was the general cut-off between beginning and seasoned players. A lot of the most interesting dungeons and quests started at level eighteen and nineteen. If my memory was correct, a lot of the big guilds required players to be at least twenty before they let them join.

Just as notable as my level gain was my infamy score. It had grown by a few hundred. That was certainly something I had little experience with as most players intentionally kept their own infamy rather low. More infamy meant higher rewards for whoever managed to kill me, but the system admins had already seen to that. My infamy might as well have been in the millions.

The most interesting thing of all was my new class: Blight of Deep Waters. Needless to say, it wasn't class I—or anyone else—had heard of before.

Eager to learn more about the class and with two levels worth of talents waiting for me, I focused on the tiny notification in the bottom of my vision and got to it:

Tainted Meat (Physical): You flesh has been corrupted, and anyone who touches your body risks infection. Defensive spines able to inject poison in your attackers grow from your back. Passive.

Part the Waters (Cunning): Your navigational abilities are greatly enhanced, and once per day you can move a body of water up to 100 cubic meters to a different nearby location. Active, consumes no energy.

Command the Fleet (Influence): You are no stranger to deep waters, and those under your command recognize your skill upon the waves. When commanding friendly naval soldiers, your underlings will work with increased speed and vigor. Passive.

Well . . . none of those felt very good. Being able to lift a bunch of water could be interesting, perhaps even useful when putting out a fire, but I had absolutely no idea how much a hundred cubic meters would actually be. A small pond? A swimming pool? A lake? Without a reference handy, there was no way to know.

Commanding a fleet felt unlikely. We didn't have any ships. But that didn't mean we *wouldn't* have any ships in the future. Each portal was located on its own continent, after all, so taking my merry band across the sea was certainly in my future. I just didn't know for sure we would be doing it in boats. It felt unlikely.

My final option, becoming a damn sea urchin, we perhaps least appealing of them all. Without Hel, I was already going to be lonely enough. I didn't need spines coming out of my back and completely precluding all possible human contact. With a sigh of contempt and disappointment, I unlocked *Part the Waters* and then quickly progressed to the next notification for my level twenty talents:

Touch of the Abyss (Physical): The body remembers what the mind dares forget. The next enemy you touch will manifest their old wounds and the pain that brought them. Consumes moderate energy.

Whisper of the Abyss (Cunning): Do not listen too long to the silence between the stars, for it is known to whisper. Once per day, you can hear the thoughts of one humanoid being already within earshot, though stronger targets may corrupt the voice you hear. Consumes massive energy.

Presence of the Abyss (Influence): They looked skyward, praying for light from the heavens. What fell upon them was not mercy. With a word, the clouds part, and the Blight of Deep Waters receives divine favor. Consumes massive energy.

Level twenty looked like one of the benchmarks for my class. Each ability was profound, to say the least. And the . . . flavor text? I didn't know what to call the short description at the beginning of each ability. Some of my previous skills had similar descriptions, but they were always relevant to what the ability actually did. These felt more dramatic, as though they were bits of added flair simply for the effect. Regardless, I had a tough decision. *Touch of the Abyss*, given the regeneration taking place on the other six continents, would almost certainly be a one-hit kill. I imagined some ridiculous guild leader trying to fight my army and killing him with a single touch. If the player had respawned a bunch, they were bound to have plenty of old—and very lethal—wounds to remember. But would it work that way? Would respawning change or reset the mechanic? I had no idea.

Whisper of the Abyss was just as incredible if perhaps a little less violent. Telepathy was not something that existed in the game, at least not to my knowledge. There were countless scenarios where it would no doubt be extremely useful.

The final ability, *Presence of the Abyss*, was the most outright enticing. Receiving Lady Kalma's divine favor had already saved my ass plenty of times. It wasn't long ago at all that *Host of Blasphemies* had transformed me into the eldritch horror I now was. But the word *presence* gave me pause. The skill did not imply that I would *become* something else, only that I would *receive* it. I would be given a divine gift. Something that could exude presence. The more I thought about it, the more it felt like it was a summon spell akin to my extremely potent *Pull from the Darkness* ability. I used the shadow pet in nearly every fight to great effect. Adding another summon to the mix felt like the right call. With a thought, I added *Presence of the Abyss* to my repertoire.

Next came the management of Undercroft Citadel itself. It was a tall task; one I was both eager to commence and somewhat dreading for the complexity of it all.

Undercroft Citadel (Raid)

Commander: Bentalÿk (Influence: 37)

Bosses: Xia (Warlock), Xollmomath (Necromancer), Elyk (Harvester), Ugg'chugg (Shaman), Kevin (undead Ranger)

Active Tiers: outer defenses, inner courtyard, necropolis, throne room

Completion Reward: Special

Active Campaigns: 673

Difficulty Rating: Challenging

Availability: Open

Time since last completion: None on record

Assign new roles to bosses? Yes | No

I nearly gasped. The raid information screen was something I was sure no one in the game had ever seen before. As far as I knew, it was extremely rare for players to lead dungeons, but raids were completely different. Raids represented the highest challenges that Wonder had to offer, and they were scripted with meticulous detail by both the game's artificial intelligence and the original programmers. Despite never seeing the panel in its current form, I had seen the player-side version of it plenty of times on the streams. Active tiers indicated the number of areas a guild would have to conquer to consider the raid complete, and four was a relatively small number. The difficulty rating was on the higher side of average but far from the kind of raids that brought millions of people to view a single stream. My heart sank as I read the number of active campaigns. Nearly seven hundred . . . nearly seven hundred groups had already declared their intentions to conquer Undercroft Citadel. If all of them showed up at once, we were certainly doomed. Our only hope was distance. The vast distances between continents would buy us time, and with time, we could grow.

What caught my attention next was the question blinking at the bottom of the stat sheet. I focused on the word 'Yes' to select it, and a new menu appeared.

Xia, available roles: Dreadhorde General, Death's Majesty, Heretical Healer

Xollmomath, available roles: Unshackled, Keeper of the Black Oath, Fallen

Elyk, available roles: Fiend-Blooded, Cosmic Imposter, Wicked Tormenter

Ugg'chugg, available roles: City Smasher, Chaos Bringer, Anarchist

Kevin, available roles: Ascended Animist, Steward of Elements, Vital Force

The options were all incredible. I burned the rest of the day mulling them over, though I only needed to make four of the selections myself. Since Elyk was still a living, breathing player, I didn't need to worry about his choice. He picked the *Fiend-Blooded* role which provided him a huge passive increase to his physical stat while also allowing him to delay a staggering amount of damage by spreading it out over time rather than taking it all at once. Now, if he was hit by some massive attack that would otherwise kill him, instead, the damage to his body would be spread out over time. A lot of raid bosses had the same mechanic, and it made their fights way harder, especially if someone was healing them.

For Xia, her three roles included buffs to commanding the undead, buffs to her personal spell casting, and adding the ability for her to heal our undead minions. All of them were tempting, all of them were certainly useful, but in the end, I elected to make her my *Dreadhorde General*. She would have full control over the entire undead army along with a handful of new spells to augment the zombies' fighting capabilities.

Xollmomath's selection was the easiest of them all. The very first one, *Unshackled*, allowed him to finally leave Undercroft Citadel. That upgrade alone was likely the most powerful thing to ever happen to Undercroft. Having Xoll by my side would mean the six remaining cities were all but doomed already.

As much as I reveled in Xollmomath's new role, I *hated* all the options for Ugg'chugg. Everything the shaman had was centered on indiscriminate wrecking. Smashing cities was useful, but I also needed the orc to not smash our own city. The same went for bringing chaos and plain old anarchy. I finally went with *Chaos Bringer*, and the role allowed the orc to cast her shaman spells with much, much greater intensity . . . albeit at random targets. I just hoped that when the time came, it wouldn't be too bad, though my confidence was low.

Kevin's roles were more like Xia's in that all three were excellent. *Ascended Animist* allowed him to create a plagued shadow of himself, essentially doubling his power in combat or close to it. *Steward of Elements* added a touch of shamanistic magic to his skillset, manipulating the ground and the elements for a whole new set of powers. The *Vital Force* role was somewhat unexpected, and I ultimately chose it for him. The role allowed Kevin to resurrect anyone lower level than him whom he killed, although the effect only lasted for ten seconds at a time. Still, despite the short duration, the resurrected enemy would be allied to Undercroft Citadel and would fight as though they were at full capabilities for the entire ten seconds. In essence, Kevin would be able to keep up a very effective continuous assault on a pack of enemies all on his own.

Before turning in for the night, there was still one part of my growing kingdom that I had yet to explore: the reflecting pool. I found it next to the bone chapel as before, and the strange pool sent a shiver up my spine. The liquid, whatever it was, shimmered with opalescent darkness. Staring into it felt like gazing at a pitch-black night sky. But that was the strange thing—there were stars overhead, but none of them were reflected in the pool. I hesitated to touch it, took a deep breath, and then swept a single tentacle-finger along its surface.

When my finger broke the surface, the liquid was not wet. It was *awake*. Something beneath the mirror-sheen noticed me, reacted to my presence. The ripples I made didn't move outward but converged inward, as if pulled to my body instead of repulsed by it. For a heartbeat, I saw the necropolis reflected not as it is, but as it was hundreds or thousands of years ago, when the first dead stars fell from the heavens and the bones of Wonder's original gods still steamed. A faint hum, resonating somewhere between the farthest reaches of my hearing and the dead space at the back of my skull, vibrated.

And then I was gone.

Or rather . . . the necropolis was gone. I felt as though I had not physically moved locations, but I had been swept along through time itself, though in which direction I had no idea. I stood in a field of swaying grasses on what *felt* like was the location of Whitechapel long before any of the houses had been built and certainly long before Undercroft Citadel had been raised. I brushed my tentacled hand through the grass, and it left an after image that slowly faded like morning fog. Light flowed off the grass as though pulled into the inky sky in flakes and ribbons. Ahead, a small structure broke the monotony of the swaying grass. I approached it slowly, finally recognizing it as a bit of crumbled brick wall. The old mortar holding the bricks together was chipped and pitted from eons of exposure to the elements. The whole structure was only about my height and no wider than a few feet. From the other side, I heard the distinct rattle of chains.

I walked around the ruined bit of wall, and there I found what I instinctively knew to be my own corpse. It was bloodied and battered, more cephalid than human, and chained around both the neck and waist. My head hung low, bent at an angle that suggested a broken neck, and a small trickle of blood dripped from the corner of my mouth.

A sense of pressure built up behind my eyes like soil settling on a coffin lid. The pressure released in a stream of whispered words. The voice was both unmistakable and unsurprising. Lady Kalma.

"I remember the taste of your breath before your lungs were woven . . . You were mine before you had a name . . . Every heartbeat you spend is a debt to the grave, and I am patient in my collection. Do you feel it, Bentalÿk? The warmth leaving your reflection? That is me, crawling backward through your veins, polishing your bones for the garden beneath the roots. All graves bloom . . . in time."

My eyes snapped open, and I was once more in the necropolis. The reflecting pool was still, silent. Xollmomath stood next to me, his depthless eyes fixed on the pool.

"Xoll," I gasped, somehow out of breath despite my lack of breathing. I took a moment to reorient my bearings. "Xoll . . . what the hell is the pool? I . . . I saw things. But I don't really know what."

He fixed me with his gaze, and I got the sinking feeling that he was not pleased by my questions. "The Stench of Corpses is not like other gods," he slowly began. He steepled his fingers in front of his chest. "She is the slow rot, the sacred decay of what was once holy. The horror of inevitability, whispered in the scent of grave dirt. The soil remembers, and so will you, Bentalÿk, when you are beneath it."

I had no idea what any of the strange necromancer's riddles could possibly mean, but I knew enough not to push the subject. And then a notification flashed in my vision, and I finally felt like I had some semblance of an answer.

Cursed: Hollow. Lady Kalma smiles upon your ambition. The soil remembers your name. Power through decay. Immortality through surrender. You are no longer merely alive; you are the echo of your own life continuing. Healing potions and other restorative magic no longer has an effect on you. Standing in the presence of corpses will steadily regenerate your body at the cost of your sanity. Those who have tasted corruption feel it like a heartbeat beneath the skin. Evil flocks to you.

I shook my head. The changes were all just *so much*. From the citadel to my physical appearance and then to my own stats and abilities—everything had changed. The last bit about evil flocking to me could either be fantastic or a horrible thorn in my side. Would other evil players like Elyk and Ministrel seek me out? Show up at the gate to pledge their allegiance to the cause?

And what about Helvegen? Hel was evil. She was most trusted advisor, after all. Would she be drawn back to my side like some scorned lover come to relive the better days? I didn't have an answer. But she was alive out there somewhere. Perhaps she would be drawn to me now. Only time would tell.

CHAPTER 3

The next morning, I went first for our production facilities. We still had more workbenches than craftsmen, and I wasn't sure how to fix that problem. What we really needed was to take over a guild of crafters or somehow entice one to come work for us, but neither of those options felt likely. Other than Geirr, we were running slim. The necro-botanist could make some potions, albeit low quality, and we had a few other zombies with enough crafting stat to at least be useful. Kulgun's death was certainly painful.

We still had a pair of gnomes from the Inventors' League, however. And Ministrel. He was their leader, and if the masks he made earlier were any indication of his crafting stat, he was bound to be a fine asset. The only problem was getting the man's attention. And getting him to focus on a task. And communicating with him. Now that I thought about it, there were a ton of problems surrounding Ministrel . . .

I found the strange wizard with his hands behind his back and counting paces in front of the walls. A host of zombies was busy repairing damage and reinforcing where they could, and I was woefully aware of just how much work the walls required if we were going to withstand another frontal assault.

"Ministrel!" I called, though I was standing directly in the man's path.

He didn't appear bothered.

"Hey, Ministrel. You have a minute? Can we talk?"

The man didn't look up from his measured pacing. He was only a few steps in front of me, and I wasn't about to move out of the way. And then he simply stepped right through me as though I didn't exist. The sensation left a tingling feeling in my gut, but it rapidly dissipated.

"Come on, man. None of your weird shit. We need to get to work!" I called after him.

Finally, the wizard crooked his head to one side and let out a sigh. I took that as a good sign. "Yes?" he said, fixing me with an unsettling grin.

"Alright, finally. First, what are you doing out here?" I asked.

He coughed into his tattered robe sleeve. "Just measuring the fathoms, boy. Nothing you need to worry over."

"Fathoms? Isn't that depth? You know what, never mind. Not important. I need to know more about your skills. What can you make? We need weapons and armor, magical items, potions—hell, we need everything!"

The crazed wizard dug around in one of his overly large pockets for a moment, then withdrew what appeared to be an egg. It was vaguely white and about the size of a normal egg, at least. "Here you go, boy. Made it fresh this morning." He tossed it to me, and then, without another word, the wizard turned on his heel and resumed counting the fathoms, whatever that possibly meant.

I caught the egg as gently as I could with my tentacle hands, and I was pleased when it didn't break. But I quickly realized it was no ordinary egg. It glimmered with the telltale sign of magic, and I accessed its description:

Doctor Malbec's Egg: When broken, this egg will release one fully grown adult chicken.

"God damnit, Ministrel," I muttered. What the hell was I supposed to do with an egg that made a chicken? That's what *all* eggs did, and I didn't have much particular use for the non-magical kind either. I decided not to try my luck with the wizard anymore and went back inside the walls to visit Geirr. I hadn't gotten much of an opportunity to speak to him lately, and a *lot* had happened.

"Hey," I said, finding him at the forge, though he wasn't slaving away with a hammer and tongs. The resurrection node had been dragged to his workshop, and it hovered a few inches off the ground. "Any ideas what we can do with it?"

Geirr shook his head. "Not yet, but there is great power inside. I just need to learn how to harness it. Here, touch the surface. You'll feel it."

I placed my strange hand on the orb, and it was warm. It thrummed with energy and heat just below its shining marble surface. "Hmmm . . . It could be some kind of energy source. Something like a battery. Or maybe a powerplant."

"That's what I'm thinking," Geirr said quietly as though he was in too much awe to speak at full volume in the orb's presence. "It is powerful, of that I have no doubt, but I don't know how to extract that power. I've tried everything I can think of, though to be fair, I don't have many options."

I wracked my own mind for ideas, though nothing sprang to the front. "Talk to Xollmomath. He won't know what it is or understand how it works, of course, but he might be able to shed some light on the power. That's my guess, at least."

Geirr nodded again. Finally, he peeled his gaze from the orb. He looked sad. "We don't have enough bodies to run all the workshops. Not even at half strength." He shrugged and stared at his boots. "What do you want me to do?"

"You're right. We need more people. I tried to recruit Ministrel to work for you, but you can guess how that went. The old man is frighteningly insane. How many people do you need?"

Geirr spread his hands wide. "The last time the necropolis expanded, we added a dozen new production facilities. We need twenty more workers, thirty or forty to be ideal. A whole guild of craftsman would be perfect."

"It's like you're reading my mind. I just don't know where to find them . . ."

"Neither do I."

"There are more towns and cities away from the coast, but leaving Undercroft without a full defensive compliment isn't going to be possible. Not yet, at least. And everyone in Echelon is bound to already be gone. The orcs are out of the question, and most of the gnomes are dead. Zombies aren't particularly useful . . ." I was running out of ideas. We simply lacked players. We had hundreds of NPC zombies, but only a handful of real humans. If we were going to survive, I *had* to remedy that problem.

"Surely there are more like . . . well . . ."

I knew what he wanted to say. "More evil players, you mean."

He gulped hard.

"No offense taken. And you're right. There weren't many, but I *know* there were some evil guilds at a few of the major cities, and there are bound to be more in the wilderness areas. Some of them will have crafters, and some of them will want to fight for the bad guys. Good thinking. We need to scout. Search them out and send envoys to negotiate."

Unfortunately, our problem with a lack of players meant we also didn't really have any scouts. Actually, we still had one scout. And a damned fine one at that. I found Alyssa, the undead arcanist, working with a few other mindless zombies at the gatehouse. I knew I couldn't give her any complex commands, but I could still order her to accomplish general tasks. And then it dawned on me: Xia's new role meant *she* could give the undead complex tasks even if I could not.

I brought the two of them together, and soon enough, we had a plan. Alyssa would use her formidable arcanist magic to scout the opposite direction from Echelon. Beyond the mine, beyond whatever was left of Tall Timbers, and to the next towns and the cities after those. It would take her some time, but it was worth it. If she found anyone evil, she couldn't exactly tell them to come back to Undercroft Citadel with her, but Xia could use her *Eye of the Necropolis* ability to give us a fix on the person's location. It was a clunky plan, perhaps far slower than I would have liked, but it was the best we had. I set her off at once.

In the meantime, I decided to finish razing Echelon. I wanted to completely destroy the city—and, more importantly, ensure that no remaining pockets of resistance existed—and then properly loot it. I also needed to take stock of their harbor. I had never left the Echelon continent in my limited time playing the game, so I wasn't very well versed in the comings and goings at the docks. If any decent ships remained, we would commandeer them, of course, though I knew my small army was still far too weak to risk a voyage to another land.

We spent four peaceful days repairing the walls, strengthening the defenses, and generally licking our wounds. Finally, I took Elyk and a hundred zombies, and we marched back to the ruins of Echelon to finish what we had started.

The city was all but abandoned. A few stragglers remained, and they were all NPCs. Of course, the non-player characters didn't quite grasp the gravity of their situation, so while most had fled with all the players, some lingered. At the first wretched survivor, I feared it was some kind of trap, but Elyk severed the man's head from his shoulders without incident. By the time my little band reached the harbor, we had butchered a good thirty or forty NPCs. Unfortunately, they were all shopkeepers or general peasants—no one useful.

I stood with Elyk at my side on a battlement overlooking the ocean. The walls at the harbor hadn't been damaged by the previous battles, and for a long moment I wondered if it would be possible to move all of Undercroft Citadel to the seaside. The walls, sturdy white stone with all manner of emplacements atop them, were leagues beyond anything we had built. But no, my city did not yet fly, and I highly doubted flight would even be possible.

A pair of ships broke up the azure monotony of the ocean, and I figured they had to be at least a mile or so out. From such a distance, I had no idea which direction they traveled. I could only guess that they were fleeing. A few smaller boats were still tied up to the docks, clearly abandoned, and all far too tiny for anything I would use them for. Only one other building really caught my attention. A lighthouse stood at the end of a rocky breakwater, and someone was inside. I watched their silhouette for a few minutes.

"Someone's up there," I said to Elyk.

He shielded his eyes from the sun and grunted. "Looks like it," he finally agreed.

"We should pay them a visit."

The man gave his anti-magic buckler a knock and led the way. The breakwater was precarious, and if the lighthouse's occupant had been so inclined, the approach would have been treacherous at best. As it was, we reached the lighthouse door unscathed and found it curiously unlocked. Elyk took a few cautious steps inside, his buckler raised on one arm and Infernum at the ready. We stopped at the base of the stairs and listened. All we heard from above was the shuffle of feet.

I pointed, and Elyk placed one slow, quiet foot on the first stair.

The shuffling feet abruptly stopped, and a man cried out. "Damned stool!" the familiar voice echoed in the tight quarters.

Elyk relaxed, and we both scampered up the stairs to find Ministrel pointing a finger at a fallen stool. With a snap, a small stream of magic erupted from the wizard's fingertip and turned half the stool to charred ash.

"Ministrel, what the hell are you doing here?" I demanded. "And *how* did you get here? We left you back at Undercroft, right?"

The man fixed us each with a crooked stare. "Forty-six fathoms from home to Echelon," he announced with a quirky smile.

I was rapidly growing tired of the old man's esoteric way of speaking. At the risk of life and limb, I grabbed him by the sides of his face and forced him to meet my gaze. "Ministrel. Speak plainly. How the *hell* did you get all the way from Echelon to this lighthouse so quickly? Tell me, or I'm going to drag you to the rail and throw you into the ocean."

"Forty-six fathoms," he frustratingly repeated. "You just walk down, of course! Forty-six!"

It was no use. The old man was simply too far gone. I let out a scream of pent of rage and slammed my tentacle fist into the wall. The thin metal bent beneath the strike.

Elyk stepped up to the wizard and placed a hand on his shoulder. "Can you get us back just as quickly, old man?" he asked.

Ministrel worked up his face into a series of odd, inscrutable expressions. "Forty-six fathoms each way," he finally answered.

"The zombies have their orders. They'll loot the city, burn whatever is left, and then make the march back to Undercroft with or without us. Let's see if the old man can take us for a ride." Elyk turned back to the wizard and held his attention much as I had, though with his hands on Ministrel's shoulders instead of his face. "Take us back to Undercroft Citadel. Forty-six . . . fathoms, or whatever. Take us for a ride!"

All at once, the world went black. I was swimming, or trying to, but the sensation only lasted for a few seconds. Then we emerged from the mysterious liquid to stand on the very spot outside Undercroft where I had attempted to extract information from Minstrel earlier. Despite performing one of the most impressive spells I had ever seen, the wizard hardly appeared fazed.

"Do it again, old man," Elyk demanded with a laugh. "Take us back to the lighthouse!"

Once more, everything went dark. We swam through some unknown, sticky liquid, and then we popped up a few seconds later back the lighthouse.

"Forty-six fathoms!" the man screamed with overt glee. I still had no idea what the phrase meant, but I didn't particularly care. We had teleportation. Teleportation! It was better than any boat we could commandeer from the harbor. Even if the spell's maximum capacity was only three—which was completely unproven—it would be the single most useful spell in my entire kingdom.

Elyk was practically hysterical with joy. "Back again, old man! Take us back!"

And back we went! We appeared once more outside Undercroft Citadel, and I held up a hand for the dizzying merry-go-round of magical teleportation to finally stop. I didn't know how much energy Ministrel had at his disposal, and it would be just our luck for it to run out at thirty fathoms or twenty-five, leaving us stranded somewhere deep underground.

Once I caught my breath, I left Ministrel to whatever it was that occupied his days and set about inspecting the wall repairs. Everything was moving along nicely despite our lack of manpower. The gaping holes had all been patched with fresh timber, and most of the tall beams were at least banded together with heavy rope if not metal. We still had our ring of fear glyphs, and the moat writhed in the afternoon sun like an inky black worm circling the entire settlement. We now sported two guard towers, one on either side of the main gate, though we didn't have any archers or crossbowman to station there. Still, some defenses were better than nothing. Most importantly, the mine was rattling along at full speed. The orcs and zombies had set up a rather efficient system, and we had a significant stockpile of ingots waiting to be crafted. But again, the lack of crafters was our downfall.

I awoke the next morning before dawn to the sound of someone banging on my door. I threw on a simple shirt and met Geirr on the steps.

"What is it?"

He didn't appear worried, just in a hurry. "A guild has come, sir, but they aren't attacking. Just . . . requesting an audience."

I immediately thought of my new curse and the final line: *evil flocks to you*. "Thanks for getting me. Is Elyk awake? I want him by my side."

Geirr offered a weak smile. "He was the first one outside the gate to meet the guild. He's with them now."

"Excellent. Get Xia and Xollmomath. Have them watch from the guard towers. If anything happens, they'll know what to do."

Geirr ran off, and I silently summoned one of the gargoyles to carry me over the walls to our new guests. Without my legendary armor, the magical stone beast's talons cut painfully into my shoulders, but I didn't really have time to think up a solution to that problem. I landed with a gentle thud about twenty or so paces from the guild.

But *guild* might not have been the best term. Six players stood in a semicircle. They wore weapons, but none of them were drawn. Each player was in the high twenties for level, and five of the six shared the assassin class. Elyk held Infernum at the ready, and the sword's magical fire provided all the light for our small rendezvous.

One of the assassins—I guessed he was their leader—stepped forward and extended a hand. "Kadorax," he said with a grin. "I lead the Blackened Blades. Syzak is a shaman, but the rest of us are assassins. We, uh, we like what you're doing. We want to help."

The shaman was a level twenty-nine hybrid race. Though he had the head and arms of a human, the rest of his body was that of a snake. A thin forked tongue darted between his teeth to taste the air.

I was instantly wary. A group of powerful assassins, no matter how small, was dangerous. But it at least made some sense. My new curse would attract other evil players, perhaps NPCs as well, and more players were bound to arrive every day. "Where are you from?" I asked.

"Olympia City," he answered.

"And how did you get here?"

"We've been on the move for about a week. Ever since the

notification that talked about real death and the continental resurrection hubs. We all made the decision join you."

Again, I couldn't help but feel like the whole set up was a trap. But if the assassins wanted to take us out, they would have attacked already. We would know their true intentions by now.

"*How* did you get to Echelon's continent?" I asked again. "A boat? Magic?"

Kadorax shrugged. "Horses to the coast, and then we stowed away on a ship that made the crossing to pick up survivors from Echelon. Well . . ." He glanced at Syzak, the snake-man shaman. "*Someone* got caught stealing food from the galley. There was a fight, and we commandeered the ship. None of us are pirates or know how to steer a ship, so we wrecked it pretty bad a few miles down the coast from Echelon. Been on foot since then."

The story at least made sense. Behind the small group, the sun was just starting to crest over the horizon. A cool breeze kicked up, and a group of white and gray birds flew overhead, noisily flapping their wings. "I take it you had more on the boat?"

The assassin sighed. "Not many. Lost two when the fighting broke out. Another to the shipwreck who apparently could not swim. Had we known she couldn't swim, we would have saved her, of course, but in the confusion of the wreck, it just . . . it was too late by time anyone noticed."

I thought of making the small group cut off a finger to show their loyalty, but the gesture felt too inconsequential. A crew of hardened assassins wouldn't be fazed by it. I needed something stronger to test their loyalty. But that plan could wait for a little while, at least. I waved to Elyk to lower his weapon. "Alright. Change your allegiance to Undercroft Citadel. You'll stay outside the walls until I trust you. And how well do you know Olympia City?"

Olympia corresponded to the portal outside Oslo in the real world, though Kadorax didn't have an accent like Helvegen and Geirr. He was clearly American.

Before he responded, Kadorax blinked about ten feet to my left, and that made Elyk reignite Infernum and nearly charge. "Walls aren't really much of a problem. We're assassins, remember? If we wanted trouble, we certainly wouldn't be standing out here in the open right now. We'd wait until night when everyone is asleep, and then we'd slit your throats one by one. Real quiet, real effective. You can trust us."

"I guess I don't have much of a choice."

He shook his head. "Not exactly, but if you don't want our help, we'll go. There are some other guilds around New Karstad and Iron Hall who are gathering armies. Evil armies like yours. They're going after the resurrection hubs. Hell, Olympia City is a full-blown warzone already. Trenches, siege gear, you name it."

The man must have read the absolutely dumbfounded expression on my face, because he laughed like I had just told the funniest joke when in reality I hadn't said a word.

"You don't get out much, do you?" Kadorax continued. "Look, I don't know how the hell you've managed to sack Echelon or how you got such a weird class, but you're not alone. Us . . . eh, *evil* players are more numerous than you might think."

I had no idea what to say. "But . . . why?"

Again, the assassin laughed. "Come on, man. The world sucks. Earth is fucking miserable. Medicine shortages, radiation, food rationing, floods. Where are you from originally? Atlanta? Shit, that's not too bad. You ever make it out west? Nevada? You should see the coast. Old skyscrapers half underwater that used to be hotels and casinos. But there's no *food* out there. Nothing grows. Not since the dust storms started a few years back. Let's just say . . . the lower the population that makes it out of Wonder and back to Earth, the more resources there will be to go around. But what's better than that?"

I shrugged.

The snake-man stepped up and finally spoke, his voice a hiss. "We never go back. Food grows here. It rains without acid stinging your skin. No radiation meds. No shortages."

I was stunned by the beautiful simplicity. It was all starting to come together, and I liked what I heard. "Ah, alright. I get it. Going back is a last resort. Yeah, agreed. And if you *do* have to go back, you'd prefer as few people making the trip as possible. That right?"

The rest of the assassins all voiced their mutual assent.

Kadorax fixed me with a smile. His shaggy brown hair was tossed on the morning breeze. The man cut a fine figure, and I had no doubt that his dark leather armor was just as powerfully crafted as the pair of wicked daggers on his belt. The Blackened Blades guild would make excellent allies. "Welcome to Undercroft Citadel," I said with a smile, extending my hand. The assassin gave it a firm shake. "We have plenty of room in the barracks. Make yourselves at home, and try to steer clear of the orcs. They're cannibals. Take a few hours to get settled, and let's meet at the gate. Oh, and maybe don't touch the reflecting pool. I don't fully understand what it does, but I got permanently cursed just by sticking in a finger."

The man gave me a nod. "Sounds good. And we've got some ideas regarding the Echelon resurrection hub if you'll listen to them."

"Of course."

Elyk and I watched the small band make their way to Undercroft, and a rising feeling took hold in my chest. We were short on manpower, but *there were others*. More players who thought like me. Well, perhaps not exactly like me, but close enough. Our goals were aligned. The Blackened Blades wanted to stop the return to Earth, if possible, and at least thin the heard otherwise.

I simply wanted everyone dead.

Close enough.

I met up with Kadorax and the snake-man shaman around noon at the gate to go over plans. Sadly, none of the assassins were skilled craftsmen. Our lack of operational production facilities was a problem that just refused to go away. What the assassins did have was knowledge, and that was damn near just as good as craftsmen. As it turned out, I basically didn't really know *anything* about the world of Wonder beyond Echelon's shores. I simply hadn't played the game long enough, and all the streamers I watched were based here.

Olympia City, the capital linked to the portal in Oslo back on Earth, was apparently deep in their own war. The evil guilds from that continent had all joined forces to attack the resurrection hub, and the city's defenders were numerous. Another thing I hadn't considered about resurrection being back online was the experience. Before, everyone had been terrified to go on quests or clear dungeons. One mistake meant truth death. Now, things were somewhat back to normal. Guilds were running dungeons and raids to outfit their players, and the war outside Olympia City was basically a farming ground for experience points. Kadorax and Syzak had seen it all on their way out of the city. For as much as the evil guilds wanted to destroy the hub, they also wanted to do it slowly. More kills meant more experience, and more experience meant more power. I wondered if I should have done something similar to the orb we captured from Echelon.

Too late now.

And Syzak had some ideas when it came to the orb itself. There were rumors that the orbs operated on in-game magic rather than purely scripted programming, and that meant the orbs followed other in-game rules. The magic could be used, in theory, to power things other than the resurrection orbs themselves. The Blackened Blades had plans to find a powerful enough wizard or other spellcaster and use them to tap into the orb's magic. If their theory was correct, a wizard would be able to super charge a single lightning bolt of blizzard spell into an absolutely cataclysmic attack if they had access to all the magic powering the orb.

With a smile, I led the two players to our own captured orb in the workshop, and they marveled. "I think you're right about the power," I said once they each had a chance to inspect it themselves. "We have a high-level wizard too, but he's essentially insane. Not much help right now. But if we can figure out how to harness the power from the orb, we'll be unstoppable."

"Limitless energy," Syzak hissed, his snake tongue flicking a few inches from the orb's shiny surface.

"Before we do anything, we need someone with answers. Someone who has played the game since day one and knows more about the orbs than we do. I don't want to start poking around and accidentally destroy it. Or worse, crack it open and release a giant explosion that kills us all." I had visions of using the gas Geirr and Kulgun had synthesized to float the orb above a capital city and drop it like a nuclear bomb. If it worked the way I saw it in my head, we would eradicate entire populations at once, just like the wars that saw the deaths of millions back on Earth. But it was all just a fantasy. We had no idea how the orb actually worked.

Kadorax smiled. "You should see the battle at Olympia City. Thousands of players. Tens of thousands. And for every player, probably ten times that number of NPCs. After the announcement, everyone rushed to the capitals to protect the orbs. Evil guilds followed. There are hundreds of wizards, powerful spellcasters on both sides. I'm sure at least some of them would know *something* about the orb and how to use it."

"Then we need to get there and capture ourselves a few wizards," I said.

"We can't take a boat. Olympia City's harbor has already been burned, and the town guard patrols it heavily. But we'll need to cross the ocean somehow. You have a plan?"

I gave the assassin a pat on the shoulder. "Remember the crazy wizard? He can blink multiple people. I don't know how far, but hopefully far enough. I'll try to get him working on it, and in the meantime, I want to see the Blackened Blades in action."

"Certainly," Kadorax said, standing a little straighter. "What do you have in mind?"

"We'll go north through the forest. There's a little lumber mill town not too far, or there *was* a town, but there will be more. We'll either run into another town or a dungeon and clear it together. Have your assassins ready tomorrow at dawn. Hopefully the zombies looting Echelon will have brought back enough horses for us by then, but it isn't a guarantee. We might be moving on foot."

"Understood." Kadorax and Syzak both snapped off crisp salutes which I hadn't really expected at all. Undercroft Citadel wasn't really a saluting kind of place. I returned the gesture as best I could, then set off to share as much of the plan with Ministrel as possible. I needed to get him working on a teleportation spell for about ten of us to Olympia City, and I needed it sooner rather than later.

◄◆►

At dawn, I was met with a welcome sight: Kadorax and his band were assembled on horseback with two more mounts. Elyk stood next to one and held the reins of mine. "The horses aren't great, just working beasts and not particularly accustomed to being ridden, but they'll do," the harvester said upon my arrival.

It took a minute for my horse to calm enough for me to mount her, but I was grateful nonetheless. The zombies had nearly finished looting Echelon, and not much had been left. Fortunately, there was a lot of livestock to be collected. Honestly, it was too much for Undercroft Citadel considering ninety percent or more of our inhabitants had no need for food. They also brought back grain and other staple crops for us to eat for at least six months. The only provisions the fleeing populace seemingly took with them were bottles of booze. Everything else had been abandoned wholesale.

I gave my unruly steed a firm pat to no effect and simply had to wait out its latest bout of resistance. Finally, after what felt like an hour but was likely only a minute or two, the horse settled enough to take a command. We started off at a slow trot, and I took stock of our merry band of adventurers. Five assassins, one shaman, a harvester outfitted in legendary gear, and then me. A class no one had seen before. We were a fearsome lot, small as we were, and I was confident that whatever we stumbled across wouldn't stand a chance.

As the others made small talk, I daydreamed of what the future would hold. If we were lucky, we'd find a dungeon with high-tier loot. If not, whatever village was closest would suffice. There would be a slaughter, looting, and then we would return home. After that: Olympia City. If Ministrel could get us across the ocean—and back again—we would destroy another resurrection hub. It wouldn't be hard with the city at war and a band of skilled assassins at my side. We'd sneak in through the chaos, bring a healthy bit more chaos, and knock out their orb before anyone realized what was happening. Then the chaos would multiply, and Olympia City would fall.

But there were more cities. Five more hubs after Olympia. New Karstad, the capital corresponding to the portal in Madrid, was already at war. And Iron Hall, too. Then we would have Bellefontaine, The Jade Spire, and Redwing's Bastion. I'd never been to any of them, but I would gaze upon each one reduced to ash beneath my boots before I died.

And if there were other evil guilds already fighting against those who would defend the orbs . . . an alliance of guilds was what I needed. Dozens of organized guilds all pursuing the same goal.

Another thought floated through my mind, and it was one I didn't know how to handle. Helvegen was still out there. We would undoubtedly meet again someday. Would I kill her? Plunge my squid-like hands through her chest once more? Or would she simply become another nameless casualty on a grand battlefield outside one of the capital cities? I thought of my curse and the group of assassins at my back. Perhaps Hel would be drawn to me the same as the assassins. Whatever happened, dealing with Hel was an issue for another day, another time.

Our group moved at a decent pace for the entire morning and half the afternoon before we came across any signs of life, though we passed two abandoned homesteads along the way. Finally, we came to a crossroads with a sign that indicated the presence of a village to our south. The town was Wolfpine, one I had never heard of before. We turned our stubborn mounts east, clopping along the meager dirt road under the shade of tall trees on both sides. Eventually, we reached the outskirts of the sleepy village, and it reminded me a lot of Tall Timbers. I supposed most of the villages in the forest would be similar to the logging town, and Wolfpine was nearly identical.

"What's the plan?" Kadorax asked.

Elyk tightened his grip on his reins. "Kill them all?"

I shook my head. "No, no need for that. Too far to get the corpses back for Xollmomath in either case." A new thought crossed my mind. "You know what, let's find their leader and see if they have a dungeon quest nearby. A town like this has to have a cave full of spiders or something else they need exterminated."

"You'd clear a cave of spiders for a random village?" Kadorax asked, incredulous.

I had to laugh. The man didn't know my style yet. "Not exactly. If there's a big bad guy lurking the woods, we'll convince it to join us. *Then* we'll raze the village."

"Ha, excellent," Kadorax said. He spurred his horse toward the tallest building in the center of town, and I lazily followed. The town didn't look like it held anything of note, at least not for us. There was a small forge that would have been useful if it was closer and that was about it.

It didn't take long for Kadorax and his assassins to find the town's NPC leader and scrounge up a quest for us, though it wasn't the most exciting thing I had ever heard. According to the town alderman, a recent shipment from the next village over that was scheduled to arrive a few days ago had not appeared. The merchant, a man named Aldo, came through Wolfpine twice a month with his big black dog to deliver an assortment of refined glass and other wares to be sold at the general store. According to local legend, there was a creature—although no one could define it—that lived deep in the woods and ate unsuspecting travelers. The townsfolk naturally believed that their unnamed and indescribable 'beast' was to blame for Aldo's late arrival. We would be paid in silver for our troubles if we were able to ascertain poor Aldo's fate.

The only thing I liked about the job was the slight chance that there was some powerful creature living in the woods that we would be able to track down and capture. Besides that, the quest wouldn't take more than a few hours, and then we could either move on or just raze and loot Wolfpine.

We set out deeper into the woods, following a pair of well-worn wagon tracks that meandered next to a small, quaint stream. The stream eventually grew wider, and we crossed an arched stone bridge decorated with a few potted flowers on either side. On the other side of the bridge, the wagon ruts carried onward, but then they veered off the expected path. They wound between some of the smaller trees, and one of the wheels clearly ricocheted off the base of a tall oak.

On the other side, half of the cart was balanced on its side with a wheel sticking up in the air. The merchant's goods were scattered across the ground, but we didn't see any blood. It only took a few seconds of investigation for one of the assassins to find at least part of our answer: a sinkhole.

"Looks like something spooked the animal, and the driver couldn't control the cart. They would have just crashed into the tree and been done with the whole ordeal, but there's a sinkhole. The animal probably fell down, and the merchant chased it," one of the Blackened Blades assassins reported. She guided us to the edge of the sinkhole, and the story seemed to line up perfectly.

"Hello? Anyone down there?" I called.

There was no response. The sinkhole looked about ten, maybe twelve feet deep. It was so muddy that it reminded me more of a heavy mudslide than a proper sinkhole, and I had seen plenty of both back in the real world. Especially in the early days of the acid rain storms after the war, sinkholes were common. Whole buildings would be devoured, and the government didn't have the resources or the motivation to prevent it.

One of the assassins uncoiled a rope and tied it around a tree, then began the slippery descent into the sinkhole. The rest of us followed suit, careful not to lose our footing in the thick, grasping mud. At the bottom, a few quick casts of assassin magic provided plenty of light.

"Not a sinkhole, then . . ." Kadorax muttered.

Elyk, flaming sword leading the way, took point. While the mudslide behind us appeared natural enough, nothing else was. We stood in a hall or some kind of antechamber to a larger stone structure. Old torch sconces hung on the walls, layers of burnt carbon streaking above them. The ceiling, now ten feet above us, was caked in mud and creeping roots from the forest floor. It smelled like dirt and trees, mold and mushrooms. And everything was wet. If there were stones beneath our boots, they were buried under more mud.

Elyk came to a wooden door banded with iron. At some point, probably hundreds of years ago, the door would have been a formidable barrier, but time had reduced it practically to splinters. The harvester gave the door a couple firm shakes, and it crumbled at his feet. The chamber beyond presented more of the same. I was about to step through behind Elyk when Kadorax stopped me.

"Need to check for traps first. Assassin's work," he said quietly. Two of his guild members scoured the hall for a few minutes before reporting that the path was clear.

We crept down the next hall, and I had to wonder what happened to the merchant. If he chased an animal down the sinkhole, he would have found the exact same area. So then why was the door intact when we arrived? It didn't make any sense.

"Be on your guard," I told the group. "Something here doesn't add up. We should have found the merchant right away."

Syzak, the snake-man shaman, came up alongside me. "Now we're in a proper dungeon. Time for a few good kills."

I supposed he was right. We were after experience, not some simple fetch mission, and it seemed we had it.

We reached a grand hall at the end of the passage, one that opened up with high, vaulted ceilings and stained-glass windows set into the walls. There was nothing but dirt on the other side of the glass, but it was curious that at least most of it was still intact. Ancient wooden supports reached toward the ceiling, and piles of fallen mortar and shingles dotted the muddy floor. On the stone walls, we found carvings too worn by the ages to be deciphered. Still, there was no sign of Aldo or the big dog he supposedly kept. If they were down here, they either didn't leave tracks or they had gone another way altogether.

We fanned out, letting the skilled assassins check for traps, and investigated the large, empty room. Beyond the layers of mud, dirt, and grime, all we found was a broken statue in one corner. It looked to originally be human, some unknown priest or other religious patron, and it had originally stood with hands clasped inside a decorated robe. Now, all that remained upright was the figure's legs. The torso had fallen, and the head was nowhere to be seen.

"Check this out, boss," one of the assassins said. He used a dagger behind the statue to pry up a thin, crumbling flagstone, and it revealed a narrow descent deeper into the ground.

My own investigation stat was only nine—absolutely terrible, but I didn't have much need for it. The assassins, on the other hand, probably trained it day in and day out. Elyk and I on our own would have never found the descent, and our pursuit of the quest would have likely ended with the broken statue and no sign of Aldo the merchant.

Kadorax sent one of his assassins down the narrow slope first, and when no cries of alarm issued forth, the rest of us followed. What remained beneath the buried building was a maze of tight, cramped tunnels and unsure footing. Tracking along behind the assassins, we soon reached a room that was perhaps a natural cave at some point, but it had clearly been worked by human hands.

The room was quiet and eerie, and ancient space that hinted at some long-lost grand designs. It was shaped as a half oval, maybe thirty feet wide and twenty deep, and untouched for centuries. The floor beneath our feet was a mixture of hard dirt and crumbling brickwork. At the far end stood a shallow basin carved from a single slab of polished basalt. Above it, another statue stood erect, though it was also curiously missing a head.

"Any ideas?" I asked, and my voice somehow felt too loud for the small, silent space. It felt like speaking would disrupt whatever eons-long process was taking place in the forgotten chamber, and if we were too loud, some malevolent entity would be roused from its eternal slumber to remedy our intrusion.

Kadorax traced a gloved finger along the edge of the basin, following an intricate relief. Images of hands cupping water, a lantern above a bowl, and a hooded figure watching it all stood out in stark contrast to the deep black basalt. Behind the headless statue, Syzak was able to translate a set of runes: *Light reflected in water reveals the truth.*

"What does it mean?" I whispered. Again, my voice felt obtrusive and insulting. A place like that was meant for silence and solitude, not words.

Syzak took a waterskin from his belt and slowly poured its contents into the basin. The water gathered and beaded into the grooves and cracks, but not by gravity. It avoided some valleys while cascading over ridges to reach others. Something was pulling the water for a purpose. I leaned over the basin to attempt to find a reflection of the 'truth' mentioned in the runes, and my image was distorted. I saw myself, but not with the tentacles and other monstrous appendages Lady Kalma had given to me. I was younger, probably from a time before Wonder even existed, and I looked happy. Or at least peaceful. Content. Then a breeze touched my skin, and I whirled, ready to fight, but nothing was there. When I looked back to the small pool, my reflection was gone.

"The walls," Syzak hissed. The shaman pointed a scaly finger at one of the ancient frescoes.

It moved. The figured carved in stone—a priest or some other robed acolyte carrying a lantern—walked toward the other end of the chamber. As the figure's lantern brightened, the illumination spells cast by the assassins dimmed. The magical being's footsteps echoed off the stone walls, though the timing was all off. The figure would take a step forward, and half a second later it would be heard in the chamber. Everything was off, just like the water in the basin. Whatever magic lingered in the place, it was powerful. But curiously, it was not malevolent. Not yet.

Our group silently followed the strange guide to the end of the oblong chamber. Where there had been nothing but stone and dirt only moments before, now there was a curved archway leading to another chamber. The figure ushered us through with a wave of its stone hand.

Again, the assassins took point, eagerly checking for traps. Watching them from the archway, I got the distinct feeling that someone had been there before. Despite the place's obvious age, it felt like we were not the first people to grace its halls. Perhaps Aldo had been there only days before, but there were no footprints. Nothing was disturbed or out of place.

Most of all, the lack of attackers worried me. This was a dungeon, I was sure of it. Dungeons were meant to be full of monsters and deadly traps. So far, we hadn't encountered a thing. Just a few esoteric puzzles that led us deeper and deeper beneath the surface. I thought back to my own measly investigation skill and wondered if this was how all the quests and dungeons were meant to be. Assassins would have incredibly high investigation, of course, and that meant they saw things that I never would. They noticed things and deciphered puzzles while I stood there like an idiot waiting for something to bash with my tentacle arms. Perhaps if I didn't have the Blackened Blades, if it was just me and Elyk, we would have found the sinkhole, found nothing inside, and then reported back to Wolfpine that their beloved merchant had simply fallen into the ground and been lost. The townsfolk would have rewarded us for the information, and that would have been it. But now . . . Clearly, there was so much more.

The lead assassins signaled back that that way was clear, and we fanned into the room. At once, I heard voices. Whispers. Echoes of things said long ago that the walls still remembered. The floor beneath us shifted, reforming from a dirty, mud-covered collection of stones into something polished and pristine. The walls straightened and seemed to breathe new life. Layers of dust and mud fell from them to vanish into thin air. Torches sprang to life in sconces all around, bathing the large room in orange and yellow.

"We're back in the first chamber," I said with confidence. "In the past. A memory. Be on your guard."

Everyone drew their weapons. Elyk ignited Infernum. Syzak stood off to the side with one of the assassins who appeared to act as his personal bodyguard.

Suddenly, a dozen or more marble statues identical to the broken one we had seen before erupted through the ground. They rose up in a perfect array, and their stone hoods fell from their bodies to reveal empty space where their heads should have been.

"Kill them all!" Kadorax bellowed.

The first pair of assassins worked perfectly in tandem, flanking the nearest statue like tigers stalking prey. They lunged, each activating a host of talents, and then crashed back to the ground. Their blades, no doubt heavily enchanted and masterfully made, were completely ineffective against the marble statues.

We didn't have time to figure out what the hell just happened. The nearest enemy was closing in with all the speed and grace of a charging bull. Syzak and I dodged out of the way, and I activated *Pull from the Darkness* as the statue skidded by. My shadow pet sapped a huge burst of energy from me, and then it launched itself at the nearest statue. I watched in horror as its attacks did absolutely nothing. The statues were just that: carved marbled. No flesh to tear, no mind to break, no will to shatter. They were perfectly impervious to both physical and mental attacks.

Before the shadow pet had a chance to drain my energy again, I dismissed it and changed tactics. *Visage of the Dark One* was an option, but if the statues had no heads or minds, I was sure they couldn't be dominated. The rest of my abilities were either poison based or just not applicable.

With a scream, I swung my powerful tentacle arms into a statue. We connected with a crash, and the force was nearly enough to break my bones. It looked like I barely chipped the marble. I had maybe two or three of those attacks left before my arms would shatter, and there were at least a dozen statues. Brute force was out of the question.

To my left, Syzak loosed a huge fireball that fully

consumed two of the statues. I held out hope that his magic was strong enough to melt the marble, but of course it was not. It only left streaks of char on their surfaces, nothing more.

Elsewhere, the assassins weren't faring any better. One of them had already broken a blade, and she resorted to dodging and evading rather than mounting any kind of offense.

"Elyk, don't risk the sword!" I yelled over the commotion. From what I could tell, he had thought the same and not been so foolish as to swing Infernum against solid stone.

Without magic strong enough to melt marble—and I wasn't even sure if such a thing existed—we were screwed. Dead. But there *had* to be another way. Dungeons were not designed to be completely unwinnable. What would be the point?

I scoured the room for any possible clues. Syzak seemed to be the only one making progress. As a shaman, he could wrench huge chunks of earth from the ground and bend them to his will, and our statue attackers struggled to climb over his makeshift earthen barriers. That, at least, bought us some time.

Deflecting a massive stone blow with the flat of one of his blades, Kadorax rolled to my side. "Any of that deathbringer magic?" he shouted.

I didn't have time to correct him on my class. "We need to search for clues. It has to be another puzzle!"

He nodded, then issued a quick stream of commands that his faithful guildmates followed at once. Two of the assassins stayed with Syzak to protect the shaman while the others quickly sheathed their weapons and went back into investigation mode.

The statues were relentless. Like the others, all I could do was dodge and hope to not get hit. Fortunately, the statues seemed to struggle with quick pivots and turns, so the assassins didn't have much problem. I, on the other hand, was slow by comparison. I took a few glancing blows, and without the legendary armor I was accustomed to, they were damn near bone shattering. I wouldn't last more than a few minutes.

"Sy, what was the riddle from the other room?" Kadorax yelled.

The snake-man glistened in sweat—a somewhat odd sight considering his scaled, reptilian body—and panted heavily. With a flourish he raised two more huge barriers of soil and stone, then scampered back in our direction. "Light reflects in water to see the truth," he said quickly. "Something like that."

I wracked my mind. *Light reflects the truth.* There had to be something there. It didn't just show us the way forward—it *had* to be the solution as well. None of the assassins had found any other clues, so I ran back the way we had come. It was dark, but I found the arched passageway easily enough and then yelled for Kadorax to follow.

"We won't be able to dodge back here," the man shouted. He was right. The tighter quarters of the first room would mean the statues held every advantage.

I stopped at the pool and stared. Nothing. No reflection at all. Maybe it was too dark. "Can you make a light?"

Kadorax didn't slow, and a little orb of light appeared right in front of my face.

The pool still showed nothing.

"Fuck!" I pounded my fists on the edge of the basalt basin. "It has to be something with the water, I just don't know what!"

"One of them is coming," Kadorax stated evenly. He held a dagger in each hand and stood on the balls of his feet like a coiled cobra ready to strike.

"Let it in," I said. "Not that our attacks do much to them

anyway. I think we need to get it in front of the pool. Maybe if it sees its reflection, it'll die. I don't know."

The assassin shrugged. "Better than nothing."

The massive statue came barreling down the tight corridor, its wide shoulders scraping rock and dirt from the walls with every step. Kadorax taunted it like a matador, then shoved it in the back right as it emerged from the tunnel.

By a stroke of good luck, I was right. The statue hurtled over the basin, and when it did, the stone melted away to flesh and bone. Where an impervious statue had once been was now just a headless priest in a loose robe. He fell dead at my feet with a complete lack of ceremony that was at least a little disappointing.

"Draw the others," I stated.

Kadorax didn't need any telling. He ran out of the tunnel, and a few seconds later he came running back with another huge statue hot on his heels.

It took a few minutes to corral all the statues into the first chamber, but it worked, and no one got injured beyond a few bumps and bruises. Unfortunately, Syzak was nearly out of mana, but that was our only real loss. He had a pair of potions that would bring him back up in a pinch, though I told him to save them. With no one to make potions at Undercroft Citadel, I felt like we needed to preserve whatever we had unless absolutely necessary.

When the killing was done, we had a pile of headless priests in black robes stacked up next to the basalt basin, and the we were finally free to explore the large chamber beyond. As I suspected, it was a mirror image of the very first room we entered after the sinkhole, albeit in pristine condition rather than tattered and crumbling.

Once more, the assassins quickly paid off with their skill in investigation. One of them found a torn shred of paper wedged into the small gap between one of the stone walls and an iron sconce. The top was singed where torch flame had reached a bit too close, but the text was still plainly legible:

I saw his lantern.

Gods, I thought it was a man.

But the light . . . wasn't light.

I looked back at me.

I hear it below.

But there's no way out . . .

"Do you think the merchant wrote it?" Elyk asked.

I shook my head. "Not likely. If he was down here alone and the statues came alive, he wouldn't have time to write anything. Something tells me the note is part of the dungeon—an item that would always be there, not a clue left behind by a fleeing merchant."

"But what does it mean?" Syzak hissed. It would take me a long time to get used to the snake-man's voice, and it sent shivers down my back.

The same assassin who found the shred of paper reached up and pulled on the sconce. The metal groaned and bent, then snapped downward with a jarring force. Bits of flaming wood sprayed across the ground where they quickly flickered and died. But something inside the pillar clicked. Then came the rattling of chains, and a slab of marble behind the pillar slowly ascended to reveal another tight passage.

I really need to work on my investigation skill . . .

The assassin grabbed the torch in one hand, a beautiful dagger in the other, and led the way. Rusted chains hung from the walls, most of them ending in broken hooks. At the far end, a faint glow flickered. It wasn't warm and orange like torchlight but dull whiteish yellow. It pulsed and moved. By the way it swayed, it was obvious that someone was carrying the light back and forth, and they hadn't yet noticed us. Our own assassin's torchlight recoiled the nearer we got to the end of the tunnel. It was as if the torch itself was hesitant to proceed any farther. Like it wanted us to go back.

We reached the room, and there was no one inside. Just a tight space dominated by a small circular pillar about waist high. Atop the pillar sat an old lantern like the ones in the frescoes from before. It held a pale-yellow candle, its extinguished wick giving off a thin stream of smoke.

All around, more frescoes and reliefs of robed acolytes stared at us. The images pressed in, adding to the already oppressive claustrophobia brought on by our large group in such a small space. Being so far underground didn't help either.

"I'm guessing that when we light the lantern, the final boss is going to come out swinging all those chains," Elyk stated.

Kadorax flipped one of his daggers around on his palm. "If it is immune to physical like the statues, we could be screwed."

"I don't think the dungeon will hit us with the same mechanic twice. That wouldn't make much sense," I said. "Besides, this is supposed to be a pretty low-level quest overall. Wolfpine isn't exactly attracting the top guilds from all across Wonder. I bet some group of level three and four players cleared this place just in the last few weeks."

Syzak pointed to the cooling lantern. "Alright, light the candle, summon the boss, and we'll just hit it with everything we have. Easy."

Everyone agreed.

We took a moment to catch our breath and steel our nerves, and then the assassin held her torch to the wick.

Elyk was right. Lighting the lantern summoned a boss, and it appeared in the narrow hallway filled with chains. A robed figure holding a lantern swept into existence with a swirl of fog and mist. Light flung wide in sizzling beams from the lantern's door, and it cut a swath right across our entire group.

But it didn't really hurt. Actually, it barely registered. The boss was simply too low level. And I wasn't even close to the highest level in our party. If the attack didn't hurt me, the assassins wouldn't have even noticed it.

None of it mattered. The boss swung his lantern again, shooting more hissing light at us all, and then a series of chains whipped out from the walls to grab the nearest assassins. They both dodged with ease, and one of them actually laughed.

"Huh," Kadorax said. He shot me a look, and then vanished in a puff of smoke. A split second later, he reappeared directly behind the robed figured.

The boss fell in a heap on the ground. One of Kadorax's daggers was lodged squarely between its shoulders. And without any further fanfare or ceremony, Kadorax retrieved his weapon, wiped it on his leather armor, and the boss vanished. "That was easy," he said after a moment.

Behind us, the pillar in the center of the small room sank. It rotated as it went, then submerged completely beneath the floor. It was lost in the shadows for a few seconds before reemerging. Now, instead of an old lantern with a candle, it held a simple iron key.

"I suppose we cleared the dungeon," I said with little mirth. I *did* get to see the assassins fight, but not in a way that really mattered. And none of us got anywhere close to earning any stat points or leveling up.

"There's still the village," Elyk added.

"Ah, you're right. Let's get out of here and see what Wolfpine has to take. With any luck, we'll make it home before midnight."

We filed back out of the small chamber, and a new door had appeared in the main room. It was simple wood with a plain lock that accepted our key without complaint. Beyond the door, a set of stairs took us back to the surface.

"No loot?" one of the assassins asked. "This place sucks."

"Too low level," Kadorax stated.

We emerged into the fading evening light and soon found ourselves on the road back toward Wolfpine. We passed the sinkhole, and then, not too far away, I caught a word on the wind.

"Shh, the merchant," I whispered. Our group stopped, but there were too many of us. Surely the merchant would have heard us coming. We crept through the trees ten paces from the road until the man came into view, and there he was with his big dog and cart of supplies. It looked like he was just finishing up repairs to the rear axle and about ready to get moving.

At my side, Elyk scoffed. "He's not a threat. Maybe he has a reward or something though."

I shrugged. He was right, of course. Our group wouldn't be in any danger from an NPC merchant and his big black dog. Honestly, I wasn't sure what number of NPCs it would take for us to really feel threatened. Another host of Echelon city guards? We had beaten them before, and we were no doubt more powerful now.

I led our small band out of the clearing and waved at who I presumed was Aldo. The merchant startled for a second, then returned my wave.

"Hello, travelers! Are you headed to Wolfpine?" the man asked with a cheery voice.

I nodded. "Sure are. We were actually sent out here to look for you. Seems you're not dead after all."

Aldo gave a hearty laugh with both hands on his rotund belly. "Oh no, not dead quite yet. Still have a few years left on these old bones, do I. Say, you've been to Wolfpine recently then, yes?"

"Just this afternoon. It was a quick trip, all things considered."

I couldn't be sure, but I got the distinct feeling the old merchant was trying to peer over my shoulder in the direction of the sinkhole. "Any new buildings in town? A morgue perhaps?"

That wasn't what I expected. ". . . A morgue?"

He smiled, and I suddenly didn't trust him. "You know the word, right? Cool place to keep a dead body from spoiling? Like a root cellar, but big enough to hold the corpses of an arrogant man and his seven dead friends?"

"What the he—" Before I got the words out of my mouth, the man lunged at full speed for my throat. He held a tiny, curved dagger in the palm of his hand. It was so small the blade barely poked out above his fingers, and I must have missed it when I first approached. I activated *Forsaken Barrier* as quickly as I could and jaunted several feet to the side as the rest of my party sprang into action.

I knew at once that this fight was going to be different. The boss below was probably level five, maybe six or seven at best. This old man was something else. He moved with speed and precision that only came from years of dedicated training and a host of potent combat abilities.

And his dog! The creature was massive. It had to be nearly the size of a horse, not a common hound. The beast gnashed its teeth in my direction, but it was merely a feint. It sprang beyond me, and it was soon lost among the flurry of assassins' blades and shamanistic magic.

As I ran to put some space between my neck and the merchant's dagger, I couldn't help but feel that something wasn't right. The merchant was an NPC. Part of a scripted quest that should have had the same ending every time. If this was it, how did any low-level player ever complete it? Between the statues and the merchant's aggression, it would have taken a miracle for someone level five to come out alive. But the man was an *NPC.* And he purposely deceived us. It wasn't impossible, just unlikely. Especially in such an effective manner.

I didn't have time to contemplate. The merchant's singular focus was on me, and he pressed his advantage with calculated maneuvers. He got close, and I activated *Malignant Putrescence*. A cloud of hazy spores leaked from my mouth right into Aldo's face.

The man was unfazed.

Behind him, Elyk swung with all the strength his legendary armor could muster. The strike—especially from a blade as powerful as Infernum—should have torn the man clean in half. Instead, it stopped just millimeters short as if the harvester had swung it into a solid steel plate.

Physical immunity. I felt like we were fighting the statues again. If my poison didn't work and Infernum couldn't cleave through the man's wards, I knew there was nothing I could do. "We need more magic!" I yelled in Syzak's general direction. I silently cursed myself for not bringing Xia or even Xollmomath with us. I made a promise not to make that mistake twice.

I caught a glimpse of the fight beyond the merchant, and I wondered if I would even have the opportunity to make that mistake a second time. The dog, completely unarmored, was somehow winning. It tore a great chunk of flesh from an assassin's arm, effectively removing one of them from the fight, then quickly pounced on the next.

The snake-man couldn't keep up. He was clearly tired, bordering on exhausted, and he could only fling spells so quickly. A thunderbolt crashed into the merchant's back followed quickly by a loud crescendo of sharp ice fired with pinpoint accuracy.

Nothing broke through.

Aldo swung his small knife again, and I backpedaled into a tree. I should have been out of his reach, but the man activated an ability at the last second, and the blade grew in size tenfold. What was a tiny dagger before was now an outright sword, and it slashed straight across my chest.

I hit my knees, my vision a blur of pain, fallen leaves, and broken sticks. Elyk stepped between us, screaming a furious warcry, and I was thankful for the reprieve.

The wound was rough, but I would live. Was this insane fight part of my curse? Surely the simple merchant and his dog were not evil. They wouldn't be drawn to me like Kadorax and his assassins. If he was a player, I would have assumed he was here to collect the massive bounty on my head, but that was also off the table. Or perhaps Wonder had somehow cranked up the difficulty?

"What the fuck is happening?" I screamed to the dirt. The effort brought a fresh wave of blood from my open wound that spilled in a hot wave over my tentacle fingers.

Above me, Elyk held the line against the man's furious assault like the last warrior standing in the breach of a great wall. I'd never seen him fighting so close, and I'd never seen him put on such a frenzied display. For every three or four strikes he parried, one found its way through his defenses, but his new Fiend-Blooded role meant he wouldn't take the damage as it came. It would be spread out over time, and I simply hoped he had enough fortitude to withstand the ordeal that was to come.

On the other side of the road, the assassins had formed a ring of sorts to keep the ferocious dog at bay. They stabbed with coordinated, practiced strokes, their attacks clearly augmented by all manner of magical enhancement, but to no avail. Nothing hurt the huge beast. Nothing even seemed to annoy it. And the assassins had taken more damage. Several of them sported bloodstains across their armor.

I wasn't about to go down in the woods outside some backwoods NPC village. If I died, it would be in a blaze of glory—preferably as the final human being to draw breath. No, it wouldn't be here. There had to be an answer.

Was it the reflecting pool again? It couldn't be. We'd be long dead by then. I slowly pushed myself up to my feet, and another wave of crimson blood oozed from my wound.

"Syzak," I yelled, hoping to catch the shaman's attention. "Need some magic. Wall him off or something." It was all I could think of, and I had no idea if it would work.

The shaman fixed me with his ophidian eyes and started to cast. Blue light shot from his clawed hands.

"No, not me!" I shouted, but it was too late. It was a healing spell, and it was useless on me. The shaman's face contorted in confusion, but there was no time to explain. "Drink your potion and wall in the merchant!"

Thankfully, he followed my command. Some vitality returned to his body with the potion, and then he dove into his spell casting with renewed vigor. A huge column of dirt erupted from the ground, cutting off the big dog from its latest target. Another series of columns burst skyward at Aldo's feet, and he finally reeled backward. It was the first time in the entire fight that the man had even staggered.

"More!" I yelled with everything I had left.

Syzak didn't hesitate. He ripped a column of earth directly beneath the merchant and sent it ten, then twenty feet into the air. He held it there, pinching it in place with an outstretched hand to control the magic, and then he did the same to the dog.

All at once, the raging, bloody battle came to a halt. Both Aldo and his dog were stranded on pillars of dirt twenty feet in the air. Whatever magic kept them from being harmed by our attacks clearly did nothing to prevent a nasty broken bone or snapped neck from a fall.

The shaman looked like he was getting ready to cast more healing on me, and I stopped him with a wave. "You can't heal me. Don't even try," I gasped, shaking my head.

Kadorax, heaving in air by the lungful but otherwise only superficially injured, stepped up to the man's pillar. "What are you? Why don't you die?" he demanded.

"Still some life on the old bones," came the man's cryptic response.

"How long can you hold the pillars?" I asked Syzak.

He didn't look confident. "Ten minutes if I don't do anything else." His tongue darted rapidly from side to side.

"Shit. Alright. Let me think." I looked back to man stuck on top of the dirt. "Are you even part of the dungeon?"

He spat at me.

"What the hell do you want?"

"I've heard stories of you. And Undercroft Citadel. You're *evil,* and I have come to purge that evil from this land. Too many have died already. I will not suffer any more." Finally, the old man was at least giving me something.

I sighed. "Heh, maybe my curse brought you too . . . You know I can't let you live, right?" I looked to Syzak. "Raise the pillar if you can."

The snake-man gave a solemn nod. The effort of holding the magic in place obviously strained him greatly. Still, the pillar rose another ten feet. It was now taller than all the surrounding trees.

"I don't think you want to fall from that height," I said as calmly as I could. "If you could survive it, you would have jumped. We've got you."

The man gave a dismissive wave to his dog, and the creature vanished. The way it evaporated made me think of my own shadow pet. The fact that the man could—presumably—summon the mighty beast at will was terrifying. I just didn't understand how he was so *damn* powerful. I needed more answers.

"Kadorax, Elyk, what do you think?"

The three of us stepped onto the road to get out of Aldo's earshot.

"Fucking invincible lunatic," Elyk muttered.

Kadorax was more controlled. "Might be something tied to the dungeon, but we would have found clues or something. That sort of thing, investigating for clues and solving puzzles, is what we do. I know we didn't miss anything."

I winced and lost another once of blood to my gaping wound. "So, what do we do about him?"

"Go to the village. See if you can find answers there. The two of us will stay with Syzak and protect him as long as we can. When the pillar gives out, he'll hopefully break his legs." Kadorax gave the harvester an unease pat on the shoulder and fixed him with a smile. "The two of us should be able to subdue an old man with broken legs, right?"

I wasn't so sure. "Just be careful. If he's still invulnerable, run. Get back to Undercroft if you can. Don't try to fight an impossible fight."

"Roger that," Elyk said with finality.

The four assassins and I set off to Wolfpine, two of them holding my shoulders to take some of the strain off my oozing belly wound. It hurt like a bitch, and I realized that if I was going to fight on the front lines, I needed to start carrying traditional bandages and other first aid material. But all of that could wait. What I needed was an answer.

We reached the village as quickly as my limping allowed, and I gave orders that were quickly followed. "Get as many people as you can. I don't care who they are, just bring them out into the street. Break bones if you have to. Round up as many as you can."

In the short span of a minute or two, the four assassins gathered two dozen NPC villagers and lined them up before me. There wasn't any resistance other than a weak punch or two, and sharp blades wielded by deft hands had a way of easily quelling that kind of rebellion.

I was starting to feel significantly weak from the blood loss. Though it slowed to a trickle, I had simply lost too much already. I pointed to the nearest row of NPC villagers. "Bring ten of them," I said to the assassin behind the peasants.

"Move," the woman said forcefully. She shoved one of them forward, and the other nine didn't resist. The stopped a few feet in front of me.

"Slit their throats."

The assassin didn't hesitate. She activated a talent that flashed with brilliant purple magic, and her dagger lashed out across all ten villagers at once. They died in the space of a heartbeat. Immediately, I felt the restorative magic of my curse hard at work. Black tendrils raked out over the corpses and latched onto their wounds. The tendrils pulsed, each wave knitting my torn gut like a skilled surgeon's needle. Behind the ten dead, the rest of the village erupted into chaos. People screamed, people ran, and the assassins cut down a handful more to eventually subdue the crowd.

When my wound fully healed, I felt *better* than healed. I felt invigorated. The dark magic was nothing short of an addicting drug, and my mind already begged for another hit. But there was too much work to do to sit there carving away at my own flesh just to drink the life from a fresh corpse.

"Where's the mayor? Or what was he called, an alderman?" I asked the crowd.

One of the assassins prodded the alderman forward with the point of his blade. "Right here, sir."

I stared at the terrified NPC for a long moment, drinking in his fear as I had done with the life force of his dead friends just seconds ago. "Who the *hell* is the merchant? Why can't I kill him?"

The man stuttered and shook his head. All that came from his lips was befuddled nonsense. I glanced at the assassin holding him roughly by the collar. "I'd like an answer."

The assassin rammed his knife into the alderman's bicep, eliciting a scream, then quickly withdrew it.

I gave the man a few moments to calm his yelling and collect himself as best he could. "One more time. If you don't answer me, my friend is going to cut off your head, and I'll simply ask the next person. And then the next. Understood?"

The man nodded, swallowing hard.

"Who was that in the woods? How is he invincible?"

The man took a long moment to get his voice under control. "Aldo is just a merchant. He-he-he visits every couple weeks from Grimshire. Just to trade and drink a few ales! I swear, that's all I know!"

"Off with his head," I ordered. Like clockwork, the assassin carried out my command. I surveyed the rest of the panicked crowd. "Anyone else?"

One man stepped forward, and the others stared at him in disbelief and awe. I respected his bravery. "Grimshire is a few miles deeper into the woods, not far. I can . . . I can take you there, if you like. Perhaps you'll find your answers."

His offer wasn't exactly what I had in mind, but I didn't hate the idea. Still, I was hoping for a much more concrete answer. "Anyone else?" I asked again.

It quickly became apparent that none of the other NPCs were going to give up any information.

"Fine. You've made your choice. I've made mine. Kill them all. Raze the town. Save that one." I pointed to the man who had offered to take us to Grimshire, and the assassin holding him dragged him off the street.

Wolfpine was not a large village. It was small, even by

village standards, and the assassins made quick work of it. Ten minutes after giving the command, the town was ablaze. Thick plumes of smoke rose from every rooftop in sight, and not a soul other than the one I had chosen to spare was left alive.

The assassins regrouped quickly. "Excellent work," I commended them. "Let's get back to Kadorax and Elyk and see what new hell that fucking merchant has unleashed."

When we arrived back at the merchant's cart, I was both relieved and a little upset to see the man dead. "How'd you kill him?" I asked the exhausted shaman.

He was so spent it took him a moment to gather the breath required to respond. "When I couldn't hold the spell any longer, I gave it everything I had left. Shot him into the air. He landed hard. Didn't move after that."

The merchant's neck and both arms were clearly broken. He probably sported a host of other internal injuries that we couldn't see.

I turned to Elyk and Kadorax, eager to let the snake-man recover. "Did you loot the body? Anything that made him immune?" I asked.

Elyk scoffed. "Take a look at this shit," he said, drawing Infernum and igniting it. He swung for the dead merchant's back, and his blade once more stopped mere millimeters from impact. "Still can't touch the fucker."

I tried myself, and my tentacle fingers, no matter how much effort I put behind them, could not touch the man or his clothing.

Finally, I grabbed the villager from Wolfpine. "Can you touch him?"

Covering his mouth with one hand, the man knelt and

proceeded to touch the merchant as though he was just some ordinary corpse. "Sir?" he said, his voice quavering behind his hand.

"Well, this is just fucked. None of us can touch the idiot, but this guy can, and Syzak's magic can. None of it makes any sense!" I paced, trying in vain to make sense of the ridiculous situation. "Search him. There must be something the bastard carried that is responsible."

The villager slowly emptied Aldo's pockets on the ground next to his twisted corpse. It was just the ordinary detritus of a merchant on the road. But then the villager found something that gave me pause: a golden amulet around the man's neck. He lifted it gingerly, then held it out for me to take. When he tried to place it in my hand, it fell to the ground as if protected by the same forcefield that had protected Aldo in life.

"That's it," I said with finality. "Can anyone analyze it? See what it does?"

One of the assassins stepped forward. "I've got that ability," he said. His eyes unfocused for a split second and then returned to normal. "Ha, no wonder. *Amulet of Forsaken Evil.* It gives him perfect immunity to anything and everything the game deems *evil.* That includes all of us."

I had to laugh. It was the perfect counter to every single one of us. "But it won't stop the ground from rising up beneath him, because the ground can't be evil. Wonderful."

"We need to destroy it," Elyk added.

I shook my head. "If only we could touch the thing." Throwing it into the ocean would be a top priority. If any player got ahold of it, we were screwed. They'd simply march through Undercroft Citadel and kill us all one by one. There wouldn't be a damned thing we could do.

"We need to get it back to—"

Before I could finish, the NPC I dragged from Wolfpine

scooped the amulet off the ground and ran. Elyk started to chase him, but he quickly gave up the effort.

"Ah . . . Well. I suppose I should have seen that coming," I said more to myself than anyone else.

CHAPTER 4

We decided to go back to Undercroft Citadel for the night. There was no point chasing the man with the amulet, and though I wanted to pay a visit to Grimshire, it could wait. I didn't like being away from home, not when there were nearly seven hundred guilds out there actively seeking to destroy us.

The morning brought disappointing news. Well . . . perhaps that wasn't exactly true. It *would* have been disappointing before, but now I wasn't sure. Xia stood on the steps to my room and waited for my reaction. I didn't know how to feel, so I couldn't react. I simply shrugged and thanked her for the report.

Vic was dead. We didn't have enough magic to keep him alive, and his wounds were far too grievous. And that meant he was truly dead. There would be no return, no second chance.

Did it matter? I wasn't sure. Vic had to die eventually, of course. Everyone did. Was it critically important *when* that happened?

Standing alone at the top of the necropolis, I could only

shrug. I didn't have the answer, and silently pondering it for a few hours wasn't likely to do much good.

Still, I wanted to lay eyes on the corpse myself. I had the gargoyles bring it to me, and the lump of flesh and bone did little to excite my mind. There was nothing left to extract from the man. Everything that had made him human was gone. I waved away the gargoyles after a minute or so and mentally commanded one of them to drop the remains near the orc encampment. If they wanted to eat him, I wasn't going to object.

More important than Vic's departure from the mortal coil, the zombies had finished bringing back everything useful that they could haul from Echelon. There was a ton of gear to sort, plenty of valuables that would likely never be useful, and enough food and livestock that we wouldn't go hungry for months, maybe years.

A trio of low-level players had also followed the zombies back to Undercroft Citadel. They stood at attention before the gatehouse, and I wasn't impressed. All three of them were only level four. The way they explained it, they had gone into Wonder only a few days before the server crash, and then once everything went down, they were too scared to keep questing and trying to level. I didn't really have much use for cowards, but that also wasn't exactly true. Despite the players having combat classes, I figured we could use them in the workshops, and I handed the trio to Geirr—basically as his slaves. If they stepped out of line, he had my permission to kill them without hesitation.

It was just another effect of my curse. The players were evil, and they were drawn to Undercroft. They could have stayed behind in the ruins of Echelon and waited out the return of the portals, then gone home and lived their lives. But not anymore. The game had influenced them, and they were just the second group of what would eventually be many. Hundreds, probably thousands would arrive.

I needed a way to process them. I needed an intake center to separate the useful players from the useless, the trusted from the treacherous. I thought of the history books and Ellis Island—back before it was lost beneath thirty feet of ocean. But Ellis Island wasn't exactly it. No, my processing center would feel more like the gates to Auschwitz. The useful would be kept and put to work. Everyone else would become a zombie.

I sighed. There was just too much damn work to do. We needed more craftsmen for the workshops. We needed better defenses. We needed more information on the other capital cities. We needed to figure out how to tap into the power of the resurrection orb. We needed to explore Grimshire and figure out how the hell an NPC ended up with an amulet that made him immune to our entire city. And there were probably a thousand other things on the list.

What I needed was my damn manager. Helvegen knew what she was doing, and I clearly didn't.

But that ship had sailed, likely in a literal sense. She was probably across the ocean in one of the other capital cities, maybe fighting against a different horde of evil players. Or perhaps she had joined them, still evil but just not on my side.

I shook the thoughts from my head. It didn't matter.

With so many people actively trying to kill us, I decided our first priority was defense. The walls were rebuilt and fortified, but they were still just wooden walls. The fear glyphs hanging on the outside were a nice touch, and the moat was incredible. What we needed next were archer ports, archers to actually shoot from them, and then we needed a second layer of stone far beyond the first.

Archers would have to wait. The zombies weren't quite dexterous enough to handle bows. But the second layer of wall was something we could start building. We still had two gnomes left from the Inventors' League, and I found them with Geirr in the workshop going through salvaged loot brought back from Echelon. Most of it was being discarded into a scrap pile to be melted down and reclaimed.

I pulled the pair aside. "What can you tell me about your abilities, specifically crafting?" I asked.

If the players were scared of being in my presence, they didn't show it. But then again, their leader was perhaps the most deranged person I had ever met in my life, and that was becoming an increasingly high bar to meet.

The players were named Berrick and Crestor, and they were both level twenty-three. They shared a class, tinkerer, and it wasn't one I was familiar with at all. The only thing I remembered about the class was that it was unique to gnomes.

"We had so many projects back in Echelon, but they're gone now," Berrick said with obvious sadness in his voice. "We're trying to restart, but we had a *proper* workshop, you know?"

"What happened to it?"

Berrick laughed. "You met Ministrel. When the servers came down, he went a little nuts. Well . . . he was always nuts. Never left Wonder from the very first day he stepped through a portal, or so he says. But he really lost it. Started kidnapping people off the streets for his experiments and killing them. Kids too. He was killing *kids*. You know what that means? The city guard arrested him and burned the workshop. We holed up in that tower where Elyk found us. You know the rest."

"What kind of experiments needed human subjects?" I knew Ministrel was useful, but perhaps he would be more akin to the necromancer than just a crazed wizard.

Crestor gave a shudder. "Terrible things. Trying to meld steel with biology. Remember the steam boars we rode? He kept trying to replace their pistons with bones. None of us knew why."

It just sounded like more craziness. "The thing I still don't understand is why keep him around? I know he's powerful, but is it worth it? I mean . . . he's really crazy."

They shared a look that told me I wasn't quite prepared for what they were about to say.

"Changing races is hard in Wonder, right?" Berrick said with a sigh.

"Yeah, for sure. Everyone usually goes elf too, not gnome. No offense."

"Ministrel changed us to gnomes on his own."

I had to take a minute to process that piece of information. From everything I knew about the game, it wasn't possible. Only NPCs with scripted pathways and quests had that kind of power. It usually took months of work to 'earn' the right to change a race, and a lot of people gave up before they ever finished. There were tons of non-human NPCs, but player characters were much, much rarer. "I have to ask . . . did you *want* to be gnomes?"

Both of them shook their heads. "Not really," Crestor answered. "We just woke up as gnomes one day. The thing is, we haven't left Wonder since it happened. The way Ministrel talks, we're worried that the change might be permanent."

I practically gasped. "Is that even possible? How the hell . . ."

"I don't know, but we're not risking it," Berrick cut in.

"Well damn. Not exactly what I expected." I filed away the information in the back of mind. If I could ever get the crazed wizard to have a few lucid hours, delving into the depths of his skills and abilities would be a high priority. If he could turn people into other races against their will . . . it opened up a lot of doors. Really terrifying doors.

"But anyway, what do you need built? We're not much

good without our supplies, a proper workshop, and, well, *more* of us," Berrick went on.

I thought over all the projects on my list. "We need to start getting ready to defend Undercroft Citadel again. More guilds are coming, and it is only a matter of time before they get here. They'll be prepared and extremely powerful. In our current state, I'm not sure we'll survive the first attack."

"What do you need from us?"

The three of us spent the next hour walking the perimeter of Undercroft and staking out the locations of the next wall. We needed stone, and instead of a simple wall, it needed all the traditional defenses of a castle. Archer ports, parapets, murder holes, and everything else the gnomes knew how to build. They could handle the design and direct the work, but getting the raw materials would be our limiting factor. I directed the orcs to get the mine producing both metal ores and stones large enough to build our wall, and they seemed eager to provide.

The project would take time, likely more time than we could actually afford, but it was better than nothing. Once enough raw stone was brought up from the mine, the zombies would be able to lend a hand maneuvering it into place, and that would speed things up, but we really needed a dozen more intelligent players who specialized in crafting if we were going to be defensible before the next guild arrived on our doorstep.

With our defenses in motion, I turned my attention to the next thing on my extensive list: I needed information about the next capital cities, especially Olympia City.

The only man who had been there recently was Kadorax, and I found him training with the other assassins just outside the walls. Geirr had been there as well, and I brought him along. I brought them both to one of the barracks rooms on the ground floor as it was the closest thing we had to a meeting space. Kadorax found some paper and a pencil from among the looted supplies from Echelon, and he got to work drawing a rough map of the city. With Geirr's help, he created enough of a map so we wouldn't be going in blind.

"How many people do you think are there?" I asked, studying the city's layout.

Kadorax rubbed his chin. "I don't know, had to be a few million before the server crash. Probably more now, especially with the fighting."

He outlined the bulk of the fighting forces on the map in red. "There was a huge guild here from New Karstad, I think. Death Hunters, or something like that. All red and black banners kind of like ours. Had to be at least ten thousand players, probably a hundred thousand NPCs. They had the entire eastern side of the city hammered with siege weapons."

I could barely even fathom that many people on the battlefield at once. "Damn. And the resistance? How many?"

The assassin sighed. "Hard to say, but more than the guild. More than all the guilds. When the announcement came through that the resurrection hubs were active, man . . . you have no idea, do you?"

I shook my head. "Everyone around here was already either dead or had fled."

"It was insane. Every single guild, no matter how far they were from the capital, started moving. A few of them probably held out and are still standing strong in the wilds, but they'll be few and far between. Everyone else went right for the capital. At first, we figured it would be peaceful. The Blackened Blades went too." Despite the gravity of his words, he spoke as though he was recounting a casual Sunday stroll through a park. "We wanted to be close to the orbs when things went back online, but that changed quickly. It was Syzak who first brought up the idea of not going back at all. That's when we joined up with some of the evil guilds right when the fighting broke out. We got a few kills—well, more than a few—then snuck onto a ship to come here and join you."

"My sister and I snuck out of Olympia City once. I can show you," Geirr added.

That was something I really needed to know. "How'd you do it?"

"There are tunnels," Geirr began, taking the pencil and sketching them. "Some of them are the sewer system that's hopefully still in place, some are old tunnels from previous iterations, and some are older yet from municipal projects no one remembers. But here . . ." He drew an X at one side of the city walls. "This is where we came out. Just next to a guard tower. It was all covered in brush, had to hack our way through a jungle just to see the sun."

"Well, if Ministrel can get us there and back, I think we should. Just a scouting mission, no heroics. What say you?"

Kadorax readily agreed. Geirr, on the other hand, was perfectly content to stay back in Undercroft with his workshops, the gnomes, and his new players.

In the end, we settled on a party of five. It would be small enough to hopefully go unnoticed while large enough to be effective. Elyk, Kadorax, Syzak, Xollmomath, and me. Our little five-man death squad. Technically, Ministrel would be making the trip as well, though I didn't really count him in the calculations. He was too . . . unpredictable.

We made a plan to leave the next day, wizard permitting, and set a goal of returning within twelve hours. Being gone any longer simply posed too much of a risk.

Our adventuring party assembled just outside the gate a few hours before dawn. Ministrel was out in the field doing his usual . . . whatever it was he did. I waved and called his name, finally catching the wizard's attention. He marched over, goosestepping with his arms crossed behind his back and counting all the while.

"Ministrel, we need you to teleport us to Olympia City. Can you do it?" I asked.

The tension in the air was palpable. Either the unpredictable wizard was about to solve our most pressing problem, or we were back to square one with a thousand miles of ocean separating Undercroft Citadel from the next resurrection orb.

Ministrel paused for a moment, his face inscrutable as ever. He breathed, and something about it wasn't natural, as if he was exhaling far more air than he brought in. I chalked it up to his general mysteriousness and didn't ask any questions.

After what felt like an eternity, Ministrel suddenly perked up. He jerked his head toward the sky, squinted, then shouted: "Eighty-eight fathoms!"

I blinked, and we were no longer outside Undercroft Citadel. Sound took an extra second to reappear, and when it did, it was instantly deafening. A confusing cacophony of noise assaulted us from every angle. I quickly realized that Ministrel had dropped us off in the middle of the battle.

Before I could get my bearings, something hit me hard in the back, and I was slammed to my knees. Fortunately, there were so many dead bodies all around that I instantly started to regenerate.

But it didn't work.

The bodies vanished in a swirl of pixels before I could harvest enough energy from them to properly heal.

"We need to get out of here!" I shouted, hoping against the odds that my voice would be heard above the din. Kadorax and Elyk were closest, and they whirled from side to side in a blaze of blood and guts. It was impossible to tell which side anyone was on. Frankly, I didn't think Kadorax cared, and I *knew* Elyk didn't.

Maybe eight or nine paces away, Xollmomath was busy conjuring magic to his ancient fingers. He gathered a huge sphere of orange and yellow fire, then loosed it directly above his head. It rocketed into the sky, arced backward, and then landed with a devastating explosion.

"That will buy us time!" the necromancer announced.

I gathered up my party the best I could and pointed for Olympia City's towering walls. "Come on, let's move!"

We scrambled through the mass of fighters, taking hits left and right but dealing out far more than we received, and finally started to see the actual battle lines. I wanted to drop a poison rune with *Shrouded Miasma* into the ground, but there wasn't any time to power it up with my life force, so I settled on a few activations of *Malignant Putrescence* instead and simply hoped to add some more chaos into the battle.

We reached the walls, bloodied and battered, and finally caught our breath.

"One, two, three . . . where the fuck is Ministrel?" I shouted. Our party was one short. A critical one short.

"No time," Elyk said. He pointed to a series of objects dotting the morning sky and rapidly growing in size.

They were either boulders from catapults, magical fireballs, or both. And I didn't want to be anywhere near the walls when they landed.

"Run!" I screamed.

I picked a direction at random, and the party followed. We ran along the wall as hard as we could, and then one of the boulders smashed into the wall maybe twenty yards behind us. The crash was immense. Shards of fractured stone flew in all directions, and the sound was enough to rattle my bones and make my teeth slam together.

We reached a protruding wall before the next volley of catapults could reach us, and it offered at least a little protection.

"Anyone see Ministrel?" I asked, but I knew it was useless. There was just too much chaos. Everyone shook their heads.

"Look alive," Elyke stated.

In front of us, a small group of the city's defenders had taken notice of our little party and turned. They were all NPCs, probably just regular city guard infantry, though they were solidly armed and armored.

"Elyk, Kadorax, take care of it," I said.

It didn't take the duo long. Infernum, fully ablaze and completely unbothered by steel and chain armor, moved like a threshing machine through a field of wheat. To Elyk's right, the high-level assassin jumped and danced with all the acrobatics of a circus performer. His daggers plunged in and out of the NPCs in a dazzling display of speed and precision. Before long, the small group of attackers was dead, and I felt my curse sucking up the energy from their corpses shortly before they vanished to respawn at the orb.

"Come on, let's keep moving." I had the map in my pocket, but I wasn't sure it would do us much good if we couldn't get somewhere high to see the city from above. As it was, we were near a guard tower, but that didn't mean much. There were dozens of guard towers. Maybe hundreds.

We scampered along the base of the walls until we put the main battle area mostly behind us, then stopped to get our bearings once more.

"Kadorax, can you scale the wall?" I pointed to the nearest guard tower. It sported a handful of archers constantly appearing at the parapet for a second or two to fire an arrow, then vanishing once more to reload. It was maybe thirty feet high, and I guessed that if anyone could climb the sheer stone wall, it would be an assassin.

He gave it a quick look and then nodded.

"Go up, kill the archers, and see if you can figure out where we are. We need to find the tunnel."

A shimmer of blue and black magic enveloped the man, and then he scaled the wall as easily as a spider would climb a tree. A few seconds later, bodies of archers started hitting the ground all around us. Within a minute, all the arrows leaving the guard tower stopped, and Kadorax peeked his head over one of the parapets. "I'll find some rope!" he called.

I watched as the bodies of the archers dissolved into pixels all around. They would respawn in a few seconds at the resurrection orb, and then they'd be right back in the fight. What was most curious was that the archers would be resurrecting right next to enemy players and NPCs fighting on the other side. Each capital only had one resurrection point, and it didn't discriminate based on alignment. Wherever the orb was, the fighting there had to be insane.

All I could think was there had to be some way to exploit it. With everyone resurrecting at the same spot, it meant the amount of experience waiting to be soaked up was immense. But would the game award such easy kills? If it did, they probably wouldn't be worth much. Still, it was an idea worth exploring.

Kadorax pulled me out of my thoughts with another shout. He found a rope ladder somewhere and had it tied around the parapet. We all scrambled up the ladder, though Xollmomath struggled with it. I hadn't considered the ancient necromancer's physical abilities before, and he was frail. Actually, he reminded me of my grandpa maybe a decade before Wonder went online, withering away in a nursing home bed without a drop of medication to be found in the entire state. We pulled the necromancer over the parapet, and he needed a few moments to catch his breath.

"What part of the walls are we on?" Elyk asked.

I spread out the map, and we tried to line it up as best we could with Geirr's drawings.

"Castle's that way," Kadorax said, pointing. He turned the map ninety degrees. "Geirr's tunnel isn't far, and that means the resurrection orb is just about perfectly across the city from where we are now."

'Across the city' meant several miles, at least from where I was standing. Echelon was huge, but it was still the smallest of the seven capitals. Olympia City, by comparison, was at least twice the size. We could probably make it all the way around the walls, slaughtering NPC archers and other guards the whole time, but I wasn't convinced that Xollmomath was up for the journey.

With a moment of temporary respite, I stood at the parapet and marveled. Olympia City was gorgeous. It boasted a Japanese style full of sweeping roofs, multi-tiered pagodas, and quaint parks dotting the landscape with huge pink trees in full bloom. Without the war raging at my back, it would have been a peaceful, serene place to live.

Elyk slapped my shoulder and stole my attention. "No one knows we're here. Not yet, at least. We can get behind the main bulk of the defenders and wreak havoc."

"Too soon," I told him, much to his dismay. "We need a plan. I don't want to give away our position until we have to, and we need to figure out a way to destroy their resurrection hub *before* we kill everyone."

"So what now?" he asked.

I wasn't exactly sure. "We need to get closer to the orb and see exactly how they're defending it. Make a definitive plan. And someone needs to find our damn wizard so we can get a ride back home." Unfortunately, making it all the way to the orb didn't seem likely with Xollmomath in such bad shape.

I turned to the necromancer. "Can you make it across the

walls? Or around the walls?" I pointed to the spot roughly opposite of us where I figured we needed to go. "Got some magic that will get you over there?"

The bald necromancer shook his head. "I'm too weak . . . This far from the citadel . . . I need magic. Something to consume."

Now we had a plan. "Alright, time to find some magic for the old man to eat!" I yelled to my party. "Kadorax and Syzak, you two protect him. Clear the nearest guard towers and raise what hell you can, but don't let him get killed. Elyk, you're with me. Let's go steal some magic."

I sprinted off to the right along the rough stone wall. It was about fifty yards to the next guard tower, and the direction I picked wasn't as heavily protected as the other. The bulk of the fighting was on the complete opposite side of the city, though a handful of NPC archers were still raining arrows on the attackers below.

Elyk and I made quick work of them. Infernum cleaved two apart at the waist, and I formed my strong tentacle arms into what basically amounted to a sledge to knock the remaining three from the parapet. "I need to find some armor," I added once the tower was clear. "Maybe a weapon, but I'm still not sure what exactly I want."

Elyk nodded. "Look for a guildhall. All their best players are probably out their fighting and farming experience. We'll hit their stores and see what we can loot."

"Any ideas what a guildhall in Olympia City looks like?"

He scanned the rooftops. "Maybe that one?" he said, pointing to a multi-story building with a swept roof and emerald green shingles. Banners flew from each of its four corners, though we were too far to see what they depicted. I shrugged. The building was indistinguishable from a dozen others not far from it, but why not? It was as good a target as any.

We flew down the stairs without meeting any other resistance. The streets were equally deserted. A few random NPCs saw us and ducked back into their houses, but no players. We reached the target building, and the banners fluttering on the walls showed a black stag rampant on a field of blue.

"A hunting lodge?" I guessed. The stag could mean anything.

Elyk just shouldered through the door in a hail of splintered wood, Infernum ready to butcher anything and everything on the other side.

A shocked attendant in a robe that matched the banners outside looked up from a stack of paperwork on a fancy desk. "What are you doing in—"

Infernum cut him in half. No one else was in the room or came charging in, so we took a moment to get our bearings.

A dozen or more desks, all finely polished and stacked with mountains of paperwork, were arranged in a neat array from wall to wall. I grabbed a few papers from the nearest one and read the heading.

"It's a tax firm. Or something like that," I said with disgust. The whole page was filled with figures and calculations from what appeared to be a butcher shop somewhere in Olympia City. I tossed the paper aside.

"Eh, probably not much magic here," Elyk grumbled.

"Maybe they have a vault like a bank. Come on, we'll just check quick." I led us to the back where a staircase ascended through the wooden ceiling to the upper level. The walls, most of which were fine paper, were ornately decorated with scenes of tigers, swans, and peafowl. It was vibrant and exquisite, obviously a mark of wealth and luxury. A place that could afford to hire such artists at least had a chance of possessing a vault.

We burst onto the top floor with no attempt at stealth.

A trio of NPC clerks or accountants or whatever they were stood from their desks in a rush of papers and screeching chairs. Elyk cut them down in the space of a few heartbeats, and then we set to scouring the room.

After a few minutes, it became clear that the accounting firm held nothing of value. Or, perhaps our investigation skills were too low. I remembered the assassins and all the cool clues and hidden mechanisms they had found in the low-level dungeon outside Wolfpine. If we had that much investigation, would we find similar contraptions?

I gave a wall sconce a yank, but nothing out of the ordinary happened. No wall raised up to reveal a hidden passage, and no plinth appeared on the floor with a magic chest full of loot. I tossed the sconce at a heap of papers and finally got an idea.

"The walls are mostly paper, and the structure itself is wood. This place is stacked with flammables . . ."

Elyk didn't need any other explanation. He willed Infernum to life and held it to a stack of papers, then the next and the next. We scrambled down the stairs and back into the street just as a tongue of orange-red flame broke through the roof.

"Over there," I said, pointing to an obvious blacksmith.

Elyk and I ran down the street and burst into the smithy in much the same manner that we had barged into the accounting firm. Instead of a single frightened NPC clerk, we found a host of NPCs working bellows and anvils along with at least two players who instantly turned and drew their weapons.

"Take the one on the left," I said quickly to Elyk, sizing up the man on the right. He was level twenty, the same as me, and had the judoka class. All in knew about the class was that it came from judo, a martial art, and that it was probably similar to karate. All I knew about karate was what I had seen in some old Chinese movies that were popular maybe a hundred years before Wonder. All that was to say I knew very, very little of what to expect.

The man grabbed a smithing implement that resembled a crowbar and charged. He didn't swing wildly as I expected, but rather wove the makeshift weapon through the air with precision that beget skill. I formed my tentacle arms into a shield of sorts and thrashed at his weapon. The judoka skipped backward, and I hit nothing but air.

Then the smithing tool smashed into my shoulder, but it wasn't a solid hit. The man was still moving backward, so he couldn't put his full strength behind the blow. I leapt over the anvil between us and bowled into the man with all of my considerable weight. We crashed the ground, knocking aside a myriad of blacksmithing tools and tipping over a bucket of hot coals that coated us both in fine ash.

The ash worked to my advantage. I didn't need to breathe, and the judoka did. He gasped for air, fighting the coal dust in his lungs and eyes, and I pressed the advantage. I launched *A Feast of Spores* into his face alongside the hot coal dust, and his coughs quickly turned to choking.

Reaching blindly to the smithing table above us, I wrapped my tentacle fingers around the first thing I could which turned out to be a heavy hammer. The man activated a series of talents in quick succession, but they were no use. He was too disoriented, and I was simply too big. Before my transformation, our brawl likely would have ended far differently. He would have quickly knocked me to the ground and held me down while his friends executed me from behind. But now, my squid-like bulk was too great, and in the fine haze of heated dust, I held every advantage.

The hammer cracked into the man's skull with a sickening clank. A second hit made the man go limp.

I shoved the corpse from my body and used the edge

of the table to pull myself back to my feet. The smithy was in total chaos. Elyk had a trio of enemies pinned with their backs to the wall, and I watched as a few more NPCs scampered out the rear door. In the cluttered space, Infernum was a bit too long to be effective, but Elyk had a host of other talents at his disposal.

He shot a ring of fire from his clenched fist that caught one of the blacksmiths in the chest. I was just about to leap to his side and join him when a bit of rustling caught my attention, and I turned back to the slain judoka. The man was rising, slowly and without any coordination, and I realized that *Reap Honor* had triggered on him. The man had no infamy, so his corpse reanimated to fight at my side.

For a brief second, I wondered how the talent would work on a continent with resurrection still in place. But there wasn't time to give it much thought, and all that mattered was that the man reanimated on my side, not a mile or two away at Olympia City's resurrection orb.

I mentally commanded the zombie to help Elyk, then chased the other NPC smiths out the back of the building. I tackled one of them to the ground, and he hit his head hard on the cobblestone road.

Dazed, he sputtered a stream of nonsense words that eventually ended in a plea for his life. I hovered my tentacle fist over his head and activated *Visage of the Dark One*. "Where can I find a powerful magic item?" I demanded.

All at once, the man's concussion-born babbling transformed into coherent speech. "Master Brenning's hammer!" he quickly answered. "It's enchanted!"

I lowered my fingers to a hair's breadth above his nose. "Something else in the city?" I yelled. "A relic? Some ancestral amulet? What's the most powerful item in Olympia?"

He sprayed a hail of spit over my hand in his haste to answer. "The silk fan! The silk fan!" he repeated over and over.

I slapped him and dismissed *Visage of the Dark One* to let his mind recover just a little. "What fan? Tell me where I can find it."

He gulped like a fish out of water. "Princess Yasha, it's her fan. The Whispersilk Fan! The most powerful relic in the city . . ." The NPC's voice trailed off as though even mentioning the object brought about a sense of awe and reverence that he could not shake. But it was more than enough information. Princess Yasha's fan was the most powerful artifact in Olympia. It would make perfect fuel for Xollmomath's magic.

"Say hello to everyone at the orb," I said.

The man's face contorted in confusion just before going blank as he died.

I tossed him aside, then took a moment to inspect the fire raging down the street. No one had yet come to extinguish it, and I figured all of Olympia City's best shaman were too busy at the walls to be bothered by a fire. The blacksmith was a few buildings down, so we had a little time.

Inside, Elyk had reduced everyone else to flaccid piles of gore. "Come on, let's find you some armor. Loot this place and get out of here," he said with a red-flecked smile.

"Couldn't agree more. Grab the smith's hammer, too. It's supposed to be pretty strong." We rooted through the shelves of finished gear, tossing almost all of it aside as useless. Most of the items were enchanted, though not powerfully. Master Brenning's hammer, on the other hand, was masterwork quality like Elyk's armor. It had a chance to raise the quality of anything produced with it to masterwork as well. If we could, I intended to take it back to Undercroft and give to Geirr in the workshop, but Xollmomath's strength came first. The old necromancer would probably have to eat it before we could put it to use.

Finally, Elyk found a chest piece that was both large

enough for my enhanced frame and decently enchanted. It consisted of a series of small leather squares fixed with flexible rivets. The cords linking all of the plates together could be adjusted at the sides meaning that not only could I put it on and take it off without any assistance, it could be tightened to fit me perfectly and would flex with my movements.

I pulled the armor over my loose shirt and snugged it into place.

Masterwork Obsidian Wreath: A fine set of lamellar armor crafted with the blessing of the Obsidian Vultures of Mount Kaju. Provides excellent protection against slashing and concussive attacks and allows the user to summon an obsidian spike at a target within fifty meters. Whenever damaged, this armor can be fully restored in the waters atop Mount Kaju. Consumes minor energy.

I turned to the zombie wrestler I had made earlier, eager to try out the new skill I acquired from the armor. I envisioned an obsidian spike launching up from the ground, and I wasn't disappointed. The spike ripped through the man horizontally more like a spear hit than a stalagmite, but it did the job nonetheless. The zombie fell to the ground in a bloody, tattered heap.

"Not bad!" Adding more offensive abilities to my arsenal was a huge. The fight against the statues had shown me that my poison abilities wouldn't always be useful, and neither would my powerful tentacles. In fact, I had chosen a *lot* of passives and talents geared toward managing and growing Undercroft Citadel. My own personal fighting had always relied on Infernum and the rest of the armor, not my abilities. That needed to change.

"Here, check out this mace," Elyk said, handing me the hilt of a weapon.

Masterwork Meteor Hammer: This weapon was once used by

Mei-Ni, Second to Walk Among the Flames of Righteousness, in her ill-fated rebellion. At night, it is imbued with the remnants of her magic and will freeze any enemy struck.

I tossed the mace back and forth, and I noticed the head wasn't exactly secured to the weapon's metal shaft. It had a little give, though it appeared to be by design. I found a small indented switch just above the leather wrapping on the handle and pushed it. The head of the mace fell about a foot on a thin iron chain that I could swing like a flail. When I let my thumb off the button, it retracted again to its normal position.

"Very cool," I said with a smile. It wasn't Infernum, but it was certainly better than using my tentacle arms for everything—especially now that I couldn't exactly be healed.

"I've got the hammer and few other items. This should be good to get Xollmomath up and running again. Come on, let's go before the fire hits us."

I followed Elyk out the front door.

To our right, a huge conflagration had overcome half a dozen buildings. A few people—I couldn't tell if they were NPCs or players—actively battled the blaze. On both sides of the street, about ten players arrayed in heavy armor stood sentinel.

From their posture, their intention was obvious. They were waiting for us. To our left, one of them stepped forward. She was tall, probably my height which meant magical augmentation, and half her face was burned down to the bone. The other half was covered in a web of scars and putrid, weeping wounds. She wore black plate armor that actively smoked. It was bent and twisted, reminding me of Vammatar. And on her back, she bore the largest double-headed axe I had ever seen in my life. It was at least as long as she was tall, and each blade was the width of her shoulders or more. It stuck out over her head, and I saw a gleaming black skull mounted between the blades with fire in its empty eyes.

The woman's name floating above her head was Faidra, Punishment Nailed Deep.

I had never seen the moniker before, and I didn't know what it meant. It wasn't her class but rather an earned title similar to my own *Host of Blasphemies*. Her class and level, displayed in onyx below her floating name, read: Level 34 Parousia.

I didn't even know what the word was. Hell, I didn't know what *language* it was in either.

She smiled and stepped closer. No, she wasn't my height, she was taller by at least a few inches. Dark ichor seeped from a line slashed across the only half of her face that still bore flesh. The other half, nothing more than a charred hunk of ruined skull, undulated in a way that made my stomach turn.

"Hello, Bentalÿk." Her voice was low like the rumble of a landslide. She spread her massive arms wide. "Around the flames of hope we gather until embers we become. Beneath a lightless star we sing for the damage we've done. The circle is open to all. Ascend and rejoice!"

At my side, Elyk nervously shifted his weight. "Uh, Ben . . . How fucked are we right now?"

CHAPTER 5

A million thoughts raced through my mind. I could charge, swing my new mace and hope for the best . . . and be torn to ribbons in a matter of heartbeats. I could run. The fire was starting to attract significant chaos, and maybe if I ran directly for it, the terrifying woman would not pursue. But her guild, I assumed, stood to either side like the pill bug statues on the stairs to my throne room. There would be no escape.

Elyk let out a heavy sigh. He hung his head.

". . . Sorry, man. End of the road for us," I said under my breath.

The harvester let Infernum slide from his grip and clatter to the ground. I followed suit and tossed my mace—a weapon that now felt comically pathetic in the presence of whatever the hell was strapped to Faidra's back—toward the woman's feet. I sank to my knees, and Elyk did the same.

Elyk, the closest thing I had to a true friend since Helvegen left, put his arm around my shoulder. "We'll respawn," he said quietly.

Fucking hell . . . respawn! I was so used to everyone I killed staying dead that the idea of spawning right outside Olympia City with all my gear and a fresh head on my shoulders had never even crossed my mind.

"Alright, grab your weapon, charge, get killed. See you on the other side," I whispered, my head still bowed.

When I looked up, I saw Faidra towering only a foot or two away. One of her underlings had scooped up both Infernum and my mace, and my heart sank again. Still, it would be a low price to pay if we escaped with our lives.

I grunted and sprang back to the trio of tentacles that had become my legs, eager to just get it over with and die.

"Enough!" Faidra bellowed, and my body froze in the air. Elyk's did as well, though I was so thoroughly paralyzed that I couldn't move my eyes to see him fully. Faidra peered down at me like a bear contemplating a fresh salmon it plucked from a rushing stream. So close to her horrid face, the smell reminded me of somewhere I had been before: Lady Kalma's temple. She smelled like the still waters of the death goddess's domain.

I tried to speak, but not a muscle in my body would move. I knew the paralysis extended to my lungs and heart, my diaphragm, and every other organ that needed contraction and expansion to work. In a single moment, the thing I feared the most was realized. I was caught, suspended in animation. Unable to move but unable to asphyxiate. It could last an eternity, and there was nothing I could do about it . . .

She leaned in close, and her putrid stench filled my nostrils. "Six voices inside," she whispered.

All at once, my body was compelled to speak. I couldn't resist the magic she cast any more than I could resist the sun rising in the east or setting in the west. Her entire will was the definition of inexorable. "My name is Ben Hales. My goal . . . is the extinction of humanity."

Next to me, Elyk was similarly compelled to speak. "My name is Kyle Jacobson. My goal . . . is to help my friends kill everyone."

Kyle Jacobson? The name would have made me laugh if I was capable of moving any muscle at all. It was just too mundane. Too plain. Too *normal.* The harvester I knew, Elyk, arrayed in legendary armor stolen from the Pyreborn Legion, would never fit the name Kyle Jacobson. But there it was, compelled from the depths of the man's psyche with but a whim and a single spell.

Finally, *thankfully*, the paralysis spell subsided. The two of us crashed to the ground. I expected to be instantly cleaved in half by Faidra's insane axe, but instead she backed away a pace before offering me her hand. I took it hesitantly, and it was ice cold against my tentacle.

"This sighting is a portent of doom," she intoned.

So far, none of her speech made a lot of sense. How was I supposed to respond?

I cleared my throat and let go of her icy hand. "Uh, thank you?" I tried.

She nodded.

Off to a great start . . . "What, uh, what exactly do you want from us? You know my name, presumably you also know about Undercroft Citadel and what will happen if you kill me." I thought of the resurrection orb just outside the city walls. "I mean, if you kill me for real."

Faidra turned her horrifying face toward the sky. "It is the hour of the nightingale. Beneath the moss, between the roots, a taste of death." She flicked her gaze to one of her underlings at her left.

A powerfully arrayed level thirty knight presented my mace back to me by the hilt. I took it, and then he did the same for Elyk with Infernum.

"Alright. I'm confused. Are you killing us or not?" I just

wanted whatever was going to happen to finally happen. Enough esoteric speech and confusing riddles.

"Everything must come to an end," she answered.

Frustrated, I turned to the knight and shrugged. "Can you translate?"

He lifted his visor, and I saw the weathered face of a man about fifty who had squeezed every ounce of life from his years. His skin was like leather and showed the faint outline of tattoos long since faded. "We've been looking for you, Ben Hales. Or waiting for your arrival, I suppose. Come, you're safe with us. My master has a proposition. You'll want to hear it."

"Where are we going?" Elyk asked, Infernum still in his grip.

The knight took a moment to gaze at the blazing fire down the street. More people had arrived, and it finally appeared contained, at least partly. "You have more people in the city?"

It was like he could read my mind. Perhaps Faidra *was* reading my mind and somehow transmitting my thoughts to the knight. Just as surely as I knew I could not defeat Faidra or her guild in an open battle, I knew it was useless to lie. If she didn't believe my answers, I would be frozen again and forced to speak, magically compelled to tell the truth.

I pointed back toward the nearest wall. "The rest of my party is up there. We came to destroy the orb, but I'm guessing you knew that already. Just scouting right now, learning what we can about the city."

"Understood. Let's go find your party, and we talk more back at our guildhall," the knight stated. There was no room for argument or suggesting an alternate plan.

Elyk and I simply fell into step with the rest of the guild—all of whom I realized were knights—and followed Faidra back to the guard tower where the rest of our party presumably awaited our return.

Once we regrouped, Faidra's guild led us down a winding knot of streets and alleyways until we came to a busted door on an unassuming building. Xollmomath consumed the blacksmith's hammer we brought him, and he was able to make the rather lengthy journey without any assistance. We still didn't know where Ministrel had gone, but there wasn't much we could do about that detail. I just hoped the wizard hadn't gotten himself killed.

One of the knights held open the broken door, and we filed inside to an equally ruined storefront that might have been a café or pastry shop in a past life.

"You know these guys?" Kadorax asked under his breath so only I could hear.

I shrugged. "Not exactly. The leader is a bit off . . . but if she wanted us dead, she would have killed us. Plus, there's the respawn orb. I'm not too worried."

Behind me, Syzak hissed.

Once our entire group was inside the building, the knight shut the door and dropped a beam across it, though what good it would do was beyond me. The place was in shambles. If anyone wanted to trespass, it wouldn't take much effort at all. Hell, the only window at the front of the building was completely devoid of any glass.

Scanning us, Faidra inhaled deeply. The smoke rising from her black armor seemed to waver and pulse with her breath. Then she snapped, and whatever illusion had concealed the room was lifted. All at once, we stood in a magnificent guildhall not all that dissimilar to Undercroft Citadel. Everything was bone and obsidian, sharp points and serrated edges. It was larger than before as well. The magic reminded me of Helvegen's painter spells, and it took my breath away.

The terrifying, imposing woman stepped directly in

front of me, though her posture was different than on the street. Instead of exuding fear and authority, she approached me as a fellow leader and held out her hand. "I am Faidra, leader of the Burned Saints." She spread her arms wide to indicate her small guild of knights. "This is my choir of nefarious tongues, and you stand where no light shines. My apologies for our previous introduction. I had to be certain before bringing you here." She knelt, and the huge shaft of her double-headed axe scraped against the ground. Even on one knee, she didn't have to crane her neck to look me in the eyes. "You, Bentalÿk, are the heir to mankind's atrocities. Humanity's castigation and rebirth. The Burned Saints seek what you seek. We will stand at your side."

She rose once more to her domineering height, and I didn't exactly know what to say. We shook hands, and a feeling of finality settled on my shoulders. We had a pact. Her name flashed into existence as another boss for Undercroft Citadel, and the difficulty rating immediately increased from 'challenging' to 'heroic.' A few seconds later, the number of active campaigns fell from well over six hundred to just under four. At the same time, my influence stat increased to thirty-nine.

Faidra motioned to the same knight who had spoken to me before. I figured he was her second in command. "I must retire for the moment. Sir Drevan will show you our home. You and your men are welcome to all that we have. Be ready to move by nightfall."

The woman turned on her heel and had to duck through a doorway to enter the next room where she quickly disappeared around a corner.

Sir Drevan took off his helm and tossed it to another knight. The rest of the choir, as Faidra had called them, began removing armor and relaxing as well. Notably, while their armor looked as though it had seen hundreds of battles, the knights themselves were altogether unscathed. I wondered how many times they had already respawned at the orb. Hundreds, no doubt.

"Hey, what's the deal with her class," I asked. "I've never seen it before."

Drevan gave me a crooked smile. "No one has seen a Blight of Deep Waters either, you know."

I had to laugh. "You got me there, but what's it even mean? I don't know the word."

"Parousia." He took a plate of food from a nearby bone table and offered me some which I politely declined. "It's an ancient language, I think. But it means 'second coming.' Faidra thinks she's a goddess, and until all the server notifications about *you*, I believed her. We all did."

"I . . . I don't really know what to make of all that. A goddess?"

He took a bite as I mulled over his words. "You aren't the only one in Wonder to get your name changed by the system. Faidra was apparently some ancient deity way back in the game's lore. Not too far from your own path, right?"

I nodded. "The similarities are uncanny."

"When we saw the notifications about your bounty, we knew we had to link up. Before the server crash, Faidra had been trying to figure out how to make Wonder *real*. How to make death permanent. And then you came along."

"I can't take credit for that part," I corrected. "But you guys just go along with her? What's in it for you?" Like the Blackened Blades, I was cautious about this new guild. Evil characters—both NPCs and players alike—weren't exactly known for their trustworthiness or honesty.

"Once she knows your name, she can kill you with relative ease," the knight explained, though his voice was much more upbeat than his words. "But it barely even matters. You see that axe? She could kill you in a heartbeat no matter what, name or otherwise. And standing behind her is much, much safer than standing in front of her."

"Yeah, I thought we were dead back there. Never seen an axe that big in my life. Or armor like that. Or any of it," I said with a laugh. "So, what's the plan for tonight? You guys going on a raid or something?"

As it turned out, the Burned Saints *were* going on a raid, and it was one that we were eager to join.

At dusk, we assembled with the Burned Saints near the wall on the opposite side of the city from our entrance. With the war going so strong outside, hardly anyone was left inside the walls to stop us. A few NPCs tried, and Faidra's knights cut them down without slowing their strides. The scene on the other side of the wall was a proper war. Guilds had brought siege engines, Olympia City's ardent defenders fired their own, and there were enough separate guilds in the mix to actually make some real battle lines.

Below, maybe a few hundred yards to our left, was the resurrection orb. It hummed and thrummed with energy, churning through dead players and NPCs at a mind-boggling pace. We watched for a few moments, and there seemed to be some kind of unspoken truce within the orb's vicinity. Attackers ran back to their lines unmolested, and defenders were allowed back to their own.

"How much experience can you farm down there?" I asked Drevan.

He shook his head. "It isn't much, especially with the siege weapons. Such a large scale means each kill doesn't take much talent. If we stayed down there for a few days, we'd probably do well, I guess."

To my right, Kadorax and Elyk were practically frothing

at the opportunity to dive into the fray and get a few dozen kills. But that wasn't the plan. Not yet, at least.

Fraida and her Burned Saints split left while I took my small party right. The guard towers were heavily defended, but none of the defenders were watching the wall itself, and we stormed them from the shadows. It didn't take long to send the defenders over the parapet to their deaths—and subsequent resurrections.

Once our two groups held both towers, Elyk gave the signal to the Burned Saints. The first phase of the plan was simple. We swiveled the ballistae downward, aiming for the nearest players who looked important enough to be guild leaders, and let loose. After the second volley, general chaos broke out in the defenders' rear ranks, and their tightly formed lines wavered.

Then came phase two. Xollmomath produced a huge sphere of conflagration in the empty space above the walls between our two towers, and then Fraida's own magic funneled into it from the other side. The fiery orb of destruction grew and grew, quickly commanding the attention of the entire battlefield below. The constant chorus of screams and clanging swords died to a low roar as the orb continued to swell. The hammer Xollmomath had consumed fed his spell immensely, and the man was nearly at full power despite being so far from Undercroft Citadel.

Phase three commenced before phase two was fully complete, and it was the riskiest of them all. Elyk, Kadorax, and the entire cadre of knights leapt from the wall. They held their weapons in front of them, just below their necks, in a beautifully coordinated suicide fall. They hit the ground with a sickening thud, and a few seconds later vanished in a huge cloud of pixels and smoke.

The assault team respawned just outside the orb, and they immediately set to work wrenching it from its marble plinth. As everyone else was busy either retreating back to their own lines or simply gawking at the apocalyptically immense fireball above their heads, our combined crews toppled the resurrection orb.

I felt the familiar twang of true death returning to the continent. It pulled at the very bottom of my gut, twisting and writhing, begging to taste death for itself.

"Now!" Syzak yelled, giving the command for the final phase.

Xollmomath and Faidra loosed their gargantuan fireball directly into the mass of soldiers. It crashed down with a thunderous force that reminded me of old propaganda movies from the wars. All it needed was the telltale screech of a jet breaking the sound barrier overhead and it would be the perfect recreation of a nuclear explosion.

When the cloud finally settled enough to peer through, the battlefield was in complete shambles. Corpses were everywhere. Thousands. Tens of thousands had died. There were still thousands left, but it would take time for the initial shock of the devastating attack to wear off enough for them to regroup and fight.

Time for phase five.

"Get us down," I commanded Xollmomath.

He nodded, and I knew his next spell would be his last until we could either get him back to Undercroft Citadel or find a magical item strong enough for him to consume. The ancient necromancer waved a hand, and a bridge of obsidian shot out of the guard tower and slammed into the ground below.

Syzak went first, using his own shaman magic to augment the necrotic bridge as Faidra and I scrambled to the battlefield.

The towering woman, half her face a ruin of burnt bone and falling ash, beamed down at me. Her smile sent a shiver through my spine. If I was evil—and that question had been answered long ago in the affirmative—the woman next to me was on a different level. Where I brought death as fulfillment of Lady Kalma's divine will, Faidra exuded downright cruelty. She wasn't killing for a goddess or revenge or some other understandable purpose. She didn't even kill for sport. No, the woman killed for the end goal of inflicting sorrow. Of bringing pain.

I shuddered again.

"Good hunting, Bentalÿk," she said with a sneer.

For a minute, my feet refused to move. I watched, completely dumbfounded, as the giantess drew her immense axe and set it to work in spectacular fashion. Bits of bone and gore exploded from her victims like fireworks. Wherever she passed, blood rolled like a silk carpet.

When I finally snapped out of it, there weren't many of Olympia City's defenders left for me to kill. But that was just fine. I followed in Faidra's wake, easily cleaning up whatever remnants of life she happened to leave behind, and we quickly broke through the defensive lines into no man's land.

Corpses stretched for hundreds of yards. The fireball had been far more effective than any of us had imagined. I felt the dead. I felt each and every one of them, their life forces stretching up from their twisted, burnt, and broken bodies. They were like dead fingers grasping one last time for a loved one, but all they found was me, and when their ethereal forms brushed against my will, I drank them in. They poured into the very center of my being, healing wounds I never knew I had and bringing a wave of reinvigoration that bordered on ecstasy.

Fifty yards ahead, Faidra picked up the pace. She charged, her axe reaching higher than any guild banner left on the battlefield, and I followed. We crashed into the attackers with the same ferocity that had dispatched the defenders. Faidra's axe threw broken pieces of human in every direction, and I swept in behind her to make sure the grim work was completed.

I didn't find many of the attackers with any real fight left in them. Almost everyone had been reduced to indiscriminate carnage. But not everyone. I crashed into a player, a knight whose level I didn't have time to read, and was instantly repelled. He held a kite shield on his left arm and a three-headed flail on the right. Judging by his armor, he was relatively unscathed. The blood splattered across his iron breastplate belonged to someone else, and he shimmered with activated talents.

I swung my newly acquired meteor hammer, and he easily parried the strike with his shield. Never taking my eyes from his flail, I backstepped out of range just as the three spiked heads sailed in front of my chest. I activated *Pull from the Darkness* and launched my shadow pet at the knight. The attack bought me a few seconds of time, and I rolled to the knight's shield side with the hope that the shield itself would restrict his vision.

My gambit paid off, and when I swung my hammer down on the knight's neck, he had no chance to react to it. I pressed the button, launching the head directly into the back of the man's gorget, and he crumpled to the bloody, muddy ground. I jumped on him before he could activate any more magic and wrapped my tentacles around his helm, easily ripping it free. I crushed his windpipe, then quickly scrambled back to my feet with every confidence that the knight would die.

Curiously, the second player I encountered completely unscathed from Faidra's assault was also a knight. This one had no shield, just a huge two-handed halberd, and charged with magically-augmented speed.

I wasn't quick enough to dodge the first strike. The long weapon's blade slashed across my armor. For a moment, I figured I was dead. *Forsaken Barrier* activated, but it wasn't quick enough for whatever magic the knight employed. Somehow, my armor held. The halberd skidded and sparked against the metal plates, and the knight flew passed me in a blur.

I whirled, and the knight executed the same maneuver again. Knowing it was coming did nothing to help me prepare. I simply wasn't quick enough. My talents were almost all focused on managing Undercroft Citadel, not single combat against a talented knight.

Miraculously, I managed to block the man's next two strikes with the haft of my meteor hammer, though the attacks still rattled all the way up my arms to my teeth. My shadow pet leeched more energy from my body—though it was instantly replaced by the limitless corpses—reminding me that I had not yet dismissed it. Amidst so much death, I knew I could keep the pet going indefinitely. I quickly commanded it to shift focus to my new opponent, then just barely got my hammer in place for yet another clumsy parry.

I was about to run, to try and put some distance between my body and the knight who so desperately wanted to cut it open, when a burst of ice erupted from the ground. The spike caught the man off balance, and I dug my heels into the ground to turn and not lose my only opportunity. I crashed into the knight, taking us both to the ground, and snaked my tentacles through the visor on his helmet. As I forced my fingers into his eyes and then beyond into the bloody brain matter, I made a mental note to acquire a dagger or stiletto to save my tentacle hands from doing the grim work themselves. Still, my rudimentary method was just as effective as it was primitive, and the knight did not survive his crude battlefield lobotomy.

I took a quick glance and saw Syzak not far off. I tried to thank him for the spot of shaman magic, but he couldn't hear me over the din of battle. When I looked back to Faidra, she had gained immense ground. We were at least a quarter of the way into the attacking army's lines. From what little I could see on the battlefield, the attackers were retreating, although it was abundantly clear that their communications were strained if not altogether broken. Some pockets of fighters still pressed onward while others right next to them fled, and commanders on tall horses rode back and forth in a vain attempt at organization.

I laughed at the absurdity of it all. There were hundreds of guilds attacking Olympia City as well as hundreds defending it. Our small group—a contingent of knights with a few other classes—had brought ruin to virtually everything. Battle lines were gone, formations broken, defenses abandoned. On both sides, the pitched battle had evaporated into chaos.

I spotted a trench line not far and waved for Syzak to follow me. "Let's clear it!" I yelled, eager for the experience and the chance to hopefully hone my clearly inadequate combat skills. The snake-man dove into the trench behind me, and we ran. The direction I picked didn't matter. We would find enemies soon enough, and we did.

Syzak and I turned a slight curve in the trench, and I caught a fleeing soldier from behind. Two blows from my mace had him sprawling on the ground, and then my powerful tentacles made quick work of his neck. We reached a small dugout with a wooden roof, and Syzak grabbed my arm to stop me.

"My turn," the snake-man hissed with obvious pleasure. He moved his fingers, and the sides of the trench exploded with shamanistic magic. They didn't just cave in on the structure, they ripped through it. All the noise coming from the room abruptly died, and Syzak and I left it as quickly as we had arrived.

We careened through the trenches, over dozens of charred corpses, and finally reached what appeared to be the command center for the entire trench operation. A dozen or more trenches met at a single confluence, the center of which was built from sturdy stone and mortar as opposed to the hasty earthen bulwarks everywhere else.

Voices came from inside. They were panicked, but someone with a level head was clearly in charge.

I had an idea. "Can you summon water? Rain or something?" I asked the snake-man.

The shaman didn't hesitate. Despite the strange nature of my request, he obeyed without question. Such loyalty and obedience, even from a player I barely knew who belonged to a different guild with a different leader, made my chest swell with pride. He looked skyward, and it began to rain in thick sheets.

"More! Flood the trenches!" I yelled.

The water pounded down relentlessly, and soon we were standing in a foot of mud, blood, and rain. "How much do you need? Rain is not hard to summon. I can keep it up," he said between torrents.

I slammed open the door to the headquarters and then cast *Part the Waters*, mentally grabbing every drop of rain in the nearest trenches and teleporting them into the room.

All at once, the room was nearly full to the very top. Tons of it flowed out of the open door, but far too slowly. After a minute or so, I was confident that everyone inside was either dead or very nearly dead, and we moved on.

We climbed a short ladder back to the battlefield, our boots caked in a thick layer of blood, and I scanned for signs of our party.

Closer to the walls, I spotted a formation of Faidra's

knights marching in unison and cleaving their way through the attackers. Behind me, Faidra herself was out of sight, though it wouldn't take any points in investigation to follow her trail of carnage.

I pointed along the path of ruin. "Come on, let's catch up."

Syzak and I traced the thirty-yard-wide swath of corpses all the way to the end of the attacking army's lines, and there we found the burned woman with her gigantic axe. She stood like a statue, her posture heroic and inspiring. All around her, the sundered remains of those who had foolishly stood in her way littered the ground.

On closer inspection, she wasn't *completely* unscathed. I saw new dings and dents in her smoldering armor that I knew weren't there before, and the line of blood running from the burnt side of her mouth and down the front of her chest was certainly hers.

She's mortal, I silently remarked, and I got the feeling that Syzak was taking stock of the same information. There would come a time when I would need to take Faidra's life, and though it would certainly not be soon, it *would* happen. Until that moment, I wasn't sure it would even be possible. But if she could bleed, she could bleed out, and that was all the confirmation of her mortality that I needed.

"What now?" I asked.

Faidra did not respond. Was she more injured than I knew? I turned to the shaman. "Can you heal her?"

Finally, Faidra turned to regard me with her gory, lifeless gaze. "Olympia City will fall. For now, the battle is concluded."

I took stock of our surroundings, and she was right. Everyone left attacking the city had fled, and everyone who had been defending it was either dead—the vast majority—or also fleeing. With the resurrection orb turned off, players would abandon the city with all possible haste. The NPCs wouldn't exactly understand what was going on, but even though they didn't know about the orb, they would react appropriately to the battle and the ensuing rout. Some small pockets of resistance would remain, just as they had in Echelon, and everyone else would abandon the town as quickly as possible.

And that presented a new set of challenges. I couldn't possibly make my way across the entire continent like a giant scythe harvesting wheat. It wasn't possible. Maybe if we have ten thousand high-level players, but even then, there were seven continents. It would take millions of man-hours to scour every inch of the continent. Billions. Maybe trillions.

I shook the bleak thoughts from my head. We needed a way to get everyone together in one spot, and the developers were already planning on giving it to us. When the portal back to the real world finally opened, I had to bet at least ninety percent of Wonder's population would be waiting. Everyone all gathered up in one spot. We would need something bigger than Xollmomath's fireball, but there was still time to work on that plan. Not much, but enough.

Kadorax, Elyk, and the Burned Saints met up with us, and I was pleased to see everyone alive. The rout had been effective, and it appeared that no one was any worse off than Faidra, and I still wasn't convinced that she was actually injured.

"Alright, we need to find Ministrel and get the orb back to Undercroft Citadel." It was dark, probably close to midnight, and I wondered how effective our search for the wizard would be. Perhaps we would need to wait until morning.

Unfortunately, the part of town where we left Ministrel was on the complete opposite side from where we stood. The city was huge, and it would take hours to trek there.

"Anyone have mounts?" I asked, aiming my question in the general direction of the Burned Saints.

One by one, the knights summoned spectral horses clad in smoking armor that matched Faidra's. Sir Drevan brought his mount close, and the stench of its sulfur breath curled my nose. "Tons of classes get summonable mounts around level twenty. I'm surprised you haven't gotten one yet," he said.

"Eh, there's a lot about my class I don't know. And the thing is, no one else knows it either. Speaking of which, I haven't gotten any points in anything during the entire battle . . ." I mentally recalled my stats just to be sure, but I was correct. No points. No stat increases. I chalked it up to more weirdness that was inherent in running a raid and shrugged. Like so many other things, it was a mystery that would have to wait for another time.

Fortunately, the Burned Saints' horses were large enough to accommodate a second rider each, and my small party was soon mounted on the beasts and heading back around Olympia City in search of our lost comrade and our only ticket home. For Olympia's resurrection orb, we decided to drag it behind Faidra's imposing mount. With a few ropes and some careful jostling, we got it to more or less stay in place behind her, though the strange object still hovered a foot or so off the ground. And Xollmomath was little better than the orb. He was so exhausted from the massive spells he cast that a pair of knights had to tie him to the back of a horse to keep him from falling.

Regardless, when I surveyed the peaceful battlefield, I smiled. Olympia City was routed. There was still work to do here, but the most challenging part was finished. And ahead of schedule too.

CHAPTER 6

It was pitch dark when we finally circumvented Olympia City. Any of the remaining combatants had fled, and I could only assume that another mass exodus was getting ready inside the walls.

Off in the distance, maybe five or six hundred yards into the battlefield, I spotted a solitary figure wearing a pointy hat with a wide brim and looting through corpses. I sighed. "That's likely our guy," I said to no one in particular. I rode behind Sir Drevan, and I pointed to the silhouette. "Let's check it out."

Once we got closer, I knew beyond a doubt it was Ministrel. A few sputtering fires flickered nearby, and it looked like the wizard himself had set up a haphazard row of torches. The firelight flickered against his unmistakable hawkish features.

I slid from the back of Sir Drevan's mount and waved. "Ministrel, you ready to go home?"

The wizard perked up, and then a bird I had not noticed before—or did it only appear just now?—flew off his shoulder and buzzed my head. Somehow, the old man was completely undamaged and unfazed by the battle. He dragged a large sack behind him, and I shuddered to think what was inside. If it was more faces . . . No, I shook the thought from my head before it made me heave.

"Hey, Ministrel . . . anyone home?" I was only a few feet from his head. It was impossible for him not to hear me. Still, the old man just kept wandering through the field of corpses and occasionally bending down to snatch some trinket from one of them.

Finally, I grabbed him by the shoulders and forced him to look at me. "Hello? Ready to go home? Do you need more time?"

He fixed me with his unnerving eyes, and I really started to question the company I kept. Between the hordes of zombies, the chaotic orcs, Ministrel, and now Faidra, I really didn't have too many 'normal' companions at my side. Elyk, perhaps, and maybe the new assassin and his shaman sidekick.

When Ministrel still didn't give me any meaningful response, I was tempted to slap him. But the man was insanely powerful, and he'd probably rip me to shreds with magic just for the attempt.

I waved for Faidra to join us, and the giantess was quick to acquiesce.

"You . . . uh . . . You mind talking to him? He's not all there, but he's our magical ticket back." What I wanted to say was: *You're both insane, maybe you share the same kind of crazy and can communicate better than I can . . .*

The huge woman snapped her fingers in front of Ministrel's pointed nose, and for a second, I assumed all hell would break lose. If the two of them ever fought, I wanted to be on a different continent.

Much to my surprise, the wizard locked onto her face. "A crystal lattice," he said, holding something out on the palm of his hand.

Faidra took it, inspected it for a brief moment, then ate whatever it was. I just shook my head.

"I hope death finds me well, wizard," the woman said flatly. "For it is a veil, flickering wicks of black, a sanguine mask and shrines of bone."

"Can anyone just speak normally? I fucking hate these—"

We were gone.

Our entire party made the ethereal jaunt through space in the blink of an eye, landing gently in some of the swaying grass not far from Undercroft Citadel. I recognized the necropolis's spire against the hazy outline of clouds obscuring the moon. My stomach churned, but the ill sensation quickly faded.

To my side, Elyk gasped. "I wish he would give us some damn warning . . ."

Again, I had no answers. Helpless confusion was a feeling to which I was rapidly becoming accustomed.

Then the notifications began, and my attention was stolen to the bottom of my vision.

Your Cunning skill has increased to 41!

Your Influence skill has increased to 41!

Your Investigation skill has increased to 10!

Your Infamy has increased to 710!

Incompatible raid boss detected: Faidra (Parousia). Faidra's allegiance cannot be changed to the allegiance required to formally join Undercroft Citadel.

I didn't earn a level, but that would come soon enough. I only needed a single additional point in either cunning or influence to tick up to twenty-one. And the bit about Faidra being incompatible with Undercroft Citadel was completely unexpected. Her name was in black, not my familiar crimson, and I assumed it was for her guild, the Burned Saints. I wouldn't necessarily expect an entire guild to change all at once, but eventually I figured they would need to in order to utilize the best perks of being in a raid.

"Drevan," I called, getting the knight's attention. "I just

got a weird message about Faidra not being able to join my raid as a boss. Any ideas?"

He lifted his visor. "Not really. I don't think anyone has ever been in their own raid before. New territory, you know?"

"Ha, preaching to the choir. I guess she can't turn off her allegiance to the Burned Saints, right?"

"Well . . . about that. Our entire guild *used* to be the Burned Saints. Now, in a very technical manner of speaking, our leader has sworn eternal allegiance to Gloandi. Once you take that path, it can never change," he explained.

"Is that a new one like Lady Kalma? I think I sort of *discovered* Lady Kalma and forced her into the game, but the jury is still out on that one."

"No," he said, shaking his head. "Gloandi is scripted into the game. There's a whole crazy backstory and tons and tons of lore." He made a big sweeping gesture like a carnival announcer at the center of a big tent. "Gloandi, the Last Glow in a Dead World. Gloandi's fire does not warm. His ash does not settle. He is the lone ember that lingers after all the stars have died. A fire not meant to cleanse but to remind all things that burning is the fate of existence. His flame does not flicker—it waits."

"Hell, that doesn't sound too far from Lady Kalma, the Stench of Corpses."

"No, no it does not. But that's why we can't officially join your raid. But . . . it does come with some other pretty cool perks." Sir Drevan produced a small golden amulet from his breastplate. He held it out from his body, then rubbed it in a circular motion. With his other hand, he pointed to a seemingly random spot in the middle of the field.

In the blink of an eye, the Burned Saints' guildhall materialized.

"We can take the guildhall wherever we go, and that's pretty helpful!" he said, beaming at the trick.

"Not bad! I'm betting you won't be able to set up inside the walls, but go ahead and claim a spot wherever you can." I looked at the necropolis and mentally summoned one of my flying gargoyles to come get me so I wouldn't have to walk all the way back. "For now, I'm tired. I need some sleep. I'm sure there will be a thousand things that need doing tomorrow. See you then."

Alyssa came back the next morning. The undead arcanist had clearly been in a fight. From what we could glean from her gesturing and overall demeanor, whoever attacked her was still in pursuit, though no one broke the horizon. Not yet, at least.

I quickly put Undercroft Citadel on high alert. A cohort of zombies sallied out beyond the walls, Xia and Xollmomath waited in the guard towers, and the rest of us simply watched. After what felt like an eternity but was likely only a few tense minutes, I ordered Xia to use her *Eye of the Necropolis* to scout. She launched the green eye the same direction Alyssa had come, and then we just had to wait.

Ellen, the final living member of the former Resurrection guild, came up behind me and startled me. I hadn't seen her approaching—actually, I hadn't seen her in days—and she caught me off guard.

"I can help," she said meekly.

My eyes still glued to the horizon, I gestured for her to continue.

"It will take most of my mana, but I can summon a raven to help scout. Would you like me to do it?"

I hated how meek she was, but it made sense. Wardens were combat classes, yes, but not on the front lines. She was accustomed to sitting behind battles and helping, healing where she could and protecting her allies, not taking proactive steps or being a decision maker. "Give it a try," I told her.

A moment later, a small black raven puffed into existence and wheeled out over the walls. Ellen collapsed to the ground at my feet, and I was baffled at the energy expenditure for such a relatively mundane spell. Either Ellen's reserves were frighteningly low or else the spell was incredibly unoptimized. Regardless, all we could do was continue to wait.

Eventually, Ellen's eyes snapped back open, and she gasped. "I saw them," she said at once between breaths. "Not many, a handful. Six at the most. They're riding in our direction."

"Players or NPCs? What level?" I demanded.

"All players, I think." She shook her head. "I didn't get a good look at them, but they're armed and armored. Blue and white checkered banners."

The banners didn't mean anything to me. Perhaps if I had played more of the game or at least watched more streams I would recognize the colors, but not now. And it didn't matter. A small group of players would be easily dispatched.

I found Elyk and Kadorax at the gate, and the three of us moved out beyond the ring of defensive zombies to form the first layer of defense. I opted to leave Faidra behind in case the attack turned out to be a ruse, but I told her knights to stay close.

"Six enemies, all mounted, three monks and three sorcerers," Xia called from the guardhouse a moment later.

"Monks and sorcerers," I repeated under my breath. I turned to Kadorax. "You know of any guilds with blue and white checkered banners? Any ideas?"

The assassin shrugged. "Thousands of guilds out there, only so many colors. Could be anyone."

"Fair point. Alright, there's a chance they're evil and

coming to join us, but we assume they are hostile until proven otherwise. Understood?"

Elyk and Kadorax both readily agree.

And then we saw them. Honestly, I was a little let down. Six riders on what appeared to be regular, non-magical horses. They were all players, and they clearly had no idea what they were coming up against. All six of them pulled hard on their reins the moment they got a good look at Undercroft Citadel. Clearly panicked, they turned to flee.

I waved to the Burned Saints. "Get some mounts, and let's run them down!"

A few seconds later, the three of us were on the backs of magical horses. We charged for the new players, and it didn't take long to close the gap. "Idiots have no idea what they're doing," I muttered, though my voice was quickly lost to the thunder of hooves.

We caught up to the players, and the fight wasn't even a challenge. Kadorax suddenly vanished from his mount and reappeared on the back of a monk's horse, a dagger running across the monk's neck. The knights didn't even bother activating any magic and simply swung their swords as we overtook the slower horses, and all three sorcerers died in a single pass.

The players were all in the single digit levels.

A sinking feeling plummeted through my gut. It *had* to be a trap. There was simply no other explanation. Why would six players throw their lives away on such a foolish task? I checked my raid panel stats, and sure enough, the number of active campaigns had dropped by one. Did that mean they weren't part of some larger plot? Would Wonder be able to make that kind of distinction with such nuance?

I shook my head and ordered the knights to leave the last monk alive.

Kadorax teleported the few feet from his position to the

monk's back, and he was instantly repelled. Some powerful magic force knocked him back as though he'd been hit by a cannon ball, and he slammed into a tree with enough force to break bone.

That was unexpected. "Nevermind about keeping him alive," I shouted. "Kill the bastard!"

Elyk and the knight he rode behind both leapt to the ground. I did as well, though I stayed far enough back from the monk to hopefully not be noticed. The player was level eight. His name was Gregg with two Gs at the end, and I hated it. He looked like he was maybe twenty-five years old. His beard was patchy, probably completely unshaven since the server crash. He wore a bit of armor that actually didn't look half bad, but nothing that should have wrecked our potent assassin so easily and so thoroughly.

Elyk circled the monk, ignited Infernum, and took a huge, heaving swing.

The legendary blade never touched Gregg. It deflected an inch from the monk's armor. After two more useless swings from Infernum, I realized what the hell was happening. It was the damned amulet that gave protection from evil. The man had somehow picked it up, and there wouldn't be a single thing we could do about it. Not without Syzak, at least.

"He has the amulet," I shouted, and Elyk lowered his guard.

Gregg the monk found his horse's reins and quickly took off. I thought of following the man, but if the ill-fated attack *was* just a ruse to lure us out of Undercroft Citadel, I wasn't keen on falling for it.

"Back to Undercroft. We can track down that wretched amulet later and figure out some way to destroy it. This whole thing could be a trap. Loot these bodies as quickly as you can, and then we ride back home." As much as I hated the prospect of letting an enemy retreat, there was just no helping it.

While the knights looted—and the monks barely had shit worth picking up—I helped Kadorax back to his feet. He probably had a few broken ribs, but it was nothing a couple easy healing spells wouldn't fix.

Once he was patched up, I finally convened what felt like my first actual war council. We met in one of the big barracks rooms on the bottom floor of the citadel. I took the head of the table. To my right were the originals: Elyk, Xollmomath, Xia, and Geirr. I left the orc leader outside for reasons of hygiene, and though I invited Ministrel, he ignored me per usual.

To my left sat our new allies: Faldra, Sir Drevan, Kadorax, and Syzak.

"First thing first, we need to figure out a way to get that amulet," I began. I looked to the snake-man for an answer. "I know your magic is technically neutral enough to work, in a sense, and I think the rest of us will be useless. But we can track it down, and then you can do your thing, right?"

He nodded, though his expression was sour. "None of us can touch the relic."

I rubbed my chin. "Well . . . you're right. I don't really have an answer for that. Not yet. Any other ideas?"

No one spoke up.

"Geirr? You know the most about magic items. How do we pick up or destroy an amulet that gives perfect protection against evil?"

The muscled engineer drummed his fingers on the bone table. Or maybe it was a bone altar, I really didn't know. "You said before that your sword couldn't touch it?"

"More or less. None of our items could harm the person wearing it, but no one tried to hit the thing with a sword, if that's what you're asking."

"It must exude some kind of aura," Geirr concluded. "Its magic protects the wearer and itself. Using weapons against it likely won't work."

"How about a contraption?" I thought of Geirr making some kind of mechanical device that we could use to smash the thing to bits.

He shrugged. "I have no idea. Worth a shot, I suppose."

"Good enough for me. Start working on a plan." I looked to Faidra and Sir Drevan next. "The Burned Saints have the best mounts in Undercroft Citadel. Work with the warden and some of the zombies, if you need them, and scout out where that monk went with the amulet. We need maps. Just don't try to fight him. Reconnaissance *only*. Make sense?"

They both nodded.

"That leaves the ongoing defensive projects, the orbs, and something else. Someone in Olympia City told me about a magic relic, a Whispersilk Fan that belongs to Princess Yasha back in Olympia. Kadorax, you know the city. Ever hear of the fan?"

The assassin laughed. "Everyone in the city knows about it, but they're all just rumors and legends. None of it is true."

"What are the rumors?"

"Just that the princess can use the fan to turn into a giant winged demon at night. She drinks the blood of innocent little girls to keep her eternal youth and beauty. It's all just a bunch of fairytale bullshit. I've never seen any winged demon in Olympia City." Kadorax spun one of his daggers on the table and scoffed.

It *did* sound a bit over the top. And what would a princess want with an item that turned her into a demon? The ruling families of each city were supposed to be *good*, not evil. It was all by design. Though the more I thought about it, the more it made sense as it actually mirrored the real world quite well. Of course, the royalty was *supposed* to be good. They couldn't just go around proclaiming to be evil and expect to stay in power very long. But that didn't mean they *weren't* evil or turning into winged demons during full moons.

"I'd like to organize one more trip back to Olympia City. There were thousands of players still alive when we left. I know most of them will have fled, but not everyone. We can wipe out the last bits of resistance and hopefully track down the princess and her magic fan. My original plan was to give it to Xollmomath to power his spells, but if it really turns you into a demon, it might be better utilized elsewhere. And that brings us to the orbs."

Geirr shook his head before I could even ask him about his progress. "I still don't know anything about them," he said with defeat. "I'm working on it, but I just don't know. Neither do the gnomes."

"Faidra? Sir Drevan? Any ideas how to harness the insane magic that powers the orbs?" I asked.

The giantess, imposing even when seated, offered a scowl. "Empty vials. Void of light. Lift your head, and death is a relief," she said, and I swore her words only came from the burned side of her face, though I knew that was impossible.

"Drevan, what's her deal?" I was tired of her and Ministrel, two of the most powerful players I had ever met, speaking in damned riddles. What good were they to me, to Undercroft Citadel, if they were both insane? They could turn on us at any moment, and I highly doubted we possessed the strength to take down either one of them.

Drevan cleared his throat. He gave his boss a fleeting glance, then finally shed some light for the rest of us. "She took a few pretty gruesome hits to the head right after the server crashed and the portals went down. As you can see, the damage was . . . extensive. But Gloandi spared her life. She sees things, and most of what she says, well, you know."

Another question popped into my mind from the battle outside Olympia. "What's her issue with knights? I saw her cleave through dozens and dozens of enemies, but she left two knights completely untouched. And all the Burned Saints are knights as well. I couldn't help but notice."

Drevan's laugh went a long way to ease the tension in the room. "Another blessing from Gloandi, you could call it. She can't hurt knights. Reminds me of that amulet, actually. Can't lift a finger against a single knight no matter how hard she tries. Some of her magic comes with a healthy dose of friendly fire, so all that's left of the Burned Saints now are knights. If you like, we could—"

Faidra cut him off with a growl, and then she took a swing at his head. I imagined her smoldering gauntlet blasting all the teeth from Drevan's skull, but the attack did nothing. The only difference between her restriction and the monk's amulet seemed to be that Faidra could still at least touch the knights. She just couldn't hurt them.

And her reaction told me another thing. While she didn't speak clearly, she *understood* everything, and that was critically important. She would be an incredible asset to the raid when the day finally came for one of the four hundred guilds actively seeking to kill us showed up. I was eager to see a demonstration of her full power, though I now knew it would likely come at the cost of a lot of friendly casualties. Though her mobile guildhall couldn't *technically* be inside the walls, Faidra and her crew were going to fit right in.

We spent the next hour or so going over defensive ideas. Keeping Undercroft secure was going to get harder and harder if we kept adding more people. More expansion meant more walls, and beyond the physical barriers, there was the issue of trust. *No honor among thieves* came to mind several times. While I trusted Kadorax and his assassins enough, Faidra was still too new, and what of the next group?

And the next? I'd only been cursed for a few days, and already we have two new guilds as allies.

I left the war council with just as many questions as answers. But everyone had their tasks, and that included me. I first went to Berrick and Crestor, our resident tinkerers, and had them draw me a detailed map. Then I got Elyk, and we took a pair of strong horses from the stables and loaded them with enough supplies for a couple days. I didn't know how long we would be gone, but I wanted to be prepared. For healing, Elyk had a vial of salve that would mend minor wounds, and I simply had to rely on being near enough corpses to regenerate.

In the back of my mind, I wondered about the 'cost of my sanity' part of the curse. Would I recognize it happening? Had it already begun? Did crazy people ever really know how crazy they were? I figured I would have my answer sooner rather than later, and I wasn't exactly keen on finding out.

As we rode toward the ruins of Echelon, I decided to pick Elyk's brain a little. Trust was becoming a higher and higher value commodity with Undercroft Citadel's growth, and I needed to know more about the man who had become my right hand.

"I sold just about everything I had back home to buy a lifetime pass right when the game went online," he explained with a laugh. "But it wasn't much. A couple guitars, a keyboard, some of my dad's old sci-fi books from before the war. You know, he had a couple boxes full of banned and censored stuff, and those old paperbacks still fetch a solid price if you know the right people."

"And you came through from Atlanta, right at Echelon?" I asked.

He nodded. "I lived pretty far from the coast. Saved up enough for a train ticket to the portal, a couple items to get me started, and then I dove in. I barely left the game unless I had to, and that was typically just when I died. Getting back was always such a pain in the ass, too. It was a *long* walk, and as more and more people stayed inside the game, it got dangerous out there. You remember how all the news feeds were constantly talking about the drop in crime?"

I remembered it well, of course. Working in the heart of the bureaucracy, I had been in the thick of those reports for most of my adult life. "Yeah, basically zero. *Humanity at peace* was the headline they kept touting. But I thought it was like that, right? No murders, no home invasion, no assaults?"

"Ha, not even close. All those stats were per capita. Sure, compared to the population of every human, crime probably did go way down. But the people who couldn't afford to go into the game . . . they turned into animals. Fucking savages."

I hadn't considered that before. Was I so insulated in my middle-management government job that I never actually understood the plight of the common man? The notion was absurd. *I* was one of the common men as well, no different than Elyk. Maybe a touch better off, but not by any significant amount. "You know, the more I think about it, the more I think you're right. I bet all the cops had enough money to play, so a lot of crime just didn't get reported or investigated."

Elyk smirked. "Bingo."

"And with no one to police the slums, they went from bad to worse."

"I got out as quickly as I could. I knew that in Wonder, in *here*, I could make something of myself. I could have a life determined by my choices, not bad luck or being born to piss-poor parents who spent more time at the virtual casinos than feeding their kids."

"With that, I can sympathize." We were reaching the outskirts of Echelon, and the giant portal loomed on the horizon. It was dim, of course, completely quiet but still standing tall. "But you know, some people would consider falling in with me to be worse luck than anything you had on the outside. Why go evil, especially after the server crash?"

He shrugged. "You're a guy who doesn't fuck around, and I like that. Always honest, right to the point. And you remember people who have done you wrong. You know how many nights I slept on the streets of Atlanta, either shivering cold or burning hot, and wished—*wished!*—I could ram a sword down the throats of everyone who had done me wrong? God . . . just that first kill after the server crash . . . I'll never forget how fucking good it felt. For the first time in my life, I was the one who decided what happened. I got to pick who lived and who died. It was unlike anything I've ever felt before, and I was instantly addicted."

We pulled up in front of the quiet, looming portal, and I contemplated Elyk's words. He was right, of course. Holding the scale of life and death *was* addicting. There was no denying it.

"Are we going to destroy the portal?" Elyk asked after a moment of silence passed between us.

"No, or at least not yet," I answered. "The day will come when the portals work once more, and everyone on this entire continent is going to flock to this portal. It will be the same on all seven continents. They will gather here like sheep, and we need to be holding the axe that takes off their heads. I just don't know exactly how we're going to do it yet."

"Right, bring the masses here, kill them all at once." Elyk craned his neck to take in the sight. Even dormant, it was still a marvel. If the marketing for Wonder was correct, the smallest portal was taller than the pyramids in Egypt—before they sank beneath the ocean. The technology that powered them was, in a very true sense, a wonder.

"Alright, enough gawking. We came here for a purpose." I pulled the gnomes' map from my pack and oriented it with the eastern wall of Echelon. Viewing the city now, deserted, brought an odd feeling. It was a vacant ruin, but it had only just fallen. It looked more like a ghost town than anything. No guards patrolled the parapets, no soldiers came rushing out the sally doors to meet us, and no civilians ran for cover at our approach. Other than a handful of birds wheeling overhead, all was quiet.

"Which direction?" Elyk asked, breaking the serenity.

I found the spot and then pointed. "It shouldn't be far. Across the main commercial district, opposite the castle. We're looking for a bed and breakfast spot called Fall of Fathom. It should have a red sign with a moon painted on it."

We kicked our horses into motion and made for the nearest gate which was now completely unmanned and left open to whatever animals wanted to explore Echelon. In a few years, the ruined city would likely be overrun by rats, and then a few years after that would come whatever it was in Wonder that fed on rats. Birds, wolves, wild dogs—Wonder had so much of earth that it was hard to believe any team of developers had actually programmed anything at all. The task was simply too monumental. Perhaps there was more to the game than what I knew, but that was a question I would almost certainly never answer.

Inside the walls, a few of the buildings showed cleared signs of having been looted after the battle, but not many. If anyone had chosen to stay, they were deeply holed up and waiting for the servers to come back online. Anyone with a bit of fighting spirit had no doubt left for another continent.

We took it slow down the main boulevards of Echelon. There was no need to hurry, and we stopped from time to time to investigate buildings that looked interesting or corpses that might have loot. We found nothing particularly useful, but it was a welcome exercise. It felt like taking a walk through a park with an old friend, albeit a touch more macabre, and the banality of it brought me a hint of peace.

It was well beyond midday when we finally reached the Fall of Fathom. The wooden sign above the door was just as the gnomes described it: a dark red field marked by a white moon. We pushed through the door, and the inside was in shambles. The place likely hadn't been looted—it was just an inn, after all—but there had been a severe panic. Tables were overturned, some of the wooden flooring was scorched, and all the glass on the rear wall had been blasted out. It looked like someone had loosed a fireball inside, though the spell was nowhere near the power of the one Faidra and Xollmomath had unleashed outside Olympia City.

"Alright, now we're looking for a bookcase." As soon as I said the words, I spotted the target bookcase standing against a far wall in what was once the inn's eating area. "That was easy. The book we need is called *Reflections of Dead Flowers*. Should have a blue spine . . ."

We scanned the spines for a few minutes until Elyk spotted the title on the second shelf from the bottom. "Just pull it out?" he asked.

"That's what they said. No magic words or anything. Pretty straightforward."

He tugged on the book, and it tipped outward, clearly hinged on a gear of some sort hidden behind it. It snapped back into place after a short pause, and then the telltale clinking of a metal chain against a wooden cog came from behind the wall. Slowly but surely, the heavy bookcase swung open to reveal our target: the entrance to the Gnomish Inventors' League. A set of worn wooden steps ascended into the second story of the building adjacent to the inn which, curiously, had no doors leading to the street. How no one in Echelon ever questioned the presence of a building without an entrance was bizarre. Surely *someone* must have noticed, but the guild had apparently gone unmolested for their entire existence until Ministrel started kidnapping people off the streets for his experiments.

At the top of the stairs, we again found very little in the way of obfuscation or security. There was another door, wooden and unlocked like the inn below, and we simply pushed it open. The guildhall looked exactly how I expected it: workbenches lined every wall, and they were stacked with papers, journals, alembics, and all sorts of other alchemical and mechanical components. I had a list from Crestor of a few notebooks and tools he had left behind, and it didn't take me long to fill my pack with them. At the far end of the long hallway, one doorway led up to a third floor where the dormitories and other trappings of everyday life were located, and the second led back to the ground level and beyond, deep under the streets of Echelon. We took the second, and Elyk ignited Infernum to give us light.

We reached the first floor, and the wooden stairs gave way to old, rusted metal arranged in a tight spiral. According to the two gnomes, the spiral staircase was the beginning of their true defensive features. Anyone attacking up or down the stairs would have a horrible time swinging a sword or aiming a weapon. We descended three or four stories beneath the surface before coming to a metal grate balanced precariously over a natural chasm that dropped some untold number of feet into utter darkness.

"What's next?" Elyk asked before risking a step on the grate.

I flipped over the map and read the directions. "There should be six levers to your left. Pull the second one, then the fourth, then the second again. A bar will brace the grate from underneath, and then we have one minute to walk across."

Elyk pulled the levers in order, and we watched as a dull

steel bar slid out from a hidden hole in the wall to reinforce the grate. Without it, the grate wouldn't fall altogether, but it would dump whoever tried to cross it to one side or the other as their weight dictated, and the fall to the pit below was more than enough to be fatal. It was a simple, effective trap that I would have loved employing at Undercroft Citadel but for the mindless zombies who would never be able to negotiate it. We would end up with a hundred rotting corpses at the bottom of a pit like that before the end of the first day.

The final trap we had to negotiate was perhaps the simplest of them all. A short passage, maybe twenty feet long in total, led to the underground laboratory's door, though it was only two and a half feet tall. The short gnomes would be able to duck a bit and still cross the passage with some semblance of speed, but any intruder of average or taller height—like the two of us—had to crawl on our bellies. All the while, murder holes had been drilled into the rock above our heads. Defenders would be able to ram spears into our backs or kill us with a dozen other things.

But we reached the opposite end without incident, of course, as the only members of the guild still alive were Ministrel, Berrick, and Crestor, and all three of them were back at Undercroft Citadel. Inside the main lab, I easily found a few more tools the gnomes requested, and then we hunted down our ultimate prize: Ministrel's private quarters. The gnomes didn't know what we would find behind his door, but I was sure it would be something worth our troubles.

Ministrel's door was made of hardwood banded with iron, and it was locked. Elyk carved through it easily. First, we encountered a pile of old rags and straw that I assumed served as Ministrel's bed, and I had to cover my mouth and nose. The stench was nearly unbearable.

"Something died in here, man," Elyk said behind his hand.

I agreed. I nudged some of the pile with my boot, but there was nothing there, and I just wanted to get away from it. The deeper we went into the room, the stronger the smell grew.

Noises came from behind one of the walls. It sounded like animals clawing at the plaster, but I couldn't tell which wall. Somehow, the sound was coming from all four walls at once. "Whatever it is, I think it is under us," I said after a moment. "The sound must be echoing from below. How do we reach it?"

Elyk and I searched the floor for any hints of a trapdoor or other access. Given the nature of the guild, I didn't think there would be a magical barrier, but I couldn't rule it out either. Finally, Elyk found a latch tucked into the far corner under another pile of rotten straw and other refuse. He lifted it, and a fresh wave of stench assaulted our nostrils. I was quite happy that I didn't *need* to breathe, but it was still nearly impossible not to simply out of habit.

Elyk held Infernum down the small shaft, illuminating a metal ladder bolted into the wall. Whatever was below, it was alive and making plenty of noise. "Sounds like a bear," I remarked, though I didn't actually know what a bear in a confined space would sound like. Actually, I had never even seen a bear in person before.

"That's not a bear." Elyk took a tentative step down the ladder, then swung Infernum behind his back to cast light on whatever it was we were about to encounter.

When it was apparent that the noise was not coming from some beast ready to claw out our insides, we both dropped down to the lower floor, and setting eyes on the device brought me no closer to identifying it.

It was the size of a wagon, maybe a touch larger, and made of gears and whirling mechanical apparatuses. At first glance, it resembled a church organ. I *had* seen a few of those in real life, though they had all been in one of the museums that displayed artifacts from before the wars. Temples, churches, and pagodas were commonplace in Wonder, but they had all been outlawed back home for at least a decade or two.

Beyond the general organ-ish appearance, the device was something entirely unholy. Instead of brass or steel pipes to channel air and produce notes, Ministrel had affixed dozens of . . . what I guessed to be human voice boxes . . . to an intricate series of pulleys, levers, bellows, and valves. A wheel maybe two feet across slowly turned on one side, and it appeared to be driving the entire contraption, though what drove the wheel itself was beyond any understanding I could hope to achieve.

And the sound . . .

Up close, it was far from the clawing or scraping that I thought I heard before. No, it was the sound of air being forced over dead vocal cords, of screams trapped in dead throats and given no choice but to sound.

I took a few hesitant steps forward and accessed the device's information. From his silence, I guessed Elyk was doing the same.

The Skin Thief: The famed and highly illegal creation of Dr. Hubert Malbec, the Skin Thief was developed in secret over several years. It contains the stolen voices of multitudes bound within its polished oak gears and brass drivetrain. Only Dr. Hubert Malbec knows exactly what the device is capable of, though he is said to have perished long before the device was completed.

The smell hit me again, and I took a step back. "What the fuck . . . I'm starting to seriously question why we keep Ministrel around . . . This is . . . *a lot*."

Elyk gave an abbreviated chuckle. There was no mirth in his voice. "Man, are you sure about this? I mean . . . he was kidnapping people off the street and cutting out their voices. That's fucked up. Even for us."

I replayed in my head what little Berrick had told me about Ministrel, and suddenly another piece snapped into place. "The gnomes said Ministrel was kidnapping kids. Not just people, he specifically said kids."

"I believe it," Elyk said. "Real messed up guy. This is some serial killer shit."

"Yeah, but *kids*, Elyk. How old do you have to be to enter Wonder?"

The silence between us hung in the air just as powerfully as the stench. Minutes elapsed. I couldn't read Elyk's mind, but I knew what he was thinking because it was a mirror of my own. Ministrel wasn't kidnapping people off the streets of Echelon. There was no surgical table in the room, no instruments that could be used to remove a human voice box from a victim. There were no discarded corpses or other indications that surgeries had taken place in the guildhall. It could only mean one thing, and for all the killing I had done, seeing such brutal slaughter up close churned my stomach.

It made me question the things I had done. Was I any different from Ministrel? Probably not. I had killed innocent people. Tortured them to death. Laughed as they pulled in their final breaths. I was a fucking monster. So was Ministrel. So was Elyk.

Not a player in Undercroft Citadel was any better or worse than Ministrel.

"It isn't right, man," Elyk said under his breath. "He . . . killed those kids back in the real world and then brought their . . . parts . . . into Wonder. I wouldn't believe it if I wasn't staring at it."

We stood in the small room for another interminable amount of time, both of us fixated on the macabre contraption, and neither of us wanting to address what would come next. We were going to take the device back to Undercroft

Citadel. Whatever it was, I had every confidence that it would be useful, though some part of me was filled with revulsion at the prospect. Bringing it back meant—at some level—that I approved of the device. Using it would only be confirmation. Was I that far gone?

Probably.

And if the Skin Thief could help further Lady Kalma's divine mission, then I was determined not to let it go to waste.

Finally, Elyk and I retreated back to the main room above to figure out how to extract the device from its chamber. We had two horses, and it didn't look heavier than what they could pull, though we would also need a wagon. That part would be simple compared to breaking down the wall and extricating it.

We spent the entirety of the night scouring Echelon for a useable wagon and plenty of rope. Fortunately, we found both to be in ample supply among the ruins. We slept in the guildhall, perfectly safe behind the gnomes' intricate defense systems, and then the real work began in the morning. It took an hour just to properly identify which wall needed to come down, and then it took the rest of the morning to find an abandoned blacksmith with a barrel of metal pitons that we could drive into the bricks.

By nightfall on the second day, we had a set of six pitons driven into the wall at various heights. Heavy ropes led from the pitons to our horses, and we began the arduous task of pulling down half the structure. Elyk and I slammed away at the bricks and mortar with sledgehammers and pickaxes while the horses pulled. It was slow work, but brick by brick, the wall began to give way. As an added bonus, my physical stat increased to forty for my efforts.

Without the added strength from Elyk's legendary gauntlets, the task likely would have taken several days, if not a week. As it was, we spent the better part of three days working at the wall until the final remnants gave way to reveal the Skin Thief still whirling away within.

The next problem was much more straightforward. The device was below ground level, though Echelon sported plenty of salvageable wooden planks to use as a ramp, and it only took an hour or so to fashion simple levers strong enough to raise the device onto the ramp. Then the horses pulled, and we had the Skin Thief on the road.

I sat down with my back against the building opposite the gnomes' guildhall and wiped the sweat from my brow. My back hurt, my legs hurt, my hands hurt, and I was hungry. Kalma's magic made it so I wouldn't starve, but my muscles still begged for food after so much physical exertion. Elyk tossed me a piece of beef jerky, and I happily ate it.

By the time we had the Skin Thief up on wheels and actually making progress back toward Undercroft Citadel, five full days had elapsed. The entire time, the only other human movement we ever saw was from a pair of NPCs who, much like us, had been rooting through some of the abandoned houses and storefronts. We hadn't bothered interfering with them, though I had at least toyed with the idea of taking them captive and hauling them back for Xollmomath to convert into zombies. In the end, it simply hadn't been worth the effort.

Elyk and I walked next to the horses out of the city, not wanting to ride them for fear of overwork. Neither of us knew much about draft animals, and we had no idea if they would be able to sustain both pulling the contraption and carrying our weight all the way back to the necropolis.

We passed through Riverside on the sixth day. That afternoon, I *felt* Undercroft Citadel long before I spotted its spires breaking up the horizon. I felt the corpses and death, the sorrow that emanated from the place like smoke from a fire.

"Something isn't right," I said aloud when I realized that

the feeling wasn't just from the necropolis itself. It was from my curse. I was feeding on corpses, regenerating the physical exhaustion I had incurred in Echelon, but it wasn't from zombies. The corpses were fresh. Wherever they were, there were a lot of them. "Let's pick up the pace. Something happened."

Elyk didn't share much of my concern. "If they were attacked, they would have sent a runner. It's nothing, I'm sure."

I shook my head. "A runner could have gotten killed. Come on, we need to move."

We left the horses and the Skin Thief to whatever fate would befall them and broke into a jog. As we got closer, I saw the remnants of a battle. We were coming in at the end, and it was obvious that my forces had been victorious. A handful of our mindless zombie soldiers had been slaughtered, but the bulk of the dead were NPCs I didn't recognize. In the middle of it all, I watched Kadorax jumping from victim to victim, his daggers and both his arms covered in gore.

I caught the assassin's attention, and he activated a speed talent to suddenly rush to my side.

"What the hell happened?"

Kadorax wiped both his blades on his thighs and slide them back into their sheaths. "Group of NPCs attacked this morning. Fifty, maybe a hundred at most. They had a catapult." He pointed to a wrecked catapult farther back. "We took them down with ease. No casualties outside a few zombies, and they'll be replaced tenfold."

I surveyed what was left of the battlefield and then pulled up my raid stats to see that the number of active campaigns had ticked down by one. Maybe a dozen of the attackers were left, but they were no match for Kadorax's Blackened Blades. The assassins cut them down with ease, and the battle concluded without much fanfare.

My first instinct was to admonish Kadorax and virtually

everyone else in Undercroft Citadel for not sending a runner to find me the moment enemies appeared at our doorstep, but I held my tongue. The battle was a simple one, and it was handled. My presence was not needed. I had to learn to trust my underlings if I was going to run a proper raid, and that meant not being involved in every single battle that took place.

"Good work," I told the assassin. "Let's get that catapult back to Geirr and see what he can make of it."

Kadorax snapped off a crisp salute, then turned for the catapult with the rest of his guild. I went back to Elyk, and we finished transporting the Skin Thief through the gate. Much to my surprise, Ministrel came wandering out of the ossuary with more haste than I had ever seen from his old bones. He threw his hands in the air and shouted with glee.

"You found her! You brought her back!" He could hardly contain his joy, and for once in his life, the things he said actually made sense. The old wizard hurriedly inspected the device, running his hands over the gears, adjusting levers, whispering incantations, and eliciting all manner of magical reaction from it.

"Well? What does it do?" I asked, hoping the man's clarity would somehow last.

Ministrel concluded his rapid inspection and then turned to me, meeting my eyes for maybe the first time. "Bring one of your zombies," he answered.

I mentally commanded the nearest zombie soldier to approach the device.

Ministrel activated the levers and gears in a specific series, his motions practiced and fluid. The voices, before only a notch or two above a whisper, grew in a rattling, terrifying crescendo. As the disembodied voices grew, so too did a faint blue-ish green aura. It pulsed and throbbed with each screech, slowly expanding outward. Ministrel 'played' the instrument with vigor, rushing from lever to lever and gear to gear, and the sound grew louder and harsher. The blue aura brushed against my cephalid foot, and it left a painful tingling sensation across my toes when I stepped back. Everyone else—all save the motionless undead—scrambled for cover before the blue aura reached them. Then it hit the zombie full in the chest, and its lifeless, pallid flesh began to slough off toward the device.

"I guess it really is stealing skin," I said to no one in particular.

The gruesome spectacle concluded with the zombie's complete flaying. The creature collapsed to the ground in a heap of bones, muscle, and sinew. Its skin continued toward the device entirely of its own accord like a fuzzy caterpillar crawling along a stick to a green, leafy dinner. When the skin reached the instrument, it was sucked up into the gears and mechanisms with a small burst of blood, and then it was gone.

"This man is your ally?" Faidra asked, and her voice made me jump. I hadn't noticed the giantess standing behind me to watch the demonstration.

All I could do was shake my head. "I guess he is. And I'm sure we'll find some horrific use for the . . . machine. For now, maybe Ministrel should join the Burned Saints at your guildhall outside the walls. What do you say?" I was only half kidding. I really didn't want Ministrel or his Skin Thief anywhere near me.

The woman scoffed, and a bit of ash fell from the burned side of her skull. "Fuck that. Fuck the wizard, and fuck that . . . whatever it is . . . twice." She turned on her heel, shaking her head and cursing under her breath.

Once the dust from both Ministrel's monstrous demonstration and the small battle had settled, Xia briefed me with a report on the citadel's progress. The walls were coming along, though we still had a lot of work to do there. More importantly, the workbenches were starting to produce useful items. We didn't have enough skilled craftsmen to make anything truly noteworthy, but the assassins and knights had been lending their hands at making gear for the zombies. The crude weapons and armor, far from noteworthy, would at least help. For the time being, we still had more raw materials than workers. Between the mine's constant production and the huge haul we took from Echelon, we would probably need at least a dozen dedicated artisans to even out the ratio.

Xia's last bit of information was the most useful: we had a general idea of where the monk likely went with the amulet. A monastery stood a day's ride beyond Wolfpine, carved into the side of a small limestone cliff face. Xollmomath, the one who had lived longest in the area, only knew bits and pieces about the place. It was old, that much he was sure, and it didn't surprise me. What *did* strike me as curious was that the monastery dedicated to one of Wonder's truly pacifist gods. Their lack of combat skill at least explained why the monks and sorcerers we fought earlier were such low level.

My best guess was that a few players had been completing quests either inside the monastery or for the NPCs who ran it when the servers crashed. They chose to hide out there, and they barely had any way to keep gaining levels. All of the quests from the NPCs would be pacifist, so they were essentially forced to stay in the single digits. Then one of them stumbled upon the amulet, and somehow it wound up in the hands of the NPC merchant we fought on the side of the road. Then one of the players got it back. Their ill-fated attack on Undercroft Citadel was probably just a quick attempt to use the amulet and take us down before we had any chance to really react, but even with the strongest defensive magic possible, the players were just too weak.

Regardless of the amulet's providence, I needed to destroy it. At the very least, I needed to possess it or lock it away where no one else could get their hands on it. I imagined a guild like Resurrection or a player like Kevin wearing it. The pathetic attack we repelled from the six players would be nothing compared to someone high level wearing it. And if, by some stroke of bad luck, more than one amulet existed . . . we were doomed.

It was best to solve that problem as quickly as possible before it ballooned out of control. As much as I still wanted to return to Olympia City and finish what we had started there, the amulet was a more pressing matter. But perhaps there was a solution. I didn't *need* to personally investigate the monastery. That was a job better left for the assassins anyway. It would require stealth and cunning, not brute force. I decided to take Elyk, Faidra, and Sir Drevan back to Olympia tomorrow at dawn, and I would delegate the task of the amulet to the Blackened Blades.

Sitting on the stairs to my bedroom and overlooking my growing empire, I missed having a manager I could trust. Helvegen would know how to assign all the tasks, and she would keep everyone's noses to the grindstones. I was trying my best, but I still felt like I was juggling a dozen tasks with one arm tied behind my back.

CHAPTER 7

In the morning, I gave Kadorax his assignment and then assembled my small team for another jaunt through Olympia City. We found Ministrel doing what appeared to be calisthenics or yoga in the midst of the orcs—a very strange sight—and it didn't take long to convince him to teleport us back across the ocean. Having a personal teleporter was certainly handy, though I still feared that we would either lose the man or he would get himself killed while we were thousands of miles from home, and that would simply be the end of Undercroft Citadel.

As before, my small party appeared in the blink of an eye just outside the city the walls. This time, there was no battle. There were corpses, thousands of them, but no battle. If it was feasible, bringing Xollmomath back to Olympia just to turn the corpses into zombies wouldn't be a bad idea, though enough time had passed that they were already decomposing. Their limbs stuck up at odd angles, frozen with rigor and reeking with an unbearable stench.

I grabbed Ministrel's shoulders and forced him to meet

my gaze. "I need you to either stick with us or at least meet us here in a few hours, ok?"

The man shrugged out of my grasp without a word.

Elyk sighed. "He'll be fine. We found him last time, we'll him again."

"I know . . . I wish we had some way to track him. Just in case," I said, shaking my head. Reasoning with the wizard was pointless. I thought of tying a bell around his neck like a cow in a pasture, but of course that wouldn't work. We simply had to trust that the man would survive and be where we needed him to be when the time came. It was a tall ask, but Ministrel had always come through before.

"Alright, let's head into the city," I said after a few agonizing moments of watching the wizard aimlessly wander among the field of corpses.

No one was left to defend the walls. Like Echelon, it would take at least another week or more for the city to be completely abandoned, but the defenses were already moot. The players had nothing left to defend, and the NPCs wouldn't take long to realize the city was as good as sacked and abandon it. My primary hope was that the royal family hadn't quite left yet.

We walked through one of the gates completely unchallenged. The main portcullis had been blasted from its vertical track, and the heavy wooden doors behind it were shattered. I peered through the murder holes above as we walked through, and I saw nothing. In a way, the silence of the town's defenses was eerie.

The castle wasn't far from our point of entry. It towered above the city with sweeping gables, fluttering banners, and all the other trappings of royalty. The castle still stood tall, and the irony of it being in the Japanese style was not lost on me. When the oceans started to rise, maybe ten or fifteen years before the bombs fell, Japan had been the only country to take it all seriously. They built huge walls and canals, spending trillions while the rest of the world laughed. Olympia City's castle, elevated on a hill at least fifty feet above the rest of the rooftops, reminded me of pictures from Tokyo. The city had survived the flooding, of course, just like the castle had survived the initial attack. What Tokyo had not survived was the war. When the rest of the world flooded, Japan refused to help. Amidst all the global chaos, China and its allies saw a quick target with its back turned to the wrong enemy, and that was the last of Japan. Whatever was left of the islands was deep inside the nuclear exclusion zone, and no one dared go near it.

What we needed was some kind of bomb. We couldn't make a nuclear reactor or anything else approximating modern technology, but there *had* to be a way to create contamination on a similar scale. We could poison the water supply or the air, and that would force everyone left into smaller and smaller territory. They would gather just like sheep in a slaughterhouse. The portals were still my best idea, though I hadn't figured it out exactly just yet. I stared at the castle, and I knew there was still time. Not a huge amount, but enough.

Once we were close enough to the castle to take stock of its defenses, we finally saw more than the errant civilian or player in the midst of fleeing. The inner keep was still guarded. Heavily guarded. Dozens of soldiers—all of them players—patrolled the parapets. More soldiers manned ballistae and other defenses. Lookouts with spyglasses scanned the streets below, and more men were positioned behind them with banners.

"They're on high alert," I said, though I knew I was stating the obvious. It was plain as day. I looked to Faidra and Sir Drevan. "Any ideas?"

"There are other entrances than the front gate, of course," Drevan said. He led us around a small building that looked like an abandoned farrier's shop as he explained the castle's general layout. He had been inside several times, as had most of the other knights, on his path to earning the class. There was an NPC who lived in the castle, the master of arms, and he was capable of bestowing the knight class, samurai, squire, retainer, and several others.

We skirted a few more buildings, taking every precaution to stay far enough away from the main keep to be of little concern, and then Drevan led us to a sewer entrance covered by brush and bramble. We cleared a path through the bushes and trees, but there was still an iron grate.

"If we blast through it, the guards will hear," I said. I was sure that Faidra's magic would be powerful enough to get us through, but it would certainly be noisy.

"I'll give you a distraction," Elyk offered.

I wasn't thrilled about the prospect of dividing our crew even further, but no one else was coming up with any ideas. "Alright. Go cause some mayhem, and we'll bust through. Meet up at the same gate where we came through the walls at dark. If you can't make it there, find a way to raise something red or throw some paint on a wall. We'll look for it."

He gave a nod, ignited Infernum, and then took off back the way we had come. Only a few moments later, we saw a plume of dark smoke rising against the blue sky. A minute or two after that, the castle's alarms were raised, and the parapet erupted with action.

"Well . . . it isn't really as loud as I expected. I don't know how well that'll mask our sound, but let's give it a shot." I stepped back alongside Sir Drevan to let the giantess cast her magic.

I was right, and the general commotion at the keep only produced a fraction of the noise that came from Faidra's spell. She cupped her hands together, charged for a short period that involved pulses of dark energy gathering into an orb around her fingertips, then let it loose into the iron bars. The explosion wasn't one of fire but something darker and colder. It enveloped the entire tunnel, then snapped back out of existence like someone had thrown a light switch. Whatever it was, it was just as effective as it was loud, and a hole large enough for Faidra to squeeze through presented itself right in the center.

"Best not to delay," I muttered, following the woman through the breach after a final glance back in Elyk's direction.

The smell inside reminded me of Ministrel's personal quarters back in Echelon. It reeked of piss, old mud, and a hundred other things I didn't want to think about. Fortunately, the slow-moving river at our feet was only a few inches deep. Any more and I wouldn't have been able to contain the contents of my stomach, sparse as they were.

"You know where you're going?" I asked Drevan, and my voice echoed off the stone walls. We also didn't have much light on account of Infernum serving as our usual torch.

"Eh, not really," the knight responded, and my heart lurched a bit in my chest. Was I being set up? Was Elyk intentionally sent off to get me alone? No, I couldn't think that way. If they wanted me dead, Faidra wouldn't have any trouble doing the deed herself. And it had been Elyk's own idea to create a distraction, not theirs.

No honor among thieves, I silently repeated. I really needed a way to ensure the loyalty of the Burned Saints. As it was, my influence score was simply too low to feel any confidence. At the moment, there was nothing I could do, so I plodded along through the muck and filth behind Sir Drevan with my head on a swivel, ready to spring into action at the first sign of danger.

We spent far too much time in the sewers, but we eventually reached another exit that released us into a small courtyard well within the inner keep's high walls. It was a tight fit, maybe only a foot and a half from top to bottom, and we had to squeeze through and then pull with all our might to get the towering Faidra to fit. Fortunately, with the castle on such high alert, no one was using the quaint alcove. It had a small stream that emptied into the sewer where we emerged, a tall pine tree, and a scenic little bench below the boughs that would be perfect for reading a book on a calm summer day. Only one window looked into the courtyard, and it was next to the only door. I didn't see anyone in the bedroom behind the hazy glass.

"We need to be quiet," I said, worried that the giantess's bulk would quickly give us away.

Sir Drevan eased open the door, and I grit my teeth when the hinge squealed. Again, luck was on our side. No guards came running for the noise, and no alarm bells were sounded.

The hallway gave us no indications of which direction to turn. Wooden doors stood at each end, both completely nondescript. I shrugged and picked the one to the right. We eased it open as we had the bedroom door, and the next area turned out to be one of the exterior parapets. There were guards, plenty of them, but they all had their attention focused squarely on the conflagration Elyk had started down below.

I shook my head to the others and slowly, gently, pulled the door shut again. At the other end of the hall, the door led deeper in to the keep. The next room was a small kitchen with a hearth, racks of cooling bread, and baskets of fresh fruit. A pair of NPC cooks slaved away at the food, and Drevan made quick work of them with his sword. Next, we entered another hallway with several doors to choose from, and I was starting to feel like we were trapped in a carnival funhouse.

Again, we had no way to tell us which door to pick, so I guessed one at random and eased it open. Luck turned against me. I creaked the door open only a few inches, just enough to get a good look at whatever was lurking on the other side, and a pair of guards met my gaze. They charged without hesitation and slammed into the door, shutting it under their body weight.

I scrambled backward, mace in hand, but in Faidra shouldered past and erupted through the door with all the force of a typhoon despite needing to duck at least several inches to keep from hitting her head.

One of the guards started to yell, but Faidra's axe cut off his voice just as easily as it sliced off his head. The second guard didn't last any longer than the first. The next room—now covered in a spray of bright red gore—looked like some sort of administrative office. Filing cabinets lined the walls, a pair of wooden desks sat in the middle with feather pens and inkwells, and stacks of parchment leaned precariously on virtually every flat surface in sight.

We pressed onward, still trying to maintain stealth, and the next room finally turned out to be something interesting: an audience hall. It was long, flanked by stained glass windows on either side, and featured a huge wooden thrown carved with delicate reliefs of swans and cranes. Voices came from our left accompanied by footfalls, and they sounded rushed.

"Charge them," I whispered.

Faidra and Drevan rushed in the direction of the footsteps, and they collided in a violent whirl of limbs and weapons with two unarmed players wearing brilliant red kimonos. They were castellans, probably the rarest class in all of Wonder, and completely unprepared for absolutely any kind of physical combat. The class, as far as I knew, was geared toward managing the castle's affairs and seeing to the royal family's needs. Why anyone in their right mind would choose to essentially play a bureaucrat in a game that let you raise corpses from the dead and sling lightning bolts with your mind was a baffling mystery. I didn't have time to ponder, however, as Faidra and Drevan butchered the two without a thought.

"Alright, one of these hallways should lead to the royal quarters," I said quietly. Despite all the killing, we still hadn't been detected by the castle at large, and I wanted to keep it that way as long as possible.

Again, all we could do was guess. Drevan picked a door, and we burst through it, opting for speed and surprise over pure stealth.

The room turned out to be an unoccupied bathroom. Other than a conspicuously large mirror on the wall, there was nothing of interest. We quickly made our way to a different door, and that one turned out to be the winner.

A woman screamed, two others cowered, and Sir Drevan quickly silenced them with a talent activation. Whatever ability he used was based on influence and intimidation, not magical silence, and the women's screams quickly diminished to quiet whimpers.

Faidra pointed at the woman in the center. "The queen," she said flatly.

I was glad the giantess recognized the queen as I had no idea what she would look like. But the queen wasn't exactly who we were after. "The princess?" I asked, hoping that one of the other two women would be Yasha.

Faidra shook her head. "Not here."

"Ah." I stepped forward, meteor hammer ready, and activated *Visage of the Dark One*. "Where is Princess Yasha?" I demanded. My augmented voice boomed off the walls, and I knew our hopes of stealth were finally dashed. We didn't have much time before the guards would come to investigate.

Whatever the queen's level of influence, it was nothing compared to the strength of my ability, and her eyes rolled so far back in her head that I feared she would go blind. The woman arched her back, her neck twisting at a cruel angle as she tried to resist the spell, and then she screamed. "My baby! My baby! Yasha is—" Her voice broke and cracked, but her will wasn't nearly strong enough to resist. "Yasha is with the king! The stable!"

The queen threw herself backward, slamming her body into a wooden dresser with a sickening crack.

I didn't want to waste any more time. I swung my hammer hard on the woman to the queen's left, and it landed squarely on her jaw. She was a player, albeit classless, and probably just one of the queen's friends from back in the real world who served as a retainer or lady in waiting. A single hit from the powerful mace was enough to send her teeth skittering across the floor like spiders. She died, but she wasn't high enough level to trigger *Reap Honor*.

The second handmaiden tried to flee, and I pushed the mace's hidden button to release the chain, and the weapon's heavy head crashed directly into the center of the woman's spine. She rocked forward, crumbling at Faidra's feet. The tall woman didn't say a word. She unhooked her huge axe, lined it up over the handmaiden's neck, and let it drop.

"Time to find the princess," I commanded.

We rushed back to the audience hall, eager to find the stables, and were finally met with resistance. A trio of guards approached from the right, all NPCs with heavy armor, steel kite shields, and flaming blue short swords. Each guard was in the thirties.

"These aren't regular NPCs pushovers," I said. As if in response, one of the soldiers launched a dark orb at us, and I was suddenly painfully aware of my lack of shield. I ducked behind Faidra's bulk, an easy task considering her immense size, but the orb didn't explode like the fireball I expected it to be. Instead, it erupted into a haze of dark, shadowy fog that was impossibly heavy. It felt as though the entire room had been bathed in sticky webs of cloying, clinging oil. I tried to lift my tentacle feet, and though they moved, they took ten times as long to respond as they should have.

Faidra instantly cast the same spell that had caught Elyk and I in suspended animation at our first meeting. The first guard in the trio froze, though the spell didn't last. The other two were seemingly unaffected. Both soldiers on the flanks broke into a charge, each one activating a host of combat talents, and the chaos that followed was impossible to track.

Sir Drevan and Faidra were players built for war. They moved with lightning speed, ducking and rolling through massive hits that would have easily killed lesser players, all the while swinging and countering with their own brutal attacks.

I lunged between the two pairs of combatants, forming my left tentacle arm into something akin to a drill while winding up my mace behind my head for a brutal overhand chop. The middle soldier activated yet another talent, and when my attacks landed, they didn't leave a mark. The man's skin had turned to stone the very instant I touched him, then quickly reverted back to supple flesh. I swung again, hoping to press what shred of an advantage I had, and I was met with the same result.

I had to skitter backward before the center guard had a chance to skewer me on his sword. Fortunately, Faidra and Drevan fared much better. The NPC attempting to parry Faidra's gargantuan axe was practically battered to pieces already, and Drevan had his man on the ropes as well.

The center guard charged, and I didn't have time to relish in my companions' success. I parried two strikes with my mace, then took a cut straight across my new armor.

Much to my surprise, the attack barely registered. I activated the armor's spike ability, aiming directly for the man's feet, and a shard of obsidian jutted up from the floor to knock him off balance. Finally, I could press the advantage. I battered him with my mace, landing strike after strike, and knocked him to the ground, bloodied from chin to waist.

I raised my mace with both tentacle arms, ready to land a killing blow, and then took a blast of dark magic from the man's fingertips that laced through my armor to chill my bones and set my teeth chattering. The frost hurt so much I couldn't think, and the mace slipped from my fingertips.

On either side, the other guards activated similar spells, and we quickly lost ground. Where our trio was clearly stronger in physical prowess, the guards held every advantage with magic. Well, perhaps not *every* advantage.

Faidra, clutching her chest and losing what appeared to be considerable volume of bone from her exposed skull, suddenly screamed with the telltale sizzle and tickle of magic lacing her words.

"Punishment!" she bellowed, and the man she had been fighting flew back into the wall. He hit it hard enough to be lethal, and then his arms flew wide as if tied tight to horses running in opposite directions.

She turned to the middle guard, and the NPC scrambled backward in fear. "Nailed!" she yelled, and the man was similarly catapulted backward into the stone wall with his arms splayed wide.

"Deep!" she screamed, and the third man met the same fate as his comrades.

Heavy spikes of pure black magic materialized around the skull mounted to the center of Faidra's axe. Twelve of them hovered in the air, slowly rotating and giving off a pungent smell of sulfur, and then they rocketed into the NPC, nailing them to the stone. Crucifying them.

Faidra gasped. It was quickly apparent that the spell had drained a massive amount of her energy, and unlike me, she couldn't just heal by standing close to the corpses. She was spent or nearly so, and her towering axe quickly doubled as a walking stick to keep her upright.

Sir Drevan rushed to the woman's side, helping her maintain balance. "Three?" he scolded. "It's too many! You'll run yourself dry!"

I didn't have time to worry. More voices came from the other side of the long hallway, and they weren't friendly. If Faidra was down for the count, so be it. Sir Drevan and I would hold the line . . . somehow.

I snatched one of the guards' shields from the floor and slid it into place over my left forearm. "I'm not great with a shield. Show me what to do."

Drevan gave me a curt nod. "Lock it with mine. No, lower. Like this." He moved my shield so it covered the lower half of my torso and most of my legs. "Too high and you'll tire. Keep it low, bring it up when you need it. Attack in time with me. You'll get the cadence."

Shields locked, we set our feet just as the new wave of guards turned the corner at the end of the hall. My heart sank. The trio crucified to the wall behind us had nearly been too much. The new group . . . they had a pair of guards similar to the ones we just defeated, and then four players stood behind them.

I shot a glance to Drevan, but he was inscrutable behind his steel helm. "What's the plan?" I quietly asked.

He didn't take his eyes from the newcomers. "Keep your shield low. Match my steps. Attack on my cadence. We move as one."

I shuddered, and a wave of magic worked its way up my spine. It originated from Drevan's armor, and I felt it linking my movements to his. We were in formation, and as long as we stayed that way, I got the feeling the boon would hold. My muscles tightened, my mind sharpened, and my weapon felt eager for blood.

Archon Phalanx (Formation): The drums of war beat steady in your chest. Your Physical stat is temporarily increased by 10. As long as the formation holds, your ability to withstand both physical and magical attacks is greatly increased.

I read the final bit of the buff scrolling across the bottom of my vision just as the first attacks landed against our shields.

Drevan and I held. The guards stabbed and slashed, but our shields moved in unison to meet each attack. More magic came in right behind the enemy swords. It thundered against our shields, and still more poured over the top to hit us, but we held.

"On three!" Drevan shouted, and I didn't know what he meant. "One, two, three!"

On the third count, he lowered his shield and stabbed forward, and I clumsily swung my mace as quickly as I could to match his cadence.

"One, two, three!"

We attacked again. This time, our movements were coordinated and precise, and I scored a weak hit on the top of a guard's metal helmet. Drevan stopped counting aloud, instead using the pounding of his heavy sabatons on the stone floor as a metronome. I imagined the entire brigade of Burned Saints locked in formation and pushing across a battlefield. Hell, I didn't need to imagine it, I had seen it with my own eyes only a week prior. Even with just two of us, I felt like we were inexorable. One, two, three, attack! We began inching forward, and the NPC guards gave up ground.

But there was still a huge problem. There were only two guards. The four players behind them hadn't yet begun attacking for fear of hitting their own allies. Even if we managed to take down the NPCs, I didn't have much confidence that we would succeed against the players.

One, two, three, attack! Drevan landed a brutal slice, and a guard went down. We closed around the last guard, and though the NPC fought ferociously, we made quick work of him as well.

One of the players stepped forward, clearly the group's leader. She was a level twenty-four shrine maiden, a class derived from the more basic cleric and monk roles, and she was arrayed in a beautiful robe of shimmering crimson and jet-black onyx.

The woman didn't waste time on introductions. She twisted her hands, and the ceiling above us turned to crystalline blue ice. It fell with a thunderous roar, and both Drevan and I were battered to the ground. Hundreds of pounds of ice kept crashing down, wave after wave, and it was all I could do to keep my stolen shield above my head. Still, the metal dented and deformed, and it was crushed around my tentacle arm until the bent edges sliced into my flesh like knives.

Suddenly, the seemingly relentless barrage quieted. I stole a quick glance over the ruined remains of my shield and saw the shrine maiden clutching her chest. The grimace on her face told me she was hurt, though I didn't know how.

"Now!" Drevan bellowed, still somehow bursting with energy despite the brutal assault we just endured.

I didn't question it. I tossed aside my shield—inadvertently ending the powerful formation spell—and charged. Faidra's towering figure filled my vision on the left. She swung her massive axe; it deflected off an unseen magical barrier and erupted against the stone wall with all the fury of a cannonball hitting the side of a ship. Stone chips exploded in all directions, and the sound was enough to make me want to drop my own weapon to cover my ears. I held on, swinging with wild abandon, and someone, I couldn't tell who, scored a hit against the shrine maiden.

The woman fell back, and her three compatriots took up the fight in her stead. What cohesion we had was quickly lost. Spells erupted all around. Fire, lightning, and more than one pulse of painful darkness slammed into my armor, and I knew I was taking hits at a pace I would never be able to sustain. Groping blindly against the onslaught, I grabbed a handful of someone's hair and pulled them toward me. I only knew it had to be an enemy simply because Sir Drevan wore a steel helm and Faidra . . . well, half her head was just a charred skull, and I wasn't tall enough to grab her in the first place.

I yanked the enemy into my chest and quickly cast *Malignant Putrescene* into their face. The player stumbled backward in a fit of coughing, but a sword strike ricocheted off my armor before I could get my bearings to attack again. I activated *Pull from Darkness* and launched my shadow pet at the newest attacker, then stumbled back myself to try and get some bearing on the battle's progress.

I wasn't so fortunate. The man I poisoned, a ninja a couple levels higher than me, pressed in with dual daggers. He stabbed in a flurry, far faster than my eyes could hope to follow. All I could do was trust my armor would hold. I took a dozen hits in the space of a single heartbeat, but I didn't die. Then the ninja stumbled again, skewered through the side by Drevan's sword, and my shadow pet tore at his throat. I swung my hammer, pressed the button, and finally wore a smile as the weapon crashed into the man's face with a burst of blood. *Finally*, the fight seemed to be turning.

I leapt on top of the man and finished him with a second blow. I mentally commanded my pet to the next enemy, then scrambled to my feet to help Faidra overpower her own opponent. The giantess was clearly gassed, practically inhaling the entire room with every painful breath, but she would not go down. We smashed another player back into the wall, and then Faidra's enormous axe loped off his head.

Then the giant woman fell back. She just didn't have enough in the tank. To our right, Sir Drevan held off two more players on his own, but he wasn't making any progress against them, merely holding his own. I activated *A Feast of Spores* and waded forward, channeling as much energy into the poison gas spewing from my mouth as I could. I batted away two strikes with my mace, and then the gas was finally too much, and both Drevan and the two players disengaged to cover their mouths.

"Pull back," I yelled, grabbing the knight by the arm. One of the attackers would explode in another wave of poison gas before long thanks to *Malignant Putrescence*, and combined with the gas I just released, I hoped it would be enough.

The two of us took a few steps back, and then a huge hit I didn't see coming crashed into my back. It knocked me down hard enough to send me skidding across the stone floor and shredding my face. The familiar taste of copper filled my mouth. I tried to stand, to at least pull myself up to my squid-like knees, but my body wouldn't move. Was my back broken? I had no idea. All I knew for sure was that it *hurt*, and my face was torn to shreds.

Then I felt the uncanny pull—the irresistible drain of life itself—as my curse drank from the three crucified NPCs on the wall. Its healing magic knit my bones back together and calmed the throbbing ache that had taken up residence in every single inch of my body. But my mind reeled. It felt like experiencing a two-day migraine in the span of a minute, and I couldn't help but scream. The magic was just too much. If it carried on for any significant amount of time, my mind would snap like a twig beneath Faidra's boot. My vision blackened, colored only by bright patches of red and orange that flashed in and out of existence.

Just as quickly as it had begun, the curse stopped siphoning the spirits of the crucified men into my body. My vision returned to normal, my body felt alive with vim and vigor, and I was able to spring to my feet with renewed violence surging through my veins.

My regeneration didn't come a moment too soon. The second I had my feet planted beneath me, the two remaining players surged forward, and Drevan and I were once again on the defensive. They were relentless, and there simply wasn't enough room or time for us to mount a coordinated counteroffensive.

I parried a quick strike from my left, then took a savage blast of ice magic directly to the chest. Suddenly, a man in red armor with a flaming sword appeared at the end of the hallway—behind our attackers and completely unseen by them. It was Elyk, and I knew we were saved.

The harvester didn't waste a second. He threw himself forward like a tornado, swinging Infernum side to side with brutal efficacy, and our attackers fell like wheat before a scythe.

Finally, the battle was over.

Faidra could barely stand. She leaned against the wall, her eyes rolled back in her burnt skull, and heaved for oxygen. Sir Drevan fared better, though he was far from unscathed. Given my recent near-full regeneration, I was in the best shape of all.

"Thank you, Elyk," I said. The harvester didn't appear too badly battered or bruised either.

"I killed a dozen of the guards down below, and when more didn't come out, I figured you would need some help here," he explained with a smile.

"Loot the bodies. They had some powerful equipment,"

I ordered, racking my brain to think back to the original plan. It felt like someone had tossed a thick blanket over my memories, and I had to fight against an unnatural weight to free them. "The princess . . . what's her name? It doesn't matter. The princess should be below. In the stables . . . I think."

Elyk fixed me with a look, but he didn't ask any questions. "There's a party getting ready to flee. Twenty or more NPCs, probably half as many players. Heavily armed." His eyes scanned Faidra, and he shook his head. "We can't take them all. Not at half strength, and not without more support."

I knew he was right. "Damn. We need Ministrel. Any sign of him? I don't want the princess to escape if we can help it."

Elyk let out a sigh that told me I wasn't going to like his answer. "That fucking mage . . ."

"Wizard," I playfully corrected.

"Yeah, wizard. That *fucking wizard* was prowling around on the parapets. Just walking back and forth without a care in the world, and it looked like he was painting."

"Painting? What do mean?"

He shook his head. "I mean painting. Paint brush, bucket of paint, and he was drawing designs on the top of the wall. I tried to get him to at least be a little less conspicuous up there, but you know he doesn't listen to me."

I had no idea what to make to Ministrel's latest proclivity, and I didn't feel like spending a ton of time trying to figure it out. "Alright, let's just get out of here. Set what fires you can start with Infernum, and let's go meet our lovely wizard friend for a ride back. As much as I want the princess and whatever magic fan she has, it isn't worth our lives."

With everyone in agreement, we made our way down the hall to the inner keep's curtain wall battlements at a slow pace. Faidra was in bad shape. The knights of her guild couldn't heal her on account of the same magic that made them immune to her also making her immune to their spells. Elyk and I didn't have any healing spells of our own, and we didn't carry any healing potions either. The woman would simply have to recover once we got back to Undercroft Citadel.

In the meantime, it took considerable effort for Sir Drevan to help her along. She was just too big, and her armor had to weigh a couple hundred pounds. It was a group effort just to get her to the wall, and then we had to negotiate thirty feet of stairs to take us back to ground level.

The stairs took far too long. I knew the princess and her retinue would be long gone by time we found the stables, and there was simply nothing we could do about it. The opportunity was missed.

Fortunately, we didn't encounter any further resistance. We stopped every few buildings to let Faidra take a break, and Elyk used the time to light fires wherever he could. Whatever was left of the city's general emergency response was either completely occupied elsewhere or already gone. And in a few hours, Olympia City would be engulfed in flame. We would leave it a ruined husk, just like Echelon, and then move on to the next. Like a swarm of locusts devouring field after field of plentiful crops, Undercroft Citadel would sweep them all aside.

And everyone in Wonder would soon know Lady Kalma's generous, permanent gift of death.

We reached a staircase leading to the top of the outer wall, and Faidra's weight became a serious issue. Getting her down a flight of stone stairs had been hard enough, but carrying the quarter ton woman *up* a flight seemed nearly impossible.

I scratched my chin. "I think we have to take off her armor," I said after a moment.

Sir Drevan had already removed his own helm, and sweat poured down his face. He collapsed onto the bottom stair with a heave and a grunt. Elyk handed him a waterskin that he drained without hesitation.

Faidra, barely conscious, had all of her considerable weight leaning against the wall, and I wasn't confident she would start moving again when the time came.

"Does your armor come off?" I asked. I didn't know what other 'blessings' her god had bestowed upon her, and being fused to her armor felt like it wasn't far from the realm of possibilities. She nodded, and I finally felt a bit of relief.

Sir Drevan and I began the slow, arduous task of unbuckling her plate. When we finally removed her chest armor, I gasped. The half-skeleton side of her face continued all the way down through her torso and to her toes. Everything on that side of her body was nothing more than charred, smoldering bones splotched with bits of stubborn muscle and sinew that had yet to slough off. And the smoke that constantly twirled up to the sky from her armor didn't stop once it was removed. The magical armament was simply smoldering, though it wasn't too hot to touch.

When we had the entire set arranged on the stairs, I finally brought up its stats in my vision:

Masterwork Ashbound Crucible of the Burned Saints: This armor, bestowed once in a generation upon the most devout of Gloandi's followers, may only be worn by the leader of the Burned Saints. Its fire does not warm, and its ash does not settle. While worn, the bearer of this relic cannot experience cold in any form. The bearer's spells are enhanced by Gloandi's divine might, radically empowering them with new effects and draining massive amounts of energy. Once per generation, the bearer may perform the Litany of Burned Saints, becoming Gloandi's avatar for twenty-four hours. The bearer will perish upon the Litany's conclusion.

"Hot damn!" I practically yelled. "You see this armor, Elyk?"

The harvester's jaw was nearly on the stone steps at his

feet. "I've never seen anything like it. I didn't even know it was possible. How . . . ? I mean . . . but . . . shit!"

We both turned to Drevan, and the man wore a huge smile. "Yeah, that's a fairly reasonable reaction. The armor is one of the highest-level relics in the game. And one of the few items that has a built-in death. You don't see that often."

"Is 'relic' an actual term of art? I've heard it before, but I just assumed it was some kind of modifier like masterwork." My thought process was simple. If Gloandi had a relic, so would Lady Kalma. And if Lady Kalm had a relic, *I* would have a relic. Eventually, at least.

Drevan nodded. "Yeah, relics are unique, of course, but so is tons of gear. You have to complete a god's highest quest to earn a relic. Only a handful of relics have been granted, as far as I know. You really didn't play the game much before the server crash, huh?"

I shrugged. "Took me a while to buy a pass," I answered. "Believe it or not, I'm still pretty new."

"Ha, imagine that. The game goes to hell, and the biggest, baddest motherfucker sending everyone to hell along with it is a total noob. No offense, of course." He held up his hands, but I knew he was kidding. And either way, it was the truth. I felt like a complete beginner, and in most ways, I was.

"Let's get all this to the top, find Ministrel, and then get out of here," Elyk said, breaking me out of my thoughts.

"Couldn't agree more," I answered.

We carefully stacked Faidra's ridiculous armor at the top of the stairs where it smoldered like a smoke signal. If anyone was looking for us and knew how the armor operated, we'd be easy to find. But fortunately, no one inside the castle who had seen her armor had lived to tell the tale.

Next came the difficult task of helping the half-skeleton giantess to the top. She weighed considerably less without the plate—at least two or three hundred pounds less—but it was still tough going. Sir Drevan mercifully took her skeleton side, and I let her drape her human arm around my shoulder. Elyk stabilized her from behind, and the three of us eventually succeeded in bringing her to the top.

Curiously, the woman barely wore any clothing beneath the smoldering armor. She had what amounted to a tattered and charred loin cloth wrapped around her waist along with a few bits of old cotton at most of her joints, and that was it. Drevan explained that any padding beneath the armor just burned away after a while, so the woman hardly bothered. And she couldn't really feel it on her skeleton side, so what was the point?

On the parapet, we were much quicker. Elyk and I could trade off every fifty yards to recover, and Faidra herself was at least a little bit more help, though that was a low bar to meet.

We found Ministrel after maybe half a mile of trekking the abandoned battlements. As Elyk reported, he was busy painting, of all things, along the parapet. I tried to get his attention before we got too close, but the man was lost in his work. When we finally reached the edge of his artistic creation, all I could do was shake my head. Part of me expected him to be painting in blood with a person's spine for a brush. It would fit the rest of the shit I had seen from the crazed wizard. But no, his painting was just that: a painting. He had a few buckets of white, green, and blue paint, and it looked like he had already exhausted a similar supply of yellow and cast the empty bucket to the street below.

The scene he painted was just as strange as the entire concept of Ministrel painting in the first place. It was a landscape. A peaceful, serene, perhaps picturesque landscape. Rolling hills rose up to meet an azure sky speckled with fluffy white clouds. Yellow dandelions swayed in a gentle breeze. A quaint little cabin stood off to one side on the edge of a delicate brook.

Elyk grabbed the man by the shoulder, but Ministrel shrugged him off. "What are you—"

"Don't even worry about it," I interrupted. Whatever answer we got from the lunatic would be meaningless. Perhaps if we had a few hours to burn, I wouldn't mind investigating the design for some deeper meaning or purpose, but I wanted to get Faidra back to her guildhall as quickly as possible.

"Alright, Ministrel. We need a ride back to Undercroft Citadel. A thousand fathoms and all that. Do you . . . uh, do you need more time to finish up here, or are you good to go home?" Honestly, I wouldn't mind leaving the man for a few days to finish his painting if he really wanted to. After all, the main threats from Olympia City were all but fully extinguished.

Finally showing a bit of lucidity, Ministrel twirled to face me, and he splattered a bit of green paint across my armor. He looked like he was about to speak, then closed his mouth again, and then pointed to somewhere inside the city. "Your princess, my liege?" he cryptically whispered. He turned back to his painting and added a nice shade of light green to one of his emerald hills to give it bit of depth.

I sighed. "Come on, Ministrel. Back home. Time to pack up and get out of dodge, yeah?"

"No, no, look!" Sir Drevan said, pointing over the interior parapet.

I followed his finger to a retinue of soldiers and wagons heading down the city's main boulevard and directly for the gate beneath us. "Well, well. What are the odds?" I crouched down below the wall with Elyk and Drevan. "If that's the princess, and it probably is, she'll be heavily defended."

Elyk pointed a thumb over his shoulder. "We've got him."

"Yeah, but what's that worth? I mean, he only listens to me because my influence stat is so high and he's sworn allegiance to Undercroft. That doesn't mean he'll fight on command, and it also doesn't mean he won't kill us all with some giant fireball if he *does* decide to fight."

"Eh, worth a shot for a fan that can turn you into a demon, right?"

I knew Elyk was right, and I couldn't help but smile. "Of course."

"That's the spirit," Drevan added.

CHAPTER 8

Faidra finally passed out, and we spent the next few minutes putting together a crude plan. The princess's entourage would pass directly beneath us, and we still had a working portcullis, though it was now painted with a gentle summer scene.

When they got close enough to count, the worry in my chest dissipated a little. It seemed the bulk of the royal family's guards were probably already dead. She traveled with six armed men that we could see, all of them NPCs, and a pair of players who both had the courtesan class. They were her ladies in waiting, or whatever the term would be in a Japanese-themed castle, and they wouldn't be a problem. The carriage itself—presumably where the princess was safely tucked away—looked far more ostentatious than practical. It was all stained wood and golden gilding, frilly silks and soft leathers. It had a roof, so we couldn't be certain the princess was inside, but I trusted Ministrel's assessment.

The woman's driver would likely be our most difficult opponent. He was a player, a level forty warlord, and he had the look of a veteran who had seen countless fights and won more of them than he lost. Strangely enough, the player was a dwarf.

We waited in silence as the retinue passed beneath our position, and Sir Drevan watched from an angle some twenty yards away that wouldn't give away his position. He lifted his hand, and when he clenched it into a fist, Elyk used the butt of Infernum's hilt to smash the portcullis release. The heavy iron grid rocketed down, landing directly on the front of the carriage and pulverizing the dwarf where he sat. It was a perfect hit. The dwarf died in a shower of blood and gore, and all of the princess's mounted guards were effectively trapped outside the city. Only the princess and her retainers remained on our side of the portcullis. Their screams quickly filled the air.

Elyk and Drevan swung over the edge, then slid as far as they could before dropping the final ten or so feet to the ground. I stayed behind with Ministrel and Faidra. The wizard, after much cajoling, was prepared to cast a spell on the carriage at my command. I wanted to see what would happen after the initial attack before I turned him free to fight, but there was no discernable reaction from the carriage. The ladies in waiting kicked their horses as hard as they could, wheeling them around and galloping back into the heart of the burning city. But the carriage remained oddly still.

Was the princess actually inside? I had no idea. Elyk and Drevan waited to either side, their weapons poised. Outside the portcullis, the princess's NPC guards were throwing a fit, hammering the iron gate with their fists and shouting every curse known to the game.

I waited for some indication of the princess inside the carriage, but nothing happened. It was quiet, and the quiet made my stomach churn. Something was wrong.

"Hit it, Ministrel," I commanded.

The crazy wizard didn't hesitate. He launched a huge burst of fire directly onto the carriage's roof. It crashed into the ornate wood and filigree with a resounding boom, and whatever protective enchantments kept the carriage safe didn't have any issue nullifying the spell.

"Ah . . . we might be in for a hell of a fight . . ." I said to no one in particular. With Faidra passed out, I was suddenly regretting my decision to ambush the princess.

As if on cue, the top of the carriage began to pull apart. The roof was actually made of two halves, and they slid sideways on hidden tracks to reveal the plush interior. It was decorated with soft velvet and cream-colored pillows. And right in the center sat a woman I assumed to be the princess. She was young, maybe in her early twenties, and radiantly beautiful. Her porcelain skin was elegantly framed by jet-black hair cascading in gentle curls down either side of her face. She wore a deep red bow on top of her head that matched her shimmering kimono. I wondered how much her ensemble cost and shook my head. Echelon had sported plenty of high-end boutiques the likes of which I had never entered, and I was sure that Olympia City was no different. Actually, being a larger city, it was probably even more expensive.

A notification scrolled across the bottom of my vision. It said something about the 'transfixed' status ailment, but I was too focused on the woman to pay it much attention. There was just something about her. No matter how much I wanted to, I couldn't look away. But no . . . that wasn't quite right. I *didn't* want to look away. What I wanted to do was go down to the carriage and apologize for attacking such innocent beauty. I wanted to help her.

I caught a glimpse of the cloven dwarf driver, absolutely rent in twain by the falling portcullis, and for a brief moment, my mind wavered.

What were we doing here? Helping this woman?

"Elyk, uh, help her down from the carriage. Don't just stand there!" I called.

The harvester didn't react. He stood still a few feet from the side of the carriage, and Infernum clattered from his grip.

"Drevan?" I called.

The knight turned a few degrees to indicate he heard, but he didn't actually look at me. His eyes were fixed on the woman, and who could blame him? She was the most beautiful creature I had ever laid eyes on. I felt dirty just being in her presence, like my homeliness somehow didn't belong so close to such magnificence. I was no better than a ragged, roach-infested street dog who had wandered into an eloquent banquet. I didn't belong.

Suddenly I remembered. My mind snapped open, and I was filled with panic.

We needed to help the princess! To get her to safety!

"You idiots!" I yelled, clambering over the parapet to drop down to the street. "Someone just killed her driver, and her retainers have all fled! What the hell are you doing just standing there staring like slack-jawed apes? Help her!"

I dangled from the parapet, then dropped with a heavy thud. Elyk finally broke out of his stupor and approached the carriage, offering his hand to the woman so she could step down with ease. The princess took his hand gently, offering her own touch with reverence, and I was suddenly jealous that I wasn't the one helping her down. I was the leader of our little party, not Elyk.

"Yoohoo!" someone called behind me, and I whirled, ready to give them hell for interrupting us.

Ministrel stood at the parapet with a dorky smile plastered over his face. "What are you doing?" he asked.

Wasn't it obvious? Was the man daft? Well . . . yes, he was. He was insane. I waved away his latest incoherent musing and decided to deal with him later.

Ministrel cleared his throat.

"Shut up!" I yelled. We didn't have time for his ramblings. The princess needed help! Couldn't he see that? Her driver was *dead*, and not just dead but brutally murdered in cold blood. Whoever did it was probably lurking in the shadows waiting to kill the rest of us and kidnap the beautiful princess.

A huge fireball crashed into the carriage, blasting Elyk onto his back. I was just barely at the limit of the fireball's radius. A wave of heat washed over my body. I ducked down to avoid the brunt of it.

"Damned fools," Ministrel yelled from the parapet.

I still had no idea what the man was talking about.

Elyk brushed off the cinder from his armor and approached the woman again. He held out his hand, and she took it once more. Her face was so radiant that I practically felt lost in its mesmerizing beauty. Was there ever a woman as pure and perfectly formed as her? Of course not. She was unique, the one flawless specimen to exist in a flawed world.

She slipped something into Elyk's hand, bent to whisper in his ear, and he staggered backward.

"You idiot!" I yelled. He was going to let her fall! I shoved him out of the way, eager to offer the woman my hand instead.

Her touch was nothing short of electrifying. It sent a dazzling bolt of incomprehensible brilliance radiating through my entire body all at once. I felt like I had somehow touched the face of god. Whatever she had given Elyk, she had one for me as well. I formed my tentacle hand into a palm, eager for any boon the woman saw fit to bestow upon me, the unworthy beggar.

She leaned in close, her breath hot on my face. She smelled sweet, like fresh flowers, cinnamon, and brown sugar. A curl of her shimmering hair brushed against my cheek.

"That's it," she whispered. "Good . . ." She drew out the word for what felt like an eternity. "You're going to help me, aren't you? You and your friends are so brave. Here, take this needle. I need you . . . I need you to just . . . just slide it into your skin. You'll do that for me, won't you?"

She placed a cold metal needle on my tentacle, and I greedily took it, eager to slip it into my flesh. I lined it up over a vein and started to push.

The needle had just barely broken the skin when another fireball broke, this time directly on my head. It blasted the needle from my grasp, and I yelled, flailing to catch it before it hit the ground and would be lost forever, but I was too slow. The fireball enveloped my head, and for a brief moment, all I knew was pain. The woman's beauty was lost to the backs of my eyelids, and all the insurmountable yearning that had grown in my chest was suddenly gone. Everything was replaced by fire.

I rolled backward, and when the fire vanished at the spell's end, I was just so confused. What was I doing? Jabbing a needle from a strange woman into my hand? What the hell was wrong with me? I looked back at the princess, and she was beautiful, sure, but certainly far from 'stranger's needle directly into a vein' beautiful.

To my right, Elyk was passed out on the street. On the other side of the carriage, Sir Drevan just stood with his arms limp at his side.

"You awake yet?" Ministrel called from the parapet.

"What?"

"Need another?"

I shook my head. The fireballs were his! "Hey, what the hell—"

Before I could finish, the beautiful woman in the carriage pulled out a fan from a pocket on her robe, opened it, and hid her face. When she lowered the fan a second later, she had transformed. Blackened, leathery wings sprang from her shoulder blades, and her face twisted with brutal fangs and hideous red eyes that were more akin to Xollmomath's than the woman I had just seen.

All at once, everything rushed through my brain. The woman was the princess, and we were specifically after her. She had transfixed me with magic, and Ministrel's fireballs were the only things that broke the hex.

"Hit Drevan with one!" I yelled. I drew my mace and charged the woman, simultaneously launching a shadow pet for her face.

I was too slow, and she leapt from the carriage before I reached her, flying twenty or thirty feet into the air before diving down like an eagle about to catch its dinner. She swooped, just barely missing with my shadow pet in her face, and I rolled to the side. She came up again, and I finally got a good look at her.

The princess was certainly a demon. Bright red horns had grown from her forehead, her face remained pale as fresh snow, but the rest of her was black like charred wood in a fire. Her arms were impossibly long, and they ended with huge talons each the size of an average sword. Her feet were the same, essentially a collection of razors, and it looked like her legs had an extra joint between the knee and the hip. She was an abomination, a true horror completely juxtaposed with the delicate beauty I witnessed just seconds before.

Ministrel hit Drevan with a fireball, and the knight suddenly shook off the stupor that had entranced us all.

"Look alive!" I yelled, but he was too late. The princess crashed into him, her huge talons scraping against his steel armor, and they were both temporarily enveloped in a deathly black orb of shadow. When the magic dissipated a second later, Drevan was on the ground clutching his chest.

Whatever the woman was, we were too beaten and

battered to fight her. "Ministrel! I need you to kill her! Give it everything you have!" I didn't know if the wizard would understand. Or if he did understand, would he obey? He'd been cooperative so far, and for that I had to thank my influence stat. He listened to me, at least on some level, and I prayed to Lady Kalma that he would again. I just needed one more, and then he could go back to being fully insane.

A huge bolt of lightning cracked the sky. It originated from nowhere—there were no clouds overhead—and ripped through the woman's body, through her carriage, and through at least ten feet of the street beneath. Rock and soil launched everywhere, and the smell burnt air filled my nostrils. The woman fell to the ground, though she was just stunned, not dead.

I quickly activated the spike ability granted by armor as many times as I could, ripping the princess apart over and over until nothing was left of her body but broken bits of bone and plenty of splattered blood.

Just as quickly as the fight had begun, Ministrel and I ended it, but not without heavy damage. I went first to Elyk. He was unconscious, and a thin line of white foam had dried on the side of his head. But he had a pulse, and I figured that was about as good as I could hope for.

Drevan fared slightly better on the other side of the now-demolished carriage. He was at least awake. "How bad are you hurt?" I asked.

He shook his head. "I don't know . . ."

"What was that sphere of darkness? The spell she cast?"

Drevan met my eyes, but his mind was a million miles away. He wasn't focused. "I'm not sure. She . . . I saw things. Horrible things."

"None of it was real," I said. "She just messed with your head." I snapped my fingers in front of his face, but his eyes didn't react. He was still lost in the visions.

After a moment, he finally exhaled and spoke. "No . . . they *were* real. They were things I had done. She showed me my past. I . . . I've done . . . horrible things."

I grabbed him by the shoulders and tried to command his attention the same as I had done to Ministrel a few times before. "Hey. Hey! We've all done shit. You just accept it and move on. No one can change the past, and as long as you're alive, the past doesn't *need* changing. Got it?"

Sir Drevan didn't respond. His mouth moved, but no words came out. His eyes were still completely unfixed.

"Shit. I'll figure you out later." I left the knight in search of our ultimate prize, the princess's magic fan, and I found it beneath a small pile of tattered clothing and gore not far from the ruined carriage.

"Alright, Ministrel. We need a ride home. Got it?"

The wizard gave me a toothy smile over the edge of the parapet. He tipped his hat, and when I blinked, I was maybe a hundred yards from Undercroft Citadel. I chalked it up to Ministrel's general insanity that I would never understand how his magic worked. He never seemed winded or spent like the rest of us, and none of his spells required the consumption of magic items like Xollmomath. He was simply an enigma, and that was that.

I saw to it that Drevan made it back to his guildhall outside the necropolis walls, and then I had a pair of gargoyles fly Elyk home. Immediately, I came across a grave problem. Syzak and the Blackened Blades still weren't back from their quest at the monastery. That left our options for healing very limited. We had a couple crude potions ready, though I opted to save those just in case we had an emergency later, and instead I sent for our other shaman: the foul-smelling Ugg'chugg. The orc cast a few spells, and she assured me that they were healing spells, but Elyk still didn't stir.

I was worried for the man. He was the closest thing I had

to a friend, and beyond that, he was incredibly powerful. I would miss him swinging Infernum through ranks of enemies just as much as I would miss having him at my side. But he wasn't dead. Not yet. And if there was one thing Lady Kalma and her towering necropolis knew, it was the command of life and death. That subtle, fragile string that bound the souls to the soulless. I had Elyk carried to the ossuary, and the gargoyles laid him out on the bone altar and stripped his armor.

Xollmomath found us in the chapel. "He is restless," the necromancer said quietly.

"What do you mean?"

His deep red eyes stared into my soul, and the hairs on my neck stood on end. "He took too much damage. It built within him, and now it is running its course. He will feel it for days . . . if he survives."

His enhanced role as a result of Undercroft Citadel upgrading to a raid meant that all the damage he took was spread out over time, and now he was finally paying the price. I supposed it was still all a net positive considering he was alive. Perhaps whatever the princess had done to him in Olympia City would have killed him on the spot. I suspected as much. Sadly, the small needle she had given me didn't make the trip home, so I couldn't analyze it to know for certain. But one thing I did know was that Elyk had been so transfixed that he pricked himself without hesitation.

To have power like that . . . I imagined pushing my influence and infamy high enough to use *Visage of the Dark One* to make someone willingly stab themself with a poisoned needle. But hell, it was so much more than that. We were powerless in her presence. Without Ministrel dropping fireballs on our heads, our entire party would have been wiped out in no time.

"He's in Lady Kalma's hands now," I said. I gave the man

a firm pat on the shoulder, then left to attend other business. There was too much to do, and I wasn't a nurse. Staying at his side was pointless.

Next on the list was my own stat sheet. As before, I gained all of my experience and notifications upon my return to Echelon's continent, and I had another level to allocate on account of my influence stat rising by one. Level twenty-one brought another three skills, and I sat on the stairs to my room to make the decision.

Pain Upon Pain (Physical): The Blight of Deep Waters can withstand physical hits that would lay others low. You no longer bleed. Passive.

Coins for the Boatman (Cunning): Lady Kalma offers you two pieces of copper, a mere pittance in exchange for your life. As long as the coins remain on your eyes, you will appear dead. Active, consumes minor energy.

The Basalt Monolith (Influence): Commanding the will of bedrock, the Blight of Deep Waters is surrounded in solid black stone. Nearby enemies will be drawn to attack you as long as the spell holds. Active, consumes moderate energy.

As was becoming the norm, all three options felt like strong choices. Not being able to bleed was perhaps the least exciting, but it was still useful. The other two had similar themes, though I felt like *The Basalt Monolith* perhaps had more practical application. Being able to turn into a pillar of stone and draw the attention of nearby enemies would have a ton of uses, especially if I had already buried a poison rune at my feet or created some other kind of trap. Would the spell pull attackers into the moat, leading them to their deaths like lemmings? Probably not. But could it get a high-level player to attack by mistake, thereby turning a fight in my favor? That seemed more plausible.

I unlocked *The Basalt Monolith*, and then an idea very quickly leapt into my head.

The Whispersilk Fan was still tucked into my belt. I pulled it out and checked the description:

Princess Yasha's Whispersilk Fan: This heirloom has been part of the Olympia City crown jewels for generations. When activated, it grants the bearer the ability to assume the form of Taured, a lesser demon from the sixth hell. The effect is easier to maintain at night. Active, consumes massive energy.

I leapt to my feet and quickly activated the item, moving it in front of my face just as the princess had done. My chest panged from the effort, and when I brought it down, leathery wings shot out of my back. My arms and legs elongated, and monstrous claws clacked against the stone stairs. It took me a few seconds to get the hang of it, and then I was flying, albeit *very* slowly and *very* clumsily.

In a display that probably looked like a drunken duck trying to take off from a pond with only one wing, I managed to fly over the walls. I cleared the moat, and then I activated my newest talent. At once, a sheath of solid black basalt encased my entire body, and I fell to the ground.

The crater I made rivaled the one from Ministrel's lightning. I was at least eight feet below the surface when I let both spells dissipate, and I had to summon more gargoyles to get me out. The combination sapped a huge amount of my stamina, so it wouldn't be a move I could count on more than once in a fight, but that *one* time I landed it would certainly be epic.

◄◆►

The next morning, I awoke a little after dawn and wished for some coffee. Sadly, there was none. What we did have was at least a fairly bustling city. Or perhaps town was a better descriptor. Village, maybe. But whatever it was, we had one, and people were up and about. Watching everyone made me smile. The defenses were coming along nicely. Our second layer of stone wall was maybe one third completed. At the workshops, Geirr and the others had the frame of a large catapult assembled, and it looked like they would be done by tomorrow.

The crops—we didn't really have enough to classify it as a farm—were coming in, though we still needed more people to help convert the flora to potions and other useful products. Near the barracks on the citadel's first floor were the storehouses, and they practically burst at the seams with food and barrels of fresh water. Looting Echelon had been incredibly productive, and we wouldn't have to worry about provisions probably ever. Especially with a good eighty percent of Undercroft Citadel being undead. Raw materials still came into the forge faster than anyone could use them, and I desperately wanted to figure out how to solve that problem. If we could find even a handful of blacksmiths to make weapons and armor, we'd be much better off. Perhaps that task would be next on my list.

First, I needed to check on Kadorax and his Blackened Blades. So far, I hadn't seen any of them around. It had only been a day, so I figured they were still handling things at the monastery. I found Xia training some of the zombies out in the fields, and she confirmed that none of the Blackened Blades had made it back yet.

I wasn't worried. Kadorax was a skilled assassin, and as long as he stuck the plan, I had every confidence that he would return.

Around noon, I went to check on Elyk in the ossuary. He was still knocked out. I didn't like his predicament, and I *hated* that I was essentially helpless. "I'm sorry, man," I told him. The gentle rise and fall of his chest gave me little comfort. "If there was anything I could do . . ."

I nearly bumped into Xollmomath on my way out of the

ossuary. The necromancer's eyes bored into me, their deep crimson color still just as unsettling as the first day I met him.

"Master," he said quietly, and I got the feeling that I wouldn't like whatever came next. "There may yet be another way. Something you can do."

There it was. I let out a heavy sigh. "Some kind of god-awful blood ritual with a thousand sacrifices to Lady Kalma, right?"

He smiled, but his expression was more of pity than amusement. "A ritual, yes, but perhaps not a sacrifice. Whatever is offered must be his own."

"Well, that's comforting, I guess. Tell me about the ritual."

Xollmomath pointed an old, withered finger at the reflecting pool. "Elyk must drink from the pool to commune with Lady Kalma. If she wishes, she will spare his life. If not . . ." He snapped his fingers and then brushed passed me without another word.

I shrugged. What harm could come of it? Well, the man could die, but that option was already on the table. Still, I wasn't sure that I wanted to roll the dice with his life just yet. My own experience with the reflecting pool had been . . . interesting, to say the least. Though I lived through it, of course. Perhaps feeding a bit of the liquid to Elyk wouldn't be such a bad idea.

I thought on it for a few more minutes and then decided that I *would* perform Xollmomath's ritual, but I wouldn't do it today. As far as I could tell, the man wasn't in critical, mortal danger right now. He could wait twenty-four hours. And if he *did* expire in that time, well, that would be my burden to bear. I'd simply have to add his death to the innumerable multitude already pressing down on my shoulders.

For the time being, I just wanted to take my mind off things. I needed a day to relax and recover, to lick my wounds and catch my breath. I figured Geirr wouldn't mind the help, and my craftsmanship stat was so woefully low that virtually any task at all in the workshop would raise it, so I spent the entire day helping him put the finishing touches on the catapult. My craftsmanship rose by three to a piddly thirteen, and I had to undo my work just as often as not, but by the time dawn broke and I was rubbing the sleep in my eyes, we had a functional device.

A siege weapon. The thing towered over our walls by at least twenty feet, and our preliminary tests showed that it possessed a range of two or three hundred yards, perhaps more with some fine tuning. We loaded it up with two barrels filled with random stones and other waste from the mine, and the resulting explosion we got when the ammunition landed was nothing short of impressive. If we could build a whole line of them to position right behind the inner wall, they'd be devastating.

Geirr agreed, and I set him to work with an order for a full dozen as soon as he could get them ready. I made my way to bed after the sun had fully crested the horizon and mentally commanded my room to wake me with the lights around noon. When it did, I was still exhausted. I laid there in the sheets for a long time considering everything I had done and how far Undercroft Citadel had come.

What weighed on my mind most was Sir Drevan. What he said echoed in my mind. The princess showed him things he had done. Real things. His own past. If she had done the same to me, would I have cared? I thought about Echelon's royal family, and no feelings of remorse crept into my brain. I just . . . did not care. What were their lives to me? Nothing. Less than nothing.

What about everyone else? There was some kid who broke into the citadel, and I chopped off his head. What was his name? I had no idea. And Vic had gotten his just desserts before his death, so that one didn't bother me either. Would I have killed him outside the game?

I thought on the question for a long time.

The man killed my daughter. My only child. Ingrid.

If Vic had done the same outside the game, I would have killed him. I wouldn't have hesitated. Perhaps Vic's death would have been less creative, but he would have died all the same.

But what of Ingrid's mother? I could barely remember her. Had Vic killed her too? No, that didn't feel right. There was a woman buried deep in my psyche, but I couldn't dig enough to free her. She was stuck somewhere, lodged in the bedrock of my mind, but I knew I loved her once.

And that sent my mind reeling to Helvegen. The pain of losing her was entirely different. Hel had been . . . what, exactly? My friend, yes. My lover, more than once. But she wasn't my wife. I knew she wasn't, and she never would be. And I had killed her. But she was still alive somewhere. Probably plotting her own revenge.

I shook the thoughts of Helvegen from my head. The woman could wait. There would be plenty of time to confront those demons later.

I rubbed the sleep from my eyes as best I could with tentacles for hands and then made my way back to the ossuary. Elyk's condition hadn't changed. His skin was cold, and small beads of sweat dripped from his arms and torso. His breathing was steady, but what good was that if the man was still unconscious after so much time? I was starting to think he would never recover.

Perhaps it was time to give Xollmomath's idea more consideration.

I paced for a few moments and tried to weigh my options. I had no real options. I could do nothing and hope for the best. Or I could get a cup from the barracks, fill it with terrifying black liquid from the reflecting pool, and force it down Elyk's mouth.

Finally, I selected option B.

I found a tin cup in the barracks, washed it a bit with some clean water, and then filled it halfway with reflecting pool liquid. I was careful not to touch any of it as I brought it to Elyk's lips. With very little fanfare, I tilted Elyk's head back and poured.

Somehow, the man drank. His throat worked, moving the dark liquid with ease just the same as if he was conscious. It didn't make any sense. Hell, half the shit around Undercroft Citadel made less sense than an unconscious man being able to drink from a cup. I shook my head and let him finish the draught.

I waited. There was nothing else I could do.

After a few minutes I thought of seeking out Xollmomath, though I didn't want to leave Elyk's side just in case.

Slowly, painfully slowly, a small black line formed on Elyk's bare left foot. It looked like a drop of thick ink, though it shined against the light inside the ossuary. It wasn't dull or matte like tattoo ink. It was reflective like polished metal. The ink grew, a perfectly straight line from his left foot up to his hip and then up his flank to his ear. It crested the top of his head and stopped right in the middle where it was lost beneath his shock of brown hair.

Elyk still did not stir. His breathing quickened, or perhaps it didn't and I only thought it did. We didn't exactly have telemetry equipment in Undercroft Citadel, so I couldn't be sure.

I waited another half an hour or better before leaving Elyk to whatever fate he had found at the hands of our death goddess. I had another grievously injured ally to attend to, though Faidra clearly fared much better than the harvester. I found her at the Burned Saints' guildhall sitting at the head of a long table and feasting on pungent, roasted meats. For some reason, seeing the half-skeleton woman eating was an odd sight. Part of me expected her to have a similar passive skill to my own, but I didn't really know much about Gloandi, so perhaps that kind of boon was outside her god's wheelhouse.

The guildhall was brilliantly lit with smoking torches and a warm blaze in a hearth behind the long table. It was an overall quaint scene, even cozy, and didn't fit the Burned Saints' aesthetic at all. I had a feeling that the place hadn't always belonged to the guild. It was likely the domain of a different guild at some point not too long ago, and the Burned Saints had killed them all and claimed it as their own.

Faidra regarded me with a simple nod and didn't speak. She seemed well enough, busily feasting away, so I left her to it and decided to explore the guildhall a bit more and hopefully find Sir Drevan.

Beyond the main great room, the next hall featured a barracks similar to the ones at the ground floor of Undercroft Citadel. A few of the knights were asleep on bunks, and another pair sat at a low table lit by a single candle and played cards. Drevan was not among them. I asked the card players if they had seen him, and one of them, a female knight, showed me to another door that led to a staircase. The guildhall was on the ground outside the walls, and the stairs led down. I wondered if there would be a huge pit left in the ground when they moved their guildhall again. If it was a big enough hole, we would need to fill it in. I sighed. Yet another task to add to my insurmountable list.

I took the stairs with a bit of caution as the light was almost completely gone. A single candle sat on a table at the bottom, and it didn't provide much for me to see. A second door greeted me at the bottom of the stairs. It was metal with a small grate set in the center, and it reminded me of a jail cell. Hesitantly, I peered through.

Sir Drevan sat in the center of a painted circle in nothing but his underclothes. A fully armored knight walked the edge of the circle around him with heavy, slow steps. I watched for a long moment as the scene unfolded. Eventually, the armored knight made a full circle around Drevan.

"What is it you seek, knight?" the armored one asked. Her voice gave away her femininity.

Drevan craned his neck to meet her eyes. "A place where we can go to mend ourselves when we feel alone."

"Somewhere no one else can reach inside."

Drevan coughed, and his voice faltered for a moment. "Bury me. I want to feel the soil."

"We all want to be glowing, golden, precious lightning. Only the moon is watching us. Flutter your wings inside my palms. I can free you, knight."

Drevan turned his face back to the floor. "Bury me. I want to feel the soil. I'll be with you when you sleep."

The female knight drew a long, slender blade from a leather sheath on her belt. She held it aloft, said a few lines in a language I did not recognize, and then—to my abject horror—thrust it deep into Drevan's chest.

I ripped open the metal door and rushed into the room. "What the—"

The woman pointed her long blade at me, and I stopped. "Do not break the circle!" she yelled.

My tentacle foot was only a few inches from the painted circle. "You killed him!"

The woman lifted her visor, and the ferocity in her eyes spoke volumes. "*Do not break the circle.*"

I held up my hands. "Alright, alright. But you killed him! What the hell?"

The woman's eyes flicked to the ceiling, and I followed.

Another painted circle mirrored the one on the ground. The dirt ceiling inside the circle rumbled. It undulated and writhed, then all at once let loose with a brutal deluge. The dirt cascaded down all around Sir Drevan like a waterfall, instantly obscuring him, but the dirt didn't stop when it the ground. It continued through the circle on the floor in one unbroken wave.

The waterfall of soil slowed to a trickle, then stopped altogether. When the room calmed, Sir Drevan was still in the same position. He was spread on the floor, his hands open and blood running freely from his gut.

Solemnly, the female knight produced a small flicker of fire on the inside of her palm with a spell. She knelt at the edge of the circle, then dropped the fire. Everything within the circle ignited. Drevan was lost in the flames for a minute, but like the soil, they subsided before long.

Then everything went dark. Whatever light had been trickling in from the other side of the metal door was gone. We were bathed in darkness and silence.

Minutes elapsed.

No one breathed.

No one moved.

Finally, a sliver of moonlight—impossible underground, but there it was—descended from the circle on the ceiling. It landed on Drevan's chest, and the bloody wound from the other knight's long blade was gone. The light grew and grew until it filled the entire circle.

The room went suddenly black again, then returned to the normal half-light of the flickering candle outside. The woman fixed me with her wild eyes once more. "The ritual is complete. You may enter the circle if you wish."

I wasn't sure I wanted to get anywhere near the circle.

Sir Drevan began to stir, and a little bit of the anxiety in my chest dissipated. At least the man was alive and moving of his own accord. That was more than I could say for Elyk still lying on a slab back inside Lady Kalma's bone chapel.

The man gasped, and I felt more relief. Breathing was a good sign.

"You alright?" I tentatively asked, though I didn't exactly expect a response.

He looked my direction and nodded.

I let out a breath that felt like it had been held in for ages.

Sir Drevan rubbed his fingers across his face, then slowly rose to his knees. The female knight offered him a hand, and with her help he was able to get back to his feet. "Hope you enjoyed the show," he said weakly. He took a few more deep breaths and seemed to steady himself. "That was my . . . fourth cleansing. They get easier, or so I am told." He tapped his temple on the right side. "It'll clear my head, you know? Best to dust the cobwebs from time to time. I'll be right as rain in a day. Just need a warm meal and a full night's sleep now."

I waited for Drevan to finish getting his bearings, then accompanied him back upstairs to the main guildhall. Faidra had finished her meal and was nowhere to be seen. Drevan sat with a heavy thud on a chair, and another knight was quick to bring him a full plate of food. Apparently, the cleansing ritual was a bigger deal than Drevan let on, and he enjoyed something akin to celebrity status, though he assured me it would fade by tomorrow. As it was, not every knight *survived* a cleansing. The fact that Drevan had made it through four of them was quite impressive. And, due to her strange circumstances regarding the knight class, Faidra could not partake in cleansings at all. But I still wasn't exactly sure what the ritual's purpose was, so it didn't mean particularly much to me.

I sat with Drevan for a while as he ate and was pleased to hear him speaking normally and not giving me any indication that whatever the princess had shown him still lingered. Part of me wanted to know what it was he saw. What could be so bad in the man's past to make him go through the ritual I had just witnessed? He didn't exactly strike me as the kind to go around butchering kids or something, but then again, I *did* watch his boss crucify three people, so perhaps the Burned Saints were a lot darker than I thought. Regardless, I knew I would see a lot more from the guild before long, and now I could trust them. They were powerful, loyal, and they would become my right hand when other guilds started attacking.

Drevan finished his meal and then retired to the barracks for some much-needed sleep, and I found myself at the top of the gatehouse before long. Construction on the outer wall was coming along, though it would still be a few weeks. More importantly, Geirr and the gnomes had the shell of a second catapult in the works.

I scanned the horizon for any sight of Kadorax and his Blackened Blades, but there was nothing. All was quiet. I watched for a while longer, envisioning grand defensive fortifications and all manner of traps and bulwarks, but I knew there wasn't nearly enough time. If Undercroft Citadel was going to survive, it would be the strength of our players and not necessarily our walls that saw us through the night.

But my closest ally, Elyk, still wasn't back to his feet, and there was nothing I could do about it.

I spent the rest of the day helping Geirr at the workshop again, and when morning broke, I went right for the bone chapel. Much to my surprise, Elyk was sitting up. He had his back against the wall, and a bit of dried blood was smeared around his mouth and his bare chest.

"You're awake!"

Elyk's eyes wavered around the ceiling for a moment before finally finding me. "Eh. Technically."

I wanted to wrap the man in a big hug, but I feared that he would crumble apart like dry leaves if I even touched him. “How are you feeling?” I asked. As soon as the question left my mouth, it felt stupid. The man had come back from the brink of death, and then whatever Lady Kalma had done to him was likely worse.

He shrugged. “I’ll make it. But we’ve got a bigger problem.” A painful cough shook his whole body. Suddenly, the man seemed frail. Small. Weak. He was a mere shadow of the brutal harvester I had fought alongside so many times before.

“I don’t even want to ask,” I said, shaking my head.

Elyk reached for my hand, and I helped him off the bone altar. “I need to move my legs. Let’s go for a walk.”

Slowly, Elyk’s balance returned, and we left the confines of Undercroft Citadel for the field between our wooden wall and the beginnings of the stone one. The whole time, Elyk kept looking over his shoulder as though someone was going to jump out with a knife and ram it through his neck. Once we were sufficiently alone, he finally eased up on the paranoia.

“What the hell is going on?” I asked.

He swallowed hard. “I didn’t know if any of the Burned Saints would be around . . . We can’t . . .”

“What is it? Just say it, and we’ll deal with it together.”

He scratched at the inky black line now tracing his entire body. “I saw Lady Kalma. I stood in her ruined temple.”

“I’m familiar. Not a particularly pleasant place, and the smell leaves quite a lot to be desired.”

He nodded. “I didn’t think any of it was real at first . . . She brought me back from the brink. Woke me up. But I had to make a deal, Ben. A *deal* with the goddess of death.”

I held out my tentacle hands as though the man had forgotten the abomination I had become. “Again, I am *painfully* familiar with Lady Kalma's brand of monkey's paw. What did you bargain away? What did she take from you?"

The man's eyes darted all around. Whatever it was, he was scared, and the Burned Saints seemed to be at the center of it. "You remember how Faidra said she's some kind of dying god coming into human flesh?"

"Vaguely. The woman has said a lot shit, and half of it hasn't left much of an impression."

He shook his head and kicked the dirt with his bare feet. "No, no. That much is true. She is slowly becoming Gloandi. The god died—or something like that—in whatever realm it is where gods live. I think . . . I think Lady Kalma killed him. And now . . ."

The implications of Lady Kalma killing another god and then that god becoming Faidra, or perhaps the other way around, were simply too much for me to figure out. "So, our goddess killed hers? You think she knows, and she'll betray us?"

"Fuck, Ben. It's so much worse than that. I'm sorry. Really, man, I'm so sorry."

"What the hell did you do? What kind of deal did you make?"

Tears streamed down his face, and his new black mark writhed beneath the top layers of his skin. "I was going to die. She offered me my life back. What was I supposed to do?"

I was tired of him dancing around the meat of it. I activated *Visage of the Dark One* and flashed a quick glimpse of Lady Kalma's face over my own. "Tell me what the *fuck* you did, Kyle Jacobson, or so help me you will die here and it will all have been for naught!"

He backpedaled, then tripped on some uneven ground and landed hard on his back. "Faidra has to die. We have to kill her. That was the price."

Somehow, it wasn't as bad as I expected. There had to be another catch. "What happens if I can't kill her?"

"Lady Kalma will kill everyone in Undercroft Citadel. Bury the entire necropolis."

There it was. "God damn, man. Shit!" I paced with my hands on my hips. Killing Faidra would be nearly fucking impossible. The woman was a half-god titan, for fuck's sake. Even without her insane armor, she'd just pick me up and crush me like a bug. I wasn't even remotely close to her level or skill. Maybe with Kevin and Ellen backing me up we'd be able to take her down, but that was only solo. With her guild? I couldn't even imagine.

"I know. I'm sorry."

I waved him off. "No, I would have done the same thing. Just . . . I'm not sure it's even possible."

A long moment of silence passed between us.

"Would you like the bad news now?" the man quietly asked.

"How the hell could it possibly get worse?"

He looked away toward the walls, his eyes anywhere but in the moment. "Lady Kalma said it has to be done in seven days. That's all we get."

I shrugged. Why not put a time limit on the impossible task? Why the hell not? "And the *we* in that statement. You and I? Everyone in the necropolis? *Who* has to kill Faidra, the unkillable half-titan, half-goddess skeleton who crucifies people to walls?"

"She just has to die. That's all Lady Kalma told me. If Faidra isn't dead in seven days, Lady Kalma is going to bury the entire necropolis and kill us all." Another long silence passed. "I'm really sorry, Ben. I know I fucked us all."

A handful of plans swirled through my mind, but none of them were guarantees. Suddenly, all of the other problems plaguing Undercroft Citadel seemed to fade a bit. The walls could wait. The catapults could as well.

"Alright, no use bitching about it now. We need to come up with a plan. Seven days is at least something. She just needs to die, right? There might be a way. Remember her armor? We just need to convince her to activate the skill. She'll become a wrecking ball for a full day, and then she'll die. And if we play it right, the Burned Saints will be none the wiser. We might be able to kill Faidra and keep her guild if all goes well."

"Hell of a bet to make," Elyk said with a mirthless smirk.

"Yeah, I know. If you come up with anything better, be sure to let me know. Meet me at dawn tomorrow at the gatehouse. If Kadorax and his assassins aren't back by then, we need to go looking for them. We'll bring the Burned Saints with us. A good fight at the monastery might just give us an opportunity . . . if we're lucky." It was the best idea I had on such short notice, and it was shit.

There was still no word by morning. I watched the horizon from the gatehouse as the sun slowly crested in the east, and there was nothing. "Let's go," I told Elyk. The Burned Saints were assembled down below, and they fell into step with us.

Outside the walls, the knights summoned their magical mounts, and Elyk and I were once again offered spots to ride behind them. I felt a little bad plotting Faidra's downfall considering her guild's overall kindness and usefulness, but it couldn't be helped. My allegiance was first to Undercroft Citadel, and that meant Lady Kalma as well. The necropolis was nothing without her. *I* was nothing without her.

We rode hard for the monastery, and we found it by nightfall, burning nearly an entire day of our very short timeline. It towered above the forest, more a fortress of stone spires and steepled roofs than a typical religious building. With a curtain wall and moat, it would be a proper castle. White pennants flew from its highest peaks, bathed in moonlight and fluttering in the cool, stiff breeze that swept in from the north. It was starting to reach fall in the game, and I tried to think back to what the date would be in the real world. I . . . couldn't remember. Did the game follow Earth's seasons? The knowledge was hazy. It existed somewhere in my mind, I knew it did, but I couldn't access it.

I told myself the locked memory wasn't important—the truth—and brought my mind back to the task at hand. Our band stood at the edge of the forest, hopefully still obscured by the tree line, and watched for any movement. As far as we could see, the monastery was silent. A few torches flickered on the outside, and some of the leaded glass windows had light behind them as well, but that was it. No porters went about their tasks in the courtyard, and no monks did whatever monks were wont to do. If I had to guess, the monastery's occupants were likely all attending to the day's final tasks indoors before retiring to their cloisters or cells for the night.

"We need to look for some sign of the assassins," I said quietly.

Faidra, smoking in her steel armor, nodded. She waved to her Burned Saints, and the knights fanned out through the woods to encircle at least the front half of the building. I stayed at Elyk's side to watch the front.

The two of us were alone. "I might have a way out," I said quietly.

Elyk breathed a sigh of relief.

"Look, with any luck, whatever has stalled or possibly even killed the assassins will get her too, and that'll be that. If Kadorax is still alive, we'll get him to help. And I have Kevin waiting in the woods. He followed us out here, and he can wait forever now that he's dead. One way or another, she's not going to make it home from this mission."

He nodded.

"I know it's a longshot. Hell, it probably won't work. But it's the only shot we have."

"Thank you," he finally said. "I owe you one."

"You mean a million. You owe me a million. Shit, look!" A shadow crossed one of the upper windows followed quickly by three or four more.

I waved to the nearest knights, and the whole Burned Saints guild came running in moments. "Movement up top," I explained, pointing to the window. "I don't know how many are up there, but that's the only movement we've seen. Just the top floor. Anyone else?"

No else had seen any movement or any other signs of the assassins. The lack of tracks made sense, at least. The assassins were experts at stealth and infiltration. If our bumbling band could pick up on their tracks, then the Blackened Blades weren't as crafty as I thought.

"Through the front then?" Faidra asked, her armor smoking like a bunch of oily candles.

Nothing better came to mind. "Let's do it. We'll stay quiet as long as we can, but once we're detected, just go. Butcher the monks and anyone else who stands in your way. Kill them all."

Nods and agreement all around. I led the team from the front, scampering up to the front door on the balls of my feet. Or what would have been the balls of my feet if I still had feet. I tested the door, and it was locked.

"Faidra?" If anyone was going to get us through the door quickly, it was her and her colossal, indefatigable physical stat.

The giantess gripped the handle with the hand on her

skeleton side and crushed. The iron bent and then crumbled, only offering a faint squeal of protest. She fished out the rest of the internal locking mechanism, and the door swung open on oiled hinges.

Inside, the monastery reminded me of the two castles we had recently purged. Wooden floors met stone walls decorated with fine tapestries and classy paintings. A coat of arms hung to the left complete with a pair of decorative crossed sabers. The place was dimly lit, and I hoped my theory of everyone going to bed for the night was correct. Only a quarter of the torches and candles were still lit. Doors lined either side of the main hallway, and a grand staircase presented itself at the far end.

"Up," I whispered.

We scampered to the staircase, and I paused for just a second to listen. Nothing. I waved for the others to follow.

The second floor was something of an art gallery. Framed paintings lined both walls, and they all depicted the same scene. It was a procession of some sort, and it reminded me of classical paintings from textbooks I had flipped through back in college. On the first few, a man was captured by soldiers in modern military gear. He was led away to a government facility where the soldiers beat him nearly to death. By the middle of the hallway, he was abandoned in a dark room, and the paintings were close to black squares.

We wandered farther down the hall, and the man in the paintings began to transform. He glowed yellow and orange, like he was bathed in fire, and then erupted from the facility in a hail of ash. By the end of the lengthy painting series, the man was enthroned at the top of a mountain. The scales of justice sat to his right, and a gargantuan sword that would rival even the size of Faidra's axe sat to his left. I assumed the man was the monastery's god, though the modern feel of the scenes didn't really line up with the game's medieval setting. Perhaps he was a real figure from Earth who had formed a cult inside the game. I thought of a man bringing his own cult into Wonder, fashioning himself into a god both inside the game and outside. The power he would wield would be immense.

Then my mind wandered back to the only other person I had known to bring things from the real world into the game, and I shuddered. Ministrel's voice boxes were the last thing I wanted filling my head.

Whatever awaited us at the top of the monastery, it needed to die. We ascended the next staircase and found a brightly illuminated corridor with cells to our right. The cells were cut directly into the mountain behind the monastery, and the area where the wooden and stone structure gave way to natural rock had been covered with fine white plaster. To the left, a long balcony separated by marble columns provided fresh night air. Torches hung from each column, and I figured we were on the same level where I had seen movement from the woods. What I had incorrectly assumed were windows turned out to just be squares open to the elements.

My party crouched at the end of the hallway, waiting for any signs of movement from the other side.

All was quiet.

We waited for several minutes before I finally motioned for everyone to ascend the stairs. I peered into the first cell, and it was empty. It featured nothing more than a stone bench that could likely double as a bed, a few books stacked to one side, and a bronze chamber pot. We slowly inched farther down the hall, and the next cell was identical to the first.

When we reached the third cell, someone stepped into the hallway at the opposite end. He was tall, though my perspective on height had changed drastically in the last few days. His head was bald, he wore no beard, and he carried no weapons or armor of any sort. His facial features struck me as vaguely Eastern, perhaps Japanese, though I was no expert there by any stretch.

"I have been expecting you, Hastalÿk." The man's voice was confident and calm.

"And you are?" I asked. The rest of my party fanned out behind me as much as they could, given the narrow confines of the hallway.

He smiled and gave a short bow. "I am Aleph, the Arbiter of Justice. You have tipped the scale too far to the side of evil, and I am the finger sent to tip the scale back." The name matched the one floating above his head, and the game told me he was a level thirty-five monk.

I quickly scanned the third and fourth cells. They were empty just like the first two. "And my friends? Where are they?"

He waved a hand as though dismissing a casual remark about the wind. "The monastery is not open to visitors at this time. Surely you must be mistaken, for you have no friends here."

"They might all be dead," I whispered to the rest of my group. If the single monk had killed the entire Blackened Blades guild, we were in trouble. But I had seen more than one shadow crossing the hall. The monk could not be alone.

"He's lying," Drevan said loud enough for the monk to hear.

"Oh?" The monk cocked an eyebrow. "I assure you; I do not lie. I am the Arbiter of Justice, not some lowlife scum as yourselves."

Next to me, Faidra unslung her colossal axe and gave it a few steady swings through the air. She twisted her neck to the side, and a loud pop echoed through the hall. "Ashes and blood. Paint the walls with his innards as the vultures circle."

I held up a hand to stop the woman from charging. I wanted to know where Kadorax and his guild were before we attacked. I just needed to buy a little time. "You're heavily outnumbered," I called, motioning to the knights behind us. "Tell me where I can find my friends, and we'll leave. Death on this continent is permanent, as I'm sure you know. I trust you would prefer to avoid such a fate, yes?"

The man's smile was unwavering. He knew something we didn't. "As I said before, you have no friends here, and I do not lie." Behind him, a wooden door creaked open and three more players stepped up beside him to fill the hallway. "And we are not as outnumbered as you may think. Though it would not matter in any case."

The glint in his eyes told me everything I needed to know. "He has the amulet," I whispered to Elyk. He grunted in response. I took a quick glance out the open wall, and it had to be thirty or forty feet to the forest floor below. Survivable, I guessed, though unlikely. "We fight, kill the other monks, shove him out the window."

"We can't touch—"

"Kill them all!" I yelled, and Faidra was the first to explode into action.

The massive woman took up nearly the entire hall. Her half-skeleton, half-armored body accelerated faster than it had any right to, and she swung her monstrous axe with all the fury of a derailed freight train. The first monk leapt with an impressively acrobatic maneuver, clearing the blade with ease, but the second wasn't so quick.

Faidra cut the man clean in half. Blood sprayed everywhere, practically drenching the so-called Arbiter of Justice. The dead monk's top half spun and flew straight out of the wall while his legs tumbled into a twisted heap where he stood.

Spells flew in every direction. The remaining monks

sprang into action, jumping and striking with open palms augmented by colorful spells, but none of it seemed to have much effect against the giantess.

"Don't engage the leader," I quickly relayed to the Burned Saints. "Corner him, force him off the ledge. He'll be immune to everything else. Go!"

Elyk stayed behind with me. There was simply not enough room for a full battle with everyone. Hell, only three or four knights could stand abreast which was their preferred fighting style. Drevan led the charge, linking his shield to two others with a fiery blue glow of magic. When they collided at the end of the hall, there was too much chaos to track.

"Come on," I said, grabbing Elyk's armored wrist. I ran down the hall toward the action, though I had no intention of fighting an unwinnable fight. I just needed to see the rest of the cells.

My heart quickly sank. Four dead assassins. They were bloodied and beaten with broken bones protruding at jagged angles. And their weapons were gone. Whatever fight they had gotten in, it hadn't been close. They were butchered. But Kadorax and Syzak weren't among the dead.

I spun back, Elyk close at my side, and went for the staircase. "We need to find Kadorax!" I shouted. I barged through the door and nearly toppled into the assassin and his shaman sidekick. The man had to activate a talent to keep from tumbling backward down the stairs.

"You can't fight him!" he yelled, and his voice was ragged. A bit of blood sprayed out with every word.

"I know! New developments!" I slammed the door shut behind me and grabbed the man's shoulders to help keep him steady. "Long story short, Lady Kalma wants Faidra dead. Let the monk guy in there kill her. With any luck, they'll both go over the edge and die together."

Kadorax's mind clearly whirled. His eyes searched mine,

but I had nothing left to give him. That was it: a shitty plan born of betrayal.

After a few long, rattling breaths, Kadorax finally nodded. "Alright. He'll kill her, of that I have no doubt."

"He'll kill us all!" Syzak added. The snake-man was better off than Kadorax, though only slightly. He was missing a huge swath of scales on his right side, and blood flowed freely from the wound.

I cracked the door to get another look at the action. I couldn't be certain, but it looked like some of the knights had already met a similar fate as Kadorax's guildmates, though the only monk still standing was the Arbiter of Justice himself. I could only watch another few seconds. Faidra's giant axe never touched the man, and his open-palm strikes were furiously denting her armor.

We needed something neutral to fight the amulet, and Syzak was out of juice. But he wasn't our only shaman. Ugg'chugg was also a shaman, and that meant her methods of manipulating the earth to do her bidding could also work. "Retreat!" I yelled. "Fall back to Undercroft!"

I didn't wait to see if any of the remaining Burned Saints would heed my warning. I took the stairs as quickly as I could, and Kadorax basically fell down them beside me. We hit the ground floor, and I was happy to see Drevan still standing along with four of his guildmates. The knights summoned their mounts, and we tossed Kadorax onto the back of one. Syzak was able to mount up on his own, and I climbed up behind Drevan.

I gave one last look to the monastery. Faidra, wherever she was, had moved from the third floor with the open walls. I hoped she was on her way down to follow, and I hoped even harder that the monk would give chase. If we could lure him back to Undercroft, there was a chance. If not . . . well, I was out of plans. Either way, the likelihood that Faidra would not survive the encounter seemed to grow every second. That would at least get Lady Kalma off my back, though I'd lose my most powerful ally in the process. I mentally ordered Kevin to shadow us through the forest, though he couldn't move nearly as fast without a mount.

We rode hard through the night, and when we finally reached home, Faidra and the monk were nowhere to be seen. But that didn't mean they wouldn't be hot on our heels. I brought Undercroft Citadel to attention as quickly as I could, mentally sounding the alarm with the help of my gargoyle statues.

Our zombie army filed out the front gate and formed a half circle formation facing the woods beyond the field. Xia and Xollmomath took up positions at our stone wall just behind the zombie army. One of my gargoyles brought Ugg'chugg to the front, and she was none too happy to be awake at such an hour.

"Hey, there's a monk coming. Probably. Well, I think he's coming. With any luck, he'll be chasing the giant skeleton woman, Faidra." I racked my brain to try and remember if Ugg'chugg had ever even met Faidra, but once more, my memories were hazy. The fucking curse was fogging my mind, and I was starting to really, really hate it.

"What you need Ugg'chugg doing?" the huge orc asked with a nasty scowl. She spat a glob of *something* revolting on the ground, and it splattered against my tentacle leg. She carried an unfinished log on her shoulder that would eventually become a support for the stone wall, but for now it would serve as a fine war club.

"When the monk arrives, kill him with magic. Got it?"

She snorted, then let out a belch that doused me in stench.

I contemplated trying to explain to the orc that it would be best if she let the monk kill our beloved half-skeleton giantess first, but I quickly decided that anything beyond pointing at an enemy and turning the shaman loose would be lost. All I could do was hope for the best.

And then we waited. An hour passed. A second.

Finally, when my eyes were all but glued shut from lack of sleep and it was nearly noon, movement broke on the horizon. "Here they come!" I yelled, though my voice was weak.

Faidra, riding her magical mount, came first. The monk trailed not far behind. He was running, probably barefoot if I had to guess, and somehow keeping up with Faidra's horse.

I looked back to Geirr and his gnomish helpers manning our one working catapult. Hitting a single target with the machine—especially a moving one—would be damn near impossible. Still, if the opportunity presented itself, we had to try.

The giantess came closer into view, and I could tell she was badly hurt. The smoke drifting off her armor came in starts and stops. She could barely hold the reins, and her massive axe dragged and skipped across the ground behind her, sending up a wave of sparks whenever it smacked into a rock.

"Zombies to the front! Slow him down!" I yelled to Xia in the guard tower.

The undead braced for impact, and the moment Faidra thundered past their line, they collapsed on the monk, swarming him with gnashing teeth and clawing hands that I knew would cause him no harm.

I turned back to Geirr. "Now!"

He fired the catapult, and it felt like my heart stopped beating as I watched the heavy rock soar through the air. It missed by fifty yards or better, just as I thought it would, and my heart returned to its previously frantic state. I waved off a second attempt. Better to save our ammunition, as plentiful as rocks were around Undercroft Citadel, than to just blindly shoot at a single moving target.

"Ugg'chugg, now!" I yelled.

The oafish orc barreled into the fight, and I was pleased when she actually followed my orders and relied on her shaman magic instead of the huge piece of lumber she called a weapon.

Great chunks of earth spasmed from the ground like the jagged remnants of a violent earthquake, and the monk finally had to turn on his heels. The magic reminded me of something else, something I had seen before. My tentacle hands gently, mindlessly fiddled with the black spider brooch fixing my cloak about my shoulders. I pulled it tighter against the gentle breeze, though it wasn't actually that cold. Not yet. In a month or two, it would probably snow. I had only ever seen snow in the game on the streams, not in person. Fortunately, Echelon and the surrounding areas were a lot more temperate than some locales, and getting frozen by a blizzard wouldn't be on the schedule.

I snapped myself out of the trance. "Damn this fucking curse," I muttered. I *knew* it was the insanity from the curse. My mind wandered, and reining it in took a concerted effort. Though the bigger problem was *recognizing* that I needed to apply the effort to recapture my mind in the first place. If I didn't realize I was going insane or drifting off to space, how could I stop it?

Again, I fought against my own brain to reel myself back down. I slammed my feet, relishing the shock that traveled up my bones in response. I tried to use the brief flash of pain to center my mind and focus my vision.

The battle. There was a battle, and it wasn't one we were likely to win. The monk had an amulet that made him immune to evil, so we had to use the closest thing to neutral magic which was shaman magic.

And my cloak.

What about my cloak?

"Fuck!" I screamed, instantly activating *The Black Goblin's Restless Vengeance*. I had the answer draped around my shoulders the entire . . . fucking . . . time. The shadowy goblin sprang to life, and I quickly commanded it to work with Ugg'chugg. More shamanistic magic filled the air as all manner of elements crashed down from the sky.

With two shaman pinning him down, the monk was trapped. He knew it, and he quickly turned to flee with terror plastered across his face.

"Raise him up!" I yelled. I wanted to capture the man if possible, just like Syzak had done with the first NPC who possessed the amulet.

The shadowy goblin raised his tiny hands, and a huge spike of earth ripped skyward under the monk's feet—and impaled him about ten feet off the ground.

"Well . . . that works too, I guess. Make sure he's dead!"

Ugg'chugg breathed a stream of fire and roasted the poor monk like a marshmallow over a summer campfire. The goblin blasted him with a lightning bolt, and that was that. The monk was certainly dead.

I dismissed the goblin back to the cloak and silently berated myself for forgetting such a powerful relic as I made my way to the monk's corpse.

I passed Faidra, and she was barely hanging on. But she was still alive, for better or worse, and I wasn't particularly thrilled. The woman had lost a chunk of collarbone from under her breastplate that looked nasty. But just like at Olympia City, the woman was more spent than physically hurt. I wondered if she had some kind of buff like Elyk where damage she took affected her slowly rather than all at once.

"Thanks for luring him back," I said quietly. She fixed me with her one human eye, inscrutable as ever, and spat a glob of blood onto the ground. It steamed and kicked off a thin trail of smoke.

The remaining knights quickly gathered their leader and took her back to the guildhall.

With the goblin gone, the piece of earth that had impaled him was also gone, so the monk's body now rested in a crumpled heap among the grasses. "Thank you, Ugg'chugg. Once we get this amulet off him, I'll let you eat the fucker's body. How's that?"

The orc seemed pleased at my offer and reached down to rip the shiny amulet from the corpse. Her meaty hands couldn't touch him. She tried again and again, all to the same result.

"Use your stick," I said, indicating her giant wooden beam. I guessed it was at least three hundred pounds, so maybe calling it a stick was wrong. Oh well.

Ugg'chugg tried to poke the corpse with it and again received the same result. She fixed me with a confused stare, and a bit of drool escaped her lips. I just shrugged. "We'll figure it out," I said.

I went back to Undercroft Citadel and the trio of engineers manning the lone catapult. "See if you guys can come up with some kind of machine that will lift the amulet from that dead monk. At least . . . I think a machine will work. It just has to be something non-evil. I'm guessing here, so cut me some slack if it doesn't work."

Geirr assured me that they would figure out a plan, and I headed back for my room. It was the middle of the day, but I hadn't slept yet, and just moving my feet was starting to become a serious task. I laid down and closed my eyes, silently urging my room to bring down the temperature so I could wrap myself in my blankets and drift off.

I wasn't asleep ten minutes before a violent explosion followed by a rumble and then a shockwave woke me.

"Damn it!" I screamed, throwing off my blankets and charging outside.

The sun was closer to the western horizon, so maybe I had slept for an hour or two. Certainly no more than that. But it didn't matter. We were under attack.

Four, five, I counted six trebuchets standing just in front of the tree line. Half our wooden wall was already destroyed, and a second volley was already in the air.

It crashed down into the first floor of the citadel, and I knew we wouldn't survive too many more volleys.

And then I saw their army.

CHAPTER 9

A horde had come to our doorstep, and we were in no shape to fight against it. Personally, I was too tired to be much good, though I already felt the adrenaline that came with imminent death filling my veins. The monk's corpse was still sitting in the middle of the open field, and he would have to wait. I only hoped that no one on the other side discovered the amulet in the meantime. Or, at the very least, if whatever guild had come to bring us down was also evil, it wouldn't matter.

Another barrage of stones smashed into the necropolis, and I feared the entire complex would come down. A few dozen zombies had already been blown to bits, and we had sustained untold damage to the actual structure itself.

I mentally commanded my gargoyles to summon all the leaders and have them meet me at the ossuary. I also commanded the pill bug statues to form a defensive ring around me, though I had no idea if they would even be able to withstand a single shot from the enemy trebuchets. Honestly, I was just betting on good luck to keep me from being blown to bits.

Xia and Xollmomath were the first to arrive amid the hail of projectiles. We ducked into the ossuary for a bit of cover, and I spotted Drevan and Kadorax not far off. A few moments later—after another brutal volley of rocks had smashed what little was left of our walls—we had the team assembled. Well, most of the team. No one knew where Syzak was, and Faidra was still down for the count at her own guildhall. Surprisingly, Ministrel had chosen to attend, though his trademark hat was apparently not big on team meetings.

"This is it," I said to the group of worried faces. "Pull out all the stops. If you have anything you've been saving, now is the time. Did anyone get a good look at the army? How many there are?"

No one had a real answer.

"Hundreds, probably thousands," Elyk said after a tense moment.

Another volley from the trebuchets rocked the necropolis, and I had to brace myself on the bone altar to keep from falling.

"Alright. Send out the zombies. Bog them down." I turned to Kadorax. "I know you're not at full strength, but tough shit. Do or die now, brother. Take whatever is left of the Burned Saints and hit the siege weapons. We won't survive the bombardment much longer."

Kadorax and Drevan both nodded and then left as quickly as they could.

Next was Ugg'chugg, leaning against the outside of the ossuary as she wasn't quite small enough to fit comfortably through the doors. I hated relying on her so much for any number of reasons, but especially because I knew her resources would be low after the fight with the monk. "Get your clan and fight. Everyone. Eat as many of them as you like. Head straight up the middle. If we can split their army in two, we can whittle the down."

She grunted and smacked her heavy hand against the wall. "We feast!" she yelled, and then she was off.

"Geirr, Berrick, Crestor—get the catapult going. The army is so big you can't miss."

"Understood," Geirr answered. He left right as another series of boulders smacked down in the middle of the courtyard, throwing up a huge rain of dirt, rock, and splintered wood.

At some point during my short sleep, the undead ranger had apparently wandered back home. "Ellen and Kevin, you're next."

The warden stood at attention, her brow already soaked in sweat from nerves. Next to her, the undead ranger didn't seem fazed.

"Go to the stone wall outside, or whatever is left of it by now. Ellen, protect him. We need a turret out there shooting arrows as fast as possible. Keep him up as long as you can, and then retreat when their army gets close. Got it?"

She nodded. "If . . . if they get to us . . ."

"Leave him. Save yourself. Get back to base and help the defenses."

She swallowed hard, and I thought the woman was going to vomit. She just wasn't cut out for this kind of thing, and it showed. Sure, she was a veteran of dozens of high-level dungeons and raids with one of the best guilds in all of Echelon, but that didn't count for shit when her actual life was on the line. "Go!" I yelled, kicking her into action.

That only left me, Elyk, and Ministrel. I rubbed my eyes, desperate to shake the last bits of exhaustion from my body, but it was no use.

"They're going to have wizards of their own," I said to Ministrel. "I need you to counter them. Whatever they send at us, either deflect it or send it back. Whatever you have to do. Just focus on defense for now. We're in no position to counterattack. Not yet, at least. Got it?"

The man nodded, said something I didn't catch, and then left.

I shrugged. "You know what we have to do," I said to the harvester.

Elyk gave me a weak smile. "Get Faidra to activate her armor, save the day, and sacrifice herself in the process?"

"Exactly. Let's get out there and do it."

We raced out of the ossuary to a scene of utter destruction. The wooden walls were completely gone. Most of the shadow moat had been destroyed as well. The outer rock wall, still incomplete, hadn't been targeted as heavily. We watched for just a few seconds as Kevin set up with Ellen at the wall's unfinished edge and began firing. Arrows streamed from his magical bow faster than I could count, though it didn't take long for our attackers to redirect their efforts toward the newest threat. I didn't know how long Ellen could hold out, but it hopefully wouldn't matter too much. Kevin's new raid boss ability, Vital Force, let him resurrect low-level enemies for ten seconds, and those new undead would automatically turn on their former allies.

Kevin would sow chaos in the ranks while also pulling their attention, and that was worth both his life and Ellen's.

The bulk of our zombie horde hit their lines a second later, and then there was simply too much happening to track any of it clearly. Elyk and I ran to the Burned Saints' guildhall, not directly in the attacking army's path but close, and found it empty. "Faidra!" I yelled.

No response.

"Come on, there's a ritual chamber thing below ground," I explained, pushing past wooden chairs toward the deeper workings of the complex.

My guess paid off, and we found Faidra in the same room where I had witnessed Drevan's cleansing. She wasn't in the midst of her own ritual, at least not that I could. The woman was alone. Her armor was stacked neatly on a wooden rack by the door. A few candles lit the space, their light reflecting poorly from Faidra's half-skeleton body.

She sat in a stone tub, motionless, soaking in dark liquid up to her chest.

A moment later, the liquid bubbled and boiled, then quickly evaporated in an intense column of steam. When the room cleared—by methods unknown as there was no ventilation I could discern—Faidra sat amidst a blaze of fire. It healed her, closing her wounds and knocking the dirt and blood from her exposed bones. Somehow, again I could not explain anything I saw in the guildhall, the fire was not hot. It raged only a few feet from us, and yet we felt nothing.

When it finally subsided, Faidra stood to her full towering height and finally seemed to take notice of us. She smiled with pale blue teeth. "Have you beheld the fevers, Ben Hales? The collapse of the mind; the silence of the heart."

I had no idea what she was getting at and no idea how to respond. "There's a battle," I said quietly.

The giantess looked beyond me, but her gaze was not fixed on Elyk either. She stared into a blackness that held meaning only to her. "He sees all. Gloandi, in a ray of darkness, in clarity and fullness, during the feverish slumber, he puts everything at risk."

Had we been discovered? Was our plan to get Faidra killed coming undone? If the woman chose to attack, even without her gargantuan axe or her armor, we were as good as dead. I'd seen her magic, and I knew it was powerful enough that Elyk's shield couldn't possibly nullify it.

I decided to press on. "There isn't much time. If the army reaches Undercroft Citadel, we're all dead. Can we . . . help you with your armor?" I didn't know if offering to essentially serve as her squire was insulting or not, but I figured the huge woman wouldn't be able to outfit herself without another set of hands.

She shook her head as though clearing cobwebs from her mind. He teeth clicked together with a noise that sent a chill shiver down the length of my spine. I was probably wrong, but I felt like more of the woman's body had been burned away to bone by the ritual. She held out her arms, and her fingertips brushed the edges of the room. I took the gesture as an acceptance of my offer.

Elyk and I spent the better part of fifteen minutes hefting the woman's heavy steel into place. The whole time, all I could do was hope that the battle above us wasn't a complete rout. I figured as long as no enemies came pouring down the steps to exterminate us, that meant the army hadn't yet reached Undercroft Citadel.

I emerged into the afternoon sunlight with Elyk and Faidra only a step behind me. The woman's axe was once more balanced across her shoulders. It was hard to tell what was going on in the battle, though I was pleased to see the that the enemy's main line had not yet advanced. The battle was still fifty or seventy-five yards out. Unfortunately, the trebuchets had not yet been silenced by Kadorax and his crew, and I winced as another volley rocketed through the sky to slam into my home. At that point, even victory would mean the near-demolition of Undercroft Citadel. And there wasn't a damned thing I could do about it.

At the front, our zombies had met the enemy and were being massacred. In the center of the mob, I spotted the tall forms of orcs swinging and smashing with their crude weapons. I knew just as many zombies would fall victim to their brutality as enemies, but I didn't care. Zombies were imminently replaceable. My necropolis, on the other hand, was not . . .

Off to the side, I watched Kevin's hail of magical arrows in amazement for a few seconds. My turret idea clearly worked. Like the orcs, he was probably hitting just as many zombies as foes, but again I simply did not care.

Another volley of trebuchet shots sailed overhead. "Alright, we have to stop those siege engines," I said. I didn't quite have to yell to be heard over the din of battle, not yet.

We rushed for the enemy's left flank and their line of trebuchets just a few feet from the trees. The siege weapons were heavily guarded, of course, and we crashed into the enemy players like thunder. I swung my meteor hammer left and right with impunity, giving absolutely no effort whatsoever to defense. Without my masterwork armor, I would have been killed in the first few seconds, but as it was, I blasted through enemies nearly as easily as Faidra and Elyk.

Weapons clattered against my armor, some of them found my legs, and I kept up a steady stream of spike activations and *Malignant Putrescence.* The three of us carved a path of destruction through the defenders, and I made sure to infect as many of them as I could with poison. In a few minutes, our small section of the battlefield would turn into a haze of toxic death.

Elyk, his small buckler neutralizing a fair amount of magic thrown our way, led the way. We reached the first trebuchet amidst a torrent of gore. With one precise blow, Faidra severed all the ropes and smashed all the pulleys on the right side of the trebuchet, easily rendering it inoperable.

Another enemy leapt at me from the side, a pair of gleaming swords flashing in the afternoon sun. I clumsily dodged and swung my own weapon, catching him in the back. The man sprawled against the broken siege weapon with a shout. The name floating above his head was dark green, and his allegiance was to a guild named Hunger God. I'd never heard of it. I swung again, battering the man back into the trebuchet, and Elyk finished him off from the side with one clean chop.

I quickly took stock of the other dead players and NPCs nearby. Many of them were from the same Hunger God guild, but still others came from a myriad of additional guilds. They all had ridiculous names—Skull Gatherers, Winter Mourning Tower, Shrouded Darkness, Howl at Night, Impending Death Premonition—and I knew the coalition was just as evil as Undercroft Citadel. They had likely come to try and claim the title of Hastalÿk for themselves, though if that was even possible, I had no idea.

In the end, their motivations were irrelevant. They attacked, and so they would be slaughtered to the man. No quarter, no mercy, no prisoners.

"To the next!" I screamed, finally filled with enough adrenaline to fully overpower my sleep deprivation. Behind me, the corpses of a dozen or more players were finally starting to explode into clouds of noxious gas. Some enemy NPCs approached as well, stumbling through the gas. We left them to the poison and charged the next trebuchet in line.

The resistance at the second trebuchet was about what we had encountered at the first, and Faidra smashed through them all with impunity. As long as the bulk of the enemy army didn't take notice of us, we could easily carve through their back line with virtually no risk at all. No player, no matter how high level or experienced, would be ready for the combined power and ferocity of Faidra and Elyk. Watching them work in tandem made me regret our ultimate plan, but there was simply no other way. I couldn't let Lady Kalma's jealousy of another god undo all the work we had done already. Nothing would stand in the way of our ultimate goal.

Our little death trio massacred our way to the third trebuchet. Again, I left a trail of festering, poisoned corpses in our wake. Faidra slammed her axe into the side of the siege weapon, and that left just one more.

"Look," Elyk said, pointing to someone on a horse behind the final trebuchet. The harvester's gauntlet was covered in gore to his elbow.

"Some kind of commander, I bet." If we could cut off the head of the beast, perhaps the army would fall apart.

We were about to move again when Kadorax, bloodied and limping, finally caught up to us. He had a trio of Burned Saints with him, all equally drenched in bits of bone and bloody sinew.

"Glad you could join us," I said with a smile.

The man didn't share my mirth. "There are just too fucking many of them," he said between heavy breaths. Glancing over his shoulder, he took stock of his meager band. "Lost two knights on the way. Not terrible, all things considered."

I shared his assessment. "Catch your breath, and let's move. The one on the horse might be a leader. We'll carve our way to the trebuchet. You take out the leader."

He nodded. "These blades still have some death left in them."

Speaking of the death, the longer we stood amidst the chaos and carnage, the more my curse healed the myriad wounds on my arms and legs. My body drank in the slaughter, and the totality of wounds that would have likely resulted in my death without the curse gently faded into nothing.

We were ready to move again, and Elyk once more led the way with his magic-dampening buckler and Infernum. We reached the final trebuchet and its compliment of players, and they were waiting for us.

Faidra broke off to the right, Elyk went left, and I charged straight up the middle into a group of players all wielding two-handed spears. Two of them were engineers by class, and I easily battered them with my mace and took them out of the fight in seconds. The others were combat classes, and they moved in unison.

I swung for the first, but the player easily parried my mace with his spear. At the same moment, the other two soldiers stabbed, and both weapons clattered off my breastplate. Reversing my arm, I swung wide and hit the button on my mace. The soldier wasn't expecting the trick, and the mace head cracked into his helmet hard enough to send him reeling. Before I could press the advantage, a ghostly silhouette of the same man appeared to take his place in the enemy formation. I swung again, and my mace passed through the ghost just to get deflected by the next spearman in line. Then all three—the ghost included—stabbed forward as one, and they struck me just beneath my breastplate. I skipped backward, but not before two of the spear points drew blood. Pain lanced through my chest and groin.

In the space a heartbeat, the damage was healed by my curse. There were so many corpses that I wondered if I could even be killed at all. My regeneration was too powerful. I swung again, using my mace more like a whip, and cracked the center spearman on the head. He didn't drop back, only reeled, and I dove for him. I wrapped him in a tentacled embrace, rendering his long spear useless. First, I activated *A Feast of Spores*, breathing toxic gas directly into his face, and then I activated the spike ability from my armor directly underneath him. After two or three hits, the man fell apart in my grasp. Sadly, given the evil nature of all the guilds, *Reap Honor* didn't activate to bring him back to fight against his allies.

My method was brutally effective, and I pounced on the last remaining spearman in the same fashion. His weapon cut deep through my right leg, though I knew it would heal before long. I grabbed him, pinned him to the ground with the weight of his own armor, and then spiked him to death.

The tactic was just as efficient as it was gory and personal. When I stood, I was practically drenched in blood. My leg healed, and I felt the familiar twinge of lunacy tugging at the back of my mind. Lady Kalma's gifts always came with caveats, and I swore I heard her whispering in the back of my skull.

Cadaverous wind blowing cold as ice . . . the voice echoed, or at least I thought that was what it said. Just as quickly as it fluttered into my mind, the voice was gone, taking the memory of its arrival with it.

I whirled to find Faidra and Elyk faring equally well. They finished their last opponents, and Faidra executed a huge swing against the last trebuchet.

Finally, I caught my breath. The biggest risk was eliminated. Our walls were already nothing but rubble, but the rest of the citadel would remain. We could repair it.

I looked to whoever was mounted not far away, and they stared back. It was a player, and the name floating above his head in bright orange read: Augustine, Level 41 Warlock, Sower of Discord.

The warlock flicked his fingers just above his saddle, and the ground between us rent in two. A wave of purple fire erupted from the fissure, and then a brass claw slammed into the edge. The claw flexed, pulling a mechanical abomination from the earth. The construct stood taller than Faidra by at least a foot, a mess of vaguely humanoid gears, spikes, metal plates, and sharp edges. It walked on two legs and bore two long arms, but it had no head or face. Its arms, twice as long as its body, ended in huge, articulated claws.

The creature swung for Elyk with lightning speed that should have been impossible for something so unnaturally large and gangly. The harvester didn't have a chance to dodge. He took the full force of the blow, his legendary armor reacted with a gout of flame, and then Elyk was throw thirty feet through the air. He landed somewhere amidst another knot of chaotic battle, and I quickly lost sight of him.

Faidra charged in, axe swinging. She hit the creature, and instead of cleaving it apart, they locked together in an epic struggle. The construct was physically larger than her, but Faidra seemed to have the upper hand—at least for now.

The warlock, still mounted on a white horse that seemed calm as ever despite the battle, turned his attention to Kadorax. The assassin moved like mist through the shadows, but the warlock still tracked him with ease. Kadorax leapt, the warlock snapped his fingers, and a burst of fire fell from the sky with needle-like precision. It hit Kadorax on the back, knocking him down and setting his cape his on fire.

I had to make a quick decision. Elyk could wait. Faidra was at least evenly matched. Kadorax was not. Without my help, he was going to die.

I rushed to the assassin, quickly activating my spike skill as many times as I could right under the warlock's mount. Much to my surprise, both the man and his steed didn't bat an eye. The ability ripped right through the horse's chest, or it *should* have, but instead it just . . . didn't do anything at all. I saw it, I was clearly activating the ability, and the spike just went in and out of the horse as easily as it would a projection.

Swinging my mace, I crashed right through the warlock and his mount. They weren't real. Just illusions, holograms, or *something* I didn't fully understand. The man could still cast spells, so it didn't exactly make sense.

"Come on!" I yelled, grabbing Kadorax by the arm and forcibly lifting him to his feet. "The warlock isn't real! The monster shouldn't be either!"

Once Kadorax was steady, I took off for the warlock's construct. I swung hard for its back, releasing the mace head for full effect, and it crashed into the creature's metal body with a resounding clang that sent painful vibrations up my tentacle arm. "What the hell?" I was so certain my weapon was going to swoosh right through it . . .

The thing shoved Faidra back a step, then turned and hit me hard. *Hard.* All the air burst from my lungs, and my vision cascaded through every color imaginable before settling on a deep shade of purple accented with floating, swirling splotches of black. I was suddenly acutely aware of not being on my feet. I was on my back. Or . . . no, I was face down. I tried to move arms, but they didn't respond.

Then that little voice in the back of my ringing skull laughed. *Won't you join me down here, Ben? It's so cold . . . I think you'd like it.*

"Get out of my head!" I screamed at the voice. The effort made my head spin even worse, and the voice only laughed again.

I groaned and rolled to my back. A shockwave of pain rattle from my toes to the back of my head, then back to my toes again. Everything hurt. But already, I felt the death all around channeling into my broken body. It filled all the new cuts and scrapes, seeped into the broken bones in both of my arms and knitted them back together.

When I finally opened my eyes, all I saw was the sky. There was dirt in my left eye, or maybe it was blood, and I painfully scooped it out. Slowly, I got to my knees, then managed to stand. The curse pumped more and more vitality into my body, sucking up dozens of corpses to make me whole.

I stood about forty yards from the mechanical construct and its illusory warlock master. My armor was dented pretty badly, but at least it wasn't completely destroyed. Kadorax was nowhere to be seen.

I rubbed my neck and tried to think of a better plan. My mind was hazy, either from the curse or the massive concussion, though it didn't matter which. All I knew was that I could barely think.

"I just need to get out of here," I finally muttered. The act of speaking, even softly, sent more pain buzzing through my jaw on both sides. I wondered if I still had all my teeth and whether the curse's healing would grow them back if the answer was no.

I sank my hands into the dirt and activated *Shrouded Miasma*. My body made the connection between the toxic rune and all the corpses. I became the conduit connecting a nearly limitless supply of energy to an ability that knew no maximum. The spell would only end when I was dead, and so long as people kept dying, that wasn't going to happen. Lady Kalma would sustain me.

Both my hands gripped the stone rune under the soil, practically melting into it, as I channeled more energy than I ever thought possible. A dozen corpses flooded my body. Then another dozen. And a third. A hundred corpses. Not all of them were enemies. Lady Kalma's unholy healing did not discriminate between the corpses of enemy players or NPCs freshly slain and those of my zombie army.

Twisting my neck, I peered over my shoulder to catch a glimpse of Faidra's epic battle. The construct she fought was mechanical and likely wouldn't even notice the poison gas. I hoped Faidra would not fare as well, though . . . she was half skeleton. Would the part of her that didn't rely on sinewy organs pumping blood and oxygen survive? I had no idea. I also had no choice. If Faidra survived the battle, we would simply have to determine another way to kill her.

Suddenly, a voice caught my attention and nearly broke my concentration on the spell. I couldn't hear what it said, and when I swiveled side to side to find the source, there was nothing there.

Then I saw it. One of my zombies, only five or so feet away, fixed me with a lifeless stare. A second one approached behind the first. Their heads were bent at odd angles, though of course a broken neck didn't mean much to a reanimated corpse that had been dead for weeks. Struggling to maintain my connection to *Shrouded Miasma*, I mentally commanded the zombies to get back into the fight.

They did not move. If anything, they shambled closer. Inches at a time, but they were coming for me. Perhaps they were not *my* zombies, but I *knew* they were. I felt them connected to me through Undercroft Citadel just as easily as I felt Xia, Xollmomath, and Elyk. The undead belonged to me, but they would not obey.

A voice whispered in the back of my skull. *Do you see them?*

I drained one more mental blast of energy into the rune, then ripped my hands free of the earth. My armor was bent and twisted, and it cut into my chest as I turned. I charged at the two zombies, swinging hard, and my mace passed straight through both of them and flew from my hands.

"Fuck!" I screamed.

More illusions from the warlock? My own insanity tugging at the edges of my frayed mind? One of Lady Kalma's twisted tricks?

"Fuck!" I screamed again.

I searched the nearest fringes of the battle for any sign of Elyk, but the man was gone. I spat a glob of phlegm and then turned my attention to Faidra's battle. She still held her own, at least from what I could tell, trading massive blows from her axe against faster, more precise attacks from the creature's brass claws.

The warlock still stood sentinel over the battle, his horse steady and calm as ever, though I knew none of it was real. But now I wasn't sure what kind of *unreal* the player was. Just a magical illusion so the real warlock could remain safe deeper behind the army's lines? Or was the warlock real at all?

I quickly glanced behind me, and the two zombies with broken necks were still there, slowly advancing with their arms outstretched like a cheap horror movie. I turned back toward Undercroft Citadel, and the horror movie theatrics continued. Standing just inches in front of my face was a little girl. Her brown hair was done in pigtails, and she held a book between her hands.

I sprinted right through her, and the girl's image swirled away like leaves in an autumn breeze.

"Ben!" someone called behind me, and I stopped in my tracks. As I turned, something hit me in the back and sent me sprawling yet again. But Lady Kalma's curse pumped through my veins, and the damage was negated.

Do you see them? the quiet voice whispered once more.

Without any other options, I fumbled at my belt for Princess Yasha's fan. I activated it, and my vision throbbed with black splotches. I was doing too much, and the toll had begun to mount. Life and energy were separate pools, and one was far deeper than the other. Still, the faint beginnings of a smile spread on my face with the growth of my magical wings, and I took to the air at once.

I flew as quickly as I could back to the heavily bombarded necropolis. From my vantage point, I saw the bulk of the damage for the first time. Our walls were simply gone. There was nothing left. At least half the moat had been filled in with boulders and wooden debris. Corpses likely littered the shadowy bottom as well.

Kevin was nowhere to be seen. His stream of magic arrows had ended. The zombies had collapsed, and the approaching army was within fifty yards of overrunning the entire citadel. The only good news was that Geirr's catapult was still firing away, though it was like shooting needles at a giant. Each one hurt, but it would take thousands to be fatal.

I reached the guard tower—what little was left of it—and landed hard amidst a pile of broken beams, splintered wood, and the bloody remains of someone I could not identify.

With a soft mental release that brought with it a shuddering wave of relief, I activated *Shrouded Miasma*. I felt the gas leaving the rune with explosive force, and the mental connection forced me to my knees. It was simply too much for my exhausted, battered mind to handle, and I passed out.

CHAPTER 10

Black gave way to purple and then red. My eyes fluttered open, and red quickly became black once more.

It was night. I was alive.

"Hello, Ben," a soft voice said. It was the same one I had heard in my skull, but this time it was real. It was behind me.

I whirled, sending a stabbing blast of pain through my side as my dented armor cut into my body.

A creature stood in the darkness. It was vaguely humanoid, but only by the barest definition as a being of about six feet with four limbs. Its arms and legs were tentacles like mine, each ending in a dozen or more black claws. In its chest, a gaping mouth filled with an impossible number of teeth dripped black ichor as it writhed and moved. It wasn't breathing but rather chewing the air in anticipation. I got the distinct impression that it was hungry.

The creature's head was a mess of thin black tentacles and bulging, bulbous eyes that glowed white—the only bit of light on the thing's pitch-black body. It sported another mouth on its head in the usual place, though it wrapped around farther than ear to ear. The mouth opened, and more teeth glinted in what little light filled the space. Thick, syrupy ichor dripped from both mouths to pool at the thing's feet.

The voice spoke again, and I was relieved when it didn't come from either of the hideous creature's mouths. "What's the matter? Seeing things?"

I spun again to find the speaker, but there was nothing amidst the rubble of the guard tower. When I looked back, the two-mouthed monster was gone.

"Get out of my mind!" I screamed into the night.

The voice laughed, always behind me no matter which direction I turned. "Oh, I think they see you too!" it called.

I scrambled to my feet, ignoring the pain with every movement, and dashed out of the rubble. I needed to see what the fuck was *actually* happening, not the wild machinations of my broken psyche.

With a quick mental command, I ordered a ride from one of my gargoyles. We ascended through the night sky, and the full scope of Undercroft Citadel's destruction came into view. The army was dead, though it was a pyrrhic victory at best.

The walls were gone, but I knew that much already. The Burned Saints' guildhall was also gone. The orc encampment was scattered. Perhaps enough of it was salvageable to rebuild, though I wasn't sure how much the orcs would even care . . . if any of them survived.

Broken bits of bone marked where the ossuary doors once stood on the first floor of the citadel. It looked like a boulder had smashed right through it. The barracks rooms next to them were completely gone. The workshop fared somewhat better. The roof would need work, but that was easy enough.

Beyond our borders, the carnage was virtually universal. A sea of corpses stretched from the former stone walls all the way to the trees a few hundred yards away. From the air, I could trace the path of our resistance directly up the middle with ease. It was like a tornado had touched down right in the army's center, scattering everything to both sides with impunity. The gargoyle dropped me down in the general area where I thought the warlock had been, but there was no sign of him. There was also no sign of Elyk, Faidra, or the summoned construct.

I ordered the gargoyle to take my busted armor back to Undercroft Citadel and then come back for me. I needed to investigate the field of death, but I also didn't want to spend much time outside the necropolis just in case. If another force hit us, we would not survive. Of that I had no doubt.

The fresh cut on my side from my bent breastplate instantly healed, and I shook my head. If there was some way to turn off the ability, I would in a heartbeat. But alas, it was a curse, not an ability.

A bit of toxic gas still lingered in the air that left a metallic taste in my mouth and made my eyes water. Everywhere I looked, people were dead. Most of them died face down, their hands covering their faces in one final attempt to survive. But the gas was heavy, and it clung to their corpses like frost or morning dew, and it filled the ruts and crevasses left by the chaos of battle. I found the epicenter, still marked by a single rune half-buried in the dirt.

It was time to retrace my steps. I found the cavernous gash left by the metal construct's summoning. One of the creature's massive arms wasn't far off. The rest of the beast was nowhere to be seen. I listened for a moment, but all I heard was the stillness of death. There was no indication at all that the construct still lived, and for that matter, there was also no indication that Faidra was alive.

Beneath the arm was a pair of heavy indents that I guessed to be from the giantess's axe. They were at least five inches wide and a foot deep. That anything, construct or otherwise, could survive even a single blow from her weapon was beyond me. To survive it twice was a miracle. I searched deeper in the direction I remembered Elyk being thrown, and there was no sign of him. I found one of the knights—dead—but that was it. Everyone else was either a zombie or one of the attackers.

No warlock, no Faidra, no Elyk, no Kadorax. Had I killed them all?

I sighed. Perhaps I had. The cost of victory was never low.

The gargoyle returned, and I was just about to command it to fly me back home when I spotted my mace among the twisted bodies of two enemy soldiers. I plucked it from the carnage, brushed off the larger pieces of gore, and dropped it back through my belt. There would be days of loot to salvage from the battlefield. Weeks. But all that could wait.

I ordered the gargoyle to fly me in a slow circle over the trees at what was the rear of the enemy's line. A patch of destroyed flora caught my attention, and we swung toward it, landing in an unnatural clearing about thirty yards into the forest. Much to my delight, Elyk sat with his back against a thick tree. He was breathing heavily, and his eyes opened at my arrival.

"You made it!" I bellowed despite the headache that had settled behind me eyes.

But . . . was it really him? Or just another trick of my mind?

He lifted a gauntlet with a meager attempt at a wave. "Alive . . . ish," he sputtered.

I took a step toward him and then hesitantly reached out a hand. When my tentacle fingers didn't pass through him like mist, I finally convinced myself that he was real. "Happy to see you, friend."

He started to speak, but I waved him off. "The gargoyle

will ferry you back to Undercroft. Get some rest. If there's anything left to heal you, you'll get it."

"No," he said with a violent cough, and I quickly called off the gargoyle taxi.

"What—"

He pointed. About ten yards to my left, her body wrapped around a pair of thin trees, was Faidra. Her smoldering armor gave off the thinnest wisp of white smoke.

"Take him back to the necropolis. Tell the other gargoyles to search for survives. Bring them all back. Come get me once you spread the word," I commanded my stone pet. It latched onto Elyk's armored shoulders and took to the air at once. Infernum, cold as the night air, dropped from his grasp to clatter next to me. I lifted the familiar blade, testing its weight in my grip, and then fixed my eyes on Faidra.

The giantess was badly wounded. Without aid, she would likely die on her own. Her guildhall had been completely obliterated by trebuchet fire, so there would be no more rituals to bring her back from the brink. Our only two shaman were an unruly orc and a member of the Blackened Blades who hadn't been seen since before the battle. Perhaps the warden could help her, assuming Ellen survived, but I had something else in mind.

It took considerable effort for me to roll Faidra off the two trees to her back. A chunk of bone fell from her exposed jaw. It still had two teeth seated on it. I kicked it aside.

The woman's single human eye opened. "Ben Hales," she said quietly. "Take me . . . to my hall . . ."

I shook my head. Her expression deepened. I leveled Infernum above her neck.

"Gloandi . . ." she muttered, but there was no strength in her voice. A tear slid down her fleshy check. Something in her countenance changed and softened. It felt like she ceased being Faidra, the titanic half-skeleton raid boss, and instead became whoever she was before the game. In the real world. A woman with a job, hopes, and aspirations. Maybe a family. I would never know that person, of course. And neither would anyone else. Her voice cracked again, and she closed her eye tight. "God help me," she whispered.

"God cannot save you now. He isn't here. I am."

I dropped Infernum, and Faidra's head rolled down the tree roots to rest against another broken part of the construct.

I didn't leave my room for a full day. I was simply too tired. Everything was quiet, Xia and Xollmomath seemed to have things relatively handled, and the prospect of starting so much damn work to rebuild was just . . . too much. When I finally did emerge, I had a handful of notifications waiting for me along with the other thousand or so tasks that required my attention. My arms and back were sore, but I wasn't hurt. Lady Kalma's curse had seen to that.

I stretched in the morning light, standing as I so often had at the top of the necropolis, and wondered if Undercroft Citadel was going to survive. We still had months left on the developers' deadline. When would the next guild come to claim the bounty? Would it be today, tomorrow, next week? The warlock on his horse came to mind, and I couldn't rule out the possibility that he was still out there, lurking just beyond the trees.

I pulled up the raid panel in my vision, and my heart sank through my chest. The number of active campaigns against us had dropped by a mere one. Faidra was gone from the list of bosses. So was Ugg'chugg. Shockingly, Kevin's name was there right next to Elyk's. Both of them were still alive—or as alive as Kevin could be—and that was a very welcome surprise.

Their survival was, perhaps, the *only* glimmer of good news. Everything else was in shambles. The walls were gone. The first floor would need rebuilt. And gazing out at what remained of the other buildings and general community, I quickly noticed a stark lack of undead. I had one of my gargoyles fly me out to the field of corpses where I found Xia and Xollmomath contemplating our next moves.

"You have returned, master," the necromancer said flatly.

"How astute."

"What would you have us do?"

I took a moment to survey the dead. There were hundreds, maybe over a thousand. Most of them were my zombies to begin with, and getting butchered and reanimated over and over again significantly reduced their fighting capabilities. "Reanimate the best of the corpses. Any too damaged to be useful . . . just loot their gear and pile them up for a fire. Let the decent corpses keep their old weapons and armor. Not like we have anyone left to make use of it anyway."

I felt my confidence slipping through my fingertips. We were good and truly fucked. There was just no other way about it. No way to sugarcoat that one. I spent an hour or so picking through the corpses for a new piece of armor, but nothing caught my eye. Or perhaps my sour mood just spoiled the task and it was paradoxically more comforting to fail than succeed.

Finally, I determined that what I needed was a good meal. I didn't *need* to eat, of course, but what was the harm?

The one thing we still had in abundance was food and drink. I went to one of the storerooms and picked through some baskets and barrels. I came up with a salted ham steak large enough to feed two or three, a few apples preserved in sugar, and a full tankard of dark, syrupy wine that smelled like a wicked hangover. I found Elyk recovering in the remains of the ossuary and fetched Geirr from his workshop.

The three of us sat at a small table in the middle of the courtyard, and I spread the food. No one said anything for a long time. All three of us needed to eat, just as much for our mental health as physical, and it felt good to do something normal for a change. Instead of demonic curses and unholy rituals performed in the name of a death goddess, we shared lunch like coworkers. Like regular people.

My mind drifted back to Faidra and her final moments. Whatever it was that had snapped inside her . . . it haunted me. For those brief couple seconds, the titanic woman was just a normal player again, terrified of death and begging me not to kill her. When the time came for me to die, would I be the same? Hell, it wouldn't take any kind of transformation on my part. I wasn't that scary to begin with—not like Faidra. Honestly, none of us were. We were evil fucking bastards, of that there was no doubt, but we weren't exactly terrifying.

"Did you find it, Ben?" Elyk asked, and from his voice I knew it wasn't the first time.

I rubbed my tentacles across my eyes and brought my thoughts back to the present. "Sorry. Find what?"

"The monk's amulet."

I shook my head. "I haven't even thought about it. Not yet."

Geirr finished what I guessed was his second or third glass of rich malbec looted from Echelon. I was still on my first. "I went out and saw those trebuchets this morning. We can salvage them. I'll have them up and running in a few days' time," the engineer said with a smile.

It was good news, but it wasn't nearly enough to lift my mood. "We need to go get Faidra's corpse," I told Elyk. "And her armor. And her axe. But speaking of which, have any of the Burned Saints survived?"

The harvester reached for another sugary apple. "I haven't seen any of them. None. I'm guessing they all went down in the gas like the orcs. Dead to a man."

"Fuck me. If anyone else attacks—"

"I know," Elyk interrupted. He winced as he sliced open the apple. His forearm sported a nasty purple bruise from the elbow nearly to his fingers.

All I could do was sigh and hope for the best.

When we finished eating, Elyk and I took a long walk back to the cleared bit of forest where I killed Faidra. The fight between her and the construct must have been unreal. Trees were scattered like twigs, and not just small ones. A huge oak had been ripped from its roots—not *with* its roots; completely shorn off near the base which struck me as monumentally more difficult—and thrown through at least fifteen other smaller trees. Amidst all the natural debris, we saw little bits of busted brass from the construct. Only a few larger pieces of the creature remained, and we sent them back with a gargoyle to be melted down as scrap.

Faidra's corpse was right where I left it. Her armor no longer smoked and smoldered. If I had any doubts that the woman had somehow survived decapitation, they were expelled. Most of the skeletal half of her was already withering away and crumbling.

"Tough way to go," Elyk said quietly.

"Just help me get her armor off."

It took the better part of an hour to strip the giantess and load up two of the gargoyles for the return trip. As one of the stone sentinels carried off her axe, it struggled under the immense weight and I thought for a moment that it wouldn't be strong enough. In the end, we got it all back home along with a few other pieces of gear that looked like they might be useful. We searched longer, and there was no sign of the warlock or anyone else still alive.

What we did find was a trail. A deep, muddy trail heading into the woods. We still had a few hours of daylight, so Elyk and I followed the path. It wound through the trees for several miles until we eventually reached the razed village of Wolfpine.

"Holy shit . . ." I said, mouth agape. In the center of the burned and ruined village stood a portal. It wasn't like any of the capital city portals at all. It was square, for one, and all the major portals I had seen before were circular. It was made of dark stone, and the horizontal beam across the top sported a painted relief of a dragon's skull breathing fire.

"Well, we know how they got here," Elyk said.

"But where does it lead?"

"Only one way to find out." Elyk took a step forward, but I grabbed his shoulder to stop him.

"We don't know if the portal works in both directions. Could have been a one-way trip." Between the square stone frame, a haze of greens and purples shimmered like the wisps of a campfire.

Elyk grabbed a bit of burnt debris and threw it into the portal. The timber disappeared without a sound. We both waited for something to happen, though I had no idea what. If someone threw the chunk of debris back to our side, we would have to run. Neither of us were in any position to fight.

"I'll just stick my hand through," Elyk said once we were both confident that chucking in the piece of debris had brought about no ill effects.

I watched with bated breath. He touched the swirling portal, his fingers disappeared, and then he pulled them back.

"Well?"

"Nothing," he answered.

Before I could protest further, Elyk jumped through the

portal. The idea of following him crossed my mind for a split second, but I held my ground. If the man couldn't make it back, which was a significant possibility, there was no reason to get us both trapped.

Only a few seconds later, Elyk emerged from the portal once more. "It's safe," he said, beaming with pride.

I wanted to slap him. But if the roles were reversed, would I have made the same reckless decision? Probably. "Where does it lead?"

"Some decent-sized guildhall outside The Jade Spire. You can see the whole spire right from the portal. No one was home at the hall—probably sent every single person they had to come kill us, and now the hall is empty."

I mulled it over in my mind. A portal to another capital city was excellent news. A portal that led to a dead guild's home base, presumably where no one would check, was even better. We could use the guildhall as a staging area to sack The Jade Spire, though attacking another massive city felt like it was weeks away. Or months. Years . . .

"Alright, we have the portal. That means The Jade Spire is our next target. We just need to regroup, recover, build our strength. As soon as we can, we use the portal to sack the city, and then we destroy it."

"Sounds like a plan," Elyk said. Though he was still heavily battered and practically on death's door, he had at least recovered a measure of his confidence. And I supposed I had as well. We had a clear plan, difficult as it would be, and that was something.

We arrived back at Undercroft Citadel sometime right around dusk. Xollmomath had resurrected a few dozen zombies, and the undead druid was busy reinforcing them with vines. Without a consciousness left in the traditional sense, the druid would carry on the last task I had given him, and that was to beef up our militia. He didn't understand the gravity of our situation, and his work was not hampered by a lack of morale. In some ways, I envied him.

Geirr found me first, and I was eager to hear what he had to say about the siege engines. But that wasn't what he had in mind. "Your armor, I'm sorry, Ben. It just . . . I'm not that good of a smith to repair it."

I had feared as much. But another idea had already sprouted in my mind, and it was an idea I very much wished to water. "Have you seen Faidra's armor?" I asked. "The gargoyles brought it back a few hours ago."

"Aye. Never held anything quite like it before." Geirr must have seen the glimmer in my eye because he shook his head. "I don't think *that's* a good idea. Lady Kalma won't take kindly to her number one servant wearing the armor of another god. Best to destroy it. Or let the necromancer consume its magic for his own needs."

"No, my good man, you're thinking too small. Think bigger. Grander."

"Elyk already has legendary armor, if that's what you mean."

I laughed. "That he does! Bring her armor to me. I'll show you what I have in mind."

A few minutes later, Geirr returned with the two gnomes. They pulled a small cart with Faidra's heavy armor inside, then dumped it unceremoniously on the ground.

"It's just a guess," I said, struggling to lift the massive steel suit. "But it can't really hurt, I think." It took considerable effort, but I managed to drop the entire suit of armor over the edge of the reflecting pool. The halcyon liquid shimmered and pulsed. A few bubbles escaped to break on the surface, but they vanished just as quickly as they formed.

For a long, tense moment, nothing happened. Then I saw a reflection. Something not quite as black as the water caught a flicker from a nearby torch. I reached in, wrapped my tentacles around the breastplate, and pulled with all my might.

The suit had to weigh nearly two hundred pounds, and it took all four of us to wrench it free, though the others had to use ropes and hooks as none of them were brave enough to let even a drop of the cursed liquid touch their skin.

I gaped in awe at the item we pulled from the depths. My plan worked, and Lady Kalma had transfigured the heavy steel from Gloandi's domain to her own. In the back of my mind, I got the feeling that the death goddess was pleased. That I was finally being rewarded after enduring so much punishment.

Masterwork Deathbound Crucible of the Bone Chapel: This armor, bestowed but once, may only be worn by the leader of Undercroft Citadel. Its enmity knows no bounds, and its hunger cannot be satiated. While worn, the bearer of this relic cannot be burned. The bearer's spells are enhanced by Lady Kalma's divine might, radically empowering them with new effects and draining massive amounts of energy. Once, the bearer may perform the Litany of Lost Souls, becoming Lady Kalma's avatar for twenty-four hours. The bearer's soul will be forfeit upon the Litany's conclusion.

Whatever lack of confidence was eating away at my mind was all but gone. Sure, there was a lot of work left to do, but damn . . . Whoever attacked us next was in for a surprise. Actually, I was eager to rush through the portal to The Jade Spire on my own just to test out my newly enhanced skills. I called up my stats, and none of the skill descriptions had changed, so I would just have to learn on the fly.

I had reached level twenty-two as well, and I was finally in the proper headspace to enjoy it and trust my decisions. Surprisingly, it was my cunning that had increased during the massive battle, and it had gone up by three to a total of forty-four. I realized just how difficult it was to reach higher levels in Wonder. If you only focused on a single stat and completely ignored the other two, you could probably get into the thirties without a huge amount of difficulty, but beyond that would take a heroic effort. Ministrel was level thirty-four, and I guessed he was built for cunning and nothing else. Faidra had been the same level, and I knew her influence was just as high as her physical. It was truly impressive.

I sat with my back against the reflecting pool, my new armor to my right, and opened the menu with my new ability choices.

Memory Eater (Physical): Lady Kalma's maw devours all. Memories are but another delicacy. With a single bite, the Blight of Deep Waters sees into the mind of the foe, navigating the brain's chambers as easily as a calm sea. Consumes minor energy.

Deceptive Rigging (Cunning): The Blight of Deep Waters can assemble objects with hidden intent and disguised purpose. This ability scales with the user's craftsmanship. Passive.

Gifts from the Sea (Influence): A fresh harvest lurks beneath every wave. All freshwater and saltwater production facilities under the command of the Blight of Deep Waters will have a chance to produce double yield. Passive.

For probably the first time since entering Wonder, I knew exactly what I had to take without question. But I was starting to question the significant aquatic focus of my abilities. And for that matter, of my very body. I hadn't tried to swim with my tentacles yet, but I imagined they would be up for the task. And with my lack of breathing, I was probably strongest underwater. But . . . I didn't particularly *like* the water. Not to mention our lack of boats for my enhanced navigational skill from *Part the Waters*.

I unlocked *Memory Eater* with a thought, and a sharp, searing pain immediately sliced through my stomach. It felt like I was being stabbed. I ripped at my tattered shirt, and there, in the center of my belly, was a brand new addition to my already hideous form: a mouth. While the one on my face was horizontal and well in accordance with human anatomy, Lady Kalma's new gift was vertical and lined with dozens of teeth. The pain quickly and mercifully subsided, and I let loose a stream of curses.

I certainly did not *want* a damned mouth in the center of my chest. And I just got new armor, perhaps the best armor the game could even generate, so the mouth wasn't even going to be useful. So much for knowing which ability to take. I cast aside my torn shirt and went to our stores of loot to find a new one.

Once more clothed, I decided it was time to try on the ridiculous armor to take my mind off my latest monumental blunder. Despite its extreme weight, I found that it slipped around my shoulders with relative ease. And perhaps it was a trick of my mind, but I swore the leather clasps on the sides fixed themselves without my touch.

The armor was made for me. I figured it had probably been the same for Faidra, forged by her god to match her towering height and skeletal body.

Then, as though the surprises were simply limitless, the center of the armor reacted to my thoughts. I was in the middle of silently cursing Lady Kalma yet again for giving me a mouth in the center of my stomach when the steel opened as if on magical hinges. The scalloped plates slid backward, and my new mouth chomped the air in anticipation.

I looked skyward to offer a weak thanks to the goddess, then quickly thought better of it and directed my half-hearted praise to the ground.

But I felt good. I felt strong. I knew my physical stat was nothing compared to Elyk's, and I barely knew how to fight in melee, but the spells were certainly coming together. I just needed to test them to be sure.

"Fuck it," I muttered. "What's one more stupid decision?"

I mentally commanded a gargoyle to find Ellen, and then the two of us headed directly for the portal to The Jade Spire.

The woman didn't say much on the journey, probably scared out of her mind and still trying to come to terms with the near-total loss of our base. But I didn't bring her along for the small talk. I needed someone with some defensive abilities, and she was quite literally our only option left.

We reached the portal sometime after dusk. Thankfully, it was still quiet. No enemy army had assembled in the ruins of Wolfpine to come finish us off. "It leads to The Jade Spire, the city with the portal from Hong Kong back in the real world," I explained.

The warden nodded. "And what are we doing here?"

I gave her a sinister smile. "I have a host of new abilities and gear. I need to test them. And honestly, I want to blow off steam."

"I take it you want me to help keep you alive?"

"Smart girl. Just don't spend all your mana. If we can get to their resurrection orb, I plan on taking it, and you'll be able to move it better than I can."

She let out a heavy sigh. Despite her obvious terror, she did her best not to show it too plainly. With morale in such low supply, I appreciated the effort.

"Come on, let's go." I stepped through the portal, and the air instantly changed. I wasn't particularly well versed in Wonder's geography, but wherever The Jade Spire was located, it was much warmer than Echelon. Almost too warm. And the air was dry, though I knew every capital city was on a coast by design.

We emerged in a small room in the former guildhall of our attackers. It was stone on three sides and open on the fourth with a waist-high banister. To our left, a set of stone stairs descended to a grassy plain. Ellen emerged behind me, and I didn't give the guildhall much more thought. All we needed to know was how to find it again when we had to leave.

On the ground, I couldn't help but marvel at The Jade Spire. It felt like the first time I stood in front of the portal in Atlanta. The city was massive, and at its center stood the eponymous green spire. It reached through the clouds, delicately swirling with an intricate helix pattern that reflected the moonlight in a thousand different directions. It was like stained glass come to life, and it took my breath away.

Unlike the other cities I had been to so far, The Jade Spire had no walls. I figured it was simply too large. The main government centers all existed inside the spire itself, and that was no doubt heavily guarded, but everything else sprawled out in a much more organic pattern that would be easy to infiltrate undetected.

I picked a nearby area at random and ran for it. Ellen would simply have to keep up. The first person I found was a low-level player carrying a sack of something that looked like rice or grain. I took the man unawares, smashing his back with my mace and knocking him to the ground. The first spell I tried was *A Feast of Spores,* one of my favorites. I reared back and breathed into the man's face, and instead of a haze of toxic spores, a trio of slimy tentacles erupted from my mouth that nearly made me gag. They latched onto the man's eyes and nose, boring through his flesh, and a foul deluge of tainted liquid followed.

The man screamed and clawed at his face, but his voice was quickly drowned by a fit of coughing that he could not control. Rapidly, much quicker than I ever would have expected, the man died. Blood seeped from the bottoms of his eyes, and a bit of pink foam escaped down his chin.

Then the spell's drain hit me. It wasn't overwhelming, but it would certainly take some getting used to. I finally understood why Faidra had been so utterly spent after every fight.

I guessed I would have five, probably six uses of the spell before I would need to rest. That was a moderate energy activation, so for something that only consumed minor energy like *Visage of the Dark One,* I would probably be able to get ten uses of it.

I dreaded to think what a spell like *Pull from the Darkness* would do. I had grown fairly accustomed to the spell, but if *A Feast of Spores* was anything to go by, the drain would be somewhere around triple what I was used to. Hell, two drains from *Pull from the Darkness* might even kill me.

Next, I needed to try out my new combo with Princess Yasha's fan. I looked around for more players, and I spotted two farther down the road that hadn't been alerted by the first man's screams. I took to the air, quickly flew about thirty or forty feet above them, then activated *The Basalt Monolith.* I fell back to the ground like a meteor, connecting with one player's shoulder and cleaving straight through it. Instead of a simple rectangular sheath of stone, I was coated in spikes sticking out in every direction like some kind of giant stone sea urchin.

The spell ripped a massive amount of stamina directly from my bones, or so it seemed. If I wasn't suspended upright by several tons of black stone, the drain would have brought me to my knees.

A wooden door banged open to my right with significant force, and I suddenly remembered the rest of the ability. It would attract enemies. A trio of players, all in the high teens for level, went to town hammering on my stone exterior. One had a club, the next had a pair of daggers, and the third man threw an ale mug before resorting to his fists.

None of it made a dent. I didn't even feel it. Not a single vibration made it through my craggy exterior. With a smile, I dismissed the spell and whirled, knocking two of the men aside as much from shock as from my mace. I grabbed the third man, the unarmed one, and ripped him in close with an oppressive bear hug.

It was time to try out Lady Kalma's most recent gift. My armor clinked open right beneath the confluence of my ribs in the center of my chest. A gaping, vertical maw gnashed out with far more teeth than any human should have anywhere, and the man wailed.

Thankfully, my new mouth was devoid of tastebuds. It chewed and chewed, ripping the man's innards into god only knew where, and then he fell from my grasp.

All I could do was laugh. The man's friends fled in terror, and then *Reap Honor* triggered, reanimating the mangled corpse at my feet.

"Do you see it?" the corpse somehow spoke, its voice raspy like rocks and sand.

I shoved it away and readied my mace. "What the hell?" My undead zombies were not supposed to speak. They simply couldn't. It wasn't possible.

The corpse cocked its head to the side, and I swore it smiled at me. Guts hung from its torn belly and touched the ground. Bits of gravel and dirt clung to its bloody intestines. "Do you see it?" the creature asked again. It turned to the building where it had left, and I followed its gaze.

The thing was referring to my reflection.

More than just my stomach had changed. I was morphing into some kind of terrible mix between cosmic horror and a seventeenth century depiction of a nightmarish mermaid. My flesh was tight and bordered on translucent. The muscle beneath pulled and writhed like waves. And my face was completely distorted. My mouth was half tentacles. I licked my lips, and my tongue was the same. I tried to dismiss the form, thinking it was just some remnant of the spell I cast earlier, but I knew deep down that it was just me. I was changing, perhaps slowly, but inevitably.

I backed away from the gruesome scene in the middle of the street and just about crashed into Ellen behind me. I hadn't noticed her approach.

"What do I look like?" I demanded perhaps a bit too harshly.

She stammered out a stream of gibberish, obviously terrified of both me and the answer.

"Just tell me!" I yelled. I wasn't convinced if what I saw in the reflection was actually real. I couldn't trust my senses.

"Uh, um. Y-you have tentacles coming out of your face!" she finally managed to say.

That much I essentially knew already. "And my skin? Can you see through it like I can?"

She nodded vigorously.

"Shit. Well . . . You're either just as insane as I am, or the transformation was real." I contemplated it all for a moment, and I quickly came to the conclusion that it actually didn't matter. At first, I was pissed because of the obvious: I was hideous. Who could ever love something so grotesque? But that didn't matter. There was no one to love. There were allies, enemies, and those caught in the crossfire. No one else. And then I feared the changes to be permanent if I ever made it back to the real world, but that was not the goal. There would never be a real world for me. Earth meant nothing.

More people were rushing down the street, and their heavy footfalls quickly snapped me out of it. "One more I really want to test," I said quietly.

I waited until the newcomers were about ten or twelve feet in front of me before activating *Visage of the Dark One*. I launched to a towering height. Faidra would have had to crane her neck to look me in the eye. I saw the rooftops of all the nearby buildings. Fire erupted from my eyes, obscuring my vision for a few seconds but quickly fading. I pointed at the suddenly terrified attackers and sneered. "Kill each other!" I commanded, my enhanced voice booming over what felt like half the city.

Two of the attackers dropped to their knees and covered their ears. Another drew his sword. He swung, easily lopping off a head. I mentally commanded my newest zombie to join the fray, and the entire group was annihilated in a matter of moments.

When I released the spell, my heart hammered in my chest. I figured I had spent about half my tank. Maybe a touch more. But *damn*. My earlier guess was right: I was powerful. I finally felt like I could hold my own against someone like Elyk or Kevin. I probably wasn't up to Faidra's former strength just yet, but I was rapidly ascending.

In that moment, I determined that The Jade Spire would know it. Who were they to have the audacity to attack Undercroft Citadel? The city needed to feel my vengeance. It needed to suffer the consequences of its foolishness. It needed to reap what it had so carelessly sown.

CHAPTER 11

"Any idea where their resurrection hub is?" I asked the warden.

She shook her head. "I haven't been here since before the server crashes. I don't know!"

"Not your fault," I said. I scanned the only parts of the city I could see, but it was no use. Based on Echelon and Olympia, the orb would be somewhere just outside the main city proper. With no walls, it was hard to tell exactly where the actual city ended and the outskirts began. What I needed was a better vantage point.

I thought of using the fan to fly to the top of the spire itself. After the last use, I wasn't sure I had enough left in the tank to even activate the ability, and if I did, I'd be completely spent after the spell expired. No, I needed another way.

"Do you have any movement abilities?" I asked.

"Just *Fleet Footed*, but it isn't very strong," Ellen answered.

I shrugged. "Better than nothing. Give it a shot."

She cast the spell, and all I felt was a slight tingle in my legs. "What exactly does it do? Make us faster on foot, I assume?"

"I said it wasn't very strong." She jumped and nearly reached my chest. "It also makes you jump higher."

"Alright, they'll be defending the orb no matter where it is. Either way we go around the city, we'll hit the harbor eventually. Fifty-fifty chance in both directions." I picked the right and started jogging.

The woman was correct. The spell kind of sucked. Sure, it made us faster, but only marginally. By the time we cleared what I guessed was a mile of ground, Ellen had to recast the spell. The only good thing with such a weak ability was that she could essentially cast it an infinite number of times.

We passed a handful of neighborhoods, merchant centers, and all the other trappings of everyday life, and I started to get the feeling that The Jade Spire was barely on alert. It was the polar opposite of Olympia City. No one was panicked, no army was defending their resurrection orb, and no alliance of evil guilds was trying to destroy it. The whole thing struck me as odd. The players who lived here were undoubtedly terrified of the prospect of losing resurrection, but yet they hadn't taken any extraordinary measures to protect it.

Perhaps they simply viewed the city as too large to defend. But that didn't make sense. The orb needed defending, not every building and street. Perhaps they were so confident in the guild that had come to destroy Undercroft Citadel that whoever had been defending it before had simply stopped.

Whatever the reason, I was determined to find the orb and destroy it.

My muscles burning but still not giving out thanks to Ellen's spell, we finally came within sight of the resurrection orb. It stood on a raised bit of earth maybe six or eight feet above the surrounding area. A handful of torches flanked it on both sides.

"No defenses," I said between breaths.

Ellen caught up to me a second later. She scanned the orb up and down. "I can probably use magic to knock it down," she said.

"Wait. Let's think it through. Investigate." The whole thing felt like an elaborate trap. Where were the guards? Where were the walls? There should have at least been NPCs from The Jade Spire, but there was no one. All was quiet. "Check for traps. Footprints. Anything," I commanded.

"My investigation skill isn't great," she said.

"Yeah, neither is mine."

We searched the nearby area without getting too close. A few minutes into the task, the orb hummed a shimmered. Someone was resurrected right in front of us. The player took a moment to catch his bearings, gave us both a friendly wave, then walked back toward the city.

"Alright, maybe they just don't know who I am," I thought aloud. But *that* didn't make sense either. Everyone in the game knew my name, or so I had thought. Perhaps I was not as infamous as the score on my stat sheet had led me to believe.

"I found something," Ellen chimed in.

She stood behind the nearest building, a pottery studio based on the sign, and held up a bent dagger. "What do you think?"

The dagger didn't have any stats or description when I tried to bring it up in my vision. It was junk. "Nothing. Just toss it."

For the next ten minutes, we didn't find anything else of interest. There were plenty of footprints, but of course there would be. The Jade Spire was home to several hundred thousand people.

Hands on my hips, I sighed. The orb hovered on its earthen plinth, taunting me with a secret I was not smart enough to deduce.

Or else the alternative: no one was defending it. The people of The Jade Spire didn't believe their orb was worth defending.

"Shit," I muttered. I checked for more players or NPCs but no one was around.

Ellen paced back and forth. "Well?"

"Alright. Do it. Knock it toward us. If we can push it back to the portal and steal it, we might as well. Though I still have no idea if they're even useful."

The warden nodded. She moved her hands in a specific pattern, and then a huge gust of wind swept toward us from the direction of the spire. It blew strong, redoubled again, and the orb slowly teetered over the edge.

The moment it skidded to a stop at my feet, another voice spoke in the back of my head. It was one I recognized, though I hadn't heard it in some time.

"Hello, Ben," Helvegen said. Her words dripped with ice.

I whirled, and there she was, arrayed in fresh armor and with an entire guild at her back. *Hunger God*, I read, and the guild name was familiar, though I couldn't quite place from where. But it didn't matter. She wasn't real. Just another trick of Lady Kalma's insufferable curse.

"Uh, w-what do we do?" Ellen stammered at my side.

"What do you mean? Use your magic to push the orb, and let's get back home. Our work here is done," I explained.

There was real fear on the woman's face. Perhaps she was just feeling the immediate effect of the continent's resurrection ability going offline, and it spooked her.

Something sharp pricked me in the side of the neck, and I slapped at it thinking it was a bug bite.

"Ben!" Ellen yelled. She turned and ran, and an arrow slammed into her back.

"Wha . . ." The color faded from my vision. It wasn't a bug bite. It was a knife. And it was buried up to the hilt in the side of my neck. Blood gushed from the wound and spilled down the inside of my new armor. It was hot against my skin.

As I hit the ground, I saw Helvegen standing over me. She casually flicked my blood from her hands before waving to someone else from the guild.

Augustine, Sower of Discord. The warlock. He wrapped a hand around her waist and kissed her cheek.

"Sorry about your new girlfriend," Hel said, bending to whisper into my ear.

"You were right. Like sheep to the slaughter," the warlock added.

All around me, my surroundings changed. More and more people flickered into view as though stepping out of a deep winter fog. They were all players, and they were armed to the teeth. I tried to focus on them, on any of them, but my eyes refused to obey.

I reached for Helvegen's armor, for anything to steady my failing mind amidst the whirl of chaos that had taken up residence inside my throbbing skull, but she brushed me away.

"When I stand upon my altar, resplendent in profane glory, I shall care not for the maggots squirming beneath me. Now squirm, Ben, squirm." She let out a laugh and twisted the knife.

I tried to speak, to get anything past my torn throat, but there was no air left to expel.

"I want you to suffer," she whispered. She ripped out the knife and sank it through my left eye. "You brought this darkness, Ben. In the deepest circle of whatever hell you're headed to, your pathetic shell will crack."

CHAPTER 12

I had just enough energy to activate *The Basalt Monolith* before it was too late. What I needed more than anything was a corpse. Even just one would give me a little spark of energy, and I knew I could cultivate that spark into a chain of spells that would—with any luck—get me out of there. And I didn't have to wait long. Hel and her new guild butchered Ellen with very little delay.

I felt the warden's powerful spirit surge through my body. It wouldn't heal the deep wounds in my neck or face, but it would stitch together those sinews and synapses of my brain enough to get me at least somewhat back into the fight. Without a need to breathe, the lack of blood flowing through my veins on account of my severed carotid wasn't a big deal. It hurt, but it wouldn't kill me on its own. My muscles didn't need oxygen the same way as everyone else. Lady Kalma's magic would sustain where biology failed.

Hel's guild, provoked by the spell, unleashed a salvo at my stone encasement that would have easily annihilated half of Undercroft Citadel. I felt each blow like the dulled vibrations of a powerful speaker a few rooms away. They thudded and reverberated, but they didn't quite reach me. The biggest issue was that I couldn't see. The basalt covered my eyes just as it covered everything else, so I had no idea what the battle—if it could even be called such a thing—looked like on the outside.

The last of Ellen's vitality ran dry. My curse consumed every ounce of energy she had, and I knew there was only one thing left to do: *Presence of the Abyss.* It was the final 'oh shit' button left in my arsenal. Memories flashed through my mind of Kevin killing me inside Echelon's castle. And then later when I activated *Host of Blasphemies*. Lady Kalma had done wonders keeping me alive, albeit at a cost, and I needed her divine intervention one more time, perhaps now more than ever.

I activated the spell, and the blackness enveloping my vision somehow deepened. What was black basalt before turned to an absolute void of light. The darkness was perfect. Complete. Inevitable.

Muffled sounds came through the stone. Screams. Terror. Agony.

I released my hold on *The Basalt Monolith*, and my craggy exterior melted away. The first thing I saw was the sky. I was on my back, staring into a magnificent red rift in the heavens. It looked like someone had taken a scalpel to the night sky and opened it from horizon to horizon. What came out was blood red and dripped like a hail of meteors. They crashed to the ground with thunderous booms, sending dirt and limbs high into the sky.

Hel's guild was already decimated. I felt the dead bodies more than I saw them—my left eye was still nothing more than a gaping wound—and the dead replenished my lifeforce with tremendous speed. Every second brought me closer to full strength.

I stood and shook the weariness from my tentacle legs.

Everywhere I looked, players were locked in battle. What rained from the wound in the sky wasn't a meteor shower. *They looked skyward, praying for light from the heavens. What fell upon them was not mercy* . . . Each crimson droplet was an angel with wings the color of blood. They rocketed toward the ground, slammed into the earth, then quickly emerged from their craters with heavy scythes ready to reap the fresh harvest of human souls.

In all the chaos, I had no idea where Helvegen or the warlock had gone. Hell, they were probably still right there, probably still fighting the same battle, but I couldn't see them. Now that I had found her again, one of my top priorities was figuring out a way to defeat her powerful painter magic.

But for the moment . . . there was slaughter to be had. Every player that fell fueled my curse, charging my muscles with unholy energy and healing my wounds better than any potion or surgeon. In less than a minute, I was back to full strength.

"You should have cut off my head," I growled, though there was no one close enough to hear it. "Now you're all going to die."

I ripped the knife from my left eye with a spurt of blood. It hurt, but only for a second. The wound closed, my vision returned, and I charged the nearest member of Hel's new guild. He was a player, a level twenty sorcerer, lightly armored and already bloodied. The man never saw me coming. He was busy throwing up defensive magic in front of him, barely keeping one of Lady Kalma's death angels from cutting him in half, and I crashed into his side.

We fell to the ground, and I didn't waste any time. My chest opened wide as I activated *Memory Eater*, and the man screamed. I felt the tentacles of my second mouth boring into his supple flesh, greedily eating both his life force and his blood. And then I tasted more than bones and guts. I tasted his memories.

I quickly sifted through the sorcerer's labyrinthine mind until I found the one I sought, the one I knew would be buried somewhere toward the back: Helvegen's arrival. She joined the guild a month ago, maybe more, only a few days after she left my continent. I blazed through the next memories in the best chronological order I could put together. Most of the memories were just snippets, fleeting moments barely worth archiving, but enough of them strung together formed an overall picture that was easy to read.

Hel arrived in The Jade Spire, from where I had no idea, and quickly used her magic to ingratiate herself into the guild. She displayed a powerful persona, but also a deeply personal one that the warlock, Augustine, quickly desired to possess. The manipulations were subtle, and the sorcerer whose mind I devoured didn't catch hardly any of them, but *I* knew Hel. I saw them plain as day. She seduced him, not just with physical attractiveness but also with her strength. The dominance of her personality.

But Augustine was already married, or that was how the sorcerer viewed it. A week elapsed, and the wife's body was discovered in their guildhall butchered like common meat. There was a fight, more manipulation, and then the warlock broke down in her arms. The guild marched against a rival. False accusations brought them to war, but it didn't matter. They still had the resurrection orb. The two guilds ran out of steam, and then the plan came together.

Hel unified them under a common goal: the eradication of Undercroft Citadel. They built the portal, assembled a handful of smaller guilds as fodder, and attacked. Secretly, Hel and the top members of Hunger God knew it wouldn't work. Their plan was to weaken Undercroft and draw me out in the process.

And the sorcerer waited with the others. Under a shroud of powerful magic, the guild's top tier laid in ambush. Then I tasted the man's fear. His unbridled terror. He had never experienced anything like it before in his life. Not even close. He had never come face to face with his own mortality, and his fear had been building to a debilitating crescendo since the moment Ellen took down the resurrection orb.

The man died in my arms, and my second mouth retreated back to its armored hiding place. By the time I had my psyche fully seated once more within my own skull, the battle had turned into a rout. The guild was broken, scattered like leaves in the wind, and dozens of them had already been butchered by angels.

I climbed the small earthen bulwark where the orb used to rest only a few moments ago and watched the slaughter. Lady Kalma's angels cleared the entire field with ease, batting away spells with counter magic of their own and then cleaving through armor as easily as the skin and bone beneath it. But the angels were not immortal. Inexorable, certainly, but not immortal. Two had fallen not far from the orb. One had been blasted apart by magic so thoroughly that only its bloody wings remained. The other had fallen to a more conventional attack, and a hand-and-a-half sword still stuck up from its torn neck.

The battle was rapidly concluding without any input whatsoever from me, so I skidded back down the slope to the dead angels. Up close, they were hideously terrifying. They wore black robes covered in chains, and their wings were red because they were translucent, much like how I envisioned my own skin would look after a few more 'treatments' by the death goddess. The blood that ran through the angels' wings was dark like wine, and it still pumped despite both specimens being dead.

I wrapped my hands around the hilt of the sword and

wrenched it free. It was heavy, probably a touch heavier than Infernum, though it felt nice in my hands. I called up its stats in my vision:

Enchanted Phase Blade: This sword was forged at the peak of The Jade Spire, mixing clouds with its steel. It passes through most armor unimpeded.

"Not bad!" I said with a smile, though my eye caught something else, and I slid the phase blade through my belt.

The dead angel's scythe was still in its grasp. I pried its bony, sinewy fingers from the hilt and hefted it to my shoulder. The thing was massive, probably on par with Faidra's colossal weapon, though its weight didn't match its size.

Bonereaper: When wielded, this scythe gives the user +15 to all stats. Enemies slain with Bonereaper are sent directly to Lady Kalma and cannot be revived or reanimated in any way.

I had to laugh at the scythe's ability. Without the server crash, it would have been fantastic. But now, with the resurrection orb sitting only a few yards away and completely inactive, all the ability meant was that I couldn't bring back anyone as a zombie. *Reap Honor* wouldn't work either. It was a net negative, given the circumstances.

As much as I wanted the huge boost to my stats, the sword was better. I tossed the scythe aside and drew the phase blade, eager to help the angels finish the rout. I found a player not far away, a wounded raider who hadn't quite been finished off by the angels yet. I charged him, and the man, to his credit, quickly brought up his own sword to parry. We clashed, the raider activated a spell that launched a gout of fire for my chest, and I rolled to the side. The man spun the opposite direction, obviously used to relying on his heavy armor to protect his back, and the phase blade went right through. I was off balance and couldn't put any strength behind the swing, but it didn't matter. The man's own momentum was his downfall, and he collapsed in a heap at my feet.

Curiously, when I ripped the sword free, the man's armor was still perfectly intact. Only a thin line of blood on the edge of my blade gave any indication that I had killed him at all.

A woman screamed behind me, and I turned just in time to take a heavy hit on my chest from a warhammer. The blow staggered me, but the woman needed a lot more than that to break through Lady Kalma's legendary armor. Normally, I would have launched my shadow pet at the woman's face and then leapt on her with a host of other spells, but I knew I couldn't afford it. And beyond the energy requirement, I simply didn't *need* to give it my all. Her warhammer was heavy and slow, just like the full plate armor she wore to match her fallen friend. I braced my sword against my waist and rammed straight ahead. She swatted at the blade, but she just wasn't quick enough, and I impaled her where she stood.

By the time I got the sword free of her corpse, the battle was all but over. The rout was complete. But the Hunger God guild was far from destroyed. Hel was still out there with the warlock. There was no way either of them would have fallen to such a straightforward battle no matter how lopsided it turned out to be. The two of them would have plans and contingencies. I knew they had escaped.

A deep silence settled over the battlefield. No one left standing even breathed, myself included. The angels slowly returned to me, and I wondered how long I would have the divine army at my command. There were probably fifty of them, and we had only lost three as far as I could tell. None of the angels appeared to be any different than the others, so I assumed there was no commander. Just me.

I looked to the towering green spire in the center of the city. It was barely visible in the dead of night. "Alright, there's a portal maybe a mile or two back that way," I said, pointing in the general direction of the guild hall. "Two of you can push the orb through it. Take it back to Undercroft Citadel, then guard the portal itself when you're done. The rest of you . . ."

I grabbed Princess Yasha's fan to give myself a set of wings to match my new army. Fortunately, the ability from the fan wasn't empowered by armor since it wasn't one of *my* abilities, so the tax on my energy reserves was just the usual debilitating surge instead of a near-death experience.

I took on the demon form and leapt into the sky. "To the spire!" I yelled. I expected the angels to yell back, to rally to my call like fresh troops eager for battle, but they were eerily silent just like the zombies. But they obeyed, and that was all that mattered.

We soared over the city in a loose square formation, and I finally saw what I had expected to see earlier. There was panic. Chaos in the dark streets. People stacked their belongings onto carts and hurriedly roped their animals to them. Others simply made a mad dash with whatever they could carry. In the distance, the harbor glistened with a streak of pale white moonlight, and several dozen boats floated at their moorings. There was even more action there, though we were too far away to really make out what was happening. Still, it was easy to guess. As many as could fit on the ships and afford passage would be taking to the sea in search of safety. Another continent, as far away as they all were, would be their goal. And they were down to just four options.

Echelon, The Jade Spire, and Olympia City had fallen. New Karstad, the city corresponding to the portal in Madrid where the game developers were located, was likely the destination for most of the refugees. It was huge, and panicked people tended to seek safety in numbers. If they were smart, and no doubt many of the people below us certainly were, they would hide out in the wilderness. The continents were also massive, and the wilds weren't *that* dangerous if you were a decent level or had a good guild to rely upon.

The task of eliminating all the refugees would have to wait. I had some ideas floating around in the back of my head for that one, and none of them were even close to ready yet. For now, I set my sights on the spire itself. It came into view in all its towering splendor, and I was happy to see that it didn't have any air defenses at all. A set of concentric rings guarded the base, but they were useless against an airborne army.

We circled the spire once before I found an entrance. A small portico jutted out near the very top, and I figured it was a balcony for one of the royal family's bedrooms. It was only wide enough for one angel at a time, so I commanded half my army to use the balcony as an entrance as quickly as they could. Once inside, they only had a single mission: kill everything that moved. Somehow, I got the mental indication that the angels would enjoy their task.

I led the rest of us to the docks.

As long as there were fleeing, panicked players, there was tons of experience waiting to be collected. And I still had another spell I hadn't yet tried in combat: *Part the Waters*. I could only cast the spell once, but I was hoping that Lady Kalma's powerful augmentation would mean that the hundred cubic meters had been multiplied.

I pulled up a good distance from the docks, hovering with my angelic death squad, and contemplated how best to use my single cast. Moving the water from directly beneath the largest ships seemed like the way to go. But then where would I set it down? I could just release it above the ships, thereby dropping and then swamping them, but I figured the sudden, violent drop would be enough on its own. Plus, the rest of the ocean would quickly rush in to capsize the vessels anyway. I wouldn't need to drop the water on them at all.

I activated the ability, and it went just as I envisioned. A huge chunk of saltwater vanished beneath half a dozen of the largest ships. The boats dropped like rocks, and the water on all sides quickly rushed in to crush their hulls from above. The ships were quickly destroyed without any hope of survivors.

My vision turned to the docks themselves. I focused on the largest mass of people, a huge group huddled in terror between two warehouses, and released the deluge. Hundreds of people were swept to sea. The warehouses shattered to splinters, no doubt crushing dozens more in the process.

I pointed at the survivors, what few there were. “No quarter,” I commanded, and my army descended with a wave of inevitability that only Lady Kalma could grant. The slaughter was nothing short of complete, and I watched it all from my position among the lowest clouds. If I could bring Xollmomath here, he would have an inexhaustible supply of corpses for zombies. Many of them would be waterlogged, but that couldn’t be helped.

I left the angels to their own devices at the docks, confident that they would simply continue causing chaos no matter where they went, and made for the spire. I landed on the balcony and finally let go of the fan’s ability, retaking my normal form. The hit to my vitality was immense, but there were so many corpses nearby that it was instantly replenished by my curse.

A wave of cold air ran down my back and made me shiver. The little voice that lived in the back of my skull returned with the chill. *How many can you eat before you no longer recognize yourself?*

I pushed through the balcony doors into the royal bedroom and quickly approached a gilded mirror hanging above a set of drawers. I was a monster. There was no denying it. Dozens of tentacles had grown out of my face, and three small openings that looked to be the start of new eyes had appeared on my forehead. My skin was getting more and more translucent. It started to remind me of pale cave fish I had seen once in a museum. My veins stood out like scars beneath the tight skin. I smiled, and the dentition that met me was equally gruesome. My teeth were filed to jagged points like daggers.

But was any of it actually real? My reflection laughed in response to the thought, and I smashed the mirror with a balled fist of slimy tentacles. It was becoming harder and harder to differentiate between my own mind, the twisted machinations of Lady Kalma's curse, and whatever painter magic Hel was capable to laying on me.

Helvegen . . .

Memories of her flashed. They were fleeting, but they brought warmth that fought the chill at my back. What had happened between us? Why were we enemies? I thought of her touch, her quiet whispers in the darkness of my room just before dawn. But I killed her. Why? My memory flickered like a TV losing its power in a violent storm. I knew the answer was there, but it was just beyond my reach.

Something with the servers, I thought, though I couldn't quite place it. And what would I care if she destroyed the servers? If anything, it would only further my goals, not hamper them. I growled and figured I would deal with my lacking memories later. For now, she was an enemy, and that was all that mattered. Enemies would die. All of them, Helvegen included.

I ripped my consciousness back to the present with considerable effort and drew my new sword. The spire's next few rooms were more of the same: royal apartments richly decorated with furs, tapestries, and oil paintings in golden frames. Blood decorated the marble floors and stained the woven carpets.

The first corpse I came across appeared to be a king. It was a man, probably in his mid-fifties, wearing a velvet house coat and matching slippers. He had been gutted from navel to nose, and his stinking innards sat in a pile next to his head. More corpses littered the residential complex. I found what I guessed to be the king's wife dead behind a reinforced door. The angels had smashed through it with impunity, impaling the woman where she cowered.

Below the apartments, I found the kitchens and other servants' quarters. There were corpses everywhere. None of them were armed with more than steak knives or chair legs, if they were armed at all. Finally, perhaps halfway down the spire, I found the military barracks that formerly housed the royal guards. Now it was home only to corpses. The angels had exterminated everyone with ruthless efficiency.

I was just about to head down to the next floor when a bit of my memory decided to rekindle. My new sword was forged at the peak of the spire. That meant there was a smithy above the royal chambers, and I raced upward as quickly as I could. Undercroft Citadel needed tools as badly as ever, and I couldn't think of a better place to loot some than an enchanted forge at the very top of The Jade Spire.

It took some hunting, but I finally found the correct door that led to another series of staircases and eventually a smithy. The place was small, but it looked neat and orderly, like someone who took great pride in their work called it home. And there were a lot of tools. Most of them appeared to be various kinds of hammers or tongs, but then others were of specialized varieties that I could not name. I rummaged through what I guessed to be the most useful and loaded up my belt. With my new sword still tucked away, I was starting to feel a bit foolish with all the other items strapped to me. What I needed was a pair of gargoyles to ferry everything back to Undercroft.

I was just about to try to summon a few of Lady Kalma's angels when a noise caught my attention. Something fell behind me, and I knocked over more tools as I turned. An NPC cowered behind one of the large coal bins. He was a blacksmith, level thirty-eight. I practically salivated at the thought of bringing him back to work for me.

I stared him down. "Do you want to live?"

The NPC nodded vigorously. It struck me as odd that an NPC would be so terrified of death, but that was their programming. They were designed to be as indistinguishable from real humans as possible, and that meant a healthy fear of death.

I thought of the old loyalty tests I used to make people do. Those days, those people . . . it was all so far behind me. I simply reached out my hand and relied on my considerable influence stat to ensure the man's loyalty.

We shook, my tentacle enveloping his fingers, his eyes wide with terror. "My n-name's Piebald. Who are you?"

"That's a weird-ass name, Piebald. I'm Ben. And you're going to work for me from now on. Hmmm . . . is there any quicker way down from here?" I stole a glance over the edge, and I had to guess we were well over two hundred feet in the air. The height made my stomach churn.

Piebald shook his head. "Three hundred and sixteen stairs, I'm afraid."

"Memorizing the stairs . . . Yeah, you're sufficiently weird. You'll fit right in. Let me get us a ride." I sent a mental commanded to the angels in the same way I had always commanded my other flying pets, and I was pleased when it worked. A handful of them flew into view, then more, and we managed to load up just about everything that wasn't a permanent fixture.

The rest of the evening was spent in logistics mode. The angels helped me loot the spire and transfer the majority of the blacksmith's shop, and then I had Xollmomath and Xia head through the portal to begin the lengthy task of resurrecting zombies. That, of course, turned out not to work. We didn't get more than a hundred. Every single angel wielded the same enchanted scythe, and that meant all their kills were essentially wasted. It was a possibility I likely should have considered beforehand, but without a time machine, remorse was as useful to me as the corpses.

When it was finally finished on the evening of the second day, I had a trio of angels topple the gate in the center of Wolfpine, shutting off access to The Jade Spire hopefully for good.

Three cities down. Four more to go. And so far, we had collected all three resurrection orbs. I still had no idea how we were going to make use of them, but it would come to me in time. Until then, Undercroft Citadel had recovered enough for me to take a full stock of our defenses. Well, 'defenses' wasn't exactly right. We had none. There was the outline of a wall, a single working catapult, and that was it.

Perhaps the lone piece of good news was that Syzak had survived after all. Using his shaman magic, he had essentially burrowed underground when the poison gas spread, and it had taken him a full day to recover enough energy to extricate himself. On top of his survival, Sir Drevan was found.

The knight had not been so fortunate. But he wasn't quite dead, either. He shambled aimlessly through the courtyard, waiting for someone to give him orders. I commanded him to come close for inspection, and the man sure took his time. Though he walked, it was with the glassy-eyed aloofness of one of the rank and file undead. Curiously, however, the name above his head wasn't gone, only changed.

Sir Drevan, Toxic Abomination.

He was an undead NPC now, and for that I was a little disappointed as I really did like the man. Still, he was in fighting shape, if a tad on the slower side. His armor, or perhaps it was his flesh beneath the steel, gave off a constant cloud of pale gas in the same way that Faidra's plate had continually smoked. I didn't need to take a deep breath of the gas to figure out that it would be poisonous.

I made the new undead Drevan show me a few swings with his sword and shield. It was nothing impressive, not like he was before. I'd have to use him sparingly, though sacrificing my closest minions seemed to be the common trend around Undercroft Citadel.

Elyk and Geirr were still alive, as was Ministrel and his gnomes, and that was it for the player base. Everyone else was either undead or an NPC. All of the orcs were gone. Not much of their encampment survived either. Piebald, our new blacksmith, took to the workshops well enough, and I was promised that the new tools and materials would soon start to bear tangible fruits. In my absence, Geirr had also brought the damaged trebuchets back, and they would be in fine working order before long.

For zombies, we were running low. Xollmomath had done what he could, but that was frighteningly little. Too many of them had been blown to bits by siege weapons or simply cut down for the third or fourth time, and while they could be reanimated without any arms or legs, what use was it? A fire burned a few hundred yards from the former walls, slowly consuming all the corpses and rubble that was no longer useful.

In the courtyard, or what was left of it, there was yet another pile of looted gear. And somewhere out in the muddy, torn up field, was the one corpse no one could touch. The monk. He was still there, and if my plan to move the amulet with a machine didn't work, he'd probably be there a lot longer.

I searched through the weapons and armor for a bit,

hoping to find a decent helmet to completement my new breastplate and tassets, but there wasn't much to choose from large enough to accommodate the tentacles growing out of my mouth. What I did find, however, brought a smile to my face. Faidra's axe had been recovered by the gargoyles, and they had left it with all the rest.

The weapon had to weigh fifty pounds. Maybe more. It wasn't as heavy as her armor, thank god, though it was perhaps too unwieldy to ever use. I guessed my new form to be somewhere around six feet five inches, and the axe was a full head taller than me. I gave it a few unbalanced swings and nearly toppled over into the pile of gear.

"Alright, time to see what you can do," I said.

Masterwork Ashbound Executioner: This axe, recovered from Gloandi's lost Chapel of Eternal Flame, carries between its blades the skull of Anaximander, Gloandi's first chosen disciple. The fire bound within its steel strikes more than flesh and armor. It pierces resolve, courage, purpose, and the very will to live. Each consecutive strike against the same foe brings the wielder closer to Gloandi's sacred immolation. Enemies slain by the Executioner are seldom remembered, even by their false gods.

My head swam with the possibilities. If I dropped it into the reflecting pool, Lady Kalma would no doubt reforge it into something that matched my armor. The prospect was tempting, *extremely tempting*, but that wouldn't solve the problem of its size. I still could barely wield the thing. Faidra had been a giantess, a titan of unnatural proportions. I was tall thanks to the tentacles that had replaced my legs, but not tall enough. Elyk was shorter than me, and he was the only other one strong enough to swing it. Perhaps if Ugg'chugg was still around . . . but she was too unpredictable in any case.

Perhaps there was another way.

Xollmomath had used bones and corpses to make a golem before, and I knew he could do it again. A bit of a plan formed, and I was giddy with excitement. If I was right, it wouldn't even take too much time to pull it off.

I took the massive axe to the ossuary and set it inside for safe keeping, though how safe it would be without doors—thanks to the siege—was up for debate. Then I found Geirr and his new blacksmith assistant diligently working on the trebuchets in front of the workshop.

"How close are you to a machine that can lift the amulet from that dead monk?" I asked, skipping pleasantries. We still had a single shaman, but that kind of magic wouldn't be precise enough to accomplish the task. I wanted something that could retrieve the amulet while also leaving the monk's corpse generally intact.

Geirr rubbed a hand through his wild hair, and I was reminded that our little settlement also lacked a barber. "By tonight, if we stop repairing these," he answered.

"Excellent. Get to it. Let me know the moment you have it ready."

He agreed, and I went to handle the final part of Undercroft Citadel's upkeep: the angels. Much to my surprise, they hadn't disappeared with the dawn or evaporated into dust after twenty-four hours. By all appearances, they were here to stay, and that was huge. Out of sheer curiosity, I commanded one to attempt to lift the amulet from the dead monk, and it didn't work. Just like everyone else, they couldn't interact with the amulet or the man's body.

The angels responded to my mental commands in the same way that the gargoyles did, and I spent a while experimenting with different formations and watching them demonstrate some magic. They were more solo fighters than anything, extremely strong in physical combat with just a few short-range spells to augment their scythes. The only thing I didn't like was the stupid ability tacked onto their weapons. If we came across a large group again, which we inevitably would, I couldn't use the angels to clear them. Regardless of the drawback, they were beyond formidable, and I knew I would be putting all forty-eight of them to the test sooner rather than later.

When dusk came, Geirr told me the good news. He had a crude device put together that resembled a small claw on the end of a long wooden arm. Pulleys moved it all, and the ropes that ran through them were manipulated by simple levers that could be easily moved by dropping weight. Technically, no one would need to touch a lever. Drop a rock, and the contraption would move.

We positioned the device over the monk's body, and it took dozens of tries to get everything lined up just right. When we finally had the accuracy drilled in, I dropped a small rock from shoulder height onto a lever, and it worked. *It fucking worked.* The claw dropped, its small metal arms wrapped around the amulet for a few seconds, and then the pressure at the back of the contraption released. Ropes pulled taught, the claw closed like a fist, and we had the amulet.

"It's a goddamn Christmas miracle!" I yelled into the night sky. Geirr gave me a high five, and I wrapped the man in a slimy tentacle hug that I knew he hated.

"Finally," the man said when I released him. "I . . . Honestly, I didn't think it would work."

"All that matters is it did. Take the machine and the amulet back to your workshop. We'll need it soon enough." For the next step of my plan, I sent a gargoyle to fetch Xollmomath.

We had corpses to reanimate.

CHAPTER 13

"I need more power, master," Xollmomath said between gritted teeth.

He looked older, withered, as though the strain of reanimation was getting to be too much for his ancient frame to take. But he was strong. He would survive.

"Is there anything left to consume?" I asked Geirr. The engineer shook his head. "Damn." Xollmomath had already consumed all the magic items we had looted from the battlefield.

Elyk stepped forward. "Get one of the orbs," he said.

Neither of us knew if it would work, but we had to try. I mentally commanded a pair of gargoyles to push over one of the resurrection orbs, and they quickly worked it into place at the necromancer's side.

"Use the orb," I told the old NPC.

He placed his withered palm against the polished stone surface, but nothing happened. We waited, dark magic swirling from Xollmomath's blackened fingertips to the forty ruined corpses arrayed outside what remained of the guardhouse . . . and nothing happened.

Finally, the old man gave up. His spirit faltered, and he collapsed to the ground. I gave him a few moments to recover his breath. "Did you get anything from the orb?" I eventually asked.

"No. It is . . . obstinate," came his slow answer.

"Shit . . . We need more power!" I yelled, but that much was already obvious. Xollmomath could easily reanimate forty corpses, but only if he did it one at a time. The spell's drain on him compounded with every simultaneous corpse, and what I proposed needed many. I knew he could do it, but we just hadn't found the right power source yet.

When the man recovered his breath, he stood to his full height and smoothed his robes. Then he fixed me with his unnerving stare. "There may be another way," he whispered. His black eyes shifted as though what he was about to tell me was not meant to be heard by human ears. "Do you remember the sacrifice my master made all those years ago?"

The memory, like so many others, was fleeting at best. I could only recall bits and pieces. There was something about a royal family, pools of blood, and porcelain.

"There is power beneath Olympia City. Great power. My master's power. I felt it when we were there, and it felt me. Take me back, and I will locate it."

It all rushed back to me. Xollmomath's story hadn't *really* happened—the game had no ancient history in that sense—but that didn't mean it wasn't programed that way. If an NPC believed something had happened in the past, the evidence of that event would almost certainly be written into the game. That meant there were huge porcelain vats of blood buried beneath Olympia City.

And now there was no one left to guard them.

Elyk, Syzak, Ministrel, and I gathered the next day at dawn. I left Xia in charge of the defenses, but we were still so vulnerable that it probably wouldn't matter one way or the other. I looked over the small crew, then turned my attention to Ministrel. "Eighty-eight fathoms, right?"

The wizard tipped his hat, flashed a crooked smile, and snapped his fingers.

When I opened my eyes, I stood in a grassy field that reminded me of the computer screensaver I used at work. The resemblance was uncanny. The grass was too green, the sun too yellow, and the flowers were too red. It all looked fake.

And there was no ruined city. "Ministrel, you idiot. Where the hell did you take us?"

The old man tipped his hat again and laughed. I wanted to punch him right in his hawkish nose, but I knew he would obliterate me before I ever had the chance. I grabbed him by the shoulders instead, forcing his eyes to find mine. "Where the hell are we?"

He gestured to open pasture of waving grasses and wildflowers with a grin. "Olympia City. Eighty-eight fathoms!"

I sighed. The man was so unreliable that I was starting to regret using him at all. But we still didn't have any other choice. "Well . . ." I looked to the others. "Any ideas?"

Elyk was the only one who looked like he knew something. He paced around, taking in the scene from every angle. "I think we're inside the scene he painted."

"What?"

"Remember the painting on the wall?" Elyk went on.

All I really remembered from that fight was getting our asses kicked and coming damn close to dying. "What are you getting at?"

He mimed Ministrel's paintbrush, and it finally clicked.

"Fucking hell. If we're *inside* his painting, we're fucked," I said. "But the distance was right, wasn't it? Eighty-eight to get to Olympia, though the fathoms bit still makes no sense."

Xollmomath hadn't said anything yet. He was busy running his withered fingers through the waving grass at our waists. "It is here, master. I feel it in my bones."

I shrugged. "Alright. Good enough for me. Lead the way."

As we walked, I figured out exactly what was going on. Beneath the tall grass, we walked among the ruins of Olympia City. We weren't inside Ministrel's painting at all. What he had painted had simply come to pass. Some of the taller buildings stuck up from the fresh layer of dirt, though everything was covered in plant life as though a thousand years had passed. In reality, it had been something like two weeks.

"Here," Xollmomath said after half a mile or better.

A few heavy stone blocks were scattered among the tall grasses, and I guessed they were from the castle, though there was no way to know. But the where and why of it all didn't matter. The important part was under our feet.

"How far down?" I asked the necromancer.

He closed his black eyes and mulled it over. "It is deep. Long forgotten. Hidden beneath both soil and time."

I looked to Syzak and nodded. The shaman was our closest thing to an excavation team. He started slow, using his magic to move only a few feet of dirt and stone at a time. It quickly became apparent that the vessels were buried far deeper than we anticipated, and Syzak cast his most powerful magic, hurling huge chunks of bedrock aside until he was nearly spent.

We found it.

Two massive porcelain vats, buried deep in the natural limestone beneath the castle, and sealed with heavy lids.

Ministrel's task was next. We needed to move the tanks

back to Undercroft Citadel as they were. It was too risky to use shaman magic to try and bring them to the surface. If one of them cracked, truth be told I had no idea what would happen, but I assumed it would be bad.

"Alright, wizard. Take us home and bring the blood!"

The man tsked at me. "I need to touch it," he said, his voice inexplicably chipper.

My stomach churned. "The . . . blood?" I wasn't particularly fond of trying to open one of the vats either. Removing a lid would require more excavation, and I was still very concerned that we would break them in the process.

Before I could ask for more clarification, the wizard took a step off the edge of the hole Syzak bored, and he lazily drifted the hundred or so feet down into the earth to land gently on one of the tanks. "Join me whenever you're ready!" he called.

A headache was starting to form between my eyes as it tended to do whenever I had to interact with Ministrel. The dull throbbing wormed its way right behind the bridge of my nose and settled in for the long haul.

I knew Syzak was too low on energy to carve a staircase for us. He was all but completely drained. Elyk wasn't cut out for it either, and I didn't have any abilities that would be relevant at all, though I spent the better part of ten minutes making sure. "I guess we climb down," I said after a long bit of thinking.

No one else had a better idea, so we climbed. It wasn't as difficult as I first thought it would be. Terrifying, sure, but not actually that challenging. Going down was easier than going up, and Syzak's imprecise magic had left plenty of holds along the jagged rock.

Still, the exercise took us over and hour. I was more pissed off than tired when we reached the bottom, and I just wanted to go home. And if for some reason Ministrel couldn't get us out, the idea of climbing all the way back to the top was something I didn't want to consider. But my fears were assuaged, and the strange wizard teleported us back to Undercroft Citadel in the blink of an eye.

The vats arrived intact, and I finally got a good look at their size. They were huge, probably each something like five hundred gallons. I didn't know how much blood the typical human body contained, but I knew that filling the vats with blood alone would have taken . . . a lot longer than I would have had the stomach to endure.

Our next problem was one I hadn't anticipated. We had no way to move the vats. They stood in the middle of the field not too far from the dead monk and the other corpses Xollmomath had arranged. Using wrecked bits of the old wall, I decided to reinforce the vats so they wouldn't accidentally tip over, and then Xollmomath needed a full day to recover his mana before trying the reanimation spell again.

In the morning, it was showtime. I was eager to see if our plan would work, and the excitement had kept me up most of the night. I rubbed the sleep in my eyes, still missing the coffee we used to brew, and watched the necromancer take up his position before the arrayed corpses once more.

Tendrils of inky black magic snaked from his fingers to the monk, then laced through the forty dead. The magic touched the eyes of each corpse, one by one, and then a second stream of it launched to the nearest blood vat. It enveloped the container, fully obscuring it like a heavy shadow during an eclipse.

And just as quickly as it had begun, the ritual completed. One vat of blood was completely gone. Vanished. Not a trace of the porcelain or its contents remained.

The bones of the forty corpses ripped free of their once-mortal shells. In eerie unison, they drifted from their former homes to the monk, where they reattached themselves in an entirely new pattern. Slowly but surely, Xollmomath's golem took shape. It towered thirty feet high, standing on legs made from entire skeletons, and when it was done, it sported four long arms. The monk's head still remained perched at the top, the only piece of the gruesome puzzle not made of bone, and a bit of blood still dripped from the loose veins and arteries swinging beneath its chin.

The monk's name changed as it came alive. Instead of Aleph, Arbiter of Justice, he was now Aleph, Cenobite of Forlorn Hope.

Aleph's name flashed onto the raid sheet for Undercroft Citadel as a new boss. Our difficulty also climbed from heroic to heroic plus. My influence stat ticked up to forty-three, and my infamy, already absurdly high, reached seven hundred twelve.

The creature bellowed and flexed its four arms. A wave of magical terror spread out from its chest, hitting all of Undercroft Citadel with a momentary spurt of fear. Honestly, I didn't need the magic to feel true terror. Aleph was the single most terrifying thing I had ever seen, either inside the game or back on Earth.

But I wasn't done. Not yet.

"Bow!" I yelled. The creature regarded me for a moment, then dipped its head and shoulders in respect. Its obedience sent another wave through my body, though it was one of joy and relief instead of awe and horror. I gave it a handful of other commands, and Aleph obeyed without question. My influence stat was high enough to perfectly command it.

Bring the axe, I silently told my gargoyles. A pair of them flapped out on heavy stone wings a few moments later and dropped the gargantuan weapon into two of Aleph's four hands. It almost looked small when compared to the megalithic construct. Almost.

"Are you really going to do it?" Elyk asked at my side.

I wasn't sure. "Maybe . . . Probably." I mulled it over another thousand times, but it was no use. I wouldn't be able to use logic to predict what would happen next. I simply didn't know. I sighed. "Yes. Either this works—"

"Or it kills us all," Elyk finished for me.

I turned to Geirr. "Bring the necklace."

The engineer nodded, his face a mask of terror. We were all scared, but if it worked, it would be worth it. The trick would be getting the amulet around the monk's head in the first place. I couldn't just have a gargoyle fly it up there.

I commanded the massive beast to lower its head, and Geirr maneuvered the small wooden crane into position as best he could with shaking hands. "You're sure?" he asked.

I wanted to say no. I wanted to tell him I was just as scared as he was. But I couldn't show any signs of trepidation. Not now. "Do it."

It took two tries to get the amulet around the dead monk's severed head, but it worked. I ordered Aleph to stand, which he did, and then I swung my phase blade as hard as I could for his leg. My blade never touched bone. It couldn't harm him at all.

Everyone breathed a collective sigh of relief. "Do not hurt anyone loyal to Undercroft Citadel without a direct command from me," I told the construct. I got the familiar mental notion that the creature understood and would obey, and I thanked whatever lucky stars I had for my incredible influence stat. Without it, I would never hope to control anything as powerful as Aleph, and I had just made it completely immune to everything and everyone I knew. But I also made it immune to probably half the players in Wonder.

As long as I kept control, we would be unstoppable. My mind went first to Hel and her guild, the warlock's indomitable construct. They were evil, and they wouldn't stand a chance. We just needed to find where they were hiding, get Aleph there, and the Hunger God guild would fall in an hour.

Having Aleph also meant I finally had something large enough and strong enough to do some heavy lifting. I had the massive creature carry the second tank of magic blood into the main part of the base, and we propped it up against the reflecting pool. I shuddered to think what would happen if I mixed the two liquids. I had no idea, but I knew it wouldn't be good.

I considered setting Aleph to work on the walls, but what was the point? We would almost certainly be attacked again before we could complete anything substantial. No, we needed to go on the offensive. Taking cities unawares was a hundred times more effective than building defenses.

Two of the remaining capitals, Iron Hall and New Karstad, were already at war. At least they were when Kadorax had gotten his information. Regardless, they would be easier to topple than Bellefontaine or Redwing's Bastion, so they were my next targets. What I really wanted was to hit another city right in the middle of a huge fight like we had done at Olympia City. If I could just take Xollmomath and Aleph, leaving all the angels behind, I could replenish our zombie army in a single day. Then I could take the army to the next city, conquering with ease and growing stronger after every battle.

We spent a week preparing. Our new blacksmith proved extremely beneficial, and along with Geirr, he was able to get all of our siege weapons into working order. He even had time to finish a few projects for the gnomes and make a few pieces of armor. Sadly, he didn't know any patterns for people of my unnatural stature, but it was nice seeing Xia in more than just a flowing red robe.

As the days passed, my physical appearance continued to alter. It was subtle, but once I started paying specific attention to it, the changes were unmistakable. What I thought were two additional eyes coming into place above my original pair turned out to be true. They didn't work particularly well in daylight, so I opted to keep them closed which didn't take a whole lot of mental effort. Based on the rest of my squid-like body, I had a feeling that the eyes were designed for underwater use. I just hadn't quite gotten around to installing a pool and clubhouse at Undercroft Citadel to give them a try. We still had half a year before the anticipated reopening of the portals, and I wondered what I would look like when that day finally came. I'd barely be recognizable as human, if it all.

But there were other players who had changed races. It wasn't just me. Before the server crashes, when players like the gnomes died, they would respawn back at their beacons in the real world as humans. The last update from the devs made me wonder, though. If I truly was their ancient cosmic god with planned crossover events into the real world, it would make sense for my form not to revert back to human. I would step through the portal and remain the same hideous monster on both sides.

At least for now, there was nothing I could do about that. Fortunately, I had other, much more pressing issues to occupy my mind than the gruesome visage I saw in the mirror.

Of the cities left to sack, Ministrel had only been to one of them. That meant he could teleport us to Iron Hall, and we were completely out of options when it came to the other three. Teleportation was inherently a wizard spell, and we needed to find other wizards who could do it. Alyssa, the undead arcanist, would perhaps be able to learn mass teleportation if she reached a high enough level, but that was now out of the question given her lack of mortal consciousness. And besides, I hadn't seen the woman in weeks. I assumed she was out somewhere in the forests and plains beyond

Wolfpine, but it was just a guess. Perhaps she had been killed. Only time would tell.

Our last information regarding Iron Hall was from Kadorax, and the assassin had described it similarly to Olympia City. Guilds were at war over the resurrection orb, and I took that as a generally good thing. War and chaos meant weaker defenses. It also meant there would be evil guilds, and we needed allies badly.

The team I assembled to hit Iron Hall was small. Elyk and I would try to discern the battle lines and make allies where we could. Xollmomath and Aleph would go together to make allies on their own. We needed corpses, and Aleph was the most adept killing machine I had ever witnessed in Wonder, so corpses he would make. For added measure, Kevin was going with the corpse harvesting team. I thought of any guilds getting in their way and had to laugh. Yes, they would make corpses. Thousands of them.

CHAPTER 14

Ministrel's spell was as instantaneous as ever. One second we stood in the morning light just outside Undercroft Citadel, and then the next moment we were deep inside Iron Hall's formidable walls. I quickly counted our squad . . . and someone was missing.

"*Fuck me . . .*"

"Aleph didn't make the trip," Elyk said.

I felt like none of us had really thought it through, but I had to take the blame. "That's on me," I said with a sigh. "The immunity to evil applied to Ministrel's spells. Shit. Well . . . New plan. I'm going solo. Elyk, you're the new butcher of Iron Hall. Get as many zombies as you can, and we'll meet back here at sundown. Got it?"

Elyk started to protest but thought better of it and just agreed. "If you aren't back by dusk—"

"We'll figure it out," I said. "Now . . . where are we?"

Ministrel traced a long, withered finger along the stone wall behind us. "Seventy-nine fathoms," he cryptically answered.

The room was stone, and it had the cool feel of an

underground chamber. The ceiling was high, and torches lined the walls about half way up. It was likely a large storage room, though for what I didn't know.

The only door was unlocked, and I cracked it open just a few inches. I had just peeked through the crack when Ministrel shouldered past me and stepped into the hallway without a care in the world. He strolled off, muttering to himself, and then turned a corner and was gone.

"Alright, meet back here at dusk. Happy hunting, friend." I gave Elyk a nod and then darted out in the opposite direction from Ministrel.

Iron Hall was built half underground on the side of a mountain. It was one of my favorite cities, but I only knew it from a handful of streams. All of those streams felt like they were from a different lifetime, as though the memories weren't actually mine but someone else's, and I could just view bits and pieces of them. Perhaps it was so long ago that I barely remembered any of it. What I did know was that the center of the mountain held a dungeon that tons of players continually farmed for experience and loot. If I was here for leisure, I'd probably find a group at one of Iron Hall's taverns and run the dungeon, but not today.

I was surprised when I turned the corner and actually found a sign with directions. Echelon only had a few street signs, and I didn't remember seeing any in Olympia City. Iron Hall was much more centrally planned as opposed to an organic metropolis, and one of the developers had seen fit to add some guides. To my left was another long subterranean hallway that led to the military quarter, and to my right was a mechanical lift. I opted first for the military area. If there were still a bunch of city guards in the barracks, it would mean the battles outside were finished. The fact that I hadn't seen anyone yet, either an NPC or another player, made me think that everyone was outside fighting.

I reached the military quarter and found the heavy iron door unlocked. No one was inside. A few odds and ends of armor and weapons were scattered about, but it wasn't much. It looked like everyone had left in a hurry, and no one had yet returned. What I needed to find was a mage quarter or wizard guild or alchemy lab—anywhere that might have an evil wizard with a teleportation spell looking for a new allegiance.

I left the military quarter and finally saw my first NPCs of Iron Hall. Three dwarves carried wooden boxes full of what appeared to be junk, and they were headed in my direction. I guessed that none of them would recognize my name so far from Echelon, and I was right. They stopped politely when I waved them down.

"Do you have a mage guild here?" I asked.

The one in the middle answered me. "Top floor, near the main gate. Look for the blue banner."

"Thanks," I said, and I let the dwarves go on their way. I found a staircase spiraling upward and took it to the highest level. I had no idea just how high that was since there were no windows to the outside world. Again, I came across a somewhat disconcerting lack of people. Where had everyone gone? It was a question to answer later.

The top of the spiral stairs presented only one option, and it was a very surprising one: a garden. Winding paths, lush lawns, and blossoming flowers stretched as far as I could see. All of it was still underground, and it was illuminated by magic lights suspended on thin wires from the ceiling. I wondered how anyone had unlocked a spell to generate UV light as it genuinely didn't seem like something that would exist in the game. Outside of a subterranean garden like the one I stood in, what benefit would the spell confer? None that I could think of.

I considered turning back. Was there really a wizard guild

at the end of the garden? I had no idea. But what other option did I have? Iron Hall was a city of thousands, hundreds of thousands, and I barely knew the first thing about the layout. I walked the serene pathways for quite some time, crossing small wooden bridges and taking in the sights like a tourist. It was peaceful, relaxing, and the more I stayed in the garden, the more I *wanted* to stay in the garden. I could live there. It had plenty of fruit trees, and I saw dozens of different species of fish populating the small streams beneath the bridges.

The garden had everything. It was perfect.

I found a small bench just beyond one of the quaint bridges, and it looked to be as good a place as any to rest my tentacles. I had been walking for . . . well, I didn't quite know. It was getting dim overhead. I sat on the bench and stretched out my legs, resting my head on the polished wooden armrest. It wasn't a bed, but it was cozy enough. A warm breeze fluttered through the area, rustling the leaves over my head.

I drifted off to sleep.

And there she was. Helvegen. She stood tall, but it wasn't an aggressive posture. She looked . . . happy. Peaceful. Beautiful. She smiled.

"What are you doing here?" I asked, and my voice echoed strangely in the dream space.

She stepped forward, and I noticed for the first time that we were no longer in the garden. We were somewhere else, somewhere completely foreign to me. A few buildings dotted the horizon, but they were too far away for any details.

Helvegen reached out a hand and gently brushed my forearm. Her touch sent an electric shiver through my entire body. How long had it been? Too long was all I knew.

"Shhh," she whispered. Her voice was just as sweet as I remembered.

"Where are we?" I wanted to look around more, to figure

out our surroundings, but something about her face had me captivated. I couldn't move my eyes to anything else.

"Somewhere safe," she answered after a moment. Her other hand found my back, and we embraced.

There was something about it all that just didn't make sense. The last time I saw Hel, I had killed her. Or . . . no, that wasn't quite right, was it? I couldn't remember. "This fucking curse," I growled under my breath.

Hel pulled back, suddenly startled. "What is it?"

I brought her in tight once more, relishing the warmth of her body pressed against mine. "I just . . . can't remember."

She nuzzled into my chest.

Where did I see her? It wasn't that long ago; I was sure of it. I forced my mind into a backward jog, recounting as much as I could from every single day in reverse order until I found it.

The Jade Spire. She was there. And she had a guild. What was their name? It didn't matter. My grip grew tighter around her shoulders, and Hel squirmed.

"Gentle now, Ben," she cooed. "Shhh . . . You're safe. No more hurting people. Just . . . close your eyes . . . relax . . . take a deep breath . . ."

I tried to do as she said, but without the need for oxygen, taking a deep breath was awkward, and my lungs stabbed with a series of sharp pains. I expected the momentary pain to fade, but it didn't. It grew.

And it grew fast.

Now I was the one trying to break off the embrace. "Something is wrong, Hel!" my dream-self shouted.

She shook her head and held tight. "Not now, Ben. It will pass. It will all be over soon. Don't fight it, just accept peace. Shhh . . ."

The woman flickered. Her form became blurry around the edges, and for a split second, I swore I saw someone else behind her. Someone familiar standing in a room I couldn't quite see.

None of it made sense. And the pain only grew sharper. It enveloped my entire chest. I'd never had a heart attack, but I had seen enough of them on television to know the signs, and I started to seriously consider it a possibility.

Was I about to die? Laid low by a simply cardiac arrest right in the middle of the greatest campaign Wonder had ever seen?

Campaign . . . the thought brought another memory. I was here for a reason, but where was *here*? I didn't know. One of the cities. It had to be.

Images of Iron Hall snapped into place. I was in the underground mountain city, and I hadn't yet sacked it. If I died, I would simply resurrect at the orb.

The pain was nearly unbearable, and Hel could no longer support my weight. I dropped hard to the ground, cracking my head against something solid that jarred my vision again. Suddenly, the dream world vanished. My eyes were open, I was awake, and I was nowhere near the pristine garden. All of it was gone. I wasn't even in Iron Hall. That much was evident simply by the visible sky above Augustine, Sower of Discord.

The man wore a smile, much the same as I had seen on him before.

My faculties returned all at once in a fiery, jumbled heap of sensory inputs and rapid neurological analysis. I had been captured. The how or when of it didn't matter. Someone was digging a knife at the base of my skull, right above my armor. Somewhere nearby, there were enough corpses to regenerate the constant damage being done by the slow decapitation, but I easily sensed that the supply of the dead was not limitless.

Someone was on top of me, pinning me down. I quickly

activated *Memory Eater*, and the last few minutes of Hel's life flashed through my memory.

The garden wasn't real. Neither were the dwarves inside the city. The city itself was an illusion. It was grand, and the woman had consumed legendary amounts of magic to pull it off, but it was all a fabrication. Somewhere in the darkness of Ministrel's teleportation spell, the warlock had caught us. The trap had already been set, and Augustine had simply redirected the teleportation right into it.

Lady Kalma's curse was the only thing keeping me alive—and neither Helvegen nor the warlock knew it existed or how it worked. In the effort of saving time, they had elected not to remove my armor, and though I saw in Hel's memories that the warlock had tried to kill me with magic first, it hadn't worked. That's when they switched to the knife. If I wasn't actively consuming corpses from somewhere nearby, they would have easily severed my spine and removed my head altogether.

Everything flashed through my mind in the span of a microsecond, and I instantly activated *The Basalt Monolith.*

Augustine screamed. I couldn't tell if it was from disappointment or terror or both. Hel issued a stream of curses as well. My addled brain swam with the exertion of casting the empowered spell, but I would recover long before its protection ever faded. From my strange, unnatural viewpoint within the hardened rock, I saw the corpse of the person who had been behind me with the knife. He was dead, impaled on one of the monolith's spikes, and his life force was the last I needed to reach full health.

I was happy to see that the rest of the Hunger God guild wasn't there. It was either a small operation, or perhaps my angels had killed more of the guild than I realized.

My black pillar of stone stood on a gentle hillside near some scraggly pines. The buildings off in the distance came into view just a little clearer, and I realized that it was Undercroft Citadel. The tall spire marking my bedroom at the very top was unmistakable. We were still on Echelon's continent. We'd barely gone half a mile, and that meant Hel and the warlock had set their trap practically on my front door.

Anger boiled inside me. Getting caught was one thing, get caught by Helvegen was another, and getting caught right outside my own home was the worst of them all.

But they didn't think it through. We were too close to Undercroft Citadel. The connection between my curse and my zombies was what kept me alive, and it also meant I could still mentally command all the undead.

Another pang of energy drained from my body, but I was so filled with rage that it barely registered. I mentally summoned Aleph, and the colossal bone golem readily obeyed. It lumbered toward me, and a host of Lady Kalma's red-winged angels supported it to either side. *Kill everyone except the painter. Leave her alive.*

I released my hold on *The Basalt Monolith* the moment my army got into range. Everything erupted into chaos. Activating *Pull from the Darkness*, I launched a massive spectral creature at the warlock and then sprinted toward the trees. Angels descended in a brutal wave of scythes and wings all around us.

As I suspected would happen, the warlock turned once again to his most powerful spell, and a gaping rift cracked through the hillside. The brass construct emerged on heavy legs made of loud pistons and whirling gears. The warlock then turned back to my shadow pet. Much to my dismay, he was able to counter the incorporeal demon with magic of his own, and my pet was quickly obliterated.

Then, amidst the fluttering of crimson wings, Aleph entered the fight.

The warlock's construct charged, and I was surprised

when it landed a hit. The creature was neutral in the same way that shaman magic manipulating the ground was. The thing didn't have any morality or consciousness to be evil regardless of who summoned it. I wondered if the same game logic would apply to Aleph itself. Hopefully we would never find a second amulet to test it.

Aleph knocked aside the construct's claws and then delivered a strike of its own with Faidra's axe. The construct dodged, but the shockwave of the attack was still enough to stagger everyone. At least thirty feet away, I felt the blow reverberate through the ground. Faidra's axe kicked up a wave of dirt, and then Aleph wrenched it free and swung again with astounding speed. The giant held the axe in its two right arms, leaving the pair on the left free to rip up huge chunks of the ground and throw them.

The battle did not last long. Aleph was simply too strong, too quick, and too large. The construct landed a handful of slashes with its huge claws that would have easily been lethal against a more normal sized opponent, but Aleph just didn't care. At the same time, the warlock hammered into the giant with spell after spell—and not a single one landed. The bone golem's flawless immunity held, and it crushed the warlock's construct into the dirt with ease. Then a heavy strike from Faidra's axe ended it altogether.

Augustine, Sower of Discord, turned and fled. The man was on foot, and his white horse quickly materialized beneath him. Aleph chased him into the woods, thrashing trees to pulp, and a host of my angels tracked the man from above. There was nowhere he could possibly run.

Bring him back alive if you can, I mentally told my entire army. *If he dies, so be it. Just make it slow.*

That brought my thoughts and attention back to Helvegen. She was somewhere close. And the woman was a master of disguise and illusion. Finding her anywhere would be a challenge, but finding her in an unfamiliar part of the forest would be nearly impossible. Only a moment later, I got the mental feeling back in response from Aleph that the warlock had been taken down. The unrefined emotion wasn't specific enough to tell me if the man was dead, only that he had been overcome. I quickly pushed the warlock from my mind.

Sweep the woods. Find her. I conjured up an image of Hel, though I wasn't sure if my connection to my underlings as a raid boss allowed for that kind of complex telepathic communication. I turned to join them, my sword at the ready, and the idea of a second ambush after the first failed so spectacularly made me laugh.

Only a minute into the search, I heard her. I would recognize her voice anywhere.

"Ben," she said quietly from somewhere to my right.

I looked, but there was no one. "Show yourself."

She flickered into view as the last bit of energy left her body. The grand illusion of Iron Hall had sapped every ounce from her body, and there was nothing left for her to maintain another spell. She collapsed against a tree only twenty or thirty yards from where I had stood to watch Aleph fight the construct.

I kept my distance. The woman was out of stamina, sure, but that didn't mean she was out of tricks. She was never out of those.

"Why are you here?"

Her eyes met mine, and part of me still longed to get lost in them again. To feel the warmth of her embrace. But I knew it was all lies, just like the dream she had used to capture me in the first place.

"To kill you," she answered quietly.

"I know that. Why are you *still* here?"

She shrugged. "I probably could have gotten away . . .

I'm just so tired. But would it have mattered in the long run? You're going to kill everyone in Wonder, aren't you?"

I wasn't sure how to interpret her words. Mentally, I called off my army and sent them back to Undercroft with whatever was left of the warlock. All but one. I wanted Aleph close just in case, and the towering amalgamation of bone and deadly magic lumbered to my side before long.

"Yes," I finally answered, though the woman knew my ultimate goals perhaps better than anyone.

Her eyes fell to my feet. "Then what does it matter? You kill me now, or you kill me in six months. Either way, I'm dead."

It was hard to argue against her logic. The only way she would ever see Earth again was if I failed. If someone like her killed me before I managed to finish the task.

"When you . . . killed me the first time," she continued, still not meeting my gaze, "I decided I wanted to live. Though I guess I always have. That's why I joined you in the first place. And now . . . the best way to survive—"

"Is to kill me."

She sighed. "Yes."

Again, it was hard to argue against her logic. It all made sense. "How do I know all this isn't another trick? Just another grand illusion, and another idiot with a knife won't jump out of the shadows to lop off my head?"

She laughed and flicked her eyes to mine. "Because it didn't fucking work the first two times! Somehow, you've become immortal. That much is clear."

I tried in vain to detect the lie. Everything made sense. It all felt honest. And I *knew* Helvegen. She wasn't some random enemy from another guild begging for her life. She was Hel. Her brother worked for me only a few hundred yards away. She had shared my bed at the top of Undercroft Citadel.

"What would you have me do?" I asked.

She pushed herself up a little bit against the tree and then held out her nine-fingered hand. "Either kill me and get it over with . . . or help me up."

CHAPTER 15

I sat on the stairs in front of my room and pondered. Or perhaps 'ruminated' was the better word. As far as I knew, rumination involved replaying the same decision over and over and over again, so it fit the bill. I sat on the stairs well into night and ruminated.

When dawn came, I was still there, though my mind no longer turned on wheels of torment. It begged for sleep instead, and I had given it some, though not much. Elyk and Ministrel were gone, lost somewhere in the vast expanse of Iron Hall. They had no idea where I was or what had happened to me. I could only hope they would return at some point to try and find an answer to that question.

Down in the ossuary, spread on Lady Kalma's altar and stiff as a board, was a corpse. Cleaved nearly in half by Faidra's huge axe, it was a ghastly sight. I regretted the death, though only partially. To Lady Kalma, even a corpse had purpose, and I was determined to make good use of the newest one to grace our chapel. With any luck, Augustine would be resurrected as another powerful warlock to add to the ranks.

That brought my mind back to Helvegen. She had filled nearly every thought I had over the last eight hours. The woman was alive, and I didn't know yet if that decision was the correct one. Perhaps I would never know. Or, more likely, I would find out decisively and all at once when she betrayed me. It wouldn't be another burst of magic against my indomitable armor or a knife at my throat. She would never make those mistakes again.

But I believed her when she said she wanted to live. And I knew she would do whatever it took to stay alive. When I killed her before, logic dictated that she would run away. I could not fault her for that. Her logic was also correct that I was the number one threat to her ongoing survival—as I was the greatest threat to *everyone* trapped in Wonder—and killing me was the best way to ensure her survival. All of it was undeniably true.

If the woman really was looking out solely for her own interests, which I had no reason to doubt, then what she told me in the woods outside Undercroft Citadel was also true: either I needed to kill her right there, or I needed to bring her back. There was no third option. If I let her go, she would have to find a new way to kill me, and we'd be back to square one.

So . . . should I have killed her?

Probably.

And I still might.

Just . . . not today. There was too much work to be done, and ever since she left, there had been no one to manage it all. No one to organize and give me daily progress reports. And perhaps there was another reason. Perhaps I still felt something for her. I didn't know. Had I ever loved anyone before? I had a daughter, Ingrid, and I loved her deeply. Hel was also at least partly responsible for Ingrid's death. But did I ever love Ingrid's mother? I couldn't even remember her name.

Did I love Hel?

I caught a glimpse of the woman before I had time to ruminate any deeper on the question. She walked with her arm draped around her brother, a cup of what I guessed was water in her hand. She had spent the night with Geirr, and he burst into tears at the first sight of her. The two had been inseparable ever since, though she'd only been back for a few hours.

I watched the two of them go to the storerooms for something to eat, and then they embraced before going their separate ways to their tasks. Geirr went back to his workshop with the gnomes and our newest NPC blacksmith, and Hel began her morning rounds with a clipboard and parchment.

For a fleeting moment, things felt normal. It bordered on placid. Then my gaze drifted to our collection of non-functioning resurrection orbs, and I was quickly reminded of the grim tasks ahead of us. We were making quick progress, but I knew the challenges would only get harder. The number of active campaigns on the raid sheet was down from nearly four hundred to just over two hundred. I didn't think it was because people were giving up. No, I knew it was the opposite. Guilds were forming larger alliances. The true difficulty of Undercroft Citadel was known to Wonder at large, and that meant rival guilds would be setting aside their differences to face a common enemy. The remaining cities would be hardening their defenses as best they could.

We got lucky with Olympia City, and I got lucky again at The Jade Spire. The rest would not be so easy. Rumors spread like wildfire, and those rumors would also grow like wildfire. Survivors from The Jade Spire would not doubt already be spreading tales of winged angels cutting down their friends with impunity. Survivors from Olympia—if there were any—would tell tales of a city that simply no longer existed.

Fear, in the short term, bred chaos and disorganization. Such faults naturally led to conquest and destruction. But over enough time, fear gave way to preparedness and shared animosity. Petty squabbles and rival factions within cities or even continents meant nothing when faced with the prospect of complete annihilation. Soon, perhaps over the next three or four weeks, I knew we would face the next challenge. It wouldn't be a single guild or even an alliance of guilds. No, it would be a true and proper army. A hundred thousand players and probably double that number of NPCs would arrive at our doorstep.

I remembered the fight against Resurrection and how close we had come to defeat, and I started to feel like I had made the correct decision when I kept Hel alive. Even if she was ultimately a dagger waiting in the shadows to kill me, we needed all the help we could get. *I* needed her. And, if I was being honest with myself, I missed her company. But we were still far from friends. It was . . . tense, to say the least.

For Hel's first day back, I was happy to see her jumping into her old role so eagerly. She was intent on getting the walls repaired and rebuilt. It was a tall task without the orcs, but not impossible. The undead knight, Sir Drevan, was still able bodied enough to swing a hammer and drag logs into place. Aleph, under Xia's command, was able to fill the same role as the charnel golem when we built the walls in the first place. Before evening, we had measurable progress, and I was happy to see it.

Still, I knew that whatever force attacked next, it would be far beyond anything a simply wooden wall could repel. For now, the wall would serve more as a simple battle line than an actual defensive structure, and that was just fine.

Sometime after dusk, I heard a fizzle and pop in the courtyard that jarred me from my inner reflection. I hadn't moved much from the stairs, but the new action had me sprinting with my sword in a moment. There, in the middle of the courtyard where I expected some new and terrible enemy, stood Elyk and Ministrel. Both of them appeared bewildered, but Elyk quickly regained his composure. A quick scan told me he was banged up, but it wasn't bad. The wizard, in usual fashion, wandered off without so much as a glance in my direction.

"What happened?" I demanded.

Elyk asked the same thing at the same time, and it took us a few seconds to sort out our questions. "I thought you were dead!" he finally exclaimed. "Ministrel and I appeared inside Iron Hall, and fucking hell broke loose. It was a war, Ben! You should have seen it! We had to retreat, but we had no idea where we were going. Just tunnel after tunnel of NPCs and players and shops and everything else. We hit a dead end and had to make a stand, but where the hell were you? What the hell happened?"

I caught a glimpse of Helvegen watching us from the doorway to the workshop and indicated her with a nod. Elyk's eyes went wide.

I cut him off before he could make a scene over her return. "It was her fault. That warlock nabbed me right out of the spell, made me think I was with you in Iron Hall, and then . . ."

"The fuck is she doing alive?" His voice came out as a growl. His eyes never left her. If there was one thing I could be certain of in the entire world, it was Elyk's undying loyalty. If I told the man to walk through hell and back for me, he'd only ask when.

"It's alright," I said, though I only half believed it myself. "She wants to live. The warlock is dead. Aleph tore him up pretty good. And her guild is all dead too. She thinks I'm immortal." I lowered my voice to a whisper. "Don't tell her about the curse . . . just in case."

The man visibly relaxed, though only a fraction.

"So, what happened in the city? You guys fled?" I asked.

He nodded. "Not much just the two of us could do without at least a map. Never even saw the resurrection orb. The city was ready for us, too. If we hadn't been teleported right into the middle, we probably wouldn't have made any dent at all. When we hit it again, we'll need an army."

"I figured as much. Speaking of which, let's get Xollmomath and resurrect a warlock, shall we?"

A few moments later, the three of us were gathered in the ossuary around Augustine's corpse. Helvegen lingered a few paces back with her brother. Neither of them said a word.

"I need him to come back with all his magic," I told the ancient necromancer. Just from recent experience, I knew he was powerfully versed in teleportation of some kind, and that was my main goal.

Xollmomath studied the rent body for a moment. "He was powerful in life. He will be powerful in death, as well."

"And the teleportation?"

The necromancer tranced a long, withered finger up the length of Augustine's bloody arm. "There is a way, though I have not performed the ritual in some time. Bring the wizard. I will require additional magic."

"Well . . . I *hate* the sound of that, but let's do it," I said more to myself than anyone in the room. Using Ministrel for virtually anything was an enormous risk, and using him to help an NPC perform a death ritual felt particularly dangerous. There were only a million different ways the crazy old man could send things off the rails.

I reluctantly shelved my hesitation, and we found Ministrel quietly meditating near the inert resurrection orbs. He didn't respond in any meaningful way when I demanded he join us at the ossuary, but thankfully my influence stat paired with an activation of *Visage of the Dark One* got his feet moving. I honestly didn't know what the hell I would do without the spell. Ministrel would be uncontrollable, that much was certain.

Back at the ossuary, Xollmomath dragged Augustine's corpse next to the reflecting pool. He propped it up against the pool with a few sticks to keep him from falling. "Once I begin the ritual, I will need you to lend your strength, wizard," he said, and his voice sounded more like a threat than an explanation.

"Do it," I added with a bit more magic to ensure Ministrel's compliance.

A circle of blue and green magic swirled to life beneath Augustine's ravaged body. Smokey tendrils grew from its edges, wrapping around the corpse until it was completely obscured. Slowly, the smoke gave way to fire, consuming Augustine's body in a pillar of bright red and orange that reached all the way to the clouds. Then Xollmomath pointed a hand at Ministrel, and the wizard was suddenly bound to him with a taut band of shimmering blue magic.

The combination of their powers wasn't anything like when Xollmomath had teamed up with Faidra to strengthen one of her spells. That had appeared consensual. Nothing about what Xollmomath was doing to Ministrel felt like the wizard had a say in the matter. Quite the opposite, Ministrel shrieked and fought, waving his hands before falling painfully to his knees, but the blue band connecting them did not falter.

Ministrel's resistance stopped altogether. He was still alive, but his eyes rolled to the back of his head, and his tongue lolled out the side of his mouth.

Another minute elapsed before the pillar of fire surrounding Augustine's corpse finally jettisoned into the sky and vanished forever. Xollmomath lowered his hands, and the blue bond connecting him to Ministrel's supply of magic evaporated as well. It was finished.

Where Augustine's corpse had been just moments before, now there stood a bone archway crafted from his remains. A spider web of pale green tendrils filled the arch. Ministrel moaned and writhed on the ground to my right. And there was no trace of Augustine whatsoever. I figured his bones had made the arch, and what was left of his organs comprised the webbing.

Xollmomath took a bow. "The warlock's magic, master," he said.

I was tempted to touch the green tendrils, but the last time I stuck my fingers where they didn't belong, I ended up cursed. "What does it do?" I asked.

The necromancer rubbed at his black eyes. The ritual had drained him as well as Ministrel, just not nearly to the same degree. "You asked for teleportation. It will take you anywhere the warlock had been in life."

"What's the drawback? I've seen enough of Lady Kalma's bullshit to know it isn't that simple," I said, imagining some brand-new hell the gate would put us through. Nothing was ever as simple as organizing a bunch of bones into an arch and then getting to waltz right through it.

"Watch your blasphemy, master. The goddess hears all," was Xollmomath's cryptic response.

Ministrel groaned and got to his knees, brushing some of the dirt from his robe. "It takes a life to turn on," he said. The wizard was still out of breath and struggling to put himself together.

"There it is. Thank you, Ministrel. And sorry about the . . . you know. My apologies."

He scowled, but he stood and tipped his hat nonetheless before sauntering off.

"He's been everywhere," someone said from behind me,

and I turned to see Hel standing sheepishly with her brother at the side of the ossuary.

"What's that?"

"Augustine. The warlock. He has been to many places. Probably every capital city. He told me stories of them. He has been to many other places as well."

I thought of Hel spending long nights with her head on a pillow next to Augustine as he regaled her with tales of the game. I expected it to make me angry, but it didn't. The man was dead. He was no threat to me now.

"Well, we need to find a few fresh sacrifices," I said to everyone. "This continent is massive. Hundreds of thousands of square miles. There might have only been one resurrection orb and one capital city, but there are thousands of other towns and hamlets out there. We'll leave on an expedition in the morning."

Everyone went back to their tasks except Hel. It was the first time I had seen her back in Undercroft without her protective brother at her side. She had the look of someone who needed to ask a question but was too afraid to raise her voice. It was a look I had seen her wear before.

"Out with it," I said, already impatient.

"Am I going with you tomorrow?"

"No—well . . ." I didn't like the idea of leaving her at the necropolis without me. Sure, I could have Elyk watch over her, but his talents were better put to use on missions that didn't involve babysitting. "Yes. You're coming with us tomorrow. Get some rest. Find a weapon if you use one." I waved her off. "You already know where everything is."

I ascended the stairs to my room in a sour mood that I knew was going to get worse before I was able to sleep. The requirement of a sacrifice for the portal to work was annoying, and perhaps it was the final straw that tipped me over the edge.

I still kicked myself for letting Hel live. Sure, I needed my manager back, but what was there to manage? Everything was still fucked from the last attack. The attack *her* guild had orchestrated. If I had any sense at all, I would go find her and ram my sword through her guts once and for all.

And what pissed me off the most was that I couldn't. I just didn't have it in me.

I sighed. At least I finally knew that I *did* feel something for her. Even if it was just the connection of friendship and loyalty, it was more than nothing.

After a long while, I determined that whatever I felt was due in large part to the fact that she was a player. A real human being. We didn't have many of those around Undercroft Citadel. Ellen was dead, Kevin was undead, and that didn't leave too many other options. Perhaps if Ministrel ever got his wits sorted, we would become friends. It was certainly a possibility, however remote. Sir Drevan and Faidra were both gone too.

I shuddered to think what I would do if Elyk died. Or worse, if he betrayed me.

In the darkness of my bedroom, I resolved to find more than just a few players to feed to Xollmomath's bone gate. I needed to find entire guilds. Evil would flock to me, as the curse said, so it shouldn't be that hard to make more allies. We would fly out in the morning, find the largest town we could, and bring back both captives and new players to swell the ranks.

Aleph was too large to fly with the angels, and on top of that, they couldn't touch him to lift him up. I opted to bring thirty of the angels, and I kept the player team to the originals: just Elyk, Helvegen, and me. The angels carried us high over the trees, and it took miles before we found anything interesting. The nearest villages were all abandoned or burned, and that didn't surprise me. I imagined the exodus after Echelon fell was significant.

We saw a few small settlements, but none of them were large enough to make it worth the stop. Two or three buildings at a crossroad, or a little farm homestead with a stable—none of them were worth our time.

The first real town we came to reminded me of Riverside. There were a few streets, some general industry, and enough houses to make me think at least a few hundred people lived there. Still, a few hundred wasn't enough. I signaled for us to land, though I had no intention of spending more than a few minutes in the town.

"I just want directions to the nearest city," I told the others. "Come on. The angels can stay here."

We marched out from the woods to the first street, and a few NPCs gave us casual waves. No one ran in panic at our presence, though none of them were players. I picked the tallest building on the street and went right for it.

Inside, a pair of NPCs were arguing over something when our arrival interrupted them. One of them, a grandfatherly type with a long beard and a bit of cloudiness to his eyes, immediately dove into what I assumed was a programmed speech about teaching the town to defend themselves from local raiders.

"Hey! We're just here for some information," I loudly interrupted. The man didn't stop his rambling, clearly trying to give us a quest, so I made quick work of him on the edge of my sword.

The second NPC, a woman probably about the same age, shrieked and tried to run, but we were standing between her and the only door. Hel caught her by the shirt and held her in place.

"Where's the nearest major city? And not Echelon," I demanded. I had to ask it two more times before the NPC stopped sputtering about her dead husband long enough for us to answer, but she did, and that was all that mattered.

We got our directions and were back up in the air only a few minutes later. The next town of any substantial size was another twelve miles north of the village which put it somewhere around thirty or so miles from Undercroft Citadel. Of course, I was completely guessing as I had no idea how quickly the angels could fly or how much time had passed.

The town stood on the edge of a lake, serenely nestled into the forest like a postcard. All it needed was a mountain in the distance with a ski lodge at the bottom and a chair lift. Streets had grown up organically among the trees, winding and snaking in harmony with the natural architecture instead of overcoming it with an artificial grid. The houses and buildings were generally the same. They fit into the forest organically. Even the farms, of which there were not many, did not make perfect squares as they did elsewhere in Wonder. Out on the lake, a fleet of fishing boats plied the waters for the day's catch.

We landed in the only small clearing we could find. It was a patch of golden wheat swaying between a row of windmills near the side of the lake. No sooner had we landed than a farmer came out from one of the mills to greet us. Unlike at the previous village, this one was a player, an elf, and he instantly knew that the army of undead angels at his doorstep wasn't there for a simple social visit. The man ran for his life, and two other players evacuated the mills in short order behind the first.

"Let them run," I said, though I didn't need to. Elyk and Hel hadn't taken a step, and the angels wouldn't attack without my command. “Let’s see what kind of resistance they can muster. I kind of want a fight. Just enough to break their spirit. We need living players for the gate, after all.”

“What do you need me to do?” Hel asked. She had the familiar battle-ready calm in her voice that I knew so well.

“When they break, show them no exit. Wall them in so they surrender.”

She nodded and set her feet. I arrayed our angels in three rows of ten with the final row flying about fifteen feet above the ground. Soon enough, the town’s guards appeared at the edge of the mill.

There weren’t many. Some were NPCs, others were players. They all looked nervous. The highest level among them was a twenty-six carpenter. The man held a sword that looked to be at least average quality, but it was obvious he wasn’t a fighter.

I’d read about places like this one on the forums. ‘Slice of life’ guilds, as they were called. Whole towns dedicated to the medieval roleplay aspect of Wonder as opposed to the dungeon delving and questing that most people enjoyed.

“I wish we would have found these people two months ago,” I said quietly. Bringing all of them into Undercroft Citadel as workers and laborers—slaves, even—would have been perfect. Now, I wasn’t sure there was time to put them to good use. Still, it was worth a shot. If nothing else, I wouldn’t shed a tear feeding them to the gate as living sacrifices.

I mentally commanded the angels to stay back. Whatever corpses were about to be strewn across the field would make fine zombies. I didn’t need the angels’ enchanted weapons mucking it up.

At my side, Elyk bristled with energy. “What’s the plan, boss?”

“Same as before. Kill the NPCs. They’re just fodder. Get them to surrender. If you have to kill a player, try not to maim them too badly. And Hel, I'm counting on you to *convince* them to surrender."

Helvegen stifled a laugh. "I don't think you'll need my help. You have an army of skeletal angels. They're farmers. Just kill a few and the rest will throw down their arms."

I took a few steps forward to try the diplomatic option first. "You know who I am?" I yelled across the field.

The carpenter tensed. He stepped forward as well. "Yes."

"Surrender, and I'll let you come work for me. All of you. Your NPCs will be killed and brought back as zombies, but all the players can live." *For a while, at least,* I completed in my head. I figured it was prudent to leave that last bit out.

The man glanced to both sides as though some valiant guild of white knights was about to break through the woods or emerge from the lake and rescue him.

No such guild appeared. There would be no last-minute salvation. "What's the choice?" I shouted.

The man tightened his grip. "We're good people, every single one of us. We'll never help you." Much to my surprise, the man found another little bit of courage and spat.

I shrugged. "Alright, back to plan A." I looked to Elyk and Hel, and neither of them were surprised. "Keep the feisty one alive. I like him."

Elyk and I charged across the field, and what resistance the villagers were able to mount would have barely stopped a low-level goblin raid. They had some players with bows and crossbows deeper in the town, but none of them were combat classes. We broke through their small line with ease, and the battle was over before it ever truly began. The hardest part was showing enough restraint to not just butcher everyone and be done with it. Still, more than a handful of players died. Most of them were slain by Infernum, not my sword.

The brawl quickly dissolved into a rout, and Helvegen

stepped forward. She cast a spell, and a towering wall of sheer stone appeared around the small village as though it had erupted from the ground itself, trapping everyone inside. Of course, if any of the villagers just kept running through it, they would have found that it didn't exist at all. As far as I could tell, only a few of them did. The rest, as predicted, threw down their arms to surrender.

It took half an hour to round up the entire village. I segregated the NPCs back into the field in front of the mills and had my angles begin the long and tedious task of ferrying them back to Undercroft Citadel. It would take all day and part of the night to move everyone, but so be it. Organizing a wagon train was out of the question.

The rest of the players numbered about a hundred and fifty. The carpenter, his name was Rowan, was the highest level among them. The slice of life players rarely ventured out of their hamlets, so none of them were bound to be high level. He had taken a bit of a beating in the short-lived scrap, and he held an old rag to his head. A bit of blood seeped out from beneath it. But the town also had healers. Many of the women had various healing classes like shaman, druids, and multiple alchemists. They even had a level twenty-one surgeon. All of those healers would have been great if my army was alive. Still, I'd happily take them.

I paraded Rowan to the front of the gathered mass and ordered everyone else to their knees. An older man near the front of the group was the only one still standing.

I stopped in front of him, my sword in my right hand and Rowan's collar in my left. The old farmer held a pitchfork in shaking hands.

"Plea—"

I rammed him through with my sword and let him fall in a heap on the ground. It would take him a while to die, but I got his lungs, so at least it would be quiet. A few people screamed. Someone tried to run, and an angel swooped down to grab them by the shoulders and deposit them with the others.

"There will be no escape," I announced, still holding Rowan. "There is nowhere left to run. None of you are strong enough to resist." The dying farmer spat up a glob of blood at my feet, and I took a step back. "Everyone is coming back to Undercroft Citadel. I know you know what it is, and we're the bad guys. Tough shit. Whatever job you did here, I'm sure it needs doing at the necropolis. Stay in line, do as you're told, and you'll be fine. If you'd rather take a shot at resistance, just do it now so I can kill you and get it over with."

I waited a long moment, and no one dared to move. Rowan was so scared that I wasn't sure he had even taken a single breath.

"Excellent. Transport is going to take some time. The angels can carry two of you at a time, but it isn't a short trip. Get whatever you need, but don't bother loading up with tons and tons of supplies. We have plenty back at your new home. Remember: if you try to run, you're dead. Got it?"

No one responded, so I waved them off, and that seemed to do the trick. The terrified mob of people scrambled back to their houses for whatever it was they wanted to bring, and I turned my attention to Rowan. His teeth clicked together as he shook with terror.

I sat him down on the small stone curb in front of a butcher shop. "Tell me about this place," I demanded.

The man's composure had barely returned, but like Hel, he wanted to live. That meant answering my questions. The town was called Laurel Cove which felt more like the name of a retirement home or an upscale neighborhood than it did a fantasy village. It was a peaceful place for slice of life players, just as I suspected, with very little need for defense.

They dealt with the occasional wild animal attack, but raiders were few and far between. Being a place geared more toward casual players, that also meant the town lacked any kind of dungeon. There was no ultimate enemy to fight, and that meant the second part of my quest for allies wouldn't be completed at the quaint hamlet of Laurel Cove.

What Rowan did know, however, was the location of a big dungeon a few miles out where I probably could find allies. Rowan knew rumors of a ruined castle deep in the woods. He didn't know exactly what was there, and the tales varied wildly. Tribes of goatmen, more orcs, a vampire, an ancient lich—the tales were limitless. And no one in Laurel Cove had ever been brave enough to venture to the castle and find out.

According to Rowan, most people who lived in the village had never even respawned before. They were so averse to combat that most of them simply never left. Those who did go back to the real world from time to time actually made the full day's journey to Echelon to go through the portal. It was completely insane. Sure, the first few deaths in the game were typically harrowing, but it got much, much easier. Though perhaps it was an indicator of Wonder's more negative effects on humanity that so many people had overcome their innate fear of falling off cliffs. I had watched plenty of streams where guilds would finish a lengthy dungeon, head back to their guildhall, and then at least half of them would kill themselves in some fashion just get back to their own place in the real world. Typically, a high fall was the method of choice.

I wondered just how terrified the poor citizens of Laurel Cove were as my angels flew them high above the trees back to Undercroft Citadel. Unlike so many others, these players still had a healthy fear of heights.

Close to nightfall, I pulled Elyk aside. "I'm going to send Hel back with the new captives."

"Think that's smart?"

I shrugged. "These people are as close to harmless as players get. If she tries to betray me with them, it'll be a bloodbath, and she'll die. If not, I'll be able to trust her a little more, I suppose."

Elyk thought it over for a second. "Alright. And what of us?"

"We're going to take two angels and find some ruined castle deep in the woods that Rowan told me about."

"More allies," Elyk correct concluded.

"Exactly."

The ruined castle only took a few hours to find. We were both tired by time we spotted it, but the magnificent sight was more than enough to reinvigorate our spirits despite the late hour. The whole structure was red stone, and it sprawled over at least a dozen acres. Giant hexagonal spires reached toward the heavens on both sides of the sloped façade. The front was terraced with ruined fountains in what was once a luxury garden but now resembled a jungle more than anything. The spire on the left was still intact, though missing all the glass from its windows, and the one on the right had fallen in on itself. Vines and other forest creepers now covered all but the highest two floors, and there was no roof.

Right in the center, a huge iron portcullis had collapsed enough for anyone to enter. I imagined the castle in all its younger splendor with banners streaming from every apex and hundreds of guards ready to defend it with their lives. Of course, that was a timeline that didn't actually exist, though I had no doubt it was programmed into the game's lore. Xollmomath would probably have a story about his master sacking the place.

Elyk and I landed a few paces from the entrance. Infernum illuminated the castle's features, and a bit of moonlight seeped through the forest canopy. "What is it we're supposed to find here?" Elyk asked, craning his neck to take it all in.

"I have no idea. Your usual ruined castle denizens would be my guess. A vampire or something similar. Rowan wasn't clear with the details." I mentally commanded the angels to do some reconnaissance around the whole structure. When they landed a few minutes later, I received the emotive answer directly into my brain that the ground floor wasn't where we should begin. There was another entrance on the rear side of the ruined spire.

We hiked around the base, again marveling at the castle's sheer magnitude. It made Undercroft Citadel look tiny. If we had a few years and several thousand workers, cleaning it up to take it over would be an incredible achievement. But there was a reason no one had done that yet.

We reached the back of the ruined tower, and a torch burned about halfway up. It hung from a short length of metal chain that had been fixed to the loose mortar with a piton. "Looks like we're not alone," I said with a smile.

Elyk matched my enthusiasm. "Perfect! Let's go make some friends."

Under normal circumstances, we would have had to either fashion a ladder or climb the ruins to reach the gaping hole that served as the dungeon's entrance. Now, all I had to do was think, and our undead angels lifted us right to it.

The dungeon began with an uncomfortable crawl. Ceiling beams had collapsed, pulling most of the thick walls in with them to form a kind of artificial cave. We squeezed through, our pair of angels in tow, and reached the first chamber. It looked like a dining hall, though it hadn't served food in centuries. Silvery platters covered in decades of dirt and grime littered the floor. Broken chairs were piled up to one side, and we finally figured out what kind of enemies called the ruins home: mushroom-men. Fungal abominations not all that dissimilar from my own zombies. The dead ones scattered near the door were small, probably young, and hadn't put up any real resistance at all. They looked like overgrown mushrooms, maybe the size of a large dog, and they had no arms or hands. Their attacks, as far as I knew, were mostly poison based much like my own. I wondered how many of the fungal enemies could cast *A Feast of Spores*.

"You ever fight against these guys?" I asked.

Elyk poked one with Infernum. The blade cut through the creature's spongey flesh with ease, though no blood poured out. "Yeah, a couple times. These tiny ones are super weak."

"And the larger ones?"

"Immobile, for the most part," he explained as we tested the next door and found it unlocked. "Mushroom bosses are usually more like trees than anything. They stay in one spot and rain toxic spores while the smaller ones mob you. Weak to fire, too."

We progressed deeper into the ruined castle and came upon a series of three jail cells set into the red brick wall. Two of them were open, and the third sported an NPC human corpse. "There's probably a rescue mission in here or something," I wondered aloud. Many of Wonder's larger dungeons had little mini quests inside that you didn't have to complete to reach the final boss. If you did them, however, you'd typically get some kind of boon during the final fight or an extra piece of gear.

More dead mushroom-men were scattered about the end of the hallway. From the looks of their sliced and diced corpses, they hadn't given the group any trouble. They were still relatively low-level enemies.

We opened the next door and found ourselves at the top

of a staircase leading down to one of the interior courtyards. Wildflowers grew from the cracks in the mortar, and rubble was piled up to either side of the main path like snow right after a plow.

It was easy enough to follow the other group's path. The mushroom-men grew larger, and by the time we reached a large set of kitchens connected to an audience chamber, we actually started seeing the remnants of battle. Scorch marks dotted the walls from fire spells, broken arrow shafts littered the ground, and a few spots of human blood were mixed in with all the fungal carnage.

"We're catching up," I mused. Before I opened the next door, I stopped to listen. Sure enough, the faint sounds of battle echoed down the stone corridor. "One more room."

We took it slow, and I kept the two undead angels a few paces back. When we finally found the guild, I didn't want them assuming the NPCs were part of the dungeon and unleashing hell on us before we could react.

The next hallway was long, lined with faded portraits of people from Wonder's lore that I would never recognize. It ended in a short staircase leading to the castle's private chapel. It was the perfect location for a boss fight. It wouldn't be the final boss, but a midway point where a lot of weaker guilds probably turned back.

We got close enough for me to take stock of the battle without being noticed. Five players, all in the mid-twenties. They were from the guild Trees of Dominion, and each of them wore a forest green tabard with a big tree of life motif over their armor. In the back, they had a cleric and a warlord directing the fight as support. Up front, a rogue danced back and forth between their two enemies in similar fashion to the late Kadorax and his assassins. The rogue was supported in melee by a blackguard swinging a huge three-headed flail and wearing jet-black steel armor. The final player, an enchanter, hovered a few inches off the ground in a magical trance. She glowed with purple energy, and streaks of lightning shot out from her body at regular intervals, striking both enemies and friendlies.

"Should we help?" Elyk whispered.

I shook my head and held a finger to my lips. I didn't want to give away our position until it was over. The guild didn't appear to be struggling, and I didn't want to interrupt their strategy. The main boss, a cleric with a two-handed mace long enough to rival Faidra's axe, was taking a beating. Behind him, a priest in flowing robes struggled to keep up the stream of healing magic flowing from his fingers into the cleric's body.

The whole fight only lasted another thirty seconds. While the cleric certainly landed a few heavy blows on the blackguard, it wasn't enough to even knock him out of the fight, much less kill him.

I gave them a few minutes to celebrate their kills and loot the bodies before stepping forward and clearing my throat. All at once, the guild leapt back into action, but it was short lived.

I kept my sword in its sheath and held up my hands. "Not here for a fight," I said quickly, and the guild relaxed a little.

"Then, uh, what *are* you here for?" the warlord asked.

I took the man for their leader. His name was Leif, and he carried a short sword and a big tower shield painted with his guild's green emblem. The cleric positioned herself behind Leif and readied a spell. Whatever it was, it didn't really scare me. There were enough corpses in the ruined castle to heal me at least once, and no matter what they had heard about me or Undercroft Citadel, I *knew* they would never be prepared for my full panoply of spells.

"Looking for allies," I answered honestly, holding out my hand.

The warlord looked at my offer of a handshake, but he didn't accept it. "We've got plenty of members," he said after a moment.

I smiled, though I knew my twisted and deformed face—sporting more than a few grotesque tentacles—did not thing to assuage his fears. "Not like that. I need guilds to join me." I waved for Elyk to step forward and mentally commanded the two angels to take up positions behind us. No matter how strong the players were, they had to recognize an overwhelming force when they saw it. "This is a one-time offer. You've no doubt heard of me and Undercroft Citadel. You know what we're capable of. I need more strong players at my side."

"We've heard of you . . ." the warlord said, and all the confidence was suddenly gone from his voice.

I made a show of mentally running the numbers on the experience I would earn killing the man and his friends, though it was all for show. "I'd probably gain a level or two killing you all, but, like I said, I need allies right now more than I need levels. Again, it's a one-time offer. And keep in mind that we watched your battle with the cleric. We could have attacked at any time. We chose not to." I took a few steps back into the hallway. "Take a few minutes to talk it over."

Elyk and I waited with the silent, undead angels, and we didn't have to wait long. The warlord sheathed his sword and set his tower shield against the wall. He extended a gloved hand, and I shook it with a smile. "Alright. We don't want to die. We'll . . . join you."

"Excellent!"

"You made the right choice," Elyk added.

"You . . . want to split the loot?" Leif asked.

I waved it off. "Not at all. You earned it!"

He seemed surprised by my answer, though in truth,

I had to imagine the loot from a mini boss like that would pale in comparison to gear Elyk and I already had.

"T-thanks," he sputtered. "What's . . . uh, what's next?"

The rest of his party looked just as scared as Leif, perhaps worse. I wasn't really sure how to set them at ease. If they joined me, performed well, and never tried to sink a dagger into my spine, we'd get along fine. There was simply no possible way for me to convey that information without it coming across as either a trap or a lie. One of the pitfalls of having a reputation as the evilest player in the game, I supposed.

One by one, I shook hands with the players and tried my best to ease their fears. I didn't think I was very successful. "How much is left of the dungeon?" I asked after the introductions.

Leif pointed to the next door. "Just a couple more rooms of mushroom-men before the final boss."

"Great! I'd love the chance to fight at your side," I told him. Again, despite being completely honest, I could tell the man didn't believe a word I spoke. But at least no one was readying spells and they all had their weapons safely stowed.

Elyk approached the blackguard, a burly man covered head to toe in black steel who reminded us both of Faidra. "I'm more of a frontline fighter like you," the harvester said. He hit his knuckles on his legendary breastplate. "Not much for big shields and dodging. Just tend to take what comes and butcher everyone in my path."

The blackguard gave his gear a long glance and nodded. "Tanks in front," he said, though he didn't lift the visor on his helm.

I wanted to explain my own role to the new team, but it was hard to put it directly into words. I wasn't a melee brawler like Elyk, that was clear enough to see, but I also wasn't a long-range caster like the enchanter or the cleric. In the end, I figured it was best to just explain by example.

The nine of us, the angels still taking up the rear, advanced up a series of spiral staircases to the highest levels of the castle's main building. It was a sprawling hall decorated with towering windows on the left and broken, grime-encrusted mirrors on the right. At the end of the hall, a dozen or more sizable mushroom-men quickly took notice and charged. They trailed streams of orange and red spores in thick clouds behind them as they ran on spongey feet.

Elyk and the blackguard met the charge, quickly cutting down four of the strange creatures in seconds. They released more clouds of toxic spores as they died, and the cleric quickly infused both frontline fighters with fortifying magic to counteract the poison.

It was oddly satisfying to fight with a real party for once. It was . . . comforting, in its own way. It felt like I was finally playing the game the way it was intended instead of flying by the seat of my pants and making whatever insane choices I thought would make Lady Kalma proud.

Elyk and the blackguard cut down the next rank of soldiers, and then the mushroom-men initiated a ranged attack. They launched globs of foul liquid from their caps, arching it over the frontline to land among the casters in the back. It would have struck home if not for the enchanter's spells neutralizing it in mid-air. Then the enchanter flashed with purple magic, and the ranged mushroom-men were locked into place by magical chains, and I charged with Leif at my side to finish them off.

As a warlord, Leif was basically seventy-five percent melee with the rest going into influence skills to help the party as a whole. He activated a talent to increase his sword speed, dicing the nearest ranged mushroom-man with brutal efficiency. I, on the other hand, was not as delicate. I had no real physical talents to activate, but I *did* have a sword that ignored armor. I braced the hilt against my hip and ran straight forward, easily impaling the mushroom-man. I thought of activating a few poison spells of my own, but I figured if any enemies in Wonder would be immune to poison, it would be these.

The rogue flashed between us to the final rank of enemies, making quick and calculated strikes right for whatever it was that served as a mushroom-man's brain.

The whole battle lasted less than a minute. The rogue, clearly well-versed in the dungeon, proceeded to manipulate a specific spot on the wall which caused a panel to fall away and reveal a small golden chest.

"You guys have done this dungeon before, probably a bunch of times, right?"

"Many, many times," Leif answered.

"What's the point? What are you hoping to gain?" I asked, though the question felt obvious. They were clearly too high level to be gaining much experience from it, and that also meant the gear probably wouldn't be very good compared to what they had.

"Well . . . Ever since the servers, you know, went down, dungeons haven't really been resetting the same way. The NPCs don't respawn like they used to. We've figured out that it'll always be the same kind of enemies, but it'll never be the *exact* same fights. Not like before. It takes a week or so before another boss comes, and we've been testing it to see how powerful they might become."

The rogue tossed the golden chest to the cleric. "That and we're bored," he added.

I shrugged. "Makes enough sense to me. What's this final boss going to look like?"

Leif ran through the final room with us, drawing a crude

diagram with his finger in the dirt. The final door opened onto a small balcony with stairs immediately to the right, and the ultimate boss was straight across a small courtyard. As soon as the door opened, we'd be assaulted by ranged attacks from the boss. We had to scramble down the stairs to the courtyard and then fight our way across through a horde of mushroom-men. Once we made it to the other side, the combination of Infernum and the enchanter's fire magic would make quick work of the boss.

We got into position, and the rogue opened the door. He darted through, easily vaulting over the balcony to the courtyard. Elyk and the blackguard filtered in behind him. It was a brutal fight right from the start, but all of us were way too high level for it to be challenging. The mushroom-men went down two at a time, barely ever registering a single hit, and what they did manage to land was far from powerful enough to break through anyone's armor. The real threat came in the form of the poison they released upon death, but the enchanter's magic kept that at bay. She produced a steady stream of water above our heads, effectively diluting the poison spores to the point of nullification.

By the time I made it through to the balcony with Leif, there wasn't much left to kill. But the sight was still something to behold. Maybe fifty yards away on its own balcony, the final boss was some kind of amalgamation of human and fungus. It looked like a huge mushroom, bright orange and covered with bulging white spots, but then it also sported a series of six arms all on the same side. They were somewhat human arms, though each had an extra joint in the middle, and their hands ended in lumps of fleshy, spore-filled sacks. The creature launched the spore sacks at us across the balcony, and each sack quickly grew back to be fired in rapid succession.

Against a newer, less-experienced squad, the fight would

have been incredibly difficult. Against us, it was somewhat trivial. Elyk and the blackguard were only a few steps behind the rogue, and thanks to the enchanter and cleric, no one had taken any serious damage.

The final boss went down in a matter of moments. Elyk carved away huge chunks of its fungal flesh, and Infernum burned what little was left. The whole battle concluded without a single spell from me or the warlord. As before, the rogue quickly looted the area.

"That's it," Leif said before I could ask him what comes next. "We wait a week or so, and then the next boss will be a notch tougher. I know it might seem lame, but the dungeon is safe. We know it well, and we aren't trying to risk any deaths by hitting something harder."

Watching the rogue pry up a flagstone to reveal a hidden cache of gold reminded me a lot of watching Kadorax and the assassins. It gave me an idea. "I know you've looted this place tons of times, but have you ever searched it for anything else?"

"What do you mean?" Leif asked.

"Well . . . there has to be a way in. The game isn't just respawning the boss like before, so the boss needs to physically get inside. I don't think the giant mushroom was mobile, so it had to get here somehow, then it *became* the mushroom boss." In my head, it sounded a lot more logical than when I said it aloud, but Leif at least seemed to get the gist.

We scoured the entire area for the better part of an hour. The rogue had the best investigation skill by far, so it was no surprise when he found a hollow stair leading up to the boss. He could pry it free from the mortar without risking damage to his blades, but the enchanter's magic was more than enough to simply obliterate it.

And there it was: a passage to another room. Once the hollow brick was gone, we easily demolished the rest of the staircase to make an opening wide enough for the whole party, though the angels still had to duck.

The descent dripped with an oily liquid too thick to be water. It seeped out of the stones above us and pooled at our feet. We descended farther and farther until we were at least a few stories beneath the ruined castle, and the passage narrowed. More and more of the thick, oily liquid coated everything, and before long it coated all of our armor as well. Finally, by the light of Infernum, we reached a heavy metal grate set into the floor and a dead end. Everything beyond the grate was too dark to see.

The rogue chipped a small piece of stone from the wall with the hilt of one of his weapons and dropped it down. "Two seconds," I said, though it was just a rough estimate. "That's got to be fifty feet."

We ran the rudimentary experiment one more time just to be sure. "I don't think the angels can get enough room to ferry us down," I said.

The rogue pulled a length of rope from the magical bag at his waist. "I've got forty feet of rope, so I hope your math is right."

In the tight confines of the oil tunnel, it took ages to pull up the metal grate and then hammer it into the stone wall so we could use it as a fixed point for the rope. When we finally had it more or less secure, I still didn't trust it, so I ordered the two angels to use their strength to brace it.

The enchanter conjured a globe of light, and then the rogue was first into the darkness. Everyone waited in silence. After a minute, we heard the telltale thump of boots on stone, and the rogue called back that there was no danger.

One by one we descended the rope into a vast stone chamber. Workbenches lined three of the four walls, and Elyk used Infernum to light a few candles and lanterns scattered among them. Everything was stacked with notebooks, beakers, vials, and all sorts of other alchemical implements that I couldn't name. The final wall resembled a prison much like the dungeon's very first room: three cells, each with an occupant.

"Are any of them . . . alive?" I asked.

The seven of us stood a few feet from the iron bars and probably all wondered the same thing. Inside the first cell was a man, or what was left of him. He had been reduced to a naked pair of legs with just a few inches of torso. His guts, red and rancid, were spilled over the rest of the cell. Intertwined with the gruesome gore was a network of pulsing, breathing fungal vines. They thrummed with vital energy, constantly inhaling and exhaling a small spore cloud.

The next cell featured more of the same, though the body had been mutilated almost beyond recognition. Little more was left other than feet and a single ankle before the fungus took over.

The third cell didn't have any human left at all. Everything had been overcome with fungus until all that remained was a vague outline of something once human.

It made me stop and think about my own transformation. What was I becoming? Some kind of squid-like abomination, as far as I could tell. And knowing Lady Kalma, the only way to stop it would be to die. With my curse, actually dying was becoming harder and harder to imagine. If someone cut off my head all at once? Sure. Well . . . probably. Actually, I didn't know. If there were enough corpses nearby . . .

I really, *really* didn't want to keep thinking about it.

"Fucking hell," I muttered, turning back from the third cell. "Let's just get as many of these notebooks—"

Movement caught my eye. I quickly counted our group, and it wasn't one of us. I held up a hand to get everyone to stop, then pointed to the shadows at the far end of the room.

"What—" Elyk started, but I cut him off with a glare.

Whatever it was moved again. I guessed it was small, maybe the size of one of the gnomes back at Undercroft Citadel, and it skittered from shadow to shadow with speed that made me uncomfortable. Whatever it was, it *had* to see us. Hell, until our arrival, the place had been dark. Whatever denizen called it home would know that, of course.

"Get ready for a fight," I said. My voice echoed off the stone walls, and I knew the thing at the other end heard.

"Celia, light it up," Leif said.

The enchanter quickly swirled a ball of pinkish magic between her hands before hurling it down the length of the room. It illuminated everything in its path—until it was promptly extinguished by the being in the shadows just before reaching it. Without missing a beat, the enchanter fired another spell, this one a lightning bolt that cracked against the far wall, and for a split second, we all saw the newcomer. It was an NPC, a haggard and deformed old dwarf covered in scars and clearly suffering from an extreme case of fungal infection. Half his body was mangled and torn, crossed through by mushrooms and whatever it was they used for roots.

"Ready for the real final boss?" I asked.

Elyk and the blackguard didn't wait. They charged, bellowing war cries and activating talents. The enchanter flung herself into action as well, casting a torrent of magic at the end of the room. One second, the boss was there at the end of the hall looking surprised at the visitors. The next, he was gone.

Then he erupted from the floor right between me and Leif. A shower of broken stone tiles cascaded around us. Mixed into the raining stone was a cloud of toxic spores. Leif was too slow to stop his breathing, and he quickly fell to the ground in a fit of coughs that sounded painful.

While the cleric started casting restorative magic, I

swung for the mushroom-man as hard as I could. My sword should have cleaved right through him, but it hit only air. He was gone.

The boss erupted from the stone again, this time right at the enchanter's feet. Before anyone could react, the mushroom-man burst out of the stone floor two more times, releasing waves of broken stone along with thick clouds of blackish-red spores. In the space of a few heartbeats, the entire room was clogged with spores. Elyk and the blackguard, our only two members wearing full helms covering their faces, seemed to fare the best, though neither of them could land a single hit. Just as quickly as the boss appeared, he was gone again.

We needed a way to stop the boss's teleportation if we were ever going to cut him down. I activated *The Black Goblin's Restless Vengeance* and instantly commanded the shadowy shaman to cover the floor in the hardest substance it could. A glimmering sheen of thick back stone rippled out from the shaman's hands, and it worked perfectly.

"Hit him now!" I yelled. The boss was stuck, trapped in place by the new layer of stone. I was the closest, and I wasted no time. As I swung, I felt a surge of powerful warlord magic fill my veins. My muscles bulged, my vision sharpened, and for a few seconds I felt the overwhelming power of having my physical stat magically doubled. My blade flew through the air and finally caught the boss. I cleaved off a huge chunk of the man's spore-ridden flesh. At the same time, Elyk reached the boss's back and drove Infernum through his chest. Then the blackguard's flail crashed down, and more chunks of spongey mushroom splattered across the room.

"Duck!" a female voice yelled somewhere behind me.

I dropped down just as a lance of fire struck the boss and engulfed him. The stench that quickly filled the room was enough to make all of us back off. Covering my mouth,

I watched as the boss burned, flailing and screaming as he died. With every tortured movement, more and more thick spores were flung into the air. When the boss finally stopped moving, there was so much smoke and poison lingering in the air that I could no longer see the corpse.

Your Cunning skill has increased to 45!

Your Influence skill has increased to 44!

Your Renown has increased to 60!

The gains that flashed through my vision weren't enough to hit the next level, so I pushed them out of my vision.

Leif was coughing so much it sounded like he would throw up a lung. The cleric and enchanter weren't much better off. The rogue downed a potion that quickly recovered his breath before handing a similar vial to the blackguard.

When the enchanter finally recovered enough to cast again, she summoned a cloud of rain at the ceiling that quickly washed the poison and smoke out of the air, though the sludge that mixed with the oil at our feet made me more than a little nervous. Whatever we were standing in, it *had* to be ridiculously toxic.

"Come on, let's grab what we can and get the hell out of here. No need to breathe this shit any longer than we have to," I said, and it didn't take any convincing. Everyone was just as eager to get out of the dungeon as I was.

We looted a ton of the notebooks, journals, and whatever alchemical implements we could safely carry before being hoisted out by the angels. I was eager to get it all back to Undercroft Citadel along with our new allies. If everything worked out how I saw it in my mind, we had made tons of progress. Fresh troops—and players, not just more zombies—plenty of interesting reading for the workshop team, and, of course, all the slaves from Laurel Cove.

There would be a lot of new faces, and that meant a lot of new managerial tasks. As I flew back over the trees toward my necropolis, I tried to quell some of the nervousness in the pit of my stomach. Either Hel would manage Undercroft Citadel again with all the vim and vigor that had kept her alive so far and we would succeed . . . or she would betray me, and we would fail. As much as I hated to admit it, everything hinged on her cooperation. She had already tried to kill me twice. I could only hope there wouldn't be a third attempt.

CHAPTER 16

It took three full days to get everyone back to Undercroft Citadel. Organizing the logistics of it all was daunting, but Hel never let me down. Using the angels as our own personal air force, we were able to fully loot everything of value from Laurel Cove *and* move all of Leif's guild. Overseeing many of the flights personally, I learned a lot about our new allies. The Seagrim Raiders, as the guild was known, made their home in a sizeable city some fifty miles north of Undercroft called Tamworth. The guild was evil, though perhaps barely on that side of the moral scale, but it was good enough for me. They numbered thirty-six, were all hardened and tested players, and would make formidable allies.

During the frequent flights, I also had a pair of angels stop at the ruined castle several times with empty barrels. We harvested as much of the toxic oil sludge from the final boss's chamber as would fill four barrels. I still didn't know what it actually did, but with Geirr's workshop running tests, I figured I would have that answer soon enough. And with all the new workers from Laurel Cove, Geirr's workshop absolutely hummed with activity. He and the blacksmith from

The Jade Spire had every single workbench and forge operating at full capacity round the clock. What the slice of life players lacked in combat experience and relevant classes, they certainly made up for in crafting ability.

I stood at the top of my stairs and watched as another panel of reinforced wooden wall was lowered into place. The entire wall was nearly rebuilt. All we needed was a few more panels and then repairs to the gatehouse towers. The second wall farther out was coming along as well. The entire outline had been dug, and a team of stonemasons were hard at work laying the foundation of what I hoped would become our primary defense.

The ranks of undead were replenished enough to last through the next siege, and now we were rapidly outfitting them with gear as well. A few of the larger, more intact zombies carried weapons and shields, but the rest weren't going unarmed. Piebald had taught a dozen of the Laurel Cove workers how to fashion spiked harnesses that the zombies could wear into battle. Since the undead mainly relied on their hands and teeth in combat, outfitting them as sea urchins felt like the best choice.

I spotted Syzak working with some of the Laurel Cover players at the wall. He was an odd sight, a snake-man standing shoulder to shoulder with all the humans. Not surprisingly, none of the slice of lifers had done the extensive quests required to change their race. I'd also noticed a significant change in the snake-man lately. Now that things had, in a general sense, calmed down a bit, his spirits were gone. He was the last surviving member of the Blackened Blades. His whole guild had been butchered either by Helvegen's attack or my poison.

I needed to keep him close. He was powerful, and all his friends were dead. Syzak reminded me of when the more popular veterans of the bureaucracy would retire. Within a few weeks, the morale around the office would falter. Then, if something wasn't done, it would die altogether, and the younger staff would leave en masse. I'd seen it happen at least two or three times. If Syzak didn't find somewhere else to fit in, he'd defect. Though I didn't think he was the type to run off and join our enemies, I simply didn't know him well enough to be certain.

I decided to bring the shaman on our return visit to Iron Hall, whenever that was actually going to take place. In the meantime, we still had massive amounts of work to do integrating all our new allies into Undercroft Citadel. First on my list was a proper visit to the guildhall of the Seagrim Raiders. They had taken over the magical, portable guildhall left behind by the Burned Saints and seemed to be settling in nicely. Two of their members had protested the move—something I had completely expected—and now the heads of those two members were jammed onto sharpened stakes to either side of the guildhall. I left the grim reminder there for two days, and I felt like it was time to remove it and make amends. My new allies would fight harder if they actually *wanted* to fight, though the fear of grisly death was no doubt a close second in terms of motivational efficacy.

Leif met me at the front. Silently, I commanded a gargoyle to take care of the heads while the warlord ushered me inside. Everyone fell quiet. A few of the Seagrim Raiders sat around the long table playing cards. Others were busy preparing food in the kitchen off to the side, but most of them just stood and gawked. For nearly all of them, it was their first time getting an up close and personal look at my twisted, disfigured face. I let them take it in.

"This . . . uh, this is Ben. He's calling the shots now, everyone," Leif said after an uncomfortable silence.

I wasn't exactly sure where to start, so I figured the truth was as good a place as any. "Thank you for the introduction."

He nodded and stepped back to let me have the room's attention. "Look, you're evil. Maybe not quite like the rest of us, but you aren't the good guys and neither are we. If you want to live, you're going to work for me. If not, just let me know, and I'll be happy to cut off your head and give your corpse to my necromancer. Those are pretty much your only options."

No one responded. All I got were hard stares all around. I had no doubt that at least half the players were thinking the same thing: there were thirty of them and only one of me. If they all got up and rushed at once, they'd easily overpower and kill me. Two things stopped them from acting on that thought. The first was my forty-foot bone golem abomination not too far from the guildhall. They knew Aleph was immune to evil, and they knew that meant them. The second, perhaps even stronger pacification, was the rumor that I was immortal. Word traveled quickly among my new guests. Elyk was the only other person who actually knew the true extent of my curse, and I very much intended to keep it that way. The more the guild talked and whispered among themselves, the more the legend of my immortality would grow, and the more their obedience would grow with it.

One of the men raised a hand. He looked scared.

"What's your question?"

"What are we doing here?" he stammered.

"The easy answer is whatever I tell you to do. But the more complex answer is . . . well, one way or another, no one is leaving Wonder when the portals finally go online. Everyone is going to die, and yes, that includes you. The only real decision you have to make is when. If you help me defend Undercroft Citadel and carry out my plans, you'll at least live to the end. If not, I'll kill you all right now."

Another long silence passed. Finally, the same man who

asked the question spoke up again. "You're . . . going to . . . kill *everyone*?"

I pointed to him with a long tentacle hand. "See, he gets it." I turned to everyone else with a smile on my gnarled face. "If you're having any trouble understanding the plan, ask him."

A clamor erupted, and I took that as my que to leave. Time would prove their loyalty or betrayal, and I had a strong feeling they were too scared to cross me. Not soon, at least. And when the first attack came from outside, they'd fight like their lives depended on it. If there was no hope of escape, just an enemy on the horizon or a worse fate in desertion, they would prefer death to flight. And once I got the guild to face death at my side, there would be nothing they wouldn't do. Nothing they could not achieve. Once their mettle was tested on the battlefield, I'd be able to trust them.

It only took two days for the attack I knew was coming to finally arrive. Three players, all high level, experienced raiders, were caught in the dead of night attempting to scale the walls. By the time the alarm was raised and I groggily stumbled out of my room into the chill night air, one of them was already dead. Aleph, having no need for sleep and happily obeying my commands, pulverized the poor player into the dirt. The second two were much harder to find.

Undercroft Citadel slowly awoke to high alert. Torches were lit and carried to every wall. Hel used her powerful magic to try and expose any deceit. But it was the enchanter from the Seagrim Raiders who finally came up with a solution. She found traces of the players and tracked them to one of the workshops.

I had my zombies surround the building, and then I sent the enchanter inside to retrieve our unwelcome guests. She came out a few minutes later covered in sweat but magically dragging two players bound in chains. They had an affiliation to some guild called Resolve, and neither of them spoke any English.

I shook my head. I had always known assassins would be coming for my head. Getting through our layer of zombie guards who had no need for sleep was impressive, though Aleph had seen them easily enough once they were over the wall. Leif volunteered to kill the two trespassers, which was fine by me, and then came the task of scouting the forest yet again.

"There might be an entire guild out there," I said, my voice still slow with sleep. "Check as much as you can, but return by noon." Closing my eyes, I mentally commanded my army of flying angels to do the same. I grabbed Leif by the arm before he could leave. "Take charge of the scouting party. Report anything to an angel and send it to me. Understood?"

The man nodded, and I let him go.

"Elyk, Hel, stay close. There could be more of them creeping out of the shadows at any moment," I said.

But there were not. The day passed without any further excitement. No one was found lurking in the woods, and no second wave of enemies sprang up within our midst. In many ways, the lack of a fight was perhaps worse than the alternative. I would never know if the three were acting alone, trying to score a quick kill in the middle of the night, or if they were part of something larger. And every single night I would go to sleep worrying. When would the next strike come? Soon, of course. It would always be 'soon' and never more specific than that.

Elyk and I began planning our next attack on Iron Hall to take my mind off it all. We had the gate and plenty of slice of life players to feed to it, but there was still one lingering problem there: I didn't know if it worked in the opposite direction. I *assumed* it would also take us home when the time came, but I had no way of knowing.

First, before we could go all the way to Iron Hall and steal its resurrection orb, Elyk volunteered to traverse the gate and report back with his findings. We picked an older woman from Laurel Cove, someone who probably wouldn't be very useful alive or dead. Elyk bashed her with Infernum's hilt and dragged her to the gate.

"I'm just guessing, but throw her through it to activate it," I said after a bit of pondering.

The harvester shrugged and heaved the woman through the bleak bone portal. The device sprang to life, instantly shimmering with a web of green and gold magic. "You got lucky," he said with a smirk.

"Alright. Think of Echelon. Surely the warlock had been there. See you in a bit."

He gave me a nod and stepped through, vanishing just as the woman had only a few seconds before. Much to my delight, the portal remained active. Its web of swirling, undulating colors continued.

Maybe an hour or so later, Elyk walked back through the portal. "I didn't know how long it would last, but I gave it some time," he said.

"What was it like?"

He shrugged. "Honestly pretty similar to Ministrel's spell, though there's a clone of the portal at the destination too. I would assume that means anyone can just waltz right through. Bit of a security risk if you ask me."

"Ministrel's spell is a bit of a risk too, just a different kind," I responded.

Elyk laughed. Behind him, the portal still swirled with brilliant colors. We ended up taking turns watching it to get an idea of how long it lasted, and we came to the conclusion that it was about six hours. It would have been great if we could have just summoned the gate's properties to our vision like I had done with the Skin Thief, but the gate was the result of a spell, not a magic item, so there was no mechanic that would easily reveal its secrets. Guess and check was the best we had.

The next morning, I assembled our team to sack Iron Hall. We were split into two groups. Leif and his guild formed the bulk of the main assault force. I was also sending a dozen of Lady Kalma's angels with him, and it was openly understood that they were going along just as much to fight as they were to keep an eye on the guild. I still didn't trust the guild, but if they succeeded in bringing back the resurrection orb, perhaps I would. Elyk and I were taking the Seagrim Raiders' enchanter and a few angels with us for a special mission. I looked over the trio of barrels we had prepared with a smile. If all went well, I'd have a much better idea of how I was going to handle the final moments when the portals went back online.

Everyone checked their supplies one last time, and then Elyk kicked a screaming old man through the portal, ripping it open in a wash of blues and violets. We filed through, instantly leaving the chill morning air of fall for the hot, humid atmosphere of Iron Hall's mountain interior.

A few terrified NPCs ran for their lives up a nearby hallway. Arrows took them in the back before I had to issue the command. "Leif, you know where to go," I said, and the warlord gave me a nod. He'd been to Iron Hall before, and though it was at least a year ago, he was confident that he remembered enough to get outside. "Everyone, remember where the portal is!"

We had emerged into a circular room with several hallways branching out radially from it, all of them ascending. The portal behind us was somewhat eerie. It showed the usual web of colorful magic, but behind it was a strange silhouette of Undercroft Citadel. The images were wrong, the angles of the buildings imprecise, and all the color was washed from it. I wondered if what I saw was only the warlock's memory of my home instead of the real thing. Either way, as long as it worked and got us home in one piece, it wouldn't matter.

I commanded two angels to guard the portal, and we split up. Leif and his crew checked a few of the tunnels before finding one that looked promising and taking it. To my right, the enchanter floated a few inches off the ground and had her eyes closed in a trance. Her hair drifted upward as though pulled by static electricity, and the air around her body thrummed with energy. Finally, she opened her eyes and pointed. "That way," she said with confidence.

I signaled for the angels, and they hoisted our three heavy barrels with serious effort. Slowly but surely, we made our way down one of the lengthy tunnels until it opened into a massive commerce district dominated by workshops on either side and a huge, ornamental pool of water in the center.

And there were people. So many people. Thousands of them. NPCs and players went about their business buying and selling all around us. Artisans plied their trades with hammers and tongs in large workshop spaces. Merchants led oxen down the center boulevard with carts laden with goods. Everything was loud, chaotic, and smelled of sweat and the stink of too many people underground.

"Perfect," I whispered, and I motioned for the angels to drop down and try to remain unseen.

Nearby, a handful of NPCs selling some kind of roasted food dish that smelled like popcorn took notice of us, and one of them screamed. The others quickly followed suit. They dropped their wares and started to run.

With a single talent activation, Elyk dashed among them in a blur of speed and precision. Infernum flashed, and all four NPCs were slaughtered before they could start a full-blown panic.

"Alright, give us some cover," I told the hovering enchanter. Hel would have been better for the task, but I still didn't want to bring her on a mission outside Undercroft Citadel, and I was fairly certain she didn't want to fight at my side. Not yet, at least.

The enchanter cast another spell, and a thin layer of fog—nearly imperceptible—wrapped around our entire group.

"You're sure it will work?" I asked.

She shrugged. "Mostly sure."

"Better than nothing. Let's move." Slowly, I led our group from the passageway into the mess of players and NPCs. People bumped into us, shouldered by on their way to wherever it was they were going, but none of them *saw* us. Not in any meaningful sense, at least. We were like a slightly obtrusive obstacle: enough to warrant altering course, but not enough of a nuisance to really notice.

We slipped through the bustling crowd until we were at the edge of the crystal-clear pond in the very center of the hall, and then we waited. And waited. Hours of grueling *nothing* went by before we finally felt the familiar sensation of being on a continent with true death.

"That's it," I said, and the enchanter instantly let down her spell. Though it didn't take much magic to keep it going, she was still all but depleted simply from the time.

All around, chaos broke out. People knew the resurrection orb had been sacked. They could feel it in their bones just as easily as we could. Elyk and the angels started prying open the barrels just as another idea flashed into my mind. "Pour them into the pond," I said.

"Wh—"

"Just do it!"

The barrels were ripped open, and we dumped all three

into the pond. The oily, toxic liquid didn't mix well with the water, but we didn't have much time to fix that before the terrified mob managed to escape. The only thing still keeping the majority of the people in the hall was their inability to organize well enough to funnel out.

"You can make it rain, right?" I asked the enchanter. I had seen her do it in the dungeon, but I didn't know how much more energy she had to cast to it now.

She gave me a weak nod. Her eyes were closed, and her chest moved with slow, heavy breaths.

"Good. Give me five seconds." I ordered two of the angels to fly low over the pond, hoping to mix the poison a little, then cast *Part the Waters*. At once, the pool's entire contents teleported to the ceiling. "Rain!" I yelled, and the enchanter gave the last bit of her mana to make it happen.

It took a few seconds to know if my plan worked. Then the screams of fear and general panic quickly gave way to screams of pain instead. Toxic oil and sludgy water rained down on everyone in the huge cavern. It only took another few seconds for the deluge to exhaust the small water supply, but it was proof that my concept worked.

"Kill them all!" I bellowed. The enchanter didn't move, but no one was coming for us anyway, so I left her. I shook the poison rain from my armor—it stung wherever it seeped through the joints and found skin—and charged into the fray.

Elyk and I, flanked to either side by scythe-wielding undead angels, slaughtered from the empty pool all the way to the back of the room. Only a handful of players even recognized what was happening. Barely any of them were armed. Players who inhaled or ingested the toxic liquid coughed and sputtered, struggling to catch their breath in the midst of the mob, though the mixture had been too diluted to cause any deaths on its own. Still, we had a working concept for a much larger, much more powerful chemical weapon.

In the span of twenty minutes or less, we completely cleared the room. Hundreds of people escaped, but thousands were dead. I even managed to bring back four of them with *Reap Honor*, though they were all NPCs with economy classes, so I ignored the new zombies and let them wander aimlessly among the sea of the other dead. Toward the front of the room, probably a hundred or more corpses had never even touched our blades. They'd been crushed from behind or trampled under the boots of those lucky enough to escape. If we had time, I'd set up a team to start moving bodies back through the tunnels to the portal for Xollmomath to swell our ranks, but it wasn't worth the immense effort.

"The portal's next," I said. I pointed to one of the blood-splattered angels. "Take the enchanter back to Undercroft. See to it that she gets help." The silent creature turned and obeyed without a second of hesitation.

"You and I, just like old times," Elyk said with a hint of a laugh.

We climbed over the mountain of crushed and suffocated bodies clogging the exit, and the rest of Iron Hall was barely any better. Chaos had overtaken the city. More bodies lined the walkways. Some were trampled; others were killed in more traditional ways. Everywhere we looked, it seemed that Iron Hall would completely turn on itself before the day's end. All the death and destruction only confirmed what I already knew. Evil people were everywhere, and the only thing keeping society from complete barbarism was the threat of punishment. As soon as the social structure was gone—and that only took the barest amount of chaos and anarchy—it was every man for himself. People said whatever they wanted, but on the inside, there were more like me who just wanted to watch it all burn than anyone would ever admit.

By the time we reached the outside, it felt like half of Iron Hall was already dead. We passed a handful of obviously evil guilds who had sprung into action the moment the orb went down, and I was tempted to try and recruit them to the cause, but not until we found the city's portal. I still had one more experiment to conduct.

Iron Hall's portal, much like the one outside Echelon, was gargantuan. It towered to half the height of the mountain itself, though instead of a circle, it formed more of a lopsided triangle. Perhaps in the months it had been offline someone else had attempted to take it down and only succeeded in damaging it. Whatever the case, I intended to succeed. When the portals came back online, it was supposed to be *all* of them. I needed it to be all but one.

Between us and the portal, a series of smaller battles had broken out. There were multiple guilds on both sides, and I didn't feel like trying to sort through them. "I'll fly above and drop down. When I land, charge. We'll kill everyone and then get to work on the portal."

Elyk gave me a nod, and I leapt into the air with an activation of *Princess Yasha's Whispersilk Fan*. As I had practiced before, I flew above the tightest knot of fighting, then activated *The Basalt Monolith* and crashed down with a thunderous explosion. At least six of the combatants died in the initial impact, and more of them reeled back wounded. I ended the spell quickly, swinging my sword in an arc, and finished off another. I took a few hits from a muscular barbarian class player, but there was so much death all around that none of it mattered. I recovered from each blow before the next had a chance to land, then activated *Forsaken Barrier* to dodge directly behind the hulking man. My phase blade sank right through his armor. The man screamed, frantically trying to both run away and pull a health potion from his belt at the same time. He accomplished neither, only dying with a pitiful groan at my feet.

Elyk and the angles hit the fight right as I wrenched my sword free, and the battle quickly devolved into a rout. No matter how much magic the other players threw at us, it simply wasn't enough. I could easily regenerate any damage sustained, Elyk had a fair bit of resistance that kept him alive, and the angels were frankly indomitable. The final pockets of resistance crumbled beneath blood red wings and the glow of Infernum's fire, and then we were alone with the portal.

I activated *The Black Goblin's Restless Vengeance*, summoning the shadowy shaman to do my bidding once more. The portal was set into a craggy, somewhat flat section of the mountainside with a paved trail leading from it to Iron Hall's entrance. Huge boulders anchored either side, and I imagined the foundation of the portal itself extended all the way to bedrock. "Rip up the ground," I commanded, pointing to the base.

The shaman waved his hands, and a pair of massive boulders slowly lifted out of the ground.

"Just throw them down the hillside," I said. The goblin obeyed, and much to my dismay, the portal didn't even sway. "More. Keep going."

The goblin ripped up three more giant sections of rock before its magic was exhausted and it blinked out of existence. What I had feared seemed to be true. The portal extended deep underground, and just removing the rock and soil around the supports wouldn't be enough. What we really needed was dynamite, but that wasn't exactly possible.

"Any ideas?" I asked Elyk.

He scratched his chin and shrugged. "Not really my area of expertise."

"Yeah, not mine either." We spent twenty minutes or so taking stock of the giant portal, and it became apparent that demolishing it from the bottom wasn't going to be an option. "The only way we'll get enough leverage to take it down is from the top," I said after throwing out a few ideas that we both knew wouldn't work.

"You could sling ropes around the top and load them with weight, pull it down the hillside," Elyk offered.

The plan was easy enough to envision, though it would take a huge amount of effort. "That, or we set up a trebuchet and bash it apart."

"Either one. But we'll have to send a team through later to handle it. Let's go find the others at the orb." I brought over the angels, and we flew around the base of the mountain until we reached the other side where the orb was situated. The back of Iron Hall was mostly undeveloped, a stark contrast to the front's grand entrance and terraced façade. It featured a few protective towers rising from the craggy slopes, and there was a series of earthen bulwarks wrapping around the resurrection orb that looked freshly constructed.

Bodies covered everything. Angels had taken care of the guard towers, though more than one of them had died in the effort, and the ground battle had been a bloodbath. Iron Hall had clearly stationed a strong contingent of fighters to protect their resurrection orb, and they had held out valiantly as far as I could tell.

We landed among the ruins not far from Leif and his surviving guild members. From the looks of it, he had sustained at least a handful of casualties. The man was breathing heavy, and a splatter of blood crossed his face from top to bottom.

"Are you hurt?" I asked.

It took his eyes a moment to focus. When he finally registered who I was, his demeanor quickly changed from shellshocked to furious. He started screaming, swinging his fists in my general direction but completely failing to land a single blow. I dodged a few more inaccurate strikes, then wrapped him in my tentacles and squeezed. "Calm down, man!" I yelled.

He kept trying to fight, and I squeezed harder. Finally, when his breath ran out and he was too crushed to draw another, I let him go. His eyes rolled back, then snapped forward again, and it looked like at least some semblance of his mind had returned.

"Snap out of it, man." I gave him a couple light slaps to either side of his face. He had a waterskin on his belt, and I pulled it free without any resistance. I splashed it on him, and that finally did the trick.

"What happened?" he asked, finally focusing on me and taking in the destruction all around him. Slowly, the rest of his guild was assembling nearby to lick their wounds and loot corpses.

"You sacked the resurrection orb just like I asked." I held out my hand, and the man very hesitantly took it.

"How many did we lose?"

I shrugged. "No idea. Probably a handful, at least. Maybe more. Get your guild together and take stock. Loot what you can. We don't have much time left before the portal closes."

He started to speak, then just nodded and closed his mouth, wandering off in the direction of his guild. I found one of the other players, a pretty high-level fencer tending to a nasty cut that had busted his leather armor. "Hey, we're running out of time," I said. I pointed to his guild leader still struggling to come to terms with the battle and what it meant. "Get him back to the portal in one piece, alright?"

The man, clutching his bloodied left arm, managed to straighten his back and look me in the eye. "Yes, sir," he said.

I gave him a nod, then turned back to my angels. I

commanded them to get the orb before assigning all but two to transport the guild to the portal and back home. Elyk and I went first, and I was eager to get back to Undercroft Citadel and take stock of everything. And I needed to talk to Geirr. If we were going to bring down the portals and not just the orbs, I would need his expertise.

As before, I got a handful of notifications the moment I returned to my home continent. I still had no idea why I couldn't level up on other continents, but it didn't really matter. As long as I still gained experience, I was fine. Toppling Iron Hall had given me another point in cunning, and that meant a level and a new set of skills.

Surge (Physical): The Blight of Deep Waters skitters forward in the blink of an eye. This ability requires no energy when used underwater. Active, requires minor energy.

Crypsis (Cunning): Once per day, the Blight of Deep Waters may take on the appearance of an NPC for one hour. Active, consumes moderate energy.

Inspire (Influence): Allies and minions under the player's control have their Trade and Craftsmanship skills increased by 10 while at the home dungeon or raid. Passive.

I didn't need to think long about my choice. I unlocked *Crypsis* with fond memories of Ministrel's extremely powerful masks.

I was pleased to see that while we were gone, no one from Iron Hall had thought to sneak through the portal. Everyone filtered back home, and then it was time to take stock. The man I had tasked with bringing back Leif had stepped up to run the Seagrim Raiders while Leif . . . dealt with whatever it was he needed to deal with. The man, a level thirty fencer, was named Soren. He typically didn't serve as any kind of second in command, but I promoted him nonetheless, and he didn't seem too upset about it. We stood with Elyk and Hel near the ossuary and watched as Leif hugged his knees tight to his chest and rocked back and forth.

"That was the first time he's ever killed someone," Soren said quietly. "I mean for real. Without respawning or resurrection."

Elyk gave him a quizzical look. "I thought you guys were an evil guild, no?"

Soren rubbed his eyes with his palms. "We are, I guess. Just . . . not really like that."

"Well, you are now," I said. I gave him a friendly pat on the shoulder. "If there was ever any doubt in your mind, or in anyone's mind, it should all be gone. No going back. The Seagrim Raiders are in it for the long haul."

The man met my gaze without wavering, but I couldn't read his expression. Was he scared? Probably. Determined to stay alive? Certainly. Finally, he reached out a hand and I took it. "We'll stay with you. To the end."

I squeezed his hand. "I appreciate that. We may seem like the underdogs, but we've sacked four capital cities. When it all finally goes down, you want to be on the right side. That's us."

The man nodded, and I let him leave to take care of his guild and account for the dead. Overall, the raid had been a success. The Seagrim Raiders had lost a dozen or so, and that was certainly unfortunate, but we were otherwise in good shape.

And the best news of all: Geirr and his new engineers had made progress with the resurrection orbs. Hel, Elyk, and I visited him at the workshop, and he practically beamed with excitement.

"They're hollow!" he said, knocking his knuckles on a spot marked with blue on one of the orbs.

"Well . . . what does that mean?" I asked. As far as I knew, being hollow wasn't particularly exciting.

He knocked on a few other places, and the tone changed drastically. "See? It is only hollow *here*, nowhere else. The orbs have channels through them."

Again, I was at a loss for the grand meaning of it all. Fortunately, Geirr had made a drawing. The orbs, according to him, had a small hollow core surrounded by denser material, and one hollow channel extended from the core to the outer shell.

"Alright, but what does any of it mean? What can the orbs actually do?" I asked. I was starting to lose my patience. There was plenty left to do around Undercroft Citadel, and waiting for Geirr to get to the point wasn't really on my list.

Finally, the man deflated. All the enthusiasm brought on by the discovery was quickly overshadowed by the mere fact that the discovery was still ultimately meaningless. "I don't know," he said quietly. "We're . . . still working on it."

Elyk perked up at my side. "Hey, do you remember what Faidra said about empty vials?"

I searched my memory, but nothing came up. "That woman said a lot of weird shit. I doubt I remember even half of it." I looked at Hel who was clearly confused. "Don't worry about Faidra. It's a long story, and she's dead now."

"Empty vials. Void of light. Lift your head, and death is a relief," Elyk recited after a moment. "Or at least I think that's what it was. I don't know, but it stuck with me. Some of her lines just sounded like poetry."

"Honestly, I didn't take you for the poetry type. You surprise me every day, Elyk," I said with a smile. "Alright, so empty vials. No light. Death. It all seems like pretty standard fare for Lady Kalma."

"Another of Lady Kalma's daughters?" Hel asked.

"Good guess, but no. And actually, that's a great point. Faidra didn't follow Lady Kalma. She had her own god, and I can't even remember his name. *Damn* this fucking awful memory." I closed my eyes and tried as hard as I knew how to recall more details of the half-skeletal woman, but it was like trying to see an unlit lighthouse through heavy fog. I knew it was there, but it was completely inaccessible.

"Maybe Drevan would know something," Elyk offered.

I sighed. "He's dead too. Or undead now. No help there, either."

Hel stifled a laugh that I didn't exactly appreciate. "What have you been doing? Just killing all your allies? Do you even want to survive?"

I knew the old Helvegen, the one I had known so well before Lady Kalma's transformation, would have never said anything like that to me. But fuck, she was right. I couldn't blame the woman for being rude if she was right. My allies came and went like ships in the night, though their departures always involved violent deaths. I sighed again, and I felt the beginning of a headache building in the back of my skull.. For whatever reason, Lady Kalma's curse apparently wouldn't fix that. It would bring me all the way back from the brink of death with my head chopped half way off, but it couldn't resolve a simple tension headache.

Elyk fired a stern look to Helvegen, then finally offered an idea. "Let's at least get them somewhere dark," he said.

"Take one to the ossuary," I added. "Helvegen, I'm sure you have plenty of managing to do. I'd like our walls rebuilt before the next attack."

I didn't wait for a response. I helped Geirr roll one of the orbs toward the ossuary and inside.

"Here, let me close the door," Elyk said. He shut it, blocking out all the light, and a soft red glow emanated from the same hollow spot Geirr had marked.

"I'll be damned," the engineer whispered. "The night probably wasn't dark enough. Not with torches all over the courtyard."

The glow was faint, but there was no mistaking it. Something magical was contained within the sphere, and it was only visible from the hollow track Geirr found, and only in the right conditions.

"We still don't know what it does, though," Elyk said with a bit of exasperation.

I shared his frustration. "Alright. We're going to run a little experiment," I said. I drew my sword, and the atmosphere in the ossuary shifted from irritation to trepidation.

Elyk and Geirr both took a step back. "You sure that's a good idea?" the engineer asked.

"No. But I'm tired of just waiting for an answer. And we only have a few months left before the portals are back online." I took a steadying breath a lined up my blade right with Geirr's mark. "Here it goes . . ."

I pushed, and the orb's shell gave way. It split, and my sword followed the hollow path Geirr had surmised. The hilt hit the edge, and I still hadn't found the orb's center. I withdrew the blade with another sigh of defeat.

"Anything?" Elyk quietly asked.

I shook my head. "Not a fucking thing. No tingle of magic, no notification in my vision, just . . . nothing."

The mood quickly turned back to frustration. "Damn," Geirr muttered.

"Empty vessels. We need to fill it with something," Elyk added after a moment of pacing the tight quarters of the dark ossuary.

It was as good of an idea as any of the three of us could come up with. "Alright, we'll make another bomb. Instead of a barrel, we'll use the orb," I said, though I was far from convinced that it would work. Even if it failed, we still had more, and maybe the experiment would finally give us the answer to unlocking the orb's magic.

Geirr and his fellow workshop staff spent the rest of the day debating on what best to load into the sphere. My vote had been for more oily sludge from the abandoned castle dungeon, but there were more factors than just toxicity that the engineer was eager to point out. Dispersion was probably the largest hurdle. If we were truly going to make a functional chemical weapon, it needed to cover a large area. The easiest way to do that was with an explosion, but gunpowder was strictly forbidden by the game's code. Much to my delight, Geirr informed me that gunpowder and other explosives were not the only ways to make an aerial explosion, especially in a world with magic.

Other challenges presented themselves as well. Two of the Laurel Cove players working with Geirr attempted to protest the entire plan. No one tried to hide the fact that we were putting together a war crime, and the slice of lifers very quickly became visibly uncomfortable. I thought about butchering one of the dissenters as an example to the others, but I had done that before. I figured the tactic would lose some of its charm if I repeated it too many times. Instead, I simply reassigned the two women from the workshops to the wall, and I told Elyk to remember their names and faces. The next two times we needed sacrifices for the bone gate, we had a pair ready to go.

That night, as I sat on the top stair to my bedroom and watched the intricate zombie and gargoyle patrols weave their patterns out in the fields beyond our defenses, Hel arrived. She wore a simple dress that was probably looted from Laurel Cove. She stood at the foot of the marble stairs, her hands clasped in front of her, and waited.

Did I want to see her? I didn't know. The only thing I *did* know was that I didn't want to send her away. I pondered for a moment in the dark, serene silence, but no answer came to me.

"Hey," I finally settled on. As soon as the word left my mouth, it felt stupid. It would have been far better to have said nothing at all.

Much to my surprise, she didn't immediately turn away and leave. "Hey," she said back.

Some of the tension at my stupidity managed to leave my shoulders, and I stood. "You can come up if you want."

She didn't say a word, just ascended the steps without ever taking her eyes off me. I opened the door, and she followed behind. Mentally, I commanded the lights to a dim glow.

"Hel, I don't—"

She took my hand and turned me back to face her, and I saw something on her face that I didn't quite recognize. Fear? Anger? Probably just nerves. I was never particularly good at reading emotions on anyone, and I was practically useless when it came to women.

Hel let out a deep breath, and her eyes fell from mine to the floor. She let go of my hand. "I just wanted to thank you for . . . for not killing me. You have every right to. No one . . . has ever given me a second chance."

Again, I didn't know what to say. The moment felt too raw for words. I wanted to wrap her in a hug, to lay with her under the sheets and talk about *anything* else, but I knew it wasn't the right time. And perhaps it never would be the right time. What happened between us was still too fresh.

"That's . . . it. That's all I wanted to say. Thank you for not killing me. You can trust me."

Before my sluggish mind could figure out how to respond, she turned and pushed through the door. I listened to her rapid footsteps on the stone stairs, and then they faded to nothing in the cool night air.

I was alone. It felt like her words echoed in the room, and I couldn't settle my mind enough to focus on anything else.

You can trust me . . .

But could I?

I wanted to trust her. Perhaps my desire to have my closest companion back at my side was clouding my judgment. Perhaps the fact that she saw my monstrous features and didn't turn away in disgust had made me drop my guard. The woman had tried to kill me, and not even once. Her guild had killed Ellen. But was Ellen even a friend? No, just a useful ally.

Would I have done anything different if the roles were reversed?

I commanded the lights to extinguish and finally sat down on the bed. Perhaps I would explain it all to Elyk in the morning. He was the only friend I truly had in Undercroft Citadel. I valued his opinion, though I had never really discussed anything so personal with him.

I shook my head and laid down. None of it truly mattered. Not in the grand scheme of things, and certainly not to Lady Kalma. What was companionship at the end of the world? Meaningless. Trite. A false sense of comfort for a dying man standing on a tall ledge. I grit my teeth and willed the room to get warmer. The fall air had turned crisp, and my room felt colder than it ever had before.

Helvegen wanted to live. For now, she would. As long as she continued to serve, she would survive. She was a useful tool, nothing more. Regardless, everything could wait until the morning.

Despite what I told myself, sleep proved elusive. The temperature never felt right, and I tossed and turned until dawn broke over the horizon. My mind was addled from stress and the lack of sleep. Somewhere out in the courtyard, someone screamed. I pulled my blanket over my head and wished for sleep, even just a few hours, but it was no use. Whatever was going on outside was too loud.

Grumbling, I sat up and rubbed my weary eyes. Someone else screamed.

CHAPTER 17

It took me several minutes to recalibrate my mind. I was tired, everything was a bit hazy, and Lady Kalma's curse was the worst perpetrator. I felt the magic clouding my thoughts and nearly blocking every last remnant of my memory. What had I been doing before I laid down? Speaking to someone, but who? To . . . I couldn't remember.

And why was I suddenly standing, my heart pounding in my chest? "Fuck this curse!" I yelled at the unadorned walls. I rubbed my temples, but it didn't help. I was just about to crawl back under the covers when another scream snapped me back to reality. How many had there been? There was no way to know. I sprinted for the door and ripped it open, expecting to see a full-scale war in the courtyard below or massive columns of fire consuming every building in sight.

Enemies were on the horizon. Not many, at least not yet.

"Get ready for a fight!" I screamed at the top of my lungs. The outer zombie patrols were already engaged, though from what little I could see in the darkness, they were losing. I commanded the gargoyles to fly out as far as they could to lend their support, then frantically searched for my lieutenants in the chaos. I found Ministrel first, but I didn't feel like dealing with his insanity when I was barely over my own.

Soren, the fencer, came running toward my stairs.

"How many are there?" I demanded.

He stopped for a second to catch his breath. "Maybe a dozen. Not a big group, but they're strong. Some guild's top raid group."

"Shit . . . Get your people and defend the inner walls. If they breach, you're the next line of defense." I didn't want to throw the Seagrim Raiders right back into another bloody fight when taking Iron Hall had cost them so much already. Leif, their actual leader, was still nowhere to be found.

I stormed down the stairs and found Xia and Xollmomath commanding the zombie army from what had been rebuilt of the guard tower. "Keep the zombies close," I yelled. I didn't want to commit the undead until I knew exactly what it was we were up against.

Elyk grabbed my shoulder. "Where do you—"

"I'll go see what we're up against," I said, cutting him off. I intended to fly out over the walls, but I had left the fan in my room. And my sword. And my armor. Hell, I was barely dressed. I looked Elyk up and down, and he had Infernum but nothing else. Just his sleeping clothes.

"Fuck, neither of us can fight," I growled. I spotted what was left of Sir Drevan dragging his weapon through the dirt and staring off into the distance. I snapped to grab his attention, then commanded him to the front.

"We need the angels," Elyk said.

"And the golem. And Kevin." I searched through the terrified mass of people—almost all of them civilians from Laurel Cove—and I didn't spot either of them.

"Zombie fight," Elyk said with a grin. He was right. None of the players were ready. A bit of magic slammed into the wall only a few feet away. The attackers were nearing.

I raced to the top of the tower, and I spotted Aleph on the other side of the wall. He was already committed to the fight and damn near upon the attackers. Faidra's massive axe, still horribly imposing even in the titan's hands, swung in a massive horizontal arc. An echoing crash of magic met his blade. Then there was another swing, and another, and pieces of human flew like confetti through the night sky. The guild rained down magic, but none of it mattered.

"They're evil," I said more to myself than the two NPCs standing in the tower with me. After another few minutes, I knew it was true. The attacking guild was evil, and Aleph was completely immune to everything they threw at him.

I had seen Elyk whirl through enemies in his full raiment of legendary armor plenty of times. His harvester class was certainly well-earned, and few had ever stood against him and lived to tell the tale. What I witnessed on the battlefield with Aleph made Elyk look like a level one player wielding his first dagger. The gargantuan bone golem was, quite literally, unstoppable. Faidra's axe claimed life after life with inexorable efficiency, and the magic bombardment directed at both our walls and Aleph rapidly died. And then it was over altogether. Quiet settled on Undercroft Citadel once more.

I turned to Xia. "Have the undead perform a thorough search. There may be more, and we need to know where they came from."

The warlock nodded and began issuing silent mental commands to the horde.

"Resurrect whatever you can," I told Xollmomath. Since the angels hadn't had time to join the fight, the entire guild would be ripe for resurrection. Though Faidra's axe had probably reduced most of the attackers to nothing more than scattered limbs, every reanimated corpse had value.

Elyk and I made our way to the small battlefield, weapons at the ready just in case. Honestly, with Aleph standing watch, the zombie horde fanning out to scout, and Xollmomath beginning to raise the dead, our own swords felt somewhat redundant.

"These guys were strong," Elyk said, picking through some of the loot. "Not just some idiot guild looking for easy fame. All this gear is raid stuff."

It didn't take long to see that he was right. Everyone had come prepared with some of the best gear the game had to offer—they just had no idea that we had a forty-foot-tall unkillable bone golem wielding a god's legendary axe. Judging by the corpses, Aleph's conquest had been thorough, and there were no survivors. That meant there was no one left to spread the word of Aleph's existence. Sure, rumors were bound to get out to the public at large sooner or later, but I wanted to try and hide our most powerful asset as long as possible. I imagined dozens of guilds making the same mistake. The closer and closer it got to the portals coming back online, the more guilds would try. Everyone wanted to be the first out. Although . . . was that even true? There were bound to be at least a few other guilds like mine. Players who never had any intention of leaving. Players who had forsaken the real world long before the server crash.

I didn't know what to do about those guilds. Perhaps I was wrong, and when the portals opened, no one would throng to them. No masses of desperate players would flood the portals all at once. If that happened, well . . . I didn't know. But it was a bridge I would have to cross later.

We looted what Aleph hadn't smashed to pieces, then waited for the zombies to finish their scouting. When they came back, none of them had a lead. As far as we knew, the guild had blinked to our doorstep, launched their assault in the middle of the night, and then been torn to pieces in short order by the bone golem.

I shrugged. There wasn't anything I could do about it

except press onward. More attacks were bound to happen. The frequency and ferocity of the attacks was bound to increase, and we needed to speed up the rate of our city conquests. The faster we took out resurrection orbs, the more other guilds on those continents would go to war with each other. Evil guilds would attack the moment an orb went down, and every slain guild now was one we wouldn't have to contend with later.

I was dead tired, but I found that clearing my head was finally easy. The attack had brought a surge of adrenaline to my veins. Elyk and I dropped off the new gear at the workshop for repairs, and then I ordered him to get another civilian for the portal.

"We're going to Bellefontaine. Now. Us and the angels."

Elyk looked like he wanted to protest, but my expression told him that I wasn't interested in hearing it. "Let me get my armor," he said.

Ten minutes later, both of us stood before the portal with a dozen angels, and Elyk shoved a screaming woman through the portal to activate it. "Let's hope that warlock had been to Bellefontaine," he said halfheartedly.

Frankly, I didn't give a shit. As long as the portal opened to a city full of players and NPCs, I would be satisfied. If we got to sack another capital in the process, even better. But I really just wanted to kill.

We stepped through, and the atmosphere on the other side was oppressively hot and humid. We weren't underground like Iron Hall but in a jungle, and the air was so heavy with humidity that taking a breath felt more like drinking water than exchanging air. Fortunately, I didn't have to breathe, but Elyk took more than a few moments to steady himself.

In every direction, all we saw was lush, verdant jungle. Trees towered toward the sky, faintly illuminated by the sun just breaking over the horizon off in the distance. The only thing I knew about Bellefontaine was that it corresponded to the portal outside Corinth, but it was abundantly obvious that the two cities shared no similarities. Even the sounds of the jungle were foreign. Insects buzzed, and more than a handful of them assaulted my body or swarmed right in front of my face. Birds wheeled overhead with bright, multi-colored plumage.

"There's a path over here," Elyk said after a moment.

"No need." I ordered the angels to lift us into the air, leaving two behind to guard the portal, and the sight above the jungle canopy was breathtaking.

A stone city rose from the trees only half a mile away. The jungle hadn't been cleared so much as conquered. Huge stepped pyramids rose hundreds of feet beyond the tallest trees. A boulevard of shorter, flat-topped ziggurats cut a perfectly straight line through the jungle to the tallest structure right at the heart of the city. Other buildings, partially obscured by the abundant foliage, spread out in a radial pattern from the center like the spokes of a great wheel. The whole city reminded me somewhat of The Jade Spire, except everything was stone and mortar, trees and vegetation.

I ordered the angels to take us higher, and the swarming insects finally left in search of their next victim. I pointed to the towering pyramid right in the center of the city. "Let's check it out."

We got closer, and the lack of people in the city became readily apparent. We saw a few here or there, but nothing that would indicate a capital city of any size.

Then it finally hit me. "The orb has already been destroyed!" I yelled. The feeling of true death was so familiar in my bones that I hadn't even realized it when we stepped out of the portal. Someone had beaten us to the orb and taken it down.

The revelation was startling. In the back of my mind, I knew it was bound to happen. I just wasn't expecting to actually see it so soon. We kept going until we reached the central pyramid, and the angels set us down right at the pinnacle. Everything was covered in blood. The dark stone was practically soaked in it. Everywhere we looked, little gobbets of what I presumed to be human flesh were stuck to the stairs. The stink of iron and the recently deceased filled my nostrils.

"What the fuck happened here?" Elyk asked. He held Infernum at the ready, but there was no one around. We could see the entire city, and though we were too far above the streets to make out any individuals, it was apparent that the only ones left were few and far between.

"A lot of people died up here," I said, though that was rather obvious. "They didn't keep the bodies though. Must have taken them somewhere."

Elyk covered his nose and mouth. "God, for what?"

There was only one idea that made it through my head. "Zombies. You don't sack a resurrection orb and ritually sacrifice the whole population on a giant stone pyramid without some kind of use for the bodies. They must have a powerful necromancer like Xollmomath. Someone is bringing them back for their own army. And we need to find them."

"You thinking about more allies?"

"It's like you can read my mind sometimes." I scanned the horizon for a moment until a thin wisp of smoke off in the distance caught my attention. "There," I said, pointing. "A fine place to start."

We flew in the direction of the fire, and I had the angels stop at a large collection of buildings and roads that resembled a neighborhood. I figured it would also be empty, and I just wanted to see for myself.

My suspicion was correct. Every house we walked into

was the same. Their stone walls were untouched, wooden doors still balanced on their hinges, and all the belongings we expected to find were there.

I stood in front of one of the houses and tried to make sense of it. "It feels like everyone just left," I said after a moment.

"That doesn't explain all the blood on that huge pyramid." Elyk had a few pieces of silver he'd looted from the last house, but he ultimately just dropped it on the ground. There was nowhere to spend it at Undercroft Citadel anyway.

"Whatever happened, there wasn't a struggle. No army came and rounded up everyone against their will. Everyone just . . . left."

"Come on," Elyk said, pointing toward the snake of fire against the horizon. "Let's go see what the hell happened."

We flew over the tall trees, and the smoke eventually came clearly into view. It rose up through a stone chimney that formed the pinnacle of yet another flat-topped ziggurat. For twenty or thirty yards around the structure, the jungle had been slashed and cleared. Instead of trees, the whole area was full of people. They were packed in closely, perhaps three or four hundred in total, and every single one of them was glued to the twirling smoke. Each of them was dressed the same in plain robes tied about their waists with simple ropes. All of them sported the same shaved head as well.

"Fucking cultists," Elyk said just loud enough for me to hear and hopefully not carry to the gathered multitude.

I shot him a glance. "They probably say that about us, too." I mentally commanded the angels to lower us into the trees before we were seen, and we dropped down on a well-beaten dirt path leading directly to the building I had now decided was a temple.

"Cremations?" Elyk wondered.

I noticed that he left my previous statement without

comment and decided not to press the issue. "Has to be," I answered. "Kill them all, drag the bodies through the jungle and burn them. But why?"

He shook his head, and we crept closer. I ordered the angels to stay behind to hopefully keep us hidden, and we made our way slowly to the very edge of the huge trees. Curiously, while the rest of the jungle had been alive with animals of all sorts, we saw nothing. Not even insects. It felt like the temple—if that was what it truly was—exuded such a force that no living thing dared to get near it.

Except the players, of course.

Every single one was the cleric class, though they varied in level from as low as two to as high as sixty. But no, I looked closer, and not *all* of them were clerics, just the vast majority. Closer to the temple, I spotted a pair of level thirty-four apostles. It was a class I had never seen before or even heard of.

"Holy . . . shit . . ." Elyk whispered under his breath. He pointed to a tall woman in a charred black robe that smoldered much the way Faidra's armor had. The woman took one of the clerics by the hand, made a series of gestures over the cleric's forehead, then ushered the player inside the temple.

A fresh burst of smoke twirled up from the top of the ziggurat, and I got the distinct feeling that the sacrifices atop the city center were only the beginning. More people were dying here . . . but they went *willingly* to the flame.

Suddenly, a hand touched the armor at my shoulder, and I nearly leapt out of my skin. I whirled, and a homely cleric stood with his hands clasped barely six inches from me.

Elyk leapt into action and brought Infernum to the man's neck in a heartbeat. "Want me to kill him?"

I waved him off. "No . . . I'll be fine." I met the man's transfixed stare. His name was Offer, which was certainly not a real human name, and his placid smile sent a wave of uneasiness down my spine. Whatever it was about the man, I didn't like standing in his presence. My whole body told me to run.

"Welcome, brother, to the Chapel of Eternal Flame," he said. As he spoke, small bursts of smoke and ash leapt from his mouth. The man didn't cough or otherwise seem bothered by it at all. "Have you come to witness the Final Glow? I am afraid that you will not be permitted to participate, however you are welcome to bear witness."

"Chapel of Eternal Flame . . . where have I—"

"Faidra," Elyk said at once. "She talked about that shit. Something about Anaximander, I think, some kind of 'chosen one' lore. I don't remember the rest."

The robed cleric smiled a bit more. "Come. The ritual's completion nears."

Elyk grabbed the cleric by his arm and whirled the man around. Instead of fear or surprise, the cleric only kept his unsettling smile. "What the fuck is the ritual? What are you doing?"

I watched as another player willingly stepped into the temple's entrance. A few seconds later, a fresh burst of smoke and ash shot from the top. "They're burning them," I said. It was the only logical conclusion.

The cleric nodded. "The pure have been accepted into the Final Glow."

"Fucking ritual sacrifice," I added. My mind conjured up pictures from history textbooks of religious cults committing mass suicide. There had been a wave of it after the last world war, then another once the oceans rose and took out all the coasts.

"Gloandi is not the god of apocalypse, brother," the strange cleric went on, gesturing to the ceremony as though either of us had taken our eyes from it at all. "He is the god of inevitability. The faithful have not been slain. The city did not die. It merely arrived early. One day . . . everything will look like this." He pointed a pale finger toward the swirling smoke and ash. "Everything will look like this, and it will be right. Other gods promise salvation or vengeance or eternal life. Gloandi promises truth. Other faiths fear the end. The faithful rehearse it."

I watched a younger player, probably in her early twenties, joyfully walk into the temple. Then another burst of smoke ejected from the top of the ziggurat, and I knew she was dead. I sighed. What did I care if the cult wanted to commit mass suicide? If anything, it made my job easier.

"Bunch of fanatics," Elyk sneered. "Want me to kill them?"

The cleric fixed Elyk with his unfaltering smile. "There is no fanaticism here, brother. No despair. Only acceptance. Better to become the last fire than to be caught in the dark."

"God, these fucking riddles. Light in the dark? Flames that never die? I'm just so sick of it." I drew my sword, and when the cleric didn't even flinch, I decided to send him to his god a few moments early and loped off his head. Much to my surprise, the rest of the players didn't budge. They quietly waited their turns, and one by one they filed into the ziggurat to be consumed. We watched in awe until nearly the entire group was gone.

"We should find the orb and get out of here," Elyk said quietly.

The silence of the jungle was unsettling, but I didn't want to leave just yet. If my memory was correct—and that was a huge question given my curse—Faidra's gear had come from the temple. And if Elyk's experience with the liquid in the reflecting pool was anything to go by, I knew that Lady Kalma wasn't very keen on allowing other gods to live. "Once they're all dead, we need to sack the temple. Bound to be some powerful loot."

"Desecrate it, you mean."

"That's just an added bonus. Too bad we don't have some cool Lady Kalma banner to drape over the whole thing." We waited until the last of the 'faithful' walked to his doom, then slowly approached. The temple entrance was a simple square door, probably four feet wide and ten feet high. Inside, all we saw was the faint reflection of dancing fire against the stone walls.

I sent one of the angels inside first to check for traps. When it returned unscathed, Elyk took the lead.

A short stone passageway led to the center of the ziggurat. Four tapered walls made a chimney, and a black bowl sat beneath it with a small fire. It was nowhere near enough of a blaze to cremate a single person, much less a few hundred. And there was nowhere else for the people to have gone. The single channel didn't split off or go anywhere. It was a ten- or twenty-foot walk to the fire, and that was it.

"What's your investigation skill?" Elyk asked with a bit of a laugh.

"Yeah, I know. I've apparently neglected all the minor stats in my haste to conquer the world. Just help me look."

I felt like investigating such a small room should have been easy. The walls were stone, the firepit was some kind of metal, and there simply wasn't anything else to investigate. Somehow, it still took what felt like all day before Elyk finally uncovered the room's secret. For one, the fire wasn't hot. It wasn't even warm. I was embarrassed that neither of us realized it until Elyk went to move the pit itself and didn't burn his hands. Beneath the firepit was a simple arrangement of five small circles. I imagined there was some clue we missed along that way that told us exactly what we needed to do with the circles, but that didn't matter. A few minutes of activating talents and recruiting the powerful angels to help, and the panel with the circles was reduced to rubble.

There was a room below the panel draped in darkness. Elyk hung Infernum down to light it, and we both saw nothing. Just a plain, square room. There were no supports to hold the ceiling aloft, and the weight of the structure above us had to be somewhere in the realm of millions of pounds. The architecture of it all didn't make sense, though I didn't really feel like taking the time to study it.

I dropped down first, and Elyk landed heavily behind me. When I stood up straight, there was a man in the center of the room who had not been there before. He sat on a simple wooden chair directly across from us.

The man lacked a head. Otherwise, he was more or less intact. He wore a robe like the clerics had during the ritual, and his skin was faintly gray like paper brushed with ash. At his sternum, a small coal was embedded through both his robe and his chest. The coal twinkled with the telltale signs of fire, but it emitted no flame, no smoke, and no heat. Only a dull red pulse. I took a hesitant step forward, and the coal brightened slightly. Or perhaps it was a trick of the low light. Maybe I was just seeing what I thought I would see. Maybe the man wasn't really there at all.

I took another step. I second guessed my vision enough that I couldn't tell if the coal changed or not, and I had no idea which outcome I wanted to be true. If the headless man was aware of us . . . well, I didn't know. Did I want the headless man to be aware of our presence? I stepped again and finally got my answer: the corpse was aware. It spoke in my mind with subtle clarity that made my teeth clench and the muscles of my back flex. From Elyk's expression, I knew he heard it as well.

When the end of your story arrives . . . will you recognize it? Do you spend your life outrunning that which does not pursue? Is survival . . . the same as living?

"What the hell, man . . ." Elyk whispered, his voice

shaking. All the color had drained from his face. "We should get out of here."

A long moment of silence passed, and neither of us moved an inch. Then the corpse spoke again.

If you were offered a beautiful ending today, in this very moment, would you refuse it? What frightens you more: oblivion or inevitability?

My heartbeat was loud in my chest and my ears. It throbbed behind my eyes. My whole body and mind felt like they were slowing to a crawl. We had come so far, accomplished so much, and it was time to rest. Time to lay down our burdens and finally embrace the end we had been striving for all along.

Elyk dropped his sword and collapsed to his knees, then to his back. He pulled off his helm, and his eyes were completely unfocused. "We could rest here. It feels . . . peaceful," he murmured.

Every fiber of my body agreed. I sheathed my sword and stumbled to the wall, eager to slide down against it and rest my head. There was no danger here. No death. Only . . . completion. An end to a life's task. I closed my eyes, and the corpse offered me a vision. It wasn't forced into my brain but offered, and my tired mind willingly accepted.

I stood on familiar ground. I was just outside Echelon, staring up at the gargantuan portal with awe. The sight was inspiring, and my literature teachers had all been right: I was a romantic at heart. The magnitude, the grandeur, it was all just so *much*. The portal swirled with life. It wasn't dead at all but alive with magic and complex computer coding. All around, for miles and miles, were corpses. Some of them were bloodied, others had been trampled to little more than sinewy pulp, but the vast majority of them showed no injury at all. They'd died by poison, I knew. And it was my poison. I killed them all.

There must have been hundreds of thousands. Millions. The field of the dead went on farther than my eyes could see.

Gazing at the endless death, I felt nothing. There was no tingle of remorse, regret, or guilt. Only emptiness. My soul was as empty as the eyes of the nearest corpse. Everyone was dead by my hand, and if anything, all that welled in my chest was satisfaction.

I tried to walk between the corpses to the portal, but there wasn't any room. I had to climb over them, and the uneven carpet of death made for slow going. I reached the portal, craning my neck beneath its splendor, and reached out a hand to brush against the magic separating worlds. My fingers slipped through the subtle gap between Wonder and Earth, between Echelon and Atlanta, and it was cold on the other side.

I took a deep breath and pushed through, stepping over a slain man with blood at the corners of his mouth.

Atlanta took my breath away. It was cold, perhaps dangerously cold, and I wrapped my arms tight around my chest. Everything had been destroyed. The skyscrapers were gone, reduced to mountains of rubble that obscured every street and sidewalk in the entire city. All the green that had once dotted the coast was gone as well. There were no trees, no vegetation, and no life at all. The waves lapping at the ruined buildings to my right provided the only movement in the entire city. Off in the distance, maybe a mile or two from the portal, was a crater.

"Bombs," I whispered, and my breath fogged the air. It was cold and getting colder. I looked to the sky and saw a heavy blanket of thick clouds that felt too low to be natural. They sagged down in places, nearly touching the ground. Everywhere I looked was more of the same. The city had been reduced to rubble, and the sun could barely break through the clouds.

The tackiness and grit that built up on my tongue told me that the clouds were not just water vapor. It was dust from the bombs. So much of it had been kicked into the air that it hung there like a pale death shroud smothering all life beneath. Without the sun, the plants had died, and animals had followed quickly.

Again . . . I felt nothing. The emptiness was there, but it was so much a part of my being that I didn't consider it alien. It was part of me, no different than my arms or legs.

I looked down, and my limbs were human once more. My transformation had not survived crossing between worlds.

I crossed my legs and sat on the edge of the portal, taking it all in. The world was gone, and I had played some role in it.

But I knew it was all a vision. None of it was real, and perhaps it never would be. I imagined the headless corpse below Gloandi's jungle temple, and when I blinked, I was back underground with Elyk at my side. The corpse was still there, quiet and unmoving.

The world is going to die, the corpse whispered into my brain. *Judgment is as inevitable as time. Now go. Take your reward and hasten the end of days. Tell the living not to despair. Tell them their long wait has concluded. Everything is finishing. Tell them . . . Tell them Gloandi and Kalma have arrived.*

If you enjoyed this book, please leave a review at your favorite online retailer's website!

Enthusiastic reviews from readers like you are incredibly helpful.

Thank you!

Discover more awesome books and authors at
www.nefhousepublishing.com

www.ingramcontent.com/pod-product-compliance
Lightning Source LLC
La Vergne TN
LVHW041103080826
845145LV00007B/1681

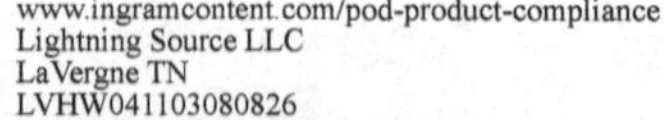

* 9 7 8 1 9 6 5 3 9 3 1 2 3 *